PRAISE FOR THE CHLOE ELLEFSON MYSTERY SERIES

A MEMORY OF MUSKETS

"Veteran Ernst provides a new perspective on the Civil War woven together with a compelling mystery." —*Kirkus Reviews*

"Extremely well-written." —*Suspense Magazine*

"Kathleen Ernst knows how to spin a tale, weave an intricate plot, and hide clues in the embroidery. *A Memory of Muskets* takes two stories separated by more than a century and knits them together into one thoroughly satisfying read." —Kathy Lynn Emerson, Agatha Award–winning author of *How to Write Killer Historical Mysteries* and *Murder in the Merchant's Hall*

DEATH ON THE PRAIRIE

"Fans of Laura Ingalls Wilder will savor the facts … Ernst does an exceptional job of sharing the kinds of character details that cozy readers relish." —*Booklist*

"A real treat for Little House fans, a fine mystery supplemented by fascinating information on the life and times of Laura Ingalls Wilder." —*Kirkus Reviews*

"'Die hard fans of Laura Ingalls Wilder' takes on a whole new meaning when Chloe and her sister embark on a 'Laura pilgrimage,' visiting all of the Laura Ingalls Wilder sites, in search of proof that a quilt given to Chloe was indeed made by Laura herself … Fans of Laura and Chloe both will enjoy *Death on the Prairie*. … Ernst spins a delightful tale of intrigue that interweaves facts about Laura's life with fan folklore, and of course, murder. I give this book an enthusiastic two thumbs up!" —Linda Halpin, author of *Quilting with Laura: Patterns Inspired by the Little House on the Prairie Series*

"The sixth installment of this incredible series … is a super read that sparks the imagination." —*Suspense Magazine*

"As superbly pieced together as a blue-ribbon quilt, *Death on the Prairie* is deft and delightful, and you don't want to miss it!" —Molly MacRae, Lovey Award–winning author of the Haunted Yarn Shop mysteries

"Suspense, intrigue, trafficking in stolen artifacts, blackmail, murder: they're all here in this fast-paced mystery thriller. Chloe Ellefson set off on a journey to visit all of the Laura Ingalls Wilder sites in search of the truth about a quilt Wilder may have made, and in the process of solving several crimes Chloe learns a lot about the beloved children's author and about herself." —John E. Miller, author of *Becoming Laura Ingalls Wilder* and *Laura Ingalls Wilder's Little Town*

TRADITION OF DECEIT

"Ernst keeps getting better with each entry in this fascinating series." —*Library Journal*

"Everybody has secrets in this action-filled cozy." —*Publishers Weekly*

"All in all, a very enjoyable reading experience." —*Mystery Scene*

"A page-turner with a clever surprise ending." —G.M. Malliet, Agatha Award–winning author of the St. Just and Max Tudor mystery series

"[A] haunting tale of two murders … This is more than a mystery. It is a plush journey into cultural time and place." —Jill Florence Lackey, PhD, author of *Milwaukee's Old South Side* and *American Ethnic Practices in the Twenty-First Century*

HERITAGE OF DARKNESS

"Chloe's fourth … provides a little mystery, a little romance, and a little more information about Norwegian folk art and tales."

—*Kirkus Reviews*

THE LIGHT KEEPER'S LEGACY

"Once again … Kathleen Ernst wraps history with mystery in a fresh and compelling read. I ignored food so I could finish this third Chloe Ellefson mystery quickly. I marvel at Kathleen's ability to deepen her series characters while deftly introducing us to a new setting and unique people on an island off the Wisconsin coast. In the fashion of Barbara Kingsolver, Kathleen weaves contemporary conflicts of commercial fishing, environmentalists, sport fisherman, and law enforcement into a web of similar conflicts in the 1880s and the two women on neighboring islands still speaking to Chloe that their stories may be remembered. It takes a skilled writer to move back and forth 100 years apart, make us care for the characters in both centuries, give us particular details of lighthouse life and early Wisconsin, not forget Chloe's love interest, and have us cheering at the end. A rich and satisfying third novel that makes me ask what all avid readers will: When's the next one?! Well done, Kathleen!"

—Jane Kirkpatrick, *New York Times* bestselling author

"Chloe's third combines a good mystery with some interesting historical information on a niche subject." —*Kirkus Reviews*

"A haunted island makes for fun escape reading. Ernst's third amateur sleuth cozy is just the ticket for lighthouse fans and genealogy buffs. Deftly flipping back and forth in time in alternating chapters, the author builds up two mystery cases and cleverly weaves them back together." —*Library Journal*

"Framed by the history of lighthouses and their keepers and the story of fishery disputes through time, the multiple plots move easily across the intertwined past and present." —*Booklist Online*

"While the mystery elements of this book are very good, what really elevates it are the historical tidbits of the real-life Pottawatomie Lighthouse and the surrounding fishing village." —*Mystery Scene*

THE HEIRLOOM MURDERS

"Chloe is an appealing character, and Ernst's depiction of work at a living museum lends authenticity and a sense of place to the involving plot." —*St. Paul Pioneer Press*

"Greed, passion, skill, and luck all figure in this surprise-filled outing." —*Publishers Weekly*

"Interesting, well-drawn characters and a complicated plot make this a very satisfying read." —*Mystery Reader*

"Entertainment and edification." —*Mystery Scene*

OLD WORLD MURDER

"[S]trongest in its charming local color and genuine love for Wisconsin's rolling hills, pastures, and woodlands … a delightful distraction for an evening or two." —*New York Journal of Books*

"Clever plot twists and credible characters make this a far from humdrum cozy." —*Publishers Weekly*

"This series debut by an author of children's mysteries rolls out nicely for readers who like a cozy with a dab of antique lore. Jeanne M. Dams fans will like the ethnic background." —*Library Journal*

"Museum masterpiece." —*Rosebud Book Reviews*

"A real find … 5 stars." —*Once Upon a Romance*

"Information on how to conduct historical research, background on Norwegian culture, and details about running an outdoor museum frame the engaging story of a woman devastated by a failed romantic relationship whose sleuthing helps her heal." —*Booklist*

"A wonderfully-woven tale that winds in and out of modern and historical Wisconsin with plenty of mysteries—both past and present. In curator Chloe Ellefson, Ernst has created a captivating character with humor, grit, and a tangled history of her own that needs unraveling. Enchanting!" —Sandi Ault, author of the WILD mystery series and recipient of the Mary Higgins Clark Award

"Propulsive and superbly written, this first entry in a dynamite new series from accomplished author Kathleen Ernst seamlessly melds the 1980s and the 19th century. Character-driven, with mystery aplenty, *Old World Murder* is a sensational read. Think Sue Grafton meets Earlene Fowler, with a dash of Elizabeth Peters."

—Julia Spencer-Fleming,
Anthony and Agatha Award–winning author of
I Shall Not Want and *One Was A Soldier*

Mining for Justice

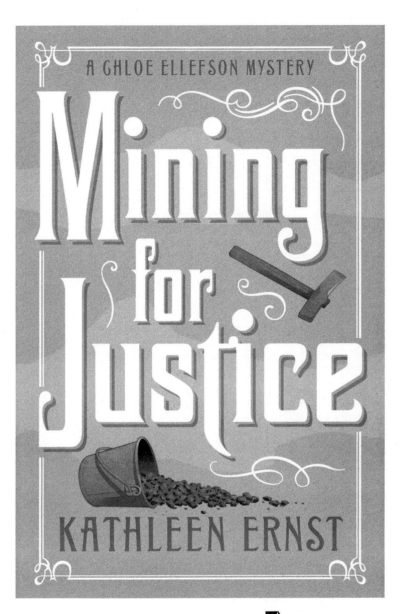

A CHLOE ELLEFSON MYSTERY

Mining for Justice

KATHLEEN ERNST

MIDNIGHT INK
WOODBURY, MINNESOTA

FIRST EDITION
First Printing, 2017

Book format by Bob Gaul
Cover design by Kevin R. Brown
Cover illustration by Charlie Griak
Editing by Nicole Nugent
Map on page xvii by Llewellyn art department
Images on pages 357–361:
   #1–2 by Wisconsin Historical Society
   #3–4 by The Mining and Rollo Jamison Museums
   #5–7 by Pendarvis Historic Site
   #8–9 by Pendarvis Historic Site, courtesy Wisconsin Decorative Arts Database

Midnight Ink, an imprint of Llewellyn Worldwide Ltd.

Library of Congress Cataloging-in-Publication Data
Names: Ernst, Kathleen, author.
Title: Mining for justice: a Chloe Ellefson mystery / Kathleen Ernst.
Description: First edition. | Woodbury, Minnesota: Midnight Ink, [2017] |
  Series: A Chloe Ellefson mystery; #8
Identifiers: LCCN 2017012759 (print) | LCCN 2017022004 (ebook) | ISBN
  9780738753652 | ISBN 9780738753348 (softcover: acid-free paper)
Subjects: LCSH: Women museum curators—Fiction. |
  Murder—Investigation—Fiction. | GSAFD: Mystery fiction.
Classification: LCC PS3605.R77 (ebook) | LCC PS3605.R77 M56 2017 (print) |
  DDC 813/.6—dc23
LC record available at https://lccn.loc.gov/2017012759

Midnight Ink
Llewellyn Worldwide Ltd.
2143 Wooddale Drive
Woodbury, MN 55125-2989
www.midnightinkbooks.com

Printed in the United States of America

DEDICATION

With thanks to the many people who have worked so hard to preserve Mineral Point's fascinating history; and in honor of those daring Cornish mining families who created new homes in the Lead Region.

AUTHOR'S NOTE

Pendarvis is a real historic site in Iowa County, Wisconsin. The buildings were originally preserved in the 1930s by Robert Neal and Edgar Hellum, who transferred the property to the State Historical Society of Wisconsin in 1970. I've tried to present an accurate picture of the site, but as always, minor details have been changed to serve the fictional plot. For example, the old mining slope is today called the Merry Christmas Mine Hill, or simply Mine Hill; I renamed it. The possible closure of the site was a point of contention in 1982, not 1983. Happily, the site is still welcoming visitors.

Pendarvis is located in Mineral Point, the first city in Wisconsin to be named to the National Register of Historic Places. Other sites mentioned in the mystery include Orchard Lawn, which is in Mineral Point; Shullsburg's Badger Mine and Museum; and Platteville's Mining Museum. Taking a mine tour at one or both of these sites perfectly complements a visit to Pendarvis. To learn more, visit:

Pendarvis
    https://pendarvis.wisconsinhistory.org

Mineral Point
    https://mineralpoint.com/live-here/why-we-love-it-here/
    history-highlights/

Orchard Lawn
    http://orchardlawn.org

Badger Mine and Museum
    http://www.badgermineandmuseum.com

The Mining and Rollo Jamison Museums
    http://mining.jamison.museum

You'll find photographs of some of the artifacts mentioned in the story on pages 357–361.

You can also find many color photographs, maps, and other resources on my website, www.kathleenernst.com.

CAST OF CHARACTERS

Contemporary Timeline (1983), Mineral Point, Wisconsin

Chloe Ellefson—curator of collections, Old World Wisconsin

Adam Bolitho—Chloe and Roelke's friend

Tamsin Bolitho—Adam's grandmother

Lowena—Adam's great-aunt

Winter—Adam's friend

Investigator Higgins—officer and investigator,
   Mineral Point Police Department

Claudia Doyle—curator, Pendarvis

Dr. Yvonne Miller—freelance historian

Gerald—interpreter, Pendarvis

Rita—interpreter, Pendarvis

Audrey—gift shop clerk, Pendarvis

Evelyn—volunteer receptionist, Pendarvis

Loren Beskeen—director, Pendarvis

Midge—archivist, Mineral Point Library Archives

Contemporary Timeline (1983), Villages of Eagle and Palmyra, Wisconsin

Roelke McKenna—officer, Village of Eagle Police Department

Libby—Roelke's cousin

Justin and Deirdre—Libby's kids

Dan Raymo—Libby's ex-husband

Chief Naborski—chief, Village of Eagle Police Department

Marie—clerk, Village of Eagle Police Department

Skeet Deardorff—officer, Village of Eagle Police Department

Greg and Marjorie Trieloff—Eagle residents suspected of selling drugs

Michelle Zietz—young woman arrested by Roelke

Troy Blakely—officer, Village of Palmyra Police Department

Historical Timeline (1827–1838, 1866), Cornwall, England, and Mineral Point, Wisconsin

Mary Pascoe —bal maiden (female mine worker)

Andrew Pascoe—Mary's older brother

Jory Pascoe —Mary's younger brother

Elizabeth and Loveday Pascoe—Mary's two younger sisters

Mr. Penhallow—surface mine boss

Mrs. Bunney—representative of the Christian Welfare Society

Ruan Trevaskis—Cornish blacksmith, the Pascoes' friend

Jago Green—itinerant painter and wood seller

Ida—Cornish girl brought to Mineral Point by her father

Will—young miner

Ezekiel—an enslaved boy

Parnell Peavey—sucker miner, slave owner

PENDARVIS
MINERAL POINT, WISCONSIN

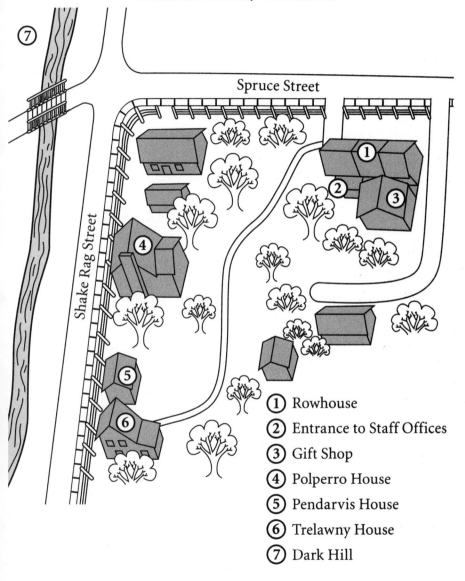

1 Rowhouse
2 Entrance to Staff Offices
3 Gift Shop
4 Polperro House
5 Pendarvis House
6 Trelawny House
7 Dark Hill

ONE

"I'm worried about Libby," Roelke said.

Chloe Ellefson glanced sideways at the man she loved. He hadn't spoken since they'd left home almost an hour ago, so she'd known *something* was on his mind. "Because she canceled at the last minute?"

"Yeah."

Chloe waited. They'd known each other for a year and half now. Been officially living together for almost two months. She'd gotten pretty good at reading his moods. Although Roelke wasn't on duty today, he was in cop mode. Mirrored sunglasses hid his eyes. His jaw was tight. Officer Roelke McKenna, Village of Eagle Police Department, looked like he wanted badly to arrest someone.

"What did Libby say when she called?" Chloe prompted. "Did her ex-husband blow off another date with the kids?"

"No. He picked them up." Roelke glanced in his truck's mirror, flicked on the blinker, and pulled out to pass. Having skirted Madison,

Wisconsin's capital, they were heading southwest to the community of Mineral Point.

"Oh." Chloe digested that. "I just assumed he had." Roelke was close to his cousin Libby, and to her kids Justin and Deirdre. Chloe loved them, too, and was accustomed to plans changing because the kids' dad was a jerk.

She swiveled in the seat. "So … why did Libby cancel?"

"She just said that something came up."

"That doesn't sound like her." Chloe wrinkled her forehead. *Blunt* was a euphemism for Libby's conversational style. "Maybe she didn't want to be two hours away from home if Dan decided he was tired of acting like a father."

"Or maybe she didn't want to see Adam."

Chloe scooched down in the seat and propped her toes on the dashboard. It was late September, but the sky was gray as slate, muting the golden maples and garnet sumacs as if in sympathy with Roelke's mood. "Did Libby and Adam have a fight?" Libby had met Roelke's friend Adam Bolitho last summer. Chloe and Roelke both thought the two would make a good couple.

"Not that I know of. But her tone was … I don't know. Funny. Something's wrong."

"We're just going to help out with the cottage he's restoring," Chloe mused. "It's not like it's a date."

"Maybe she felt like it was. She did tell me that she wasn't willing to date anybody until her kids were grown."

Chloe sighed. "Since Deirdre's only four years old, that seems a little harsh."

"Yeah."

And I thought this was going to be such a nice day, Chloe thought. She seriously needed a nice day. Maybe even two or three.

2

Mineral Point was a charming town she was eager to explore. She didn't know Adam well, but he seemed like a nice guy. He'd helped fix up the old family farmhouse Roelke had recently purchased, where she and Roelke now lived. Since Adam worked construction and ran a small contracting business from his Eagle apartment, his help had been invaluable. Now he'd invited them and Libby to see the old stone cottage he was restoring in his hometown.

"Do you want to cancel the trip?" she asked. "Go back and see what's going on with Libby?"

Roelke's thumbs beat a mindless rhythm on the steering wheel. "It's not fair for us to bail on Adam too. Beside, you've got the work thing."

"I do." Mineral Point was home to Pendarvis, one of the historic sites administered by the State Historical Society of Wisconsin. Chloe was employed as curator of collections at Old World Wisconsin, a sister site located just outside Eagle. With over fifty furnished structures to manage, she had more than enough to keep herself busy. Still, when site director Ralph Petty announced that he was loaning her to Pendarvis as part of a "sites support" initiative, she'd been pleased. It would be fun to help out at another site. September was a quiet-ish month at Old World, so this was a good time to be away.

Besides, she and Petty despised each other.

Her maniac boss had wanted to fire her pretty much since the day she'd started working at Old World sixteen months earlier, in May 1982. Back in July she'd given him good reason to do so, and she'd felt herself teetering on the edge of unemployment. Inexplicably, he hadn't acted. She'd spent two months tiptoeing around, wondering if today would be the day. It was exhausting.

"This is going to be a good week for me," she announced. "Claudia Doyle, the Pendarvis curator, is a friend. I'm ready for a break. It will be restorative."

Roelke threw her a sardonic look. "I know it will be a break from Old World, but you're still working at a historic site. It seems to me that there's a good chance you'll get sucked into *some* kind of mess. Site politics or something."

"No, I won't," Chloe vowed. "I'm just a guest. I will not get involved in anything even faintly problematic. If something comes up, I will refuse to take delivery." She was determined. Being on loan to Pendarvis wouldn't just give her the chance to learn more about this community's history and help out a colleague. She desperately needed to engage in museum work without having a micromanaging megalomaniac hovering over her shoulder. And she needed a chance to gain back a little curatorial credit. I'll show the Pendarvis director that I'm good at my job, she thought. If he made a good report of her time here to the Historic Sites Division Director, it would make it that much harder for Petty to malign her.

And that was essential. She'd made a commitment to Old World Wisconsin. She'd also made a commitment to Roelke. The farmhouse they now shared had been built by his ancestors near Palmyra—a short commute from Old World. She'd have a very hard time finding any other museum job within driving distance of the farm.

She tried to rid herself of gloomy thoughts. "Well," she said, "talk to Libby when you get home tonight. If something's going on, you'll both feel better when it's out in the open."

"Yeah," Roelke said. "I will." But his thumbs still beat a troubled tattoo.

———

Less than an hour later, Chloe pointed to a sign: Shake Rag Street. "Turn here."

Roelke did. "What kind of name is Shake Rag Street?"

"It has to do with the area's mining history," Chloe said. "Supposedly women stepped outside and waved rags to let their men know a meal was ready."

"Well, hunh."

"That may be just a legend. Miners working underground couldn't see women waving rags. But it's very cool that Adam's house is on Shake Rag Street. He must be close to Pendarvis."

The narrow road descended through a shady ravine. Despite a few modern houses, the road had an old feel.

"There's Adam's truck," Roelke said. He pulled over and parked in front of a small one-and-a-half-story stone cottage built into the hillside behind it. A ladder stood against the eaves, the windows were empty holes, and piles of rubble were visible in the side yard. A low stone wall ran along the sidewalk.

"*Oh*," Chloe breathed reverently as she slid from the truck. The disrepair didn't hide the magnificent stonework.

"Hey, guys!" Adam strode from the open front door, wiping his hands on his jeans. "Welcome to *Chy Looan*." He met Roelke with a handshake before turning to Chloe. She leaned in and kissed his cheek.

Adam Bolitho was wiry, well-muscled, deeply tanned, not classically handsome but good-looking in a rugged kind of way. He had dark hair, a thin face, and blue eyes that often sparkled.

They weren't sparkling today. "I'm sorry Libby couldn't come." Adam's tone strove for casual but didn't quite make it.

"Yeah," Roelke muttered. "Something came up." His tone wasn't even remotely casual.

Chloe felt compelled to intervene. "What does *Chy Looan* mean, Adam?"

"It means … well, it's Cornish, but I don't actually know what it means." He shrugged apologetically. "This house has been called that as long as I can remember. Look." He pointed to a stone above the door.

Squinting, Chloe made out chiseled letters, weathered and worn but still visible. "*Very* cool. Adam, your cottage is charming."

He looked pleased. "I'm not moving back to Mineral Point full time, so once this place is restored you'll be welcome to stay here."

Chloe grinned. "When was it built?"

"Sometime in the 1830s."

Roelke whistled. "Holy toboggans. My ancestors came from Germany in the 1850s, and I thought that was early."

"The Cornish weren't the first white people here," Adam said. "Miners, mostly Americans from the Southern states, started arriving in the 1820s to look for lead. But the Cornish, who were world-class miners, showed up in the 1830s after word of mineral deposits here started circulating. And unlike most of the original miners, who were single men looking to strike it rich and move on, many of the Cornish immigrants brought their families and settled down. Lots of descendants still live in the area. The first Bolithos got here in 1837."

Chloe felt her spirits rise. Immigrant history was her specialty. Her passion, really. She especially loved searching out evidence of everyday people whose stories would otherwise be lost.

Roelke studied the cottage. "Has this place always been in your family?"

"No. We're not sure where my mother's people settled. The Bolithos had a place that dated back to the same period, but it was across the road." He gestured widely with his arm. "In the 1820s and '30s, that whole hillside was being mined. At first the men scratched about, looking for easy hauls. The Cornish introduced deep mining to the region."

Chloe eyed the wooded hill. There was something compelling about it, something that made her want to leave the men to their rehabbing and go exploring. If she squinted her eyes, she could almost see the miners digging for lead. "How lovely that you've got such a great view," she said. "Pretty much all rocky ridge and prairie landscape back then, I take it?"

"Right. Not many trees in the area, and what wood there was went to smelters or cookfires. But Cornish stonemasons in that first wave of immigrants had no trouble building cottages—and later on, bigger homes—from local limestone and sandstone. There were maybe thirty little homes along Shake Rag Street at one time, plus the ones over on the hill." Adam's gaze became faraway. "I'd give anything to have the original Bolitho place, but it was destroyed in the 1930s. They built the municipal pool with local limestone— including stones from the old cottages. It was one of Franklin Roosevelt's projects to put men to work."

Chloe's shoulders slumped. "I'm glad the men got work, but … I hate stories like that."

"Me too," Adam agreed. "But I did enjoy swimming there when I was a kid. And my grandparents were able to purchase this cottage, which likely saved it from destruction. My grandpa died about ten years ago, but my grandma lived here until last spring. It wasn't easy, but we finally talked her into an apartment."

"My family went through something similar with my great-aunt Birgitta," Chloe said sympathetically. Birgitta had been, at ninety-four years old, alone on a farm. Still, she'd fought the move to a senior citizens' complex.

"Grandma's guest room is ready for you," Adam told her.

"It's *very* nice of her to let me stay with her while I'm in town."

"She loves having company, especially since my folks moved to California to be close to my sister's family." Adam cocked his head toward *Chy Looan*. "I get here more often now that I'm restoring the cottage. I had to make it a priority. Years of deferred maintenance were taking a toll."

"I'm here to help," Roelke said. "I don't know a thing about stonework, but I'm a quick study."

"Actually, I've got another job in mind for you two," Adam said. "Want a tour?"

Chloe and Roelke followed Adam up two steps carved from massive slabs of stone and into the empty cottage.

"Watch your step," he cautioned. "I had to take up the original floorboards, and I've shut off the electricity. The structure itself is stable … "

Of necessity, Chloe tuned out of Adam's tour and tuned in to the space itself. Since childhood, she had occasionally perceived lingering emotions in old structures. Most often she felt only a vague jumble, as easily ignored as background chatter in a coffee shop. Sometimes, though, a mood punched like a fist. It might be anything, but the bad ones—anger, fear, despair, hatred—could render her unable to stay inside.

"This lower room was originally used as living space, kitchen, and dining room, with a bed too," Adam was saying.

Chloe opened herself to anything that might remain within the old stone walls. There *was* something here in Adam's cottage, something stronger than a faint muddle. But to her relief, what she perceived was contentment. Thank you, thank you, she murmured silently to whomever had left behind such good vibes. She would not have to make excuses to Adam after fleeing white-faced from his grandparents' home.

"I've been tuck-pointing … "

Roelke nudged Chloe, a question in his eyes: *Any problems?*

She smiled, and gave a tiny shake of her head: *Everything's fine.*

He nodded: *Good.*

Chloe reached for his hand, trying to telegraph just how much she appreciated his acceptance of something he didn't understand.

Adam patted a wall. "The local yellow sand gives it this nice warm hue."

"It *is* nice," Chloe agreed, and the tour continued.

"Families were used to living together in one open space in Cornwall," Adam told them. "The kids would sleep upstairs, under the eaves."

"This place is awesome," Chloe said happily, admiring a huge fireplace.

Adam looked pleased. "I knew you'd like it. And you haven't even seen the really cool stuff yet." He walked to a plywood-on-sawhorses table and with great ceremony turned back the tarp covering it. "Look what I've found."

Chloe stepped closer, her mouth opening with surprised delight as she surveyed dozens of artifacts neatly lined up for inspection. She scrabbled in her totebag for the penlight she carried for such emergencies, and flicked it on. The treasures included a clay pipe bowl, a slate pencil, what appeared to be an ivory brush handle, several clay marbles, a whistle, and a porcelain doll head. The collection also included innumerable shards of glazed pottery.

These were tangible scraps of real peoples' lives. Who touched you last? she asked silently, considering the toys, the jagged bits of cookware. What were your stories?

"This is really cool." Adam reverently unwrapped a towel from an odd cast iron tool.

Chloe didn't recognize it. "What the heck is that?"

"A candleholder. The miners called them 'sticking tommies.' This sharp end could be thrust into a crevice, see?" Adam pointed. "Or this hook could be hung from a spike."

Chloe picked up the candleholder. The cast iron was pitted with age, but the device showed surprising craftsmanship. What blacksmith had taken the time to add that decorative twist? What miner had thrust the spike into a crevice, lit a candle, and gotten to work with pick and shovel in the scant light underground?

"Do you mind if I borrow this?" Chloe asked. "This decorative work is distinctive. I'd like to compare yours with whatever sticking tommies are in the collection at Pendarvis. I might be able to identify the maker."

"That would be great," Adam said. He turned to a curved piece of earthenware, glazed a yellowish-cream with brown spots. "This one *I* can identify. Bernard Klais was a well-known potter in Mineral Point. He made roofing tiles, but also crocks and flowerpots."

"But … where did you find all these things?" Chloe asked.

Adam walked to a door in the back wall. "Some early occupant dug a big root cellar into the hill, accessed through here. The floor is packed earth, and over the years a foot of sand and gravel sifted into the space. My grandparents eventually blocked the cellar off to keep damp out of the rest of the house. Flooding used to be a problem in this area until the city engineered a drainage system along the road." He looked like a little boy ready to burst with the need to share a secret. "*Anyway*, I started shoveling out the sand, and the pipe bowl turned up pretty quick. After that I was a whole lot more careful."

He opened the door. Roelke followed him into the root cellar, and Chloe trailed behind. Inside she got an instant's look at the windowless space—shelves built around the walls, dirt and sand floor, the wheelbarrow and shovel Adam had been using—before a jolt of something almost electric shot through her solar plexus.

Something very dark, very... very *bad*, was buried among the artifacts in Adam's root cellar.

Chloe bit her tongue hard to keep from yelping. After stumbling backwards through the doorway, the blackness receded.

Roelke glanced over his shoulder with a questioning look. Chloe gave him a tiny, helpless shrug: *I was too quick to believe all was well.*

"There's no telling what else might turn up, so I thought you guys might enjoy working back here," Adam was saying. "I'm getting down to the bottom of the sand." He turned and discovered that fifty percent of his team had retreated. "Chloe? Is something wrong?"

Shit, Chloe thought, because she had no idea what to say.

Thankfully, someone intervened before her silence became awkward. "Adam?" a feminine voice called. "You in there?" A woman in faded denim overalls stood on the front step, peering in the open door. She held several folded newspapers.

"Winter?" Adam emerged from the root cellar's nether reaches. "Come meet Roelke and Chloe. Guys, this is my friend Winter. She's a potter."

Winter looked like a potter, Chloe thought. Some kind of artist, anyway. Her light brown hair was twisted into an untidy bun behind her head. Escaping tendrils framed a heart-shaped face. She had big eyes that should have given her a waifish look, but there

11

was a tension to her, a tightness about the mouth, that was most un-elfin.

"Nice to meet you," Winter said. "And I'm sorry to intrude, but—Adam, have you seen this? Today's *Democrat-Tribune*." She slapped a newspaper into his hand.

Adam's smile faded as he unfolded the paper. "What the hell?" He held it so Roelke and Chloe could see the headline: PENDARVIS THREATENED WITH CLOSURE.

"What?" Chloe gasped. "Pendarvis is a state-owned site. Why on earth would it be closed?"

"Closing Pendarvis would kill Mineral Point," Adam muttered. "This is an artists' town, and everyone depends on tourism. Lots of visitors come tour Pendarvis, then spend the rest of their time visiting galleries and studios."

"You can keep the paper," Winter said. "I wanted to be sure you got the news. A bunch of us are going to meet tomorrow evening. Seven p.m. at the Walker House. We can't let this happen."

Adam was still staring at the headline. "I'll be there."

"See you tomorrow, then." Winter nodded at Chloe and Roelke. "Nice to meet you."

After Winter left, no one spoke for a long moment. Then Adam put the newspaper on the makeshift table. "I'll look at this later. I don't want to get sidetracked while you're here."

"Let's get to work," Roelke agreed affably.

Chloe couldn't acquiesce. "I'm sorry, but I need to read this," she said. After all, she was an employee of the Historic Sites Division. Besides, evil energy lingered in the root cellar. Reading the paper would give her at least fleeting cover for not following the men.

Adam and Roelke left her alone. She leaned against a wall and read the lead article.

September 18, 1983

Pendarvis, the historical site on Shake Rag Street, is in danger of being closed. State Historical Society of Wisconsin officials have announced that financial shortfalls have forced them to consider the drastic measure.

The historic complex includes Polperro, Pendarvis, and Trelawny Houses. These historic structures were restored in the 1930s by Robert Neal and Edgar Hellum, who were alarmed to see Mineral Point's architectural heritage disappearing. Neal and Hellum operated a popular restaurant there for thirty-five years. When they retired in 1970 the property was transferred to the historical society.

The state has operated the popular historic site for the past thirteen years without problem. However, the development of Old World Wisconsin, a huge outdoor ethnic museum near Eagle, has drained the Historic Sites Division's resources.

"Oh, no." Chloe felt a hollow sensation in her stomach. "No, no, *no*." News that Pendarvis was on the chopping block was heart-breaking; discovering that her beloved Old World Wisconsin was being blamed made that even worse.

The news did not bode well for her having a happy week as guest curator at Pendarvis.

I bet Petty knew, she thought. The news hadn't trickled down to curators yet, but surely the site directors had been involved in the Division's budget process, or at least informed. Chloe could just imagine the SOB's self-satisfied smile as he made arrangements to exile her into the Mineral Point lion's den—the very week the news became public. Another Petty atrocity.

Well, this day is sucking more and more, she thought morosely. She was ready to get back into Roelke's truck and—

"Jesus!" Adam exclaimed from the root cellar.

Chloe darted to the doorway. Roelke was crouching in a back corner, gently brushing sand away from something. Adam watched with an expression of horror.

"What's wrong?" she demanded.

Adam pointed. "We were just going along, keeping an eye out for pottery and stuff, and then we found ... "

"And then you found *what*?" She couldn't see.

Roelke stood slowly. "And then we found human remains."

TWO

WELL, ROELKE THOUGHT, THIS day is going to hell in a handbasket.

"You found human remains?" Chloe echoed from the doorway. "Seriously?"

"Human bones," he confirmed, eyeing her. She'd been freaked about something in the root cellar even before this discovery.

Then—well, duh, he thought. Chloe had felt some strong negative emotion lingering back here; somebody with a bashed-in skull was buried back here. Even he could connect those particular dots.

"I'll go next door and call the police," Adam said.

After he left, Roelke went to Chloe and gathered her into his arms. "You okay?" He inhaled her sweet Chloe-scent, felt her long blond braid beneath his forearm. She was nothing like the vague image of the woman he'd once thought he wanted. She was four years older than he was, had a graduate degree, and spent her days immersed in her history-world, responding passionately to events that at times seemed incomprehensible. He loved her so much it sometimes made his chest ache.

"Well, it's been quite the ten minutes," she said a little shakily, "but I'm okay. You found the bones?"

"Yeah. We'd gotten down to what appears to be the original dirt floor back there, packed hard. I scraped away some dirt and hit what looked like a neck vertebrae, so I kept going until I'd exposed the skull. It was lying on its left side. A portion of the skull, in the back, is crushed."

Chloe winced. "Oh my God."

Adam returned, and five minutes later a police car pulled to the curb. The officer who emerged was a tall, solidly built man with weary eyes and a competent air. He had a flashlight in his hand. "Good to see you, Adam. You're making progress, I see."

"Well, we *were*," Adam said, and introduced Chloe and Roelke. "This is Officer Gene Higgins."

"Investigator Higgins, actually," the older man clarified.

Roelke extended a hand. "Mineral Point has an investigator?" He realized that might sound rude. "Just curious."

"Most of the time I'm on patrol," Higgins explained. "But my extra training comes in handy on calls like this. Let's take a look. First thing to do is see if we can tell whether it's a human bone or what."

Roelke didn't blame Higgins for saying that. It wasn't unusual for homeowners to find the remains of someone's pet buried in the garden. He'd once discovered that the bone which had prompted a panicked 911 call was a moldy old stick. But he was pretty sure that Higgins would reach the same conclusion he had, and just as quickly.

Adam led the way and trained his own flashlight on their discovery. Higgins crouched to get a closer look, and whistled softly. "That's human, all right."

"Yeah," Roelke said. "And look here." He stepped around Higgins and pointed to the shattered spot.

Higgins studied the skull. "When did your grandparents buy this place, Adam?"

"Sometime during the Great Depression." Adam shifted his weight from one foot to the other. "My grandma could tell you."

"What happens now?" Chloe asked from the doorway.

Higgins straightened. "The first thing we need to do is make sure this body isn't connected with a missing persons case. I'll call the coroner and the state crime lab." He rubbed his chin with the thumb and forefinger of his left hand. "Once we're sure this clandestine grave doesn't involve a relatively recent crime—"

"Of course this doesn't involve a recent crime!" Adam looked incredulous. "For God's sake, until last spring my grandmother lived in this house."

Higgins pressed his palms down several times, as if trying to subdue rising air. "I'm not accusing Miss Tamsin of anything. But there are procedures I have to follow."

Roelke had been trying to stay out of it, but now he felt compelled to step close to Adam. "Let the man do his job, buddy."

"Of course. I just—I—of course."

While Higgins conducted a preliminary investigation of the scene, Chloe, Roelke, and Adam sat outside on the wall. Adam drummed the heels of his workboots against the stone. "Since I do construction work, it's not like I've never thought about something like this. But it never occurred to me that it would happen on family property."

Chloe put a hand on his arm. "Of course not."

"I'm sure we'll learn that the body was buried a very long time ago," Roelke added.

"But *somebody* ... well, I saw what the back of the skull looked like."

Chloe hugged her arms across her chest. Roelke put an arm around her shoulders.

Higgins emerged from the cottage. "I have everything I need, for now—ah. There's the coroner."

The coroner, a pudgy man with a Moe Howard haircut, didn't linger long. "I think it's safe to issue a death certificate," he said sardonically. He conferred briefly with Higgins and departed.

The investigator spent some time on the radio in the squad car. "How long will this take?" Adam asked after about twenty minutes.

"A while," Roelke told him. Chloe leaned her head against his shoulder. No one found anything else to say.

———

The crime scene techs arrived two hours later. "So, what all does this involve?" Adam asked, watching them carry equipment into the cottage.

"They'll document the scene," Roelke told him. "Photographs, measurements, stuff like that. They'll probably excavate farther, looking for any other human remains. They'll recover and preserve whatever they find, and take it all back to the lab for study."

Adam sighed. "Unbelievable."

Higgins overheard the exchange. "You're staying with your grandmother? I'll keep you posted," he told Adam. "I'll oversee these guys, so there's no need for you to hang around."

Adam hesitated.

Roelke understood his reluctance to leave the property, but he also understood that sitting on the wall all evening wouldn't accomplish anything. "I think we should go."

Higgins shook his head. "You know, Mineral Point's a pretty quiet town. It's not perfect. We've got our share of domestic abuse calls, speeders, kids on drugs. But I've been a cop for a long time, and I've never seen anything like this." He went back inside.

"Well," Adam said, "this day didn't go at all like I thought it would." He tipped his head toward his truck. "My grandma is expecting us for dinner. Besides, I want her to hear about this from me."

Roelke and Chloe followed as Adam drove through town. "You know, you could come home with me tonight, instead of staying," Roelke said.

Chloe frowned at him. "I'm expected at Pendarvis tomorrow."

"After what happened … " He let his voice trail away, not even sure if he was referring to what they'd found in Adam's cellar or what they'd read in the newspaper.

She patted his thigh. "I'm staying."

"It's supposed to rain all week." That was feeble, but all he had left.

"I'm *staying*, Roelke."

Adam pulled over in front of a modern four-plex, and Roelke parked behind him. As they all got out of their vehicles Adam said, "We talked her into a ground-floor apartment, at least. Her older sister Lowena lives in a nursing home, but Grandma says she's not ready to spend all of her time with, and I quote, 'old people.' At eight-eight she was still climbing the stairs at *Chy Looan*, can you imagine?"

Go Grandma Bolitho, Roelke thought. All of his grandparents were dead. He wished they weren't.

Adam's grandmother greeted her guests with a joyful smile. She wore stretchy pants and sensible shoes and a brown cardigan with autumn leaves knit into the design. Behind plastic-framed glasses, her eyes gleamed with warmth.

Adam's hug lifted her a few inches from the ground. "Hey, Grandma. These are my friends, Chloe and Roelke."

"Nice to meet you, ma'am," Roelke said.

"Rell-kee?" Mrs. Bolitho repeated. "How is that spelled?"

Roelke told her. "It was my mother's birth name."

Mrs. Bolitho nodded approval. "I've always liked that custom."

"It's kind of you to have us for dinner," Chloe said. "And you're especially kind to let me stay here, Mrs. Bolitho."

"Oh, we'll have fun! And you must call me Tamsin." She ushered them inside.

Tamsin's apartment was immaculate, if a bit over-furnished for Roelke's tastes. Gewgaws were displayed on shelves. Artwork and family photos covered the walls. But a juicy aroma made him forget everything else. The picnic lunch they'd planned had been forgotten, and he suddenly realized how hungry he was. "Something smells heavenly!"

Tamsin looked pleased. "Beef pasties. Homemade, of course. They're Adam's favorite."

"Um ... " Chloe began uncomfortably.

"Oh, don't worry, dear." Tamsin patted her hand. "Adam told me about your special diet. I made an herby pasty for you. Dinner won't be ready for a bit, though. Please, make yourselves at home."

Chloe gravitated to an antique rocking chair like metal to a magnet. Roelke settled on the couch, but Adam lingered on his feet. "Grandma, there's something I have to tell you." He took a deep breath. "This afternoon, when we were cleaning more sand and gravel from the root cellar, we found ... we found a skeleton."

The old woman pressed a hand against her chest. "You found ... *what*?"

"We called the police, and Gene Higgins came. A team from the Madison crime lab will excavate the bones. That's all I know."

"Are you trying to tell me that all the years we lived in *Chy Looan*...my children and grandchildren...and all the while..." Her hands worked together with agitation.

Roelke and Chloe exchanged an uneasy glance. He could completely understand Tamsin's reaction. He would be aghast to discover a skeleton in the cellar of his farmhouse, and he'd only been living there for a couple of months.

"When did you and Grandpa buy *Chy Looan*?" Adam asked.

"In 1936. Nobody wanted those old cottages then, but it was all we could afford."

"Did you ever use the old root cellar?"

"Of course I did!" Tamsin wailed. "We didn't have an icebox at first. Dear God, are you saying that the whole time I was walking over..."

Adam reached over and took her hand. "I'm sorry, Grandma. But it does seem that the bones were buried in the root cellar all along."

"What if people think otherwise?" Her voice rose. "What if people think *we*—"

"Grandma," Adam said gently, "I really don't think anyone will believe that we did someone in and buried them in the root cellar."

A sheen of tears glazed Tamsin's eyes. "We don't know that, do we."

Roelke and Chloe exchanged another stricken glance. He was used to handling upset people, but in a professional capacity. It felt wrong to be sitting on this sweet lady's couch as she neared meltdown.

"I'm sure the police will get to the bottom of this situation quickly," Chloe tried.

Tamsin shook her head. "The death *must* have taken place before we moved into the cottage. I don't think the police will have time and knowledge to pursue something that happened over fifty years ago, do you?"

"Well … perhaps not," Chloe admitted. "Maybe the news will jog someone's memory."

"Such news about my house!" Tamsin's tone rose to a wail again.

Adam began to pace. "I wish I'd never decided to excavate the cellar."

Surprisingly, Adam's remorse did more than anything else to calm Tamsin down. She drew a deep breath, exhaled slowly. Then she shook her head. "No, I'm glad you did. That poor soul, whoever it was, deserves a decent burial and resting place."

She's got a good heart, Roelke thought, and felt a little better about leaving Chloe there.

"We need to know what happened." Tamsin abruptly turned to Chloe. "You're a historian. I know you'll be busy at Pendarvis, but maybe, if you have a little spare time, you could do some research?"

Chloe clearly hadn't seen *that* request coming. "Research about what?"

"Old crimes, I suppose. Someone gone missing."

"But I … It's not that I don't want to help, but I'm a newcomer here. Surely a local historian would be better suited."

Tamsin sat down beside Chloe. "I shouldn't have asked. It's just that I can't bear the idea of being the subject of gossip, so I hoped … well. I'll think of something."

Roelke was starting to wonder if Tamsin Bolitho was a lot more shrewd than she looked. Chloe held her elders in high esteem. She loved talking with them, loved hearing their stories, loved seeing the things they considered precious. Loved helping them, if she could. He didn't think she could hold out for long.

"Well, I can probably do a little checking," Chloe said helplessly.

Okay, she couldn't hold out at all. New record.

"I'd be ever so grateful," Tamsin told her.

"I can't promise I'll find anything."

A timer dinged in the kitchen. Tamsin patted Chloe's hand again and bustled away.

Roelke leaned toward Chloe. "That was kind of you."

"What was I supposed to do?" she whispered. "Geez. This puts a different spin on the week."

Adam carried a platter of pasties from the kitchen, and Tamsin followed with a bowl of applesauce. They settled at a round table covered with a linen cloth. Tamsin said a brief grace, then smiled at her guests. "Dig in."

Roelke helped himself to a pasty, cut into it with his fork, and scooped up a bite. "Holy toboggans," he mumbled. "This tastes even better than it smells." He'd been eating less meat lately. Chloe's deal with him, when she moved in, had been short and sweet. "I don't care if you cook meat," she'd said. "But *I* won't cook meat." She was a better cook than he was, so he was happy to let her loose in the kitchen more often than not. He almost always liked what she prepared, and he knew he was healthier for it. But meals like this Cornish meat pie only proved that he was not on the verge of becoming a vegetarian.

"Mine is delicious too," Chloe assured Tamsin. "Pasties are quite traditional in Cornish cooking, aren't they?"

Tamsin nodded. "Cornish people have been eating pasties for centuries, I expect. There are different kinds, but most are filled with chopped meat, potatoes, onion, and swede."

Roelke studied his pasty, completely baffled. "Swede?"

"Yellow turnips. You call them rutabagas."

This lady was born in Wisconsin, Roelke thought, but *we're* the ones who call them rutabagas.

"Of course, the truly poor people had to make do with hoggans," Tamsin was saying.

"Hoggans?" Chloe mumbled around a mouthful of herby pasty.

"Flatbread with a morsel or two of pork baked into it," Tamsin explained. "My father said they were hard as rocks. Women made them of barley flour when wheat was too dear." She glanced at Chloe. "Don't worry, dear. I won't serve you hoggans. Although I think you'd enjoy figgy hobbin, a sweeter version made with wheat flour and raisins and caramel sauce. I understand the dish has almost disappeared from Cornish tables, but it's still popular here in Mineral Point."

That perked Chloe up, and her thin face grew animated. "I can't wait to try it!" Roelke was pleased to see her genuine smile, and the shine in her chicory-blue eyes.

"Tell me more about your visit," Tamsin urged her. "Adam said you're working at Pendarvis."

"I'm here to help the curator. It's part of a project to make people at the state's smaller sites, like Pendarvis, feel less isolated." Her smile faded, and she put down her fork. "At least that's what I thought it was about."

"Did you see the paper today, Grandma?" Adam asked.

Tamsin's smile had faded too. "All this new commotion almost put it out of my mind, but I did, indeed."

"I didn't know anything about it," Chloe said, sounding only a little defensive. Roelke patted her knee beneath the table.

"Winter is organizing a meeting for tomorrow evening at the Walker House," Adam told his grandmother.

"I wouldn't miss it," Tamsin said.

"I was planning to go home tonight, but I want to check on *Chy Looan* tomorrow after the cops are finished there." Adam scooped up some applesauce. "I might as well stay in town until Tuesday morning so I can attend the meeting. My guys will be fine on their own at the worksite for a day."

Chloe fiddled with her fork. "Would you two mind if I tagged along? I feel like I should be there, but I would be grateful if I didn't have to sit alone. I can't expect locals to feel too kindly about me being here. I might get run out of town on a rail."

"Of course you can come with us," Tamsin said. "But Mineral Point people are generally kind. I think you'll be alright."

Chloe clearly was not convinced. "Well, I'll see how things go at the site tomorrow."

"If Loren Beskeen is anything less than gracious," Tamsin said pertly, "you report back to me."

Loren Beskeen is the site director, Roelke reminded himself.

"I'll set him straight," Tamsin promised. "I taught Loren when he was in third grade."

Adam reached for a second pasty. "Grandma taught everyone when they were in third grade."

"Forty-five years in the same school will do that," Tamsin agreed.

"I understand you have deep family roots in Mineral Point." Chloe pinched up a bit of pastry that had fallen on the tablecloth and popped it into her mouth.

Tamsin nodded. "My family came about the time the first Bolithos arrived. I'm proud of my ancestors. They were strong people. My husband, God rest his soul, took me to Cornwall twice. It's a wild, beautiful place. Most Cornish people don't consider themselves English, you know. We're one of the Celtic nations—just like the Welsh and the Scots and the Irish. We have our own heritage, and our own culture."

"Were your ancestors miners in Cornwall?"

"Oh, yes. They mined tin. With a bit of pilchard fishing."

"Pilchards are grown-up sardines," Adam told his friends. "I keep asking Grandma if we have smugglers on the family tree, but she won't say." He winked.

"Oh, hush, Adam." Tamsin shot him a look of affectionate exasperation. "Certainly no one on *my* side of the family ever did such a thing."

When the dishes were done Roelke knew he shouldn't linger. "I best get on the road," he said reluctantly. He thanked Tamsin for the fine meal.

Chloe walked out to his truck with him. He set her suitcase on the sidewalk, then regarded her soberly. "I wish I could stay with you, but I have to be at work tomorrow morning. And then there's Libby—I need to find out what's going on with her. And—"

"Roelke, why are you so anxious? Is it the skeleton? It's disturbing, but whoever it was died a long time ago. And it's Adam's house, not mine. It has nothing to do with me."

"But that newspaper article has something to do with you. You said yourself that you're nervous about the meeting tomorrow."

Chloe looked away, as if choosing her words. "I'm uncomfortable about the situation," she said finally. "But I don't *really* expect to be tarred and feathered."

Roelke tried and failed to come up with a new argument against her staying in Mineral Point. "Call me," he said at last.

"Of course I'll call you," she said, and wrapped her arms around him. They stood that way for so long that in the end, it was Roelke who felt compelled to pull away. She's sorry to see me go, he thought, and had to content himself with that.

THREE

THE BREAKFAST TAMSIN PREPARED on Monday morning—scrambled eggs, oatmeal with apples and brown sugar, pumpkin rolls, juice, and coffee—suggested that Chloe and Adam were heading to the mines for a day of manual labor. Chloe was okay with that.

"So, I've been thinking about your cottage," she told them. "Do you have any old records about the building? Tamsin, do you remember anything about the previous owners?"

Tamsin frowned thoughtfully. "No. The cottage had been empty for five or six years when we bought it."

"Maybe the death and burial happened while it was abandoned," Adam suggested.

"I can't bear to think about it." Tamsin shuddered, then looked at Chloe. "And I'm not being any help to you at all."

"Don't despair yet," Chloe said, with more good cheer than she felt. "There are lots of ways to go at this."

After breakfast, Adam and Chloe said goodbye to Tamsin and walked to the curb. "Want a ride?" Adam asked.

She shook her head. "No, thanks. I can walk from here. Have a good morning." She pictured crime scene techs, barricades, police tape. "If that's possible. I'll stop by the cottage at lunchtime and see how you're doing." She started to turn away.

"Chloe, wait." Adam put a hand on her arm. "I'm sorry Grandma put you on the spot last night. About doing research."

"It's okay." Chloe remembered the stricken look in Tamsin's eyes. "I can't promise I'll find anything, but I'm happy to look."

Adam held her gaze. "Thank you. I wouldn't have a clue where to begin."

"It's what I do," Chloe said. "See you later."

Chloe enjoyed the walk through Mineral Point, home to Wisconsin's first National Register Historic District. Almost every building downtown had been restored to its original stone or brick façade. She didn't linger, though, and arrived at Pendarvis at seven forty-five a.m. Fifteen minutes early. Not that she was nervous or anything.

The historic site was situated on four and a half acres in the right angle created by Shake Rag Street and Spruce Street. It was best known for the three historic homes mentioned in the newspaper article: Polperro House, Pendarvis House, and Trelawny House. Those structures backed into the same craggy limestone wall that rose behind Adam's cottage.

An old rowhouse consisting of several other historic structures had been preserved against the hill on the upper property. A cabin on one end was restored and open to visitors, and the lower level also included a re-created traditional Cornish pub. The upper level of the rowhouse included staff offices and a large room for the gift shop and ticket counter—a warren of spaces all under one roof. The "Staff Only" entrance led into a room that had once been a kitchen, and now held bookshelves and a rack of reproduction 1840s clothing. Chloe wandered past the director's closed door and knocked on the second office's open one.

Site curator Claudia Doyle greeted her with a hug. "Chloe! Good to see you."

"It's good to be here," Chloe assured her. "And to see you somewhere *other* than a collections committee meeting."

Because the Historic Sites Division staff was spread out geographically, meetings were regularly scheduled at the historical society's headquarters in Madison. Site directors and curators attended monthly collections committee meetings. Each curator made a presentation about artifacts offered for donation, along with a recommendation about whether to accept the gift or not. Many of the people now stationed at other sites had once worked at Old World Wisconsin, which had enjoyed a larger staff during the frantic development years in the late 1970s. When curators from other sites presented their conclusions about potential donations, everyone else generally nodded. When Chloe made *her* presentation, the room crackled to life with dissent and observations from people who knew her site better than she did. "Your predecessor had decided *against* using tea leaf china in the Four Mile Inn ... Doesn't the Pedersen Farm research report refer specifically to a *blue* quilt? ... I'm surprised you want to accept another *tine*, since your storage is so tight ... "

Chloe hated collections committee meeting days.

The bright spot was seeing Claudia, who'd been employed by the society for only a few months longer than Chloe had. As the two newbies, they habitually sat next to each other, providing moral support. They'd been known to connect by phone the day after the

Madison gatherings to commiserate and kvetch. Claudia often felt as overwhelmed as Chloe did at the wretched meetings.

Now she gestured Chloe into a cramped office that felt almost familiar: two desks, a wall of file cabinets, plastic milk crates on the deep windowsills holding overflow files, a plank shelf crammed with interpretive manuals, local histories, and collections care how-tos.

"Want some coffee?"

"Yes, please." Chloe rubbed her palms on her trousers.

Claudia took a red mug from a shelf and poured coffee from the percolator sitting on one corner of her crowded desk. She was a plump woman in her early forties, with gray hair worn in a Gibson Girl–style bun, a round face, and wide hazel eyes behind wire-rimmed glasses. She wore a cotton dress with a small floral pattern and canvas Mary Jane shoes. In addition to collections care, Claudia trained and supervised the interpretive staff, was responsible for educational programming, and stocked the site's gift shop.

Life at a small site, Chloe thought, as she accepted the steaming mug. "Thanks." A framed photograph of a girl with dark pigtails on her friend's desk caught her eye. "What a pretty child."

"That's my daughter, Holly. She's nine. She adores the site, so I'm sure you'll meet her while you're here."

Chloe decided to mention the elephant in the room. "After reading that article in the newspaper yesterday, I was half afraid that I'd arrive to find a *Chloe go home* sign."

Claudia sank into her desk chair and motioned Chloe into another. "That news was quite a shock."

"You didn't know it was coming?"

"I assume Loren did, but I found out when the reporter called my house for a comment." She shoved a loose strand of hair away from her face. "It was all I could do to keep from losing it on the phone."

"I'm so sorry."

"Holly has special needs, Chloe. She doesn't handle change well, and after moving here, I swore to myself that I would never uproot her again. And she gets special therapy that is not covered by insurance. *And* my new husband is having second thoughts about raising a child with a brain development disorder." She sighed. "Suffice it to say that I cannot afford to lose my job."

This was the first Chloe had heard about these personal problems. "Oh, Claudia. Are things here really so bad?"

Claudia sighed. "Pendarvis opened thirteen years ago, in 1971. Attendance peaked at about 30,000 in 1976. When the site opened there was only one permanent person on staff, who had to do everything. I was the first curator hired. The position is absolutely essential, but obviously my salary is an additional expense. Last year wasn't great, but we worked hard on trimming the budget. I've been aligning staff with visitor traffic, for example. And this season we're relying on a volunteer receptionist, when we've always had an LTE during the season."

Chloe nodded. Limited Term Employment, she meant. LTEs were limited to 1040 hours of work in a calendar year, and had no benefits or protections. The historic sites were open seasonally, so LTEs were critically important—and the most vulnerable for cuts.

"We'll be okay if we have good weather this fall," Claudia said. "But obviously, things are tight."

"Yeah." Chloe had thought Old World's budget was tight. Evidently she didn't know a good thing when she saw it.

Claudia summoned a determined smile. "Well, it's too early for dirges. I am glad you're here this week. Loren and I get along fine, but I've really been looking forward to having another curator to talk to."

Chloe thought about all the times she traded sad stories with Byron, Old World's curator of interpretation. Or Dellyn, who managed the site's historic gardens. "I'm here to help in any way I can," she said earnestly.

"As you know, my background is in education, not collections management." Claudia stirred creamer into her own mug. "I've got a list of artifact questions. And I want to talk to you about creating a permanent storage facility."

"Sure."

For a moment Claudia looked excited. "I dream of putting together a subset of items documented to nineteenth-century Mineral Point. In the early days, this was a pretty lawless place. Lots of scandals about bogus mine leases, gambling, claim-jumping, duels, bribery, you name it. But if I can find the right artifacts, I can show that Mineral Point was not a frontier town for long. The Cornish people saw to that." She hesitated, and the flicker of excitement drained away. "If it even makes sense to do any long-term planning..."

"It does," Chloe said firmly.

"I don't mean to overwhelm you. I'm just really glad you're here."

Chloe felt something tight inside her ease. She'd been lamenting the ill fortune that had deposited her here just as the announcement came of possible doom for Pendarvis, supposedly all because Old World Wisconsin had with malicious greed sucked every penny from state coffers. It hadn't occurred to her that the terrible news might make Claudia even more desperate for a colleague and friend.

"You'll want to start by getting to know the site. I'll get you a copy of our interpretive plan, and tour you through the buildings."

"Do you have any accounts written by Cornish women?" Chloe asked eagerly.

Claudia shook her head. "Sorry. I'd give anything for a primary source glimpse into domestic life. But most of the immigrants from Cornwall were illiterate."

"How about artifacts?"

"Nope. We have some kitchenware that might have been owned by Cornish women, but nothing's documented." She gave Chloe a *What can I say?* look. "If you happen to discover any clues to life for the early Cornish women in Mineral Point, I'd be eternally grateful."

A firm knock sounded on the office door. Chloe turned and saw a slender thirty-ish woman standing in the doorway with a briefcase in one hand and an expensive-looking notebook bound in green leather in the other. Her black hair was clipped in a bob, and she wore dressy jeans and a dramatic scarlet blouse. "I'm sorry for interrupting," the newcomer said in a tone that held not even a jot of sorrow. "But Mr. Beskeen said I could use your research files this morning."

"Certainly," Claudia said. "He's not in today, but it's no problem." She gestured toward Chloe. "This is Chloe Ellefson, curator of collections at Old World Wisconsin. Chloe, this is Yvonne Miller."

Chloe stood, extending a hand. "Hi, Yvonne."

The other woman hesitated before pressing Chloe's fingers for a nanosecond. "I prefer 'Dr. Miller,' actually," she said. "I have a Ph.D."

Well, golly gee, Chloe thought. Aren't you special.

"You're welcome to work at my desk," Claudia said with admirable grace. "Chloe, it's about time to meet the interpreters anyway, and get the day started." She led the way out of the building.

"So," Chloe murmured, "who was that?"

"Yvonne? She's a 'freelance historian.'" Claudia made little quote marks in the air with her fingers.

"What's she working on?"

"A book."

"About Pendarvis?"

"I'm not sure. She hasn't deigned to explain the focus of her work." Claudia rolled her eyes. "She's been making regular appearances here as long as I've been on staff. I think she's trying to convince Loren to hire her as a project researcher or something." She snorted. "That's even less likely to happen now. Even the threat to close Pendarvis has a silver lining."

"Ah," Chloe said, which was the most tactful response she could come up with.

Claudia took a well-worn path behind the rowhouse. "I meet with the staff every morning in the gift shop," she explained. "Same building, but there's no inside access. Bob and Edgar—you know about Bob and Edgar, right?"

"The guys who saved these buildings?" They'd been mentioned in the newspaper article.

"Right. Bob Neal and Edgar Hellum added the gift shop room and used it as studio and entertaining space." She smiled. "They were both very creative, very clever. A natural spring runs under the building, and they created a little fish pond right in the floor. We have it covered now, but one day I'd like to—"

"She has no business here!" An angry male voice drifted through the open door as they approached the shop.

"It's not her fault that the historical society is threatening to close Pendarvis." That was a younger voice, female.

Damn, Chloe thought.

"First her site vampires all the resources from ours," the older man snapped. "Then they send her here to—"

Claudia marched through the door. "Good *morning*."

35

Straggling in behind her, Chloe found herself facing three seasonal employees. A white-haired woman in street clothes stood behind the ticket and sales counter. Two people wearing 1840s-style clothing were obviously the day's tour guides: a diminutive young blond woman, and a man in his sixties with gray hair and beard. The woman looked anxious. The man looked pissed.

After a few seconds of unhappy silence, Claudia introduced Chloe. "She'll be helping me this week."

"Hi," said the young woman.

"Good to meet you," the cash register lady echoed.

"I hope you're satisfied," the man said, "now that Old World Wisconsin has diverted the funds Pendarvis needs to stay open."

"Gerald!" Claudia snapped. "Chloe is our guest. I expect you to treat her with respect."

Gerald folded his arms.

"I understand why you're angry," Chloe tried. "I was horrified when I read that article yesterday."

Gerald didn't deign to respond.

Claudia shot Chloe a mortified glance: *I'm so sorry!*

Chloe gave a tiny shake of her head: *Let it go.*

Claudia shared a few updates—scheduled school tours, a request to use quiet time for sweeping and dusting the buildings, an update on maintenance work being done at Trelawny House. Only when business was complete did she circle back to what was on everyone's mind. "At this point, I don't know anything more about our status than you do. Loren is in Madison today, but he'll be back in time for the meeting at the Walker House this evening. We all need to make an effort to put the uncertainty out of our minds for now."

"But—" Gerald began.

"The first school bus will arrive any minute," Claudia said firmly. "Let's get to work."

The two interpreters went to meet the expected bus. The older woman began cleaning the counter with commendable zeal.

"Let's head down to Polperro House," Claudia suggested to Chloe. "I should be able to give you the nickel tour before the kids descend." They left the building and started down a fern-lined path. "I apologize for Gerald's comments. I'll talk to him."

Chloe ran her fingers along a frond shimmering with lingering rain droplets. "Don't scold on my behalf. The threat of closing Pendarvis came as a horrible shock. I'd feel bad if staff members *weren't* upset. I take it Gerald has been here for a while?" He'd been wearing reproduction shoes, and his glasses were in antique frames. Unless Pendarvis had a whole lot more money in its period clothing budget than Old World Wisconsin did—which clearly was not the case—interpreters either purchased those expensive items themselves or went without.

"Since the site opened," Claudia agreed. "He's a great interpreter. Rita, the young woman, is too. She graduated from Marquette last spring with a history degree, and signed on here for the summer. She hasn't been able to find a permanent job, so she decided to stay through the fall season. And I'm grateful she did." All of the state historic sites closed at the end of October, but the autumn could be busy with tours. "And Audrey, who manages the gift shop, has been here for years."

Chloe let Gerald's attitude slide away. It was a beautiful September morning. Birds chittered in the trees. Goldenrod bloomed in the sprawling gardens. The sky was that deep blue that only came in autumn.

The Depression-era swimming pool Adam had mentioned was clearly visible across Shake Rag Street. Happily, south of the pool was the undeveloped hillside Chloe had admired from Adam's front step the day before. "I'm so glad that at least part of the hill was left alone," she said.

"This area was part of the Michigan Territory when mining by whites began," Claudia told her. "That hill was placed on the National Register of Historic Places in 1972 because it was one of the most densely mined places in the region. And it's ours! The state recently transferred forty-three acres to us. We're restoring the landscape to prairie and creating self-guided interpretive trails."

"That sounds fantastic," Chloe said. "Would it be okay if I go wandering over there sometime? Something about it calls to me."

"Sure, if you want to. The Cornish miners called the hill *Mena Dhu*. It means 'Dark Hill.'"

Chloe felt a tiny frisson down her spine as she gazed across the street. Dark Hill. Evocative, she thought.

They reached Polperro, an unusual three-story house. The lowest level and back had been constructed of stone, with two additional stories at the front constructed of logs. Approaching from the side, the house looked as if it had grown out of the tall stone outcrop behind it, with lush plants spilling from cracks and crevices.

"The Polperro family lived here?"

"There was no Polperro family." Claudia fished two keys from her pocket and handed one to Chloe. "Here. This will open any site building. The front doors are sealed since the houses are right on the street, so use the back doors. Anyway, when Bob and Edgar acquired the house they named it for a fishing village on the southeast coast of Cornwall." She unlocked the door and ushered Chloe inside. "We start our tours by talking about mining. That provides context for all of the other stories." She led the way through a small entryway into a room with mining hand tools mounted on the walls. Larger pieces of equipment stood around the periphery.

Chloe pointed at a shovel. "That seems awfully short," she said as she tried to surreptitiously check for any lingering emotions. Nothing unusual, thank goodness.

"Men working on their knees didn't need long shovels."

"I suppose." Chloe stopped by an array of miners' candleholders. "Sticking tommies."

"That's right!" Claudia said approvingly.

Chloe studied the display, but without Adam's candleholder in hand, she couldn't be sure if any of these might have been made by the same smith. "Do you have more of these?"

"There may be more in storage."

Chloe made a mental note to check. "It's difficult to imagine working underground with such scant light."

"Lead was the prime ore here, of course, but the miners who immigrated from Cornwall likely learned their trade working in tin mines, or copper at deeper levels. They were used to it. They'd stick a candle into a lump of clay on their hat."

"Such a hard life," Chloe murmured. She'd attended West Virginia University, where a few of her fellow students took classes during the day and worked coal mines at night. She'd heard stories.

"It absolutely was. But I suspect most miners did a bit better financially than fishermen or peasant farmers, at least when mineral prices were good. The Cornish miners were the best in the world. Shafts around here were no more than maybe a hundred feet, but in Cornwall their shafts went down as far as three thousand feet."

"Seriously?"

"Absolutely. But, as you say, conditions were brutal. Some boys and girls began doing surface work as early as six or seven years old—"

"Just *children*." That hurt Chloe's heart. "Boys *and* girls?"

"The girls stayed above, sorting and breaking the ore. Bal maidens, they were called, which means 'mine girls.' But when a boy turned ten or so, he went underground to start learning true mining from his father. Or an older brother or uncle, if his father was dead, because families worked together. The miners' health started failing when they were still in their twenties. The average lifespan of a Cornish miner back then was forty-seven years."

Such a hard life, Chloe thought again. And she'd had no idea that little boys—and little girls—had worn themselves out at the Cornish mines.

FOUR

"Wage day tomorrow, Mary," one of the other girls said. "Want to go to the shops with us?"

Another bal maiden looked up from the ore heap and scoffed, "Mary never wants to go to the shops. She fancies herself too good for the likes of us."

"No, that's not so," Mary protested. She was eleven now, and the thought of visiting the shops was appealing. "I just pass what I earn to my father."

In truth, though, it wasn't quite so simple. When Mary began working at the mine, her parents had decided that she could keep any overtime pay. "I want you to have a bit of money that's all your own," Mama had told her, hands on Mary's shoulders. "Keep it for something important. You're a hard worker, but you're also smart, and I pray you won't be a bal maiden forever." She tipped her head with a sad smile. "Oh, Mary. I do *so* want a different life for you."

Mary, who'd been all of six at the time, hadn't any idea what "different life" meant. But after Mama died, Mary had continued to mouse away extra pence in an old stocking. Her mother was in heaven, and spending precious coins on lace mitts or silk ribbons would be disrespectful.

"*Mary Pascoe!*"

The bellow brought Mary back from her memories. When she saw the mine's surface captain approaching, her heart began pounding like a cobbing hammer. "Is one of my brothers hurt? Or my father?"

"No," Mr. Penhallow snapped. "Just come with me."

Mary followed the boss away from the other girls on the picking floor. What had she done to catch his attention? She couldn't think of anything. She was as strong as any girl her age. She worked hard.

A freckled lad caught her eye behind Penhallow's back. He didn't dare make a lewd comment in the boss's hearing, so he cupped one hand in front of his private parts with a jerking motion. Mary rolled her eyes and kept walking. Penhallow usually picked weaker girls for his unwanted attentions. The ones without a father or brother working underground. The ones who didn't fill their daily quota but desperately needed to keep their jobs.

He led her first to the washbasins by the dinner shed. "Scrub your hands and face."

She did her best to splash off the grit, but her wariness grew when he turned toward the counthouse. At the door he stepped back so she might enter first.

She paused, fiercely holding his gaze: *You will not touch me.*

"Be quick, you silly chit," he hissed, pushing her through.

The office was not empty. A woman with brown hair sat in Penhallow's chair. No, Mary corrected herself, a *lady*. Her pretty purple-striped dress was clean. A bonnet with lace peeking from beneath the brim sat on the desk. Mary quickly pulled off her *gook*—the huge bonnet with shoulder flaps she wore for protection from flying chips of rock—but it was too late to remove the wool strips she'd wound around her legs for the same reason, or to slap dust from her rough wool dress. Her shoes were stained red with iron oxide.

Penhallow gripped Mary's arm and pushed her into the empty chair in front of the desk. "Mrs. Bunney wants to ask you some questions. Mind you answer fitty."

Mary couldn't imagine what questions this lady could possibly have for her.

"This here's Mary Pascoe," Penhallow announced. Then he stepped back and folded his arms across his chest. He was a stocky man with thick neck and shoulders. His close-cropped hair was gray, his hands and arms scarred from his own days below ground. He planted his feet as if settling in for a brawl.

"Good afternoon," Mary said politely.

Mrs. Bunney ignored her. "That will be all for now, Mr. Penhallow," she said coolly in formal English. Mary, used to her region's Cornish dialect, had to concentrate to understand.

Penhallow didn't move.

Mrs. Bunney raised her eyebrows. "I desire hot tea."

Penhallow's jaw worked, but in the end, he walked out of his office.

Ordered out by a woman! Mary marveled. How had Mrs. Bunney accomplished it? It had been more than her tone, her posture. Mrs. Bunney's authority came from someplace inside. From a sense of knowing who she was—and of understanding, Mary thought, that she was not beholden to a greasy dobeck like Jake Penhallow, surface captain of Wheal Blackstone in Camborne, Cornwall.

For the first time, Mary thought she might have glimpsed the "different life" her mother had wished for her.

Mrs. Bunney turned to her. "Did Mr. Penhallow explain why I am here?"

Mary licked lips suddenly gone dry and buried her scarred hands in her skirt. "No, ma'am."

"I am here on behalf of the Christian Welfare Society." Mrs. Bunney laced long fingers on the desk. "We are concerned about the welfare of helpless children like yourself employed in the mines. How old were you when you began working here, Mary?"

"Six, ma'am."

"Six!" Mrs. Bunney said sorrowfully. "Such a tender age."

Not so tender, Mary thought. Hungry, more like. Most girls were a bit older when they started, but ore falling from an overloaded bucket had broken Mary's father's arm, and the family needed the money.

Still … her sister Elizabeth was six, sturdy like Mary was, and could become a bal maiden any time. Since their mother was dead and their father too tired and sad to take notice, it was Mary who'd decided that Elizabeth would stay home. "She can mind Loveday," she'd told her father, even though a neighbor had offered to take Loveday, just three, in with her brood during the day. Truth was, Mary had vowed to herself that Elizabeth and Loveday would never come to the mine. She'd done all right, but Mama's voice still whispered in her ear. Mary wanted better for her sisters too.

Mrs. Bunney pulled a pencil and a small leather-bound journal from her basket and began making notes. "What are your duties?"

"I'm a picker. We pick out the good stones of ore from the waste. I've filled in cobbing if need be too. Soon I'll move over there for good."

Mrs. Bunney's brow crinkled in confusion. Evidently this was the first mine she'd visited.

"See, the ore can't be smelted until it's broken down. Spallers break large stones into smaller ones. Cobbers chip the waste stone away from lumps of ore. Like this." Mary held out one fist to demonstrate the desired size. "Buckers smash those stones."

Penhallow returned from the kitchen, carrying a tin coffeepot with a dirty rag wrapped around the handle and a rusty tin cup. Mrs. Bunney reached back into her basket and removed a teacup and saucer made of blue and white china. Suddenly Mary could hardly breathe. That china was the prettiest thing she'd ever seen. For a glorious moment she thought a second teacup would follow, and she would be invited to share tea with Mrs. Bunney.

Mrs. Bunney pulled out a single small china plate and a cloth napkin. A yellow saffron bun wrapped in greased paper followed. Mary had only tasted saffron a few times when the price fell in the shops because smugglers had brought it. Mary thought saffron tasted exquisite. Like the sunrise, if sunrise could be tasted.

"Shall I pour?" Penhallow asked, like he was some fine toff.

Mrs. Bunney gestured, and he carefully filled her cup with steaming, fragrant tea. Mary realized that there was naught but one cup, one bun.

"That's all, Mr. Penhallow," Mrs. Bunney said and made a little shooing gesture with one hand. He retreated with obvious reluctance. Mrs. Bunney nibbled her saffron bun and sipped her tea before turning back to Mary. "Do you like being a picker?"

Mary struggled to tear her gaze from that delicate teacup. How her mother would have loved such a pretty thing! How Elizabeth's and Loveday's eyes would shine if Mary brought something so lovely home! If I had such a teacup, Mary thought, I wouldn't carry it in a basket to be bumped and chipped. Such a cup belonged on the mantel, to be used only on special days.

"Mary?"

Remembering the question, Mary shrugged. "I like it well enough." She was strong and did well. She got paid.

Scribble, scribble. "Do you work indoors or out?"

"Out. Sometimes under a roof, sometimes not."

"Are you warm enough?"

"It's raw in winter," Mary admitted. "It takes a lot of water to wash the ore, so my feet are usually wet."

Mrs. Bunney shook her head. "How far do you have to walk to get here? What time do you start in the morning?"

"I live a bit over two miles away, ma'am. I leave home at five thirty."

Mrs. Bunney made a clucking noise with her tongue. "Dreadful."

Mary shifted in her chair. Unless the weather was horrid, the morning walks were the best part of her day. She liked the peace of it, liked seeing bits of light converge as mine workers carrying lanterns met on the path, liked singing Methodist hymns with the others as they walked. In summer, when days were long, she liked seeing the distant high tors watching over the moor. She liked passing gravestones left from ancient times, huge slabs of weathered granite. She liked smelling primroses when they bloomed in the hedges.

But Mary didn't try to explain. She was starting to figure out that Mrs. Bunney had brought decided opinions about the mine workers with her.

"What do you eat?"

Mary wondered what would happen if she said she didn't want to answer any more questions. Nothing good, surely, as Penhallow was no doubt listening from the next room. "I bring a pasty with meat for dinner most days," she said with a touch of pride, although honesty compelled her to add, "or a hoggan. At home we have barley bread and milk for breakfast, usually. And boiled potatoes for supper."

"That hardly seems enough for a ten-hour shift," Mrs. Bunney said. "You must feel weak and sickly all the time."

"No, ma'am." Mary held her gaze. "I do just fine."

By the time Mary had answered all of Mrs. Bunney's questions, the marvelous teacup was empty and the plate littered with crumbs. Mrs. Bunney closed her notebook, laced her fingers together again, and leaned over the desk. "Mary, on behalf of the Christian Welfare Society, I am worried about you."

You just met me, Mary thought.

"It's not only the danger inherent in mining work that troubles me. I'm worried about your soul. You are surrounded daily by rough men who use foul language. Young ladies like yourself should be cultivating modesty and grace. How can you do that here?"

Mary had no idea where she was supposed to cultivate modesty and grace.

"And you left your mother's side at such a young age." Mrs. Bunney shook her head mournfully. "You've had no education."

Mary didn't answer. Girls the likes of her didn't have much chance for schooling.

"Have you even learned any domestic arts? Are you prepared to become a decent wife and mother? Of course not! How can a girl who has known nothing but manual labor and rough company accomplish anything in polite society? If you do marry, your husband will surely find no comfort by his own hearth. And that, my girl, means he will search for it at the pub."

Mary's cheeks burned. Something hot formed inside, too, and built like steam in a boiler. She gripped the edges of her chair until her fingers ached.

"Child, I beseech you to take my words to heart. Pray over them. And I will pray that you see the error of your ways. A mine is no place for children, especially girls. Don't be tempted by earnings. Don't be distracted by the fine clothes and fripperies you girls dream of. You simply have no hope of becoming a respectable woman unless you give up mining."

A whistle blew. Mary unclenched her fingers by sheer will and stood. She was leaving the office. Otherwise all that steam inside her chest would blow too.

Penhallow hurried into the room. His jaw was tight, and he didn't seem quite so eager to fawn all over Mrs. Bunney of the Christian Welfare Society. "Mary's shift is over, and she must be on her way."

"I have what I need from Mary," Mrs. Bunney told him. "You may bring the next girl in."

"But ... all of the girls are finished now," he protested.

"Surely a few extra minutes won't matter. Bring three more girls, at the least. I haven't come all this way to interview just one bal maiden."

Mary left them to it. Outside, the other girls were already drifting away. Hurry, Mary wanted to say. Escape while you can.

She wanted to get away too—not because of Mrs. Bunney, but because Elizabeth and Loveday had been home alone all day. Loveday had always been a weakly child. Mary had learned to bundle her worries aside while she worked, but when the whistle blew and she could turn toward home, the fear came flooding back. What if Loveday had taken a sudden fever? Or fallen? Elizabeth had a good head on her shoulders, but would she know what to do? Usually

Mary hurried home, kissed Loveday and Elizabeth, and hung a kettle over the hearth fire so dinner would be ready by the time her father and two brothers got home.

But not today. Today was the first day that her younger brother Jory, who'd been doing surface work for several years, had gone underground.

That morning Jory had donned flannel trousers and a new hat that was rubbed with resin, with a dish-shaped crown where he could fix a candle with a lump of clay. At the mine she'd watched her father tie a rope around his own waist, then tie the other end around Jory's. Father had gone into the shaft first, pockets bulging with candles, his feet in their hobnailed boots descending slowly down the ladder, rung by rung. Jory followed, trying to pretend he wasn't scared. Then Andrew, a year older than she was, had disappeared into the earth.

Now she wanted to welcome Jory when he emerged from his shift underground. She watched as men climbed from the shaft, one by one.

"So, how was it?" someone leered just behind her. It was the freckled young man who'd watched Penhallow take her into the counthouse.

"Giss on," Mary said. Don't speak rubbish. Any stronger reaction only encouraged men like this.

Young ladies like yourself should be cultivating modesty and grace. How can you do that here?

And what do you know about it, anyway? Mary thought angrily. Fie on Mrs. Bunney, with her lace-edged bonnet and fancy airs and fragile teacup. One day, she thought, when I do better, I shall buy a whole china set so I can serve other people.

The stream of tired miners reaching the surface slowed, then stopped. Mary began to pace, too irritated and anxious to stand still.

Finally a small hand curled around the top rung of the ladder. Then Jory's head appeared. His face was filthy and he looked inexpressibly weary, but he managed a grin as he climbed from the shaft. Father followed him, with Andrew again bringing up the rear.

Jory made a big show of sprawling on the ground ... but Mary had seen how he'd struggled to manage the last few rungs. "I was starting to worry," she whispered to Andrew.

"Father knew he'd be slow, so we waited till last."

"He's all right?" Mary cocked her head toward Jory.

"Just trembly. We've been climbing for almost an hour, I figure. First climb, after his first shift below ... " Andrew smiled. "Jory did well."

Father stood nearby, bent over with hands on knees. "He *did* do well," he agreed, straightening. "I'm proud of—" Suddenly his voice broke, and he staggered a few steps.

"Father!" Andrew jumped to his side and grasped his arm.

"I'm all right." Father gently shook his son free. "Just dizzy for a moment." He extended a hand to Jory. "On your feet, son. You need to get home before your muscles seize up."

But Mary's heart seized as Jory slowly climbed to his feet. Andrew looked stricken too. The air in deep mines was bad, often thick with dust from the blasting. She'd seen Father cough up black stuff, which was a sign of miner's disease. Dizziness was another sign of miner's disease. Miners said that once the dizziness came on a man, his days were numbered.

Suddenly she wanted to sprawl on the ground too.

But there was no room for that. "Let's get on home. I'll cook supper and make tea." It wouldn't be served in fine china with lovely saffron buns, but barley bread and tea would hearten them all.

It took longer than usual to walk home because Jory was that wobbly kneed. Finally they crested the last rise. Their little thatch-roofed stone cottage, last in a row of three, came into view.

"Something's wrong," Mary hissed. "There's no smoke." Elizabeth always had a fire going by the time she got home—and they were late today.

She began to run. Andrew was on her heels.

The neighbor woman was waiting by the garden, red-eyed and sniffling. Mary felt as if someone had dropped her heart down a mineshaft. "Loveday?" she gasped.

"Loveday's fine. She's inside with my girls. But—oh, Mary." The older woman began to sob. "It's Elizabeth."

FIVE

"OFFICER MCKENNA?" CHIEF NABORSKI stood in his office doorway. "A word?"

"Sure." Roelke put aside the report he was working on and followed his boss. He couldn't think of anything he'd screwed up lately, but this kind of summons always made him feel like a truant kid getting called into the principal's office.

"Shut the door."

Roelke did, then sat in the chair facing the chief's desk. The older man didn't *look* pissed. Always an encouraging sign.

Chief Naborski tipped his chair back on two legs. He was a good chief who knew the Village of Eagle well. Residents respected him. The cops who worked for him respected him too. He had a craggy face and had evidently worn his gray hair buzzed in a flat-top since serving in the Korean War. His job had more to do with community politics and supervision than action now, but Roelke knew the man could hold his own and then some in a bar brawl. Naborski's calm demeanor hid a core of iron.

Chief twiddled a pencil in his fingers. "Have you had a chance to follow up on that Hackberry Lane problem?"

Roelke had recently taken a call from a concerned citizen who reported lots of people coming and going at the house across the street. "I think they're selling drugs over there," she'd concluded indignantly. "I won't have that going on anywhere near my kids."

"I'm keeping an eye on the place," Roelke reported now. "It could take a little while to establish any kind of pattern."

"Keep me posted," Chief Naborski said. "Now. On the topic of drug activity, I just got a call from Dorothy Blevins." Dorothy Blevins was the Village Board member who chaired the Police Committee. "They're granting my request for funds to send one officer to a Criminal Drug Interdiction training program for patrol officers."

"Great!" Roelke said eagerly. He'd asked several times for more training. In his first job with the Milwaukee Police Department, he'd spent most of his time walking a beat. After transferring to Eagle, he'd found himself spending most of his time in a patrol car. His second day on the job he'd pulled a woman over for speeding and sent her on her merry way with ticket in hand, feeling rather pleased with himself. The next day he learned that a cop in Jefferson County, after pulling over the same vehicle, had found bundles of cash and a whole lot of drugs in the trunk. "I'm chalking it up to lack of experience, but you screwed up," Chief had said to Roelke. "The Jefferson guy spotted something you missed."

Roelke didn't want to kick his skills up a notch just to make up for his mistake. He wanted to be proactive in protecting the community he was sworn to serve. Comedian John Belushi's death the year before from a speedball—cocaine and heroin—had brought awareness to the problem, but cocaine traffic was spreading, and Eric Clapton's ode still got plenty of airtime. Cocaine use wasn't confined to Hollywood, or even big cities like Milwaukee and Chicago, much as some people in small towns like Eagle wanted to believe. So much cocaine was flooding the market that prices had dropped. Instead of being discouraged, dealers started converting the powder to crack. Small quantities of the solid, smokeable stuff could be sold to more people. For dealers, crack was easy to produce and very profitable. For users, crack was cheap and horribly addictive. Roelke was particularly worried about bored teens who were curious, susceptible to peer pressure, and convinced they were invincible.

Suddenly he realized what Chief Naborski hadn't said. Who was going? It should be me, Roelke thought. This was a great opportunity, and he really, really wanted it.

"The catch," Naborski said, "is that the Police Committee wants to be involved in choosing the recipient."

Roelke's right knee began to bounce. "Why?"

"I don't know," Naborski admitted. "And I don't like it. But Ms. Blevins was adamant on that condition."

Was this Ralph Petty's handiwork? Roelke wondered, gritting his teeth. Petty was not on the Board, but it was no secret that Chloe's boss was contemplating a run in the next election. Roelke had found a way to cut Petty down to size last summer during a murder investigation. Was this his revenge? Had he made nice with the Committee members and managed to set Roelke up for failure?

"I was asked to recommend two officers for consideration." Naborski's gaze was steady. "I gave them your name and Skeet's."

Officer Skeet Deardorff was not a permanent employee of the EPD, as Roelke was. But that was only because the funds for another full-time officer—with benefits—didn't exist. Skeet worked as many hours as Roelke did. And Roelke knew that Skeet was hungry for any opportunity like this. For Skeet, extra training and certification made it that much more likely that he would get hired in a permanent status in Eagle, or with another force.

"Is there some kind of evaluation process?" Roelke asked.

"The Police Committee will call each of you in for an interview one day this week."

Roelke hated having to compete with Skeet for this, but there it was. "Alright."

"One more thing." Chief brought the front legs of his chair to the floor with a bang. "You're a good cop, Roelke. But if you want this one, you gotta fly straight. Do you understand me?"

"Yes," Roelke said, although he didn't, not fully. Was Naborski's comment a general statement? Or did it hint at something more? Since joining the EPD he had crossed the boundaries a couple of times. He'd once kicked a killer after he was cuffed. I'm a better cop now, he thought. Nothing like that would ever happen again.

"Any questions?" Chief asked.

Roelke's knee was working like a piston. He forced it to stillness and stood. "No sir."

————

At Polperro House, excited voices signaled the approach of the first school group. "We can make our escape this way," Claudia told Chloe, opening a door that led to a steep, narrow staircase. Upstairs Chloe got a quick glimpse of an 1840s-style kitchen before following her friend out another door. "The benefit of building into such a steep hill," Claudia said. "Both floors are ground floors."

Chloe paused, looking back at the old house. She wanted to get a better feel for the people who had once walked the floors of the homes now preserved at Pendarvis, and she wasn't sure how. "Is there an old Cornish cemetery? Maybe at one of the churches?"

"Your best bet is the old city cemetery." Claudia kicked a fallen stick from the walkway. "Burials date back to the 1830s. Take Second Street just a few blocks south of High Street."

"Great. When I have a chance I'll wander through, see what I can find of the Cornish immigrants."

"Feel free to do that on state time. I'd welcome any information you discover."

"Thanks, I will." Chloe glanced at her watch as they walked up steps that led to the upper property. "Claudia, I need to tell you something." She summarized what had happened at *Chy Looan* the day before.

"Dear God!" Claudia stopped walking. "A skeleton? *Really?*"

"As you can imagine, Tamsin Bolitho was disturbed by the news," Chloe said. "She asked if I'd do some research, in hopes of somehow identifying the body."

Claudia looked dubious. "How are you going to do that?"

"I think it's most likely that the death and burial took place in the early 1930s, when the cottage sat empty. Maybe I can find some record of a missing person." She gave a regretful shrug. "I'm hardly the best choice for the job, but I was handy, and I'm glad to help if I can. Any suggestions on where I should begin?"

"The Mineral Point Archives," Claudia said promptly. "Bob Neal donated his collection of documents and photographs to the public library before he died, which formed the nucleus of the collection. What he saved is priceless. And Midge, the archivist, is a dynamo."

They continued walking up the hill. Back in the office, an elderly woman with ramrod posture and silver hair swept back from her face in permed patrician waves sat at the second desk. A cane was propped within easy reach. She swiveled in her chair to greet them.

"Chloe, this is Evelyn Bainbridge," Claudia said. "She helped out in the gift shop last year. This year she has kindly given us a *lot* of volunteer hours as receptionist."

"Hi, Evelyn," Chloe said, hoping she wasn't stepping in it this time.

Evelyn extended a hand with manicured nails. Chloe caught a faint whiff of lavender. "It's good to meet you, Chloe."

"We'd be lost without her," Claudia added. "Not only is she great with callers, but she's lived in Mineral Point her whole life."

"My husband did too, God rest his soul." Evelyn's voice was wistful. "We shared a love of history. He collected military antiques. Anyway, I'm grateful I can be helpful here."

"We're grateful too," Claudia told her, then looked around. "Was Yvonne Miller here when you arrived?"

"She just left." Evelyn looked annoyed. "But she didn't have the courtesy to put back the files she pulled! As if we have room to store things for her." She gestured indignantly at a new stack of folders. "Don't worry, Claudia. I'll put them away."

Another member of the Dr. Yvonne Miller fan club, Chloe thought.

"If I can, in between calls," Evelyn amended. "The phone's been ringing off the hook." She held out a stack of little *While You Were Out* slips.

Claudia took them and dropped into her desk chair with a stifled groan. "Let me guess, people are upset about the newspaper article."

"That's putting it mildly. I've been hearing them out, explaining that I don't have any additional information, and reminding them about the meeting this evening at the Walker House."

Every site needs an Evelyn, Chloe thought.

"I have to deal with these," Claudia said. "Chloe, maybe you should start with our site interpretive plan, and some of the general research files."

"Sounds good," Chloe said. She truly wanted to contribute something useful while she was here. She also wanted to keep so busy today that she didn't stew about the meeting this evening.

At noon she slipped away and walked the short distance to *Chy Looan*. Adam's truck was the only vehicle parked in front. He stepped outside as she approached.

"Where is everyone?" Chloe called.

"Just left." He sank onto the stone wall. "You should see the root cellar. They moved a lot of dirt."

Chloe didn't want to see the root cellar. "Did they find anything else?"

"A few odds and ends. No more bodies, thank God."

"Thank God," she echoed fervently.

Adam rubbed his palms on his thighs, looking frustrated. "Yesterday I was shocked. Today I'm furious. Who would have buried a body in my cottage?"

He doesn't want to say the word, Chloe thought. But burial was the lesser crime. Whoever dug that rough grave had likely been a murderer.

———

Roelke had gotten home too late the night before to talk with his cousin. At lunchtime he drove straight to the modest ranch house in Palmyra that Libby had shared with her kids since her marriage ended two years ago. The divorce had been so ugly that Roelke had moved to Palmyra to lend support. Since he'd rented a tiny soulless walk-up flat, this house had been his de facto home until he bought his ancestral farmhouse last summer.

Libby's car was in the drive. Justin's bike lay abandoned in the front yard, which needed mowing. Roelke would have been glad to mow Libby's grass, but she wouldn't let him.

He had a key and let himself inside. "Libby?"

"In here."

He walked into the kitchen. A typewriter and several file folders sat on the table. Dirty dishes were stacked in the sink. Libby stood at the counter, measuring flour into a big yellow bowl. She wore a long-sleeved t-shirt and shorts.

"Hey." Libby glanced at the clock. "I have to pick up Deirdre from preschool in about fifteen minutes. What are you doing here?"

"I think you know."

Libby did not meet his gaze. "If you have something to say, Roelke, just say it."

"Why did you cancel on Adam and the trip to Mineral Point?"

"Stuff came up." Libby opened a drawer and pulled out a set of metal measuring spoons.

Roelke rarely got pissed at his cousin, but he was getting pissed now. Libby was never evasive. Never coy or secretive. "'Stuff came up?' That's a lousy excuse for disappointing Adam at the last minute."

"Look, I know he's your friend, and I'm sorry if that makes things awkward. But it's just not going to work out with Adam and me."

He frowned. "I thought things were going okay."

She shrugged and stirred cinnamon into the flour.

Roelke reached over and took the spoon from her hand. "Tell me what you're leaving out."

"I'm not—"

"Libby." He waited until she finally, reluctantly, looked at him. "You and I don't always agree, but we are always straight with each other. What the hell is going on?"

Libby blew out a long sigh and leaned against the counter. She ran her fingers through short gray-shot dark hair, leaving little spikes sticking out. Finally she said, "Roelke, I told you last summer that I didn't want to date until my children are older. A lot older. After all the turmoil, they need stability."

Roelke considered her with narrowed eyes. He remembered the conversation. But he'd also seen Libby and Adam together several times over the past few weeks. They were taking things slowly, but there had been a growing ease in their conversations. "Something has changed. You agreed to go down to Mineral Point and see Adam's cottage. You were looking forward to it. So—what gives?"

Libby walked to the window and shoved her hands into her pockets. "I'll only tell you if you promise not to get angry."

"I promise," Roelke said automatically.

"It's Dan."

Roelke was instantly angry. "What does your ex have to do with anything?"

"Dan doesn't want me to date."

"I don't give a rat's ass what Dan does or doesn't want. And neither should you."

"I wouldn't," Libby said evenly, "if Justin and Deirdre weren't involved. But they are."

"What happened?" Roelke growled.

She sighed. "Adam and I sat together at one of Justin's T-ball games. That's *it*. We talked, we laughed, we cheered on Justin's team. Well, unbeknownst to me, Dan actually showed up. He'd never come to one of Justin's games before."

"That's because Dan sucks at being a parent." Deirdre went with the flow but Justin's heart had been broken by his father over and over.

"After the game Adam gave Justin a high-five, said goodbye, and left. Then I see Dan walking up. Justin wraps his arms around him. He was so happy that his dad had come to see him play. It should have been a nice moment."

"And?"

"And Dan looks at me over Justin's head and says, 'I see your new boyfriend is spending time with my son.'" Libby's voice was tight. "I know Dan, and the look in his eyes when he said it—"

"Dan Raymo abused you and has been indifferent to his kids." Heat flamed inside Roelke's chest. "Whether any friend of yours spends time with Justin is none of his concern. You have every right to—"

"But I won't. Dan still wants to punish me for divorcing him, and it's the kids who will suffer. Maybe he'll file for joint custody."

"Maybe you should try to get a restraining order."

"On what grounds?" Libby demanded. "I know that he was making a threat. But he didn't actually say anything threatening."

Roelke knew that. He also knew that beating the crap out of Justin's father, which he sorely wanted to do, was not the way to go. He began to pace the room, almost tripping over a stuffed unicorn. "This isn't right, Libby. Adam's a great guy, and—"

"And I can't see him anymore. End of story."

"But—"

"Justin's fragile enough already," Libby snapped. "You *know* that, Roelke."

He knew that too. Justin was small for his size, not particularly athletic, not particularly good at making friends. He wore glasses and could be moody and still desperately wanted to believe that his father actually cared about him. Roelke had spent a lot of time with Justin and Deirdre and couldn't possibly love them any more than he did.

"He's such a good kid," Roelke said. His heart hurt.

"He is."

"They're both good kids."

"I agree."

"You're giving Dan too much power."

"He already has power. He knows nothing hurts me more than involving the kids in the ugliness."

"I'll talk to him. No threats. Just talk—"

"No, you won't." Libby grabbed his arm, fingers digging into the skin. "I will handle my ex."

But this is what I do, Roelke wanted to say. He did his damnedest to take care of people he loved. The look in Libby's eyes—and the bruises surely already forming on his arm—were painful reminders that he had work to do.

But he didn't argue. Instead he put on his best impassive cop face. "Adam deserves an explanation, Libby."

She sighed. "I know. I'll call him."

Roelke had to be satisfied with that. "When's Justin's next T-ball game?"

"Tomorrow. Seven p.m."

"Unless something messy comes up, I'm off work at three tomorrow. How about I pick you up? It's been way too long since I went to one of his games."

Libby's shoulders relaxed, and she rewarded him with a genuine smile. "That would be *great*."

Roelke couldn't manage a smile in return. One pleasant evening wouldn't wipe away the damage Dan Raymo was doing.

SIX

AFTER LEAVING *CHY LOOAN*, Chloe detoured south. The old city cemetery sprawled over maybe two acres on top of a hill. The years had not been kind to the tombstones, many of which were not only worn, but broken. But like most cemeteries it was peaceful. Chloe believed that those who had suffered during their earthly days were now free of pain, reunited with loved ones.

She was wandering when a voice surprised her. "Can I help you find something?" A balding, white-haired man sat on the ground beside a broken headstone. He held a clipboard. "I'm a volunteer with the cemetery restoration committee."

"I'm looking for any gravestones of early Cornish immigrants."

The man got to his feet. "The majority of burials here took place before 1860. Lots of victims of mining accidents, and the cholera epidemics of 1849 and 1851. But there's no official burial map."

Of course there's not, Chloe thought. That would have been way too easy.

"Before statehood in 1848, death records weren't even collected. I'm trying to document the stones here before any more become illegible. Are you a descendant?"

She shook her head. "No, sir. Just doing some research." That seemed safer than saying she'd come in hopes of somehow connecting with the old Cornish souls.

"I'm afraid there's no logic to the layout," the gentleman added. "And lots of people from Cornwall listed England as their birthplace. Good luck."

Chloe thanked him and walked away, checking those stones she could read for early burials and Cornish surnames. She hadn't gone far when she spotted a young woman crouched near an oak tree, doing a gravestone rubbing. Her back was turned, but the cap of black hair, the scarlet shirt, and the green journal lying in the grass unmistakably belonged to Dr. Yvonne Miller.

Really? Chloe thought, vexed. *You pick the one day I'm here, looking for peace and quiet, to do cemetery research?* She stood for a long moment, willing Yvonne to go away.

It didn't work. Finally Chloe turned, leaving the dead to Yvonne's scrutiny, and retraced her steps. She'd come back to the cemetery another time.

———

Roelke worked a double shift that day, picking up the extra hours as a favor to Skeet. Evidently Skeet had something better to do that evening. Evidently Skeet's wife was not spending a week as guest curator a hundred miles away. Well, Roelke thought, I wanted to keep an eye on the suspected drug house anyway.

Once on Hackberry Lane, he cruised past the house that the observant mom had reported for suspicious activity. It was just a house—well kept up, bushes pruned, grass mowed. He'd learned what he could about the couple who owned it. Greg and Marjorie Trieloff, both thirty-eight. No kids, thank God. Greg worked in the Waukesha warehouse of a food distribution company. Marjorie worked at a day care facility in Mukwonago. Not bad jobs, but not high-paying either. Did Mr. and Mrs. Apple Pie America decide they wanted a ritzier lifestyle than warehouse work and teaching ABCs allowed? Evidently, because Roelke's gut sense agreed with the mom who'd made the report. Too many cars came and went. Something hinky was going on.

An old-model blue Mercury he didn't recognize sat in the drive. He committed the license plate to memory, drove around the corner, and pulled over so he could call it in. Three minutes later Marie, the EPD clerk, called back on the radio. "George 220. I ran the plate. License and registration up to date, no outstanding warrants."

"Thanks. George 220 out."

He'd hoped the Mercury owner was driving with expired registration or something. He needed to talk to one of the visitors, but he couldn't pull the driver over and search the vehicle without cause.

In the course of an hour a young couple in a Ford sedan came and went, and a single man in a black pickup. Neither party gave him reason to stop the vehicle. Well, druggies weren't the sharpest pencils in the box. Sooner or later somebody would screw up.

———

"I'll carry the food basket, Grandma," Adam said as he helped Tamsin from his car.

"And I've got the flowers," Chloe added. The three of them had left early for the meeting about Pendarvis so they could stop at the nursing home where Tamsin's sister Lowena lived.

"It's nice of you to come up, Chloe," Tamsin said.

"My pleasure," Chloe said honestly. If it wasn't for the meeting about saving Pendarvis, she would have been content to settle in for a nice chat.

"Lowena recently had her hundred-and-first birthday. She has good days and bad days, but visitors are always a nice distraction."

"Has anyone interviewed Lowena?" Chloe asked. "Done an oral history?"

"Not that I know of, dear."

"Somebody should," Chloe said. Surely the local historical society would be interested in Lowena's memories. Pendarvis staff too.

The nursing home was much like others she'd visited. Cheerful prints of children and gardens decorated the walls. A hint of Lysol lingered in the corridors. Someone was playing "Moon River" on a piano in the lounge.

They found Lowena sitting in a chair in her room, staring out the window, but a smile lit her face when her company arrived. Tamsin waved Chloe forward. "Lowena, this is Chloe. She's a museum curator, and a new friend of mine."

Chloe smiled. Lowena studied her. She was a tiny woman with thin white hair. She wore a blue sweatshirt and sweatpants—easy to put on and take off—and matching slippers. Glasses with thick lenses were perched on her nose. But behind the plastic there was a spark in the old woman's blue eyes. Her body might be frail, Chloe thought, but there's still a real person inside.

"I'm glad you've come." Lowena's voice was thin, quavering. "I've been waiting for you."

Tamsin caught Chloe's eye and gave a little shake of her head: *She's confused.* Chloe nodded. But she wished she knew who the elderly woman had been waiting for.

Adam leaned in and kissed Lowena's wrinkled cheek. "It's good to see you, Aunt Lowena."

Lowena looked up at him. "Adam? They were talking about you today. Something about the cottage ... ?"

Tamsin and Adam exchanged a resigned look. "The nurses must have been gossiping," Tamsin murmured, before pulling a spare chair close and taking a seat. "Lowena, Adam found some old bones buried in the cottage today. It's nothing to worry about. The police will take care of it. Now, are you hungry?"

Lowena's gaze grew cloudy. "Is Billy coming?" she asked, with a mixture of hope and confusion and wistfulness that broke Chloe's heart.

Adam patted Lowena's arm. "Not today, sweetie." He picked up a framed black-and-white photograph from the dresser and gently placed it in Lowena's hands. Chloe glimpsed the portrait of a young soldier posed in a uniform from the First World War.

"Oh, yes," Lowena said. "He's still at the front."

Tamsin began excavating the basket. "I brought you supper." She removed foil from a pasty and placed it on a plastic plate.

"Sit," Lowena told Chloe, gesturing at an empty chair. "We'll have a nice dish o' tay."

"Now, we can't stay long enough for tea," Tamsin interjected, while Chloe was still deciphering Lowena's comment. "We have a meeting to attend. But I'll visit you tomorrow, all right?"

After Adam and Tamsin said their farewells, Chloe took one of Lowena's fragile hands in hers. "It was lovely to meet you."

"I'm glad you've come," Lowena said again. Her gaze held Chloe's. The clouds seemed to be gone.

"I'll be in town all week," Chloe told her. "Perhaps I can visit again."

They left the old woman with her memories. "She does get a bit confused," Tamsin murmured to Chloe apologetically.

"Was Billy a husband, or a sweetheart?" Chloe asked. "Did he die in the Great War?"

"He was her first husband. She was in her early thirties when they met, quite old for a first wedding in those days." Tamsin gave Chloe a wry smile. "I never knew him. Lowena and I are half sisters, you see, and didn't grow up together. Anyway, he survived the war only to come home and die of influenza, poor thing. Her second husband died in a mine cave-in."

Chloe imagined how it must have been for Lowena to see her husband home safe from the war, only to lose him in the pandemic; to marry again, only to lose her second husband in a mine accident. And yet she survived, Chloe thought, and was still going … well, if not strong, pretty darn good, considering. Cornish women were made of sturdy stuff.

In fact … Lowena might be a good person to ask about old stories of a missing person in Mineral Point. Chloe made a mental note to do just that.

The Walker House was a huge old stone structure built against the southern end of Dark Hill, with dining and lodging on the second and third floors and an atmospheric pub on the ground floor. Tamsin, Adam, and Chloe arrived in time to eat dinner before the meeting started. "It's always good to support a local business," Tamsin said.

"Absolutely," Chloe agreed. She'd just noticed that the menu featured Babcock Hall ice cream, made at the University of Wisconsin Dairy, so she was feeling slightly more optimistic about the evening.

Lots of people stopped by their table to greet Adam and Tamsin. Chloe also spotted the two interpreters she'd met that day: Gerald, still in period clothes; and Rita, the young college graduate, who had changed into jeans and a rugby shirt. Super-volunteer Evelyn Bainbridge was there, and Audrey from the gift shop. To Chloe's surprise, Dr. Yvonne Miller, Ph.D., came too. She did not stop to say hello, and seemed to be taking notes.

Claudia approached with her daughter, who wore an 1840s dress made of yellow cotton, with pantalets peeking out beneath the hem, and black ankle boots. "May we join you?" Claudia asked. "My husband is out of town for business all week, so I brought Holly with me."

"Please do," Tamsin urged. "Holly, you look lovely."

"I'm sure you remember Miss Tamsin and Mr. Bolitho," Claudia told her daughter. "And this is my friend, Ms. Ellefson. She's helping me at Pendarvis this week."

"Hi, Holly." Chloe smiled.

Holly leaned against her mother, avoiding eye contact. She had delicate features. Her eyes were wide and green. Her shyness, her prettiness, and her period clothing gave her an almost fey air.

Claudia and her daughter slid into empty chairs. Holly had brought a set of dominoes in a cloth bag, and she carefully placed them on the table and began arranging them. Chloe debated trying to start a conversation with the girl, maybe even help with the dominoes, but she wasn't sure if that was a good idea.

By seven o'clock the place was packed. Adam's friend Winter, the potter, stepped to a podium at one end of the room. She wore overalls again, with big earrings and what looked like a hand-dyed scarf holding back her hair.

"Thank you for coming," she began. "We all were shocked to read that the state historical society is considering closing Pendarvis. The historic site contributes to Mineral Point's economy, but it's not all about money. Pendarvis reflects a vital period in Wisconsin's history. We simply can not let bureaucrats make such an arbitrary decision."

That prompted a wave of applause.

"Most of you know Loren Beskeen, site director at Pendarvis," Winter continued. "Loren, what can you tell us about the situation? Is it true that Pendarvis funds got siphoned off to Old World Wisconsin?"

Chloe concentrated on scraping up the last molecule of butter pecan from her dish.

Loren, seated at a corner table, got to his feet. He was a man of middling height, in his thirties, going soft around the middle. Unruly chestnut hair flopped over his forehead, touching his wire-rimmed glasses. Chloe didn't know Loren well, but he was the youngest and most energetic site director, outgoing and friendly at meetings. She liked him.

"That's probably a bit too simplistic," he said. "But it is true that development costs at Old World Wisconsin exceeded original estimates. It's also true that Old World's annual operating costs exceed the budget for the society's five other historic sites combined."

A low collective grumble rolled through the room.

"The state historical society is governed by a board of curators," Loren continued. "At the present time there are thirty-six curators serving on the board. Only one of them comes from southwest

Wisconsin, even though half of the state's historic sites are in southwest Wisconsin."

More unhappy rumbles.

"What we must remember," Loren said, "is that the State Historical Society of Wisconsin is both a state agency and a membership organization. Members have power. Members must speak up." He took his seat again. Chloe had to admire his probably rehearsed remarks. Fire up the crowd, then place much of the power squarely on their shoulders.

A woman sitting near the front waved her hand. "My family donated some valuable heirlooms to Pendarvis when it opened a decade ago," she said. "If the state is going to close Pendarvis, I want to get them back before they go to Old World Wisconsin. How can I do that?"

Oh, geez, Chloe thought. This could get very ugly, very fast.

"Claudia?" Winter stepped back from the podium with an *It's all yours* gesture.

"I'll be back," Claudia whispered to her daughter, then rose and made her way forward. "As many of you know, I'm the Pendarvis curator. At this time I don't have any reason to think that our artifacts are going *anywhere*."

Chloe felt a warm presence at her shoulder—Holly. Astonishingly, she slid onto Chloe's lap. She was heavy and warm, and her hair smelled of shampoo. Chloe felt something in her heart hitch, as if a bow had just been tightened.

"Anyone with a specific concern should call the site," Claudia was saying. "I'll be happy to discuss the situation with you."

"I'd like to say something," someone called.

Oh, this oughta be good, Chloe thought, recognizing the voice.

"I'm Dr. Yvonne Miller, Ph.D.," Miller said to the crowd, before turning back to Claudia. "I'd just like to point out that you may have brought this situation upon yourselves. Research and interpretation at Pendarvis are derisory."

Stunned silence settled on the room. Claudia's mouth opened, but no words emerged. Chloe narrowed her eyes at Yvonne. What a witch, she thought. *Witch* with a *B*.

Tamsin raised her hand and spoke directly to Yvonne. "My dear, that's both unkind and inaccurate. You are of course entitled to your opinion, but the rest of us are here because we're proud of the wonderful work done at Pendarvis."

"I agree," Winter said quickly, before Miller could respond. "Let's open the floor to anyone with a *positive* suggestion for action."

Claudia returned to the table, and Holly slid from Chloe's lap and snuggled next to her mother. Over the girl's head, Claudia and Chloe exchanged an incredulous look: *Can you believe Miller actually said what she said?*

Two hours later, a pad on the large easel by the podium was covered with suggestions. "We've done good work tonight," Winter said. "Let me summarize the main points. We're forming a support group called Protect and Preserve Pendarvis. We're appealing to our political representatives to demand increased funding for Pendarvis. We're inviting leaders from the historical society to come and explain their vision for the future of Pendarvis. And we're going to collaborate with the other southwestern historic sites to increase regional tourism." She stepped back, studying her own scrawls. "Did I miss anything?"

For a moment it appeared that nobody thought Winter had missed anything.

"I am impressed," Chloe whispered to Adam. "I expected angry rants, but instead the community is coming together to get the job done."

Then Gerald slowly rose to his feet. "I believe we should get ownership of Pendarvis back from the state."

Hoo-boy, Chloe thought.

"The state obviously doesn't really want it," Gerald pressed. "As far as I can tell, the state considers Old World Wisconsin the only site worth investing in." He leveled a baleful stare at Chloe. Heads turned as others looked to see who he was glaring at. Chloe forced herself to refrain from sliding down in her chair like a guilty child.

"What would happen if the state was willing to give it up?" somebody asked.

Gerald shrugged, clearly unconcerned about the finer points of his plan. "The town can manage the site. Or the Mineral Point Historical Society." He sat down again.

"The Mineral Point Historical Society already has its hands full running Orchard Lawn," another man called from the back of the room.

Claudia leaned close to Chloe and murmured, "Orchard Lawn is a gorgeous nineteenth-century Italianate mansion."

Chloe nodded. Managing one historic building was plenty for most local historical societies.

The sound level rose as people discussed the proposal. Finally Winter grabbed a knife and tapped it against her water glass. Other people took it up until conversation died.

"Maybe the thing to do is raise money for a special fund," she said. "The idea would be that if the State Historical Society of Wisconsin announces that they are definitely closing Pendarvis, we'll try to buy them out. If you would like to explore that further, Gerald, and learn what would be involved, you can present your findings at our next meeting. Thanks for coming, everyone. I've got a clipboard up here with a signup sheet for anyone who wants to get more involved."

Chloe fished a bill from her wallet and laid it by her plate to cover her sandwich and the ice cream. "I'd say that was a productive meeting."

Adam helped his grandmother shrug into her sweater. "Once Winter gets her teeth into a problem," he said, "she doesn't let go."

"This will turn out well. You wait and see," Tamsin added. "This town cherishes its history."

Chloe concluded that Tamsin was right. Winter was engulfed with supporters.

But Dr. Yvonne Miller, Ph.D., sailed from the room with a serene expression on her face. Chloe frowned after her. What was *up* with that woman?

Then she became aware of Gerald. He stood leaning against one wall, arms folded, glowering at Chloe.

Chloe raised her eyebrows: *Yes, I do see you.* Then she turned her back with a nonchalance she didn't quite feel.

She understood completely why the idea of closure was extremely upsetting to a devoted Pendarvis interpreter. She just wished that Gerald didn't seem to hold her personally responsible.

SEVEN

ADAM HEADED BACK TO Eagle at first light the next morning. "I'm glad you're here," he told Chloe quietly when, yawning, she said goodbye. "It's good for Grandma to have company this week."

Chloe walked to Pendarvis early. She'd had a restless night in Tamsin's guest bedroom, her mind bouncing from producing images of an open-mouthed skull to replaying Dr. Yvonne Miller's caustic comments. It had rained in the night, but the clouds had moved on. A fortifying walk in the woods on Dark Hill, across the road from Pendarvis, seemed like a good plan.

She crossed Shake Rag Street and found a path leading up the hill. Walking where the miners walked, she thought. It was sobering. Those Cornish men had tunneled into the bowels of the earth—lonely and scary work, to her mind. Was it truly in their genes, or did each young man have to make peace with years spent laboring inside the dark earth? Chloe had done some caving in West Virginia. Long, wet belly crawls had provided bragging rights after the fact, but also pushed her to the edge of her comfort zone.

She only went with experienced cavers. No way would she ever venture underground—under crushing eons of rock—alone.

But this was not a morning for melancholy, she decided. Goldenrod and purple asters grew in clumps among the bur oaks. A blue jay scolded, and a warbler's more melodic song filled the morning. Then a faint, unfamiliar birdcall drifted down the slope. She froze, straining to hear it again. She was pretty good at identifying birds by sound alone, but this call was new. It almost sounded like a crying child.

The fine hairs on the back of her neck quivered. Minutes ticked by as she waited for the sound to repeat itself, but she heard only the breeze stirring the leaves overhead.

Finally she began climbing again. The name "Dark Hill" was messing with her. She didn't know every Wisconsin bird's call, and the sound had been barely audible. Sometimes she really was *way* too suggestible. If she was going to imagine hearing anything on this slope, it would most likely be echoes of the men who'd labored so hard—

A scraping sound sent her heart racing. Images of filthy miners attacking the hillside with picks and shovels filled her mind. She forced herself to take a cautious step, and peered around a shrubby thicket. A shovel flashed in the sun and a bladeful of dirt sailed through the air.

She took another step, and the imagined miners of long ago disappeared. Loren, glib site director, and Gerald, belligerent interpreter, stood shoulders-deep in a hole just downslope of a limestone outcrop. Loren wore gray trousers and a calico shirt and suspenders. He thrust the shovel into the ground again and heaved the earth aside.

Then he spotted her and rested the shovel. "Chloe, good morning!" he called, wiping his forehead with one sleeve.

"Good morning," she echoed, walking closer to the hole they were excavating. "Good morning, Gerald. I'm just out for a walk."

Gerald nodded curtly.

"This hillside has lots of stories to tell," Loren said. "Over the years hundreds of zinc and lead mineshafts were dug here."

Chloe considered the implications of that. "Are there any open mineshafts I should be aware of?"

"Don't worry. All the mines in the area should have been barricaded or filled years ago." He grabbed his shovel.

Should have been, Chloe thought. Lovely. She waved her hand in a vague gesture. "Um ... what are you doing?"

Gerald rolled his eyes and got back to work. Clearly he thought it should be obvious.

"We're creating a badger hole," Loren explained. "There are plenty of original badger holes on this hillside, but—"

"There are?" Chloe looked around, alert for yawning holes all over again. "Isn't that dangerous?"

Loren climbed a wooden ladder out of his badger hole and joined her. "Badger holes weren't mines. Some of the early miners who needed temporary shelter simply burrowed into the ground." He pointed. "Look there."

At first Chloe didn't see anything unexpected. Then her eye caught the unusual depression Loren was indicating. "I see it! And— there's another one. ... And another." The holes were shallow, and filled with new growth, but they were obvious once she knew what to look for.

"The miners would cover the holes with logs, or maybe brush and sod," Loren explained. "Most of the first men here were from

Illinois or southern states, and they generally didn't winter over. They were called suckers because they came and went, and they lived in sucker holes. Miners from New York and New England who overwintered were called badgers because of the shelters they dug. Hence Wisconsin is called the Badger State."

Chloe tried to imagine holding her head high in the Sucker State. The sway-backed but fierce badger so beloved by UW sports fans was, she had to admit, a much better mascot than a fish.

"Anyway, since there's little left to see, we're re-creating a badger hole," Loren said. "It was Gerald's idea. We're going to shore it up and create a roof. Visitors will see how tenuous a shelter they were."

If Gerald hadn't been shoveling away with such gusto, Chloe would have told him how impressed she was with that plan. Actually, seeing Loren out here, sweat-stained and solitary, was also impressive. Most administrators had neither the inclination nor the time to stray far from their desks and telephones. At Old World Wisconsin, Director Ralph Petty didn't venture onto the site in period clothing unless there was a photographer or television camera on hand.

"Visitors will love this," she said. "It's awesome to see the depressions left from the actual miners, but your reproduction badger hole will make it possible for people to truly imagine what it was like for the men."

"This hill has incredible interpretive potential," Loren said eagerly. "We need to get rid of the buckthorn and other invasive vegetation. I'm partnering with the Department of Natural Resources on that. In time we can use the hillside for environmental education too."

"Say," Chloe said, "speaking of environmental stuff—have you by chance heard a bird that sounds like a crying child?"

Gerald stopped shoveling. He and Loren exchanged a long, silent glance.

"What?" Chloe demanded.

"We haven't heard anything unusual." Loren began backing down the ladder. "Well, back to it. Enjoy your walk."

Chloe wanted to do just that. But she'd only gone a few feet when she realized that this excursion—like her visit to the cemetery—had been spoiled. She wanted solitude, not Gerald's bad energy. I'll try again another time, she thought, and looped back to Shake Rag Street.

———

Roelke's day began with a trip to Jefferson, seat of an adjacent county, to talk with local officers about a spree of vehicle break-ins that had included several cars in Eagle. After a collegial meeting, all Roelke had to do was head southeast toward Eagle and call back into service.

He didn't do it.

Instead he drove two blocks west and parked on South Gardener Street, directly across from an office building. Painted on the big window on the first floor: *Dan Raymo, Insurance.* Roelke couldn't see Raymo through the window, but his car was parked outside. A black Pontiac Firebird. Raymo liked to think he was cooler than he was.

Roelke sat for a long time, staring across traffic at the office. He didn't know what he thought eyeing the building would accomplish. Since he was in uniform, driving the Eagle squad, he had no business wasting time in Jefferson. He was aware of a faint sense of sliding, just a bit, like a toe inching over the edge of a precipice that should not be approached.

But he couldn't help it. He felt compelled to send a steely stare across the street to Libby's ex. You're watching Libby? he thought. Well, I'm watching you.

———

Clouds were building as Chloe crossed the road. Dr. Yvonne Miller stood on the sidewalk in front of Polperro House, staring at the old building. Her journal was in hand.

"Dagnabbit," Chloe mumbled. She wasn't in the mood for Miller's unique brand of toxic discourse.

Still. Chloe felt a certain sense of challenge as she regarded the other woman. Why did she carry so much animosity? It wasn't healthy. Squaring her shoulders, Chloe approached Miller. "Good morning!" she called brightly.

"Oh!" Miller whirled. "Good morning." She slapped the journal closed.

Chloe was distracted by the journal, which was a beautiful shade of deep green. Not that Chloe would ever choose a leather notebook. But Dr. Yvonne Miller should carry something dyed a shrill, discordant color. Hot pink, maybe. Or neon orange.

"Do you want something?" Miller asked.

Chloe realized the pause had become awkward, and produced her most chipper smile. "How is your research coming?"

"My research is fine."

"So, what exactly is your topic?"

"The lead region."

Well, Chloe thought, that covers a whole lot of ground, literally and figuratively. "Do the structures here at Pendarvis play a role? You seem particularly interested in the historic site."

"If I do," Miller snapped, "it's only because interpretation here is so inadequate."

"That's a bit harsh," Chloe said mildly. "You said last night, and I quote, 'research and interpretation at Pendarvis are derisory.' I strongly disagree. What is your problem with the site?"

"The interpreters tell the wrong stories. An entire building is devoted to talking about Bob Neal and Edgar Hellum. Those men weren't even historians!"

"No, but they saved the buildings that comprise the historic site, and as I understand it, created the local preservation ethic that has given Mineral Point such a distinct identity. What they did is inspiring, and we owe them a huge debt of gratitude. Their story is just as important as what happened here in the 1830s and '40s."

Miller's cheeks were growing flushed. "How can you say that? What about the Black Hawk War? What about men like Henry Atkinson and Henry Dodge?"

Chloe was struggling to keep up. Henry Dodge had been the first territorial governor of Wisconsin. In 1832, he'd fought Sauk and Fox Indians in what turned out to be a final, tragic clash between US land policy in the area and the Native Americans' way of life. But she didn't know much more about him than that. "What about Henry Dodge?"

"The last time I toured Pendarvis, the interpreter didn't even mention him! It's all Cornification."

"Cornification?" Chloe was falling further behind.

"Glorifying nameless Cornish immigrants," Miller said, with an air of *Must I explain everything?* "Dodge arrived in 1827 with his family and some enslaved workers. He played a critical role during the Blackhawk War, which should be explained in depth, and—"

"Hold on." Chloe held up one hand. "Dr. Miller, visitors to historic sites haven't come for a lecture. Many are parents touring with children. Interpreters have to gear their presentations to their audience—"

"The audience doesn't know what they need to hear! Site educators have an obligation to instruct their visitors."

"Site educators have an obligation to *intrigue* their visitors," Chloe countered. "If kids have a good time and want to come back, if adults hear something that provokes them to learn more about lead mining or Cornish immigrants or the success of Bob and Edgar's work, then the interpreters have done their jobs."

"Pardon me," someone said. Chloe stepped aside to let a man walking a white poodle pass. The interruption forced a pause in the debate, and Chloe was grateful. She'd been getting more wound up than she'd intended.

"Look, Dr. Miller," she said when they were alone again. "I've read the Pendarvis interpretive plan. It's very thorough, very thoughtful. But at any historic site, there are *always* more stories that can be told. Sometimes inexperienced interpreters make the mistake of trying to share everything they know, but most visitors don't want that. Good interpreters tailor their presentation to the visitors' interests."

"That Doyle woman has made poor choices."

Chloe thought Claudia had made excellent choices about interpretive themes and information. "There's no one right way to tell a story. Is it possible that you're critical of Pendarvis interpretation simply because the planners made different decisions than *you* would make?"

Miller sniffed. "You're eliminating the role of scholarship."

Okay, Chloe thought, we're about done here. "Absolutely not," she said firmly. "Once the research is done, however, educators have to address the needs of visitors of all ages, with different learning styles, different reasons for visiting the historic site in the first place. If guests are overwhelmed with an avalanche of information, their eyes will glaze over and they'll never come back."

After bestowing Miller with another fake-chipper smile—*I so enjoyed our discussion*—Chloe turned and walked away.

She found Claudia in the office, talking on the telephone. "Yes ma'am, I do understand your concerns... No ma'am, at this time I don't have any reason to believe that Pendarvis's artifacts will be given to Old World Wisconsin... Yes ma'am, but since Old World Wisconsin doesn't interpret lead mining, I can't imagine that staff there would even *want*... Yes ma'am. I'll check on the gad your family donated."

Claudia hung up the phone and swiveled to look at Chloe, who'd dropped into the guest chair. "Are you lusting after a gad to spirit away to Old World Wisconsin?"

"What's a gad?"

"A long, sharp chisel miners used for breaking ore. Sort of like a primitive drill."

"I'll pass."

Claudia rubbed her hands over her face. "The phone was ringing when I walked in here at ten before eight." She picked up a stack of message slips. "I was so looking forward to working with you! But I've got all these calls to return... " She sighed.

"Want my help?" Chloe twisted her mouth. "Not making the phone calls, I guess. I doubt anyone wants to hear from Old World Wisconsin's curator right now."

"No. Besides, it's my responsibility. But thanks."

Chloe stretched out her legs, knocked over a stack of files, and quickly tidied the mess. "I enjoyed meeting Holly last night. She's a real sweetie."

"I was surprised but delighted that she took such a shine to you."

"Is there anything I need to know? Should I try to engage her, or leave her alone?"

"It's kind of you to ask." Claudia picked up a pen and clicked the button absently. "Holly has trouble communicating. Her father and I realized something was wrong when she didn't start talking when other children her age did." She shook her head. "When I don't understand what she needs to tell me, she gets so frustrated…"

Chloe hated knowing that Holly faced such challenges.

"But she's been getting speech therapy since she was four years old. The first word she got out was *mama*." Claudia looked fiercely proud. "She can read and write. She's very smart, and she's usually very sweet. But she's pretty much a loner, and she still struggles to communicate verbally. Her father couldn't handle it, and took off."

Jerk, Chloe thought.

Claudia stared blindly at the pen in her hand. "Holly loved her dad. His betrayal turned everything inside out." She paused. "My new husband doesn't always know what to do with her either."

"That must be so tough."

"Yeah," Claudia agreed. "You saw her with her dominoes last night? She loves arranging them into stacks or patterns, over and over. My husband keeps trying to teach her to actually play a *game* of dominoes. What difference does it make, as long as she's content? But he can't let it go, can't stop saying that he hadn't realized…" She swallowed hard and gazed out the window. "I'm starting to wonder if I'm going to lose another husband. I'm terrified about what that would do to Holly."

Chloe leaned forward and squeezed her friend's hand. "I hope it won't come to that. You don't deserve that, and neither does your daughter."

"There's nothing I wouldn't do for Holly. It's wonderful to share my love of history with her. I've made her several 1840s dresses, which she adores. She's always on her best behavior here." Claudia clicked the pen again, then looked startled, as if she hadn't known she was still holding it. "She loves roaming the site, even Dark Hill."

"Speaking of Dark Hill," Chloe said, "I was over there this morning and heard a bird or something that sounded like a crying child."

"Really?" Claudia looked impressed. "You've tapped into a local legend. Every once in a while someone comes down from the hill saying they've heard a child crying."

Chloe mulled that over. "I asked Loren about it, and all I got was a strange look."

"Loren is not a fanciful person."

"How about you?"

"I've never heard weeping," Claudia said, "but I'm open to the possibility."

Chloe felt a prickling sensation skitter over her skin as she remembered the sound. Me too, she thought.

Okay, enough of that. "I don't know if I should tell you this or not, but I just had an … intense conversation with Yvonne. I asked how her research was coming along and somehow we ended up debating the site's interpretive focus. She thinks you're telling the wrong stories."

Claudia shook her head. "That woman is making me crazy. I've done my best to be polite, but her criticism is starting to feel personal."

"Do you two have some bad history or something?"

"Hardly." Claudia spread her hands, clearly at a loss. "I married into the community two years ago, so it's not like we've been feuding for years. I barely know her."

"I tried ever so politely to help Dr. Miller see that her vision of successful interpretation at Pendarvis is not the only model."

"Any success?" Claudia looked skeptical.

"No," Chloe admitted. "The word *hubris* comes to mind. But it was worth a try."

For a moment they sat in silence, pondering the incomprehensible Yvonne Miller. "Did you notice her sly little smile when she left the meeting last night?" Claudia asked. "I think she wants Pendarvis to close." Her eyes narrowed at the thought. Then she took a deep breath and swiveled back toward her desk. "Well, I better start returning some phone calls. Can you entertain yourself?"

"I think I'll head over to Pendarvis House and get to know that building."

"It's Holly's favorite." Claudia smiled. Then the phone began to ring. She lightly pounded her forehead with her fist before reaching for the receiver.

Chloe slipped out of the office and made her way down the hill toward Pendarvis House, middle and smallest of the three cottages restored along Shake Rag Street. From the upper property, stone stairs descended to the back door. She stepped inside a narrow kitchen, and on into the main room. No one was inside the old stone structure. The house held no strong sensations to trouble her, just a faint muddle in the background that was easy to ignore. It was peaceful.

Chloe sat on the floor and simply took in the space. It was furnished to suggest the multiuse function Adam had described as the custom in Cornwall. A bed and trundle filled one corner, a table and chairs another. Two more chairs near the hearth along with a large embroidery hoop, suggesting cozy evenings of tea and handwork. A small hatch in the ceiling over the bed suggested only the most minimal of storage space above. They didn't need much, Chloe thought.

The most striking artifact in the room was a woman's portrait hanging over the fireplace. She looked to be perhaps fifty, although her hair was still dark. She wore a black dress and cap with a lovely lace collar and a necklace, suggesting a woman of comfortable means. She was not smiling, but the artist had captured something striking. This was not a flat likeness, but the portrait of a woman who had seen a lot of life and, Chloe fancied, done all right for herself.

What was your life here like? Chloe asked the woman silently. Did you ever stop missing the old country? Or had life in Cornwall been so hard that you wanted to leave?

EIGHT

DECEMBER 1833

"Try to keep up, Loveday," Mary called. "You'll stay warmer if you walk faster." They were heading home from the mine with Andrew and Jory. The December night was bitter, and the wind howling across the moorland fierce. Mary was eager to get home to their stone cottage and start a fire.

"I'm too tired to walk faster," Loveday whimpered. "Truly, Mary."

Andrew crouched. "Here, Love. I'll carry you on my shoulders for a spell."

"You're wisht too," Mary told her older brother, but with a grateful glance. He did look exhausted from the day's labor. At least Loveday, now nine years old, was still puny for her age.

They started off again. To hearten them all, Mary began to sing her favorite hymn. "*Away with our fears! The Godhead appears, in Christ reconciled, the Father of mercies in Jesus the Child...*" Jory joined in, then the others, and they made their way home.

Mary built up a fire of fragrant dried gorse in the hearth. "Rest while I fix supper, Loveday," she suggested. Loveday crawled onto the bed, tugged the blankets around her, and was soon asleep.

Jory and Andrew pulled stools close to the fire. Mary chopped potatoes into a kettle of water. She wished fiercely for some flour, and a pinch of saffron, so she could make buns. Instead, at the last minute, she slipped a few dried pilchard into the pot. She'd been saving the fish for Christmas, but ... she'd think about a Christmas treat later.

The boys stared silently at the flames until the fire popped and sparked. Andrew started, added two pieces of peat, and rubbed his palms on his trousers. "Don't know if you've heard," he said in a low voice. "Some of the boys are talking about immigrating."

"Aye?" Mary shivered, as if the flames had grown cold. "Andrew, you're not ... you *wouldn't*."

"There are better opportunities in other places. Australia, maybe. Or America."

"No," Mary said.

He frowned at her. "You could at least think about it."

"I don't want you to leave." She tried to keep her voice steady, but she was cold and tired and hungry and, now, afraid. Afraid she couldn't manage if Andrew left. Jory was sixteen, almost a man now. But what about Loveday? Loveday was Mary's responsibility.

"I wouldn't leave you to fend for yourselves," Andrew said defensively. "If I go, we all go."

"But to leave this place ... " Mary thought of her mother teaching her how to make pasties and star-gazy pie, and Elizabeth reciting Bible verses before Sunday School, and the tobacco smell of her father's pipe. She thought of the way dew glowed on the grasses when the sun rose over the moors, and walking to church on hoarfrost mornings, and the harsh call of rooks in the trees.

Their father had been dead for almost five years. "Father, tell the captain you need to work on the surface," Andrew had urged, as the dizziness became more frequent. "You shouldn't be climbing the ladders."

"I won't be here for much longer, son," Father had said gently. "Working on the surface would mean a cut in pay. I need to do the best I can for you children, while I can." And he had done just that, until the day he fell to his death. Had a dizzy spell come upon him? Or had he been just too weary, too lonely for his wife? Mary didn't know.

Andrew rubbed his filthy hands over his face. "I thought to pick up a bit of money on the boats when the mine was closed, but since the pilchard didn't run last year, no one was hiring. What would you have me do, Mary?"

"I don't know." Mary fanned her hands closer to the flames. The mine had been closed for two weeks after some equipment broke, costing them dearly in wages. Local crop failures had driven up prices. Their own soil was too rocky to plant a cash crop.

"I'd consider immigrating," Jory told Andrew. "If it meant good digging." Andrew dreamed of better prospects. Jory just liked mine work.

"We are not immigrating!" Mary snapped. Their parents and Elizabeth were dead. She had nothing left but memories, and the memories were here in Cornwall.

"Mary," Jory began, "you should—"

Andrew stopped him with a waved hand. "Let her be," Andrew advised softly. "Mary knows her own mind."

———

"Loveday Pascoe!" The words drifting from the dressing floor were faint but clear against the dull staccato of cobbing hammers striking rock.

Not again, Mary moaned silently.

"Penhallow's hollering at your sister again," the girl next to Mary said sympathetically. "She's not the worker you are."

"She does her best." Mary flicked waste from the fist-sized rocks she'd reduced to gravel. She beat the next rocks with more vigor than absolutely necessary.

Two of the older girls trudged up carrying a handbarrow between them. They dumped the load of ore in front of the cobbers. Then one of them put her end of the barrow down and rubbed her back.

"Beatrice," Mary called, "would you like to trade for a while? I'll handle the barrow and you take my hammer."

"Thank you," Beatrice said gratefully. "Even a short rest would help."

Mary and her partner made two more trips to supply the cobbers. Then the other girl said, "We should take a load of ore to the dressing floor. The pickers are likely running low."

Staying clear of the men dumping heavy ore buckets on the pile, they shoveled a load onto their barrow and delivered it to the pickers. "Give me a moment," Mary said and sidled close to Loveday. Loveday didn't stop working but she glanced up, all hollow cheeks and big tear-stained eyes. She was shivering, and Mary rubbed the girl's arms briskly. "I heard Penhallow scolding," she whispered. "What happened?"

"I took a bite of my hoggan," Loveday told her. "I was that hungry! But he saw me, and yelled."

One day, Mary thought, I will come to Wheal Blackstone in a coach, and I will take beautiful teacups from my basket and make

Penhallow serve tea to me and all the bal maidens. And I will tell him that if he doesn't treat them better I shall have him arrested.

"She's been fearful cold all morning, Mary," the girl sitting next to Loveday said, her hands flying as she picked waste stone from the ore. "I tried to huddle close but I have to get my own work done."

"I know, Daisy." Daisy was a big girl, and kind-hearted. Mary was grateful that she tried to look out for Loveday.

Mary looked over her shoulders. No sign of Penhallow. "Loveday, go stand in the boiler house for a few minutes to get warm. Don't let Penhallow see you."

"Thank you, Mary," Loveday breathed gratefully. Then she scurried away.

"Mary," her barrow partner said impatiently, "Penhallow's going to come down on us if we don't get back to work."

"I know." Mary rewound her woolen scarf around her neck and picked up her two handles.

They were shoveling rocks onto their barrow at the ore pile when the afternoon exploded. The impact knocked Mary from her feet, roared in her ears, sent reverberations shuddering through the air. And, when she made sense of it, shattered her heart like a stone.

NINE

Roelke drove back to Eagle wondering what mistakes he was making, what he didn't know. Wondering if he should have walked into that insurance office and had a talk with Dan Raymo. Wondering what Chloe was doing at Pendarvis, and how a body had come to be buried in what became the Bolitho family home. By the time he reached the village he was *not* in a good mood. He'd brought a lunch from home but didn't feel like chatting with Marie, so he decided to eat at Sasso's.

The popular tavern was a village institution. When Roelke arrived he nodded toward the regulars at the bar, friendly but disinterested, and headed toward an empty table in the corner. After ordering a burger and fries, he saw someone approaching in his peripheral vision. Damn, he thought, hoping it wasn't a half-drunk citizen bent on complaining about a speeding ticket or some other police atrocity.

The other man pulled out a chair. "Mind if I join you?"

"Oh—hey, Adam. Of course not."

"You looked lost in thought."

"Just trying to avoid anyone I might have arrested recently. You working on a job in Eagle?"

"Building a deck. Not my favorite kind of work, but it pays the bills." Adam swirled ice cubes in the glass of tea he'd brought with him. "Roelke, I'm glad I saw you. I was hoping we could talk."

That doesn't sound good, Roelke thought.

"What's going on with Libby?"

Roelke wished he'd opted for small talk with Marie. "Didn't she call you?"

"She did, yeah. Last night. All she'd say was that she couldn't see me anymore. I was so frustrated by the conversation that I drove over to her house." Adam leaned back in his chair and crossed his arms. "She still didn't say much. 'You're a great guy but it just isn't going to work out, blah blah blah.'"

Dammit, Roelke thought.

"I'd like to know what changed her mind," Adam said. "We were getting along great. Then all of a sudden—bang, we're done."

Roelke didn't know why Libby hadn't explained what was going on. Pride, maybe? Didn't want to admit that she'd married an asshole? But Adam was indeed a good guy, and a friend. He deserved the truth.

The waitress brought their food, and Roelke unfolded his napkin. "Has Libby ever mentioned her ex?"

"No."

"Dan Raymo is a real SOB. He works in Jefferson but lives in Palmyra, and the divorce was so ugly that I left the Milwaukee PD and moved out here. Most of the time Raymo ignores his kids. It's been particularly hard on Justin."

Adam's eyes had narrowed. "I will never understand men—parents—who don't make their children top priority."

"Yeah," Roelke said grimly. "Anyway, Raymo showed up at that T-ball game you went to, and saw you with Libby and Justin. He said something to Libby that she took as a veiled threat, and—"

"What did he say?" Adam demanded.

"Just that he'd seen you all together. Libby said it wasn't the words, but the way he said them that made her uneasy. So she decided that she can't see you—can't see anyone—until the kids are older."

"That's crazy! She can't let him dictate her life."

"I agree. I tried talking to her, but she wouldn't budge."

Adam looked away, face hard, hands clenched into fists. "I want to talk to this guy."

"No." Roelke leaned across the table. "Believe me, there's nothing I'd rather do. And if he didn't promise to back off, beat some sense into him. But—"

"It isn't right," Adam insisted. "So let's go."

"*But*," Roelke said, "that is not the way to handle this. Libby thinks he'll calm down again, and I have to respect her wishes."

"And what if he doesn't calm down?"

"Then he'll eventually cross the line, and the Palmyra cops will handle it."

Adam shook his head.

"Stay away from Raymo, Adam. You have to. We both have to."

Adam looked stunned. "Libby's your cousin! How can you just sit there and do nothing?"

Roelke was starting to realize that maybe he shouldn't have shared this information with Adam. "Because I respect Libby's ability to make decisions for herself and her children. And because I'm a police officer."

"But—"

"We have to trust the Palmyra cops to deal with Raymo if he goes too far. The fact that Libby is family doesn't change that."

Adam looked out the window again. His burger was getting cold on the plate.

Roelke didn't feel like finishing his lunch either. He'd confided in Adam in hopes of smoothing things over. Now he was pretty sure he'd made things worse.

———

At lunchtime Chloe dashed to the library to check out the Mineral Point archives. Upstairs she introduced herself to the friendly archivist, a woman with long gray hair captured in a green barrette, and reading glasses with bright blue frames. Her face was lined, as if she spent a lot of time in the sun, but it was an interesting face. Best of all, she exuded an air of calm knowledge. Her plastic nametag said MIDGE.

Chloe wanted to be low-key. "Are you by chance familiar with any old stories about someone disappearing?"

"Is this about the bones Adam Bolitho found in his family cottage?" Midge asked.

So much for being low-key. "Um … " Chloe hesitated, remembering Tamsin's distress about gossip.

Midge smiled. "It's a small town. Everyone will know before the next edition of the newspaper carries the story."

"It is about the remains Adam found," Chloe admitted. "I'm a friend of the family, just trying to help out."

"I'm afraid I don't know of any stories that would explain *that*." Midge shook her head. "Poor Tamsin. She must be beside herself."

"Kinda," Chloe admitted. "The cottage had been empty for five or six years when Tamsin and her husband bought it in 1936, so I thought I'd look at newspaper accounts from the early '30s."

Midge produced the appropriate reel of microfilm. Chloe settled at the reader and made herself dizzy scanning the headlines as quickly as possible. She got through 1930 and part of 1931 before she had to quit.

"Any luck?" Midge asked.

"No, but I'm out of time. Thanks for your help. I'll come back tomorrow."

Chloe jogged back to Pendarvis, and the sense of accomplishment that gave her—it was at least half a mile—ameliorated the sting of failure. She hadn't really expected to find, in forty minutes, anything concrete about someone disappearing under suspicious circumstances. Research didn't work that way. Still, quick results would have come in handy.

When she got back to the office, Claudia was waiting for her in the entry room. "Let's get out of here before the phone rings. I want to show you our collections storage."

"Sounds good to me." Chloe dropped her totebag on the counter, grabbed her notebook, and headed back out the door.

They went to Trelawny House, last in the row on Shake Rag Street. "This was where Bob and Edgar lived for thirty-seven years," Claudia said as she opened the door. "We show it as it looked about 1940."

Chloe wanted to peer into the sitting room, but Claudia was already starting up the stairs. "Most of the objects that aren't on display in one of the historic houses are up here, which is off-limits to visitors," she said over her shoulder. "It's not ideal."

"No," Chloe conceded as they reached the second floor. A winding, crabbed corridor led from bedroom to bedroom to bathroom. Artifacts were everywhere—on shelves, on the beds, even in the bathtub.

"This is what I inherited," Claudia said bleakly. "Almost three thousand objects."

"Honestly, my collections storage space at Old World isn't much better," Chloe said.

For a moment they regarded the cramped space in silence. "Philosophical question," Claudia finally said. "Should the historical society accept buildings or artifacts without ideal storage or enough funds for preservation if it means they get saved? Or should the society turn down whatever can't be protected according to modern museum standards?"

Questions like that made Chloe's head hurt. Her heart too. Finally she said, "I know it cost a lot of money to move all of the buildings to Old World Wisconsin and restore them. But the thought of letting them be destroyed . . . I can't accept that. We have to save as much as we can, and then do our best."

"Most of our collections were acquired by Edgar and Bob," Claudia said. "The guy who ran the town dump called them whenever somebody tossed out something old, and they'd go get it. The collections needs here are overwhelming, but I'm enormously grateful that Bob and Edgar saved as much as they did."

"What kind of records came with their collection?"

"Not what we'd wish. Bob and Edgar were antiques dealers and collectors. They bought and accepted what they liked. The year before my position got funded, curators from HQ cataloged the collection, creating an inventory and assigning object numbers. I keep photocopies in binders down in my office." Claudia lifted her hands, dropped them again.

"Do you happen to know if there's any information about that woman's portrait on display in Pendarvis House?"

"None, I'm afraid. We don't even know if the woman was Cornish."

Bummer, Chloe thought. "I'm still interested in sticking tommies too."

"Ask Loren or Gerald," Claudia suggested. "They know a lot more about tools than I do. Maybe we'll stumble over some packed away up here. Otherwise, you can check the inventory records."

"Will do."

Claudia blew out a long breath. "Anyway, this space is not climate-controlled. I want to create proper storage in one of Bob and Edgar's guest cabins. But it would only hold a fraction of our collection. I don't know where to even begin."

Chloe considered the jammed space with hands on hips. "Then we better get busy. We'll do a sort of triage to determine which objects are most vulnerable, or significant, and therefore top priority for a move."

Claudia looked glum. "Are we wasting our time?"

"You never know when funds might appear," Chloe reminded her friend. "Perhaps from a private donor. Or you may see a grant prospect with a tight deadline. Getting a general plan organized now means you can jump when the opportunity presents itself."

They spent the afternoon peeking under protective sheets, poking into closets, opening boxes. Chloe helped Claudia determine which objects were most at risk, which ideally should be moved, those that were stable where they were.

Claudia peppered Chloe with questions: "Should I try to clean this shawl? … How can I store this map until we can afford to buy a case for flat storage? … Have you ever seen this type of cutwork before?" Chloe didn't have all the answers, but it was fun to talk curatorial stuff with a colleague. Nice to be needed.

They were finishing up one of the bedrooms when a beautiful flowerpot, pale yellow with brown streaks, caught her eye. "Is this Klais pottery?"

Claudia looked startled. "It is. Do you study pottery in particular?"

"Hardly. But Adam found a few pieces in the root cellar at *Chy Looan*. I thought it was pretty."

"I've talked with Winter about reproducing this piece for site use. She's excited about it. But there's no money to make repros."

"There's no money *yet*."

They worked until the late afternoon. "We got a good start," Claudia said.

Chloe stepped to the lone window. "It looks like it might rain. Clouds are—oh!"

"What?"

"I just caught a glimpse of a girl in period clothing running into the woods." Chloe gestured toward a grove of trees on top of the upper property. "I assume that was Holly?"

"Without a doubt. She gets to come here after school."

"Lucky girl."

Claudia began folding a linen tablecloth, carefully cushioning the textile with acid-free tissue. "Loren gave his okay. She has to wear period clothing, she can't bother me while I'm working, and she can't go to Dark Hill alone. In the summer she plays quoits on the lawn with visiting kids. She must be in hundreds of photo albums."

"I wish I could have wandered around some historic site when I was nine." Chloe sighed wistfully.

Claudia's shoulders relaxed. "Thank you, Chloe."

Chloe wasn't sure what she was being thanked for, but she was glad—once again—that she could help.

———

When Roelke turned the corner onto Hackberry Lane late that afternoon, he saw a yellow two-door Ford Fiesta hatchback parked in front of the house he'd been watching. He pulled over well behind the Ford and called Marie to run the plates. "George 220," she responded. "License and registration up to date, no outstanding warrants."

"Thanks," Roelke said. "George 220 out." This was getting old.

The driver, a skinny white woman wearing blue jeans and a pink sweater, came out of the house, slid into the car, and drove away. Then she paused at the corner, displaying one burned out brake light.

Bingo. He hit the flashers and went after her. She pulled over on the next block.

Roelke reported his status to Marie before approaching the car. "Good afternoon," he said in his pleasant-but-serious cop voice.

The woman stared ahead. She was about twenty, with blond hair feathered in poufy layers. She looked like a college student or kindergarten teacher. But a blister on her lower lip was probably caused by a too-hot crack pipe.

"What's the problem, officer?" She didn't meet his gaze. Sitting rigid, pressed against the seat, she gripped the steering wheel with white-knuckled fingers.

"Your left rear brake light is burned out. May I see your license and registration please?"

"I'll get the light fixed right away."

"Good. May I see your license and registration?"

She grabbed a purse from the passenger seat and dug out her license. "Here."

Roelke glanced at it. The name matched what Marie had given him: Michelle Zietz of Oconomowoc. "And the registration?"

"It's in the glove compartment."

"Get it out."

For a moment he thought Zietz wasn't going to move. Finally she reached for it, moving stiffly, slowly. Had she stashed drugs in there? A weapon? He let his hand rest on his own gun.

Then he spotted the triangle of plastic emerging behind her hip. He opened the door. "Get out of the car."

"But—"

"Out of the car, now!"

Zietz got out of the car. The baggie of crack cocaine she'd tried to hide behind her back fell to the seat.

Busted, Roelke thought, and reached for his handcuffs.

After searching the car and finding no more drugs, he drove Zietz back to the PD in silence. It was good to let her stew for a few minutes. Ultimately, he didn't want her. He wanted the people she'd been buying from, and he needed her help.

The station was empty. Roelke pointed at the chair beside the officers' desk. Zietz sat, her hands twisting together anxiously in her lap.

Roelke took the desk chair. "So, Michelle. Tell me about yourself."

"Wh-what do you want to know?" she quavered.

Prompting her along, he learned that she lived with her parents and younger brother. She was a freshman at Carroll College in Waukesha, on a partial scholarship, and planned to major in political science. She had never been arrested before, she assured him earnestly.

When she'd run down, Roelke leaned forward and regarded her intently. "Michelle, I don't think you realize how much trouble you're in. Prosecutors consider possession of a controlled substance a very serious crime, and Wisconsin law regulates strict consequences."

Zietz's eyes grew wider.

"All drug offenses trigger a mandatory driver's license suspension for up to five years. Convicted felons are not eligible for academic grants or other forms of financial aid. And felony possession of cocaine leads to a ten-thousand-dollar fine plus three and a half years in prison."

"Oh my God! My parents are going to kill me." She looked dazed, and her skin had turned blotchy. "Oh, my, *God*."

"I might be able to help minimize the damage you've done to your future," Roelke continued, "but it depends on the choices you make now—"

"I'll do anything!"

"We're going to have three conversations. The first is the one we're having now, just exchanging information. Next, we're going to go on the record. You must be completely honest so I can testify in court that you are a reliable witness. You will provide an oral statement, and then a written statement. Third, and only if I believe your statement was truthful and thorough, we will talk about what you can do to maybe get yourself out of this trouble."

"What do you need to know?" the young woman asked frantically. "I'll tell you everything."

Zietz's story held no surprises. She'd never done drugs in high school, but new college friends got her started. ("I was such an idiot!") One of them pointed her toward the house on Hackberry

Lane. She'd bought crack there three times, counting today. ("How could I have been so stupid!") She didn't know the dealers' names but she'd seen a man and a woman. ("You won't have to take me to prison because my parents are going to kill me!") The descriptions she provided matched the homeowners, Greg and Marjorie Trieloff.

"Okay," Roelke said, when her written statement was complete. "On to conversation number three. I have to emphasize that I can't promise anything. Do you understand?"

She wiped away a tear. "Yes."

"I believe you are capable of helping me out as a CI. A confidential informant."

"I've already told you everything I know!"

"But I want to nail the dealers, and I need more help. If you agree to participate, you will sign an agreement spelling out your role as a CI. I will need you to go back to that house several times. Each time you will buy more crack with money that I provide. You will be wired to record the conversations. If you agree to the plan, I will hold all charges against you while you complete the buys."

Zietz chewed her lower lip.

"Then I will write a letter to the DA's office and explain in detail how helpful you were, and your willingness to attend a drug-treatment program. The amount of crack found in your possession suggests personal use, not resale, and that's in your favor too. I will explain how I believe your assistance and remorse should be rewarded by permanently dropping the charges." He folded his arms. "Think hard about—"

"I'll do it," Michelle Zietz said.

———

Chloe and Claudia emerged from Trelawny House at the end of the afternoon. "Ooh, definitely looks like rain," Claudia said. "I've got to get today's take from Audrey in the gift shop, then round up Holly and scoot home. She knows she has to come by my office by five. You coming?"

Chloe looked toward Dark Hill, then she squinted at the black clouds sailing overhead. A breeze had kicked up, but the energy appealed to her. She didn't want to think about skeletons with crushed skulls, or Gerald's glares, or Dr. Yvonne Miller's criticisms, or overwhelming curatorial needs.

"I'm not quite ready to head back to Tamsin's place," she said. "I'm going to take a quick walk before it rains."

"See you tomorrow." Claudia hurried away.

As Chloe lifted a hand in farewell a blue Mustang—battered but still cool—pulled up at the curb down the street. Rita, the young interpreter, hurried toward the car. She still wore period garb, and a glowing smile lit her face. She slid into the car, and she and the driver indulged in a passionate embrace. When they finally separated and he drove past, neither glanced in Chloe's direction. She got only a glimpse of the guy, who was wearing a rakish red bandana pirate-style on his head.

Young love, Chloe thought wistfully. She didn't want Roelke to drive a Mustang or start wearing a bandana. But she did miss her guy. It would be good to talk with him that evening.

She crossed Shake Rag Street and took the trail she'd followed that morning. There was no birdsong now, just the wind sighing through the trees. The temperature was dropping and the air smelled damp. She grinned, soaking it all in. Maybe the old miners were beckoning her: *Don't be content with the houses. Tell our stories too.*

Or maybe it was something more elemental. She was of pure Norwegian descent, and while she didn't make nearly as big a deal about that as her parents did, she did embrace the notion of *frilufts-liv*—free air life. It had compelled her to attend forestry school and earn a degree in nature interpretation before beginning her history career. It was one of the reasons she loved Old World Wisconsin, which sprawled on 576 acres within the Kettle Moraine State Forest. And it was one of the reasons she loved the old Roelke farm, which was bounded on two sides by that same forest. After this break she'd be better able to think, to talk with Tamsin that evening, to face Gerald's scowls the next day.

She climbed until she reached the badger hole Loren and Gerald were constructing. She stepped over the orange safety rope they'd strung and looked down from the edge. The badger hole was a tidy rectangle over five feet deep. Once Loren got a brush-and-sod roof in place, it would be impressive. She imagined Gerald interpreting here, perhaps cooking—

A gentle pressure glanced against her back. Then she was falling.

Before her brain accepted *that*, she hit bottom. Really, really hard. She flopped onto her back and lay motionless for a moment, gasping and stunned, staring at black clouds and whipping tree limbs. Tears of pain blurred her vision.

Finally breathing came more easily, and she collected her addled thoughts. The first thing she did was indulge in a little heartfelt whimpering.

The second thing she did was cautiously move her fingers, her toes; her arms, her legs. She ached all over, but nothing seemed badly damaged. Slowly she curled back on her side, testing the whole idea of motion, not at all sure it was a good concept. After a moment she pushed herself to a sitting position. That seemed to go okay, so she staggered to her feet, and looked around for Loren's ladder.

No ladder. The men had taken it, and their shovels, with them. She'd left her totebag at the historic site. She had nothing, no tools, just a tissue and the site key and half a roll of Life Savers in one pocket.

Chloe stepped to the wall. She could see over it. She laid her forearms on the ground and strained upwards, teeth gritted, the toes of her shoes scrabbling against the earth. She raised her body an inch, another inch, legs cycling like the cartoon roadrunner ... and could go no farther. She was nowhere near high enough to get a hip or a knee over the edge. She dropped back down.

She prowled the pit with a growing frenzy. There had to be something she could use to hoist herself out of here. A protruding rock or root. *Something.*

There was not. It seemed she was trapped in the badger hole.

Well, this sucks, she thought. She bit off a cherry Life Saver and tried to think of a plan, but came up empty. Damn.

A fierce burst of wind howled over the hill. A fat raindrop hit her face. Another, and another. Then the deluge began.

TEN

The deluge ended just as Mary and her traveling companions reached Mineral Point. "I think this is it," Andrew said. "We're here."

Mary pushed her gook back from her face so she could get her first good look at the Mineral Point diggings. "I do wish it weren't such a dummity day," she said, eyeing the dreary gray sky. They had traveled so far, and for so long, that she'd almost stopped believing there would be a "here" for them. Now her feet hurt, her skirt was muddy to the knees, and her bodice was stained with sweat. She and the men had pushed hard to make Mineral Point this evening.

This is my future, she thought, overwhelmed with the enormity of it. From the moment she and her brothers had agreed to emigrate from Cornwall, she had fixed all hope on a new home in Mineral Point, in the Michigan Territory. She was seventeen years old and determined to create the life her mother had wanted for her.

The last leg had been made on foot, with their precious belongings in a small handcart. Jory, who'd had the last stint pulling the cart, rubbed his hands. "Doesn't look like so much."

"It looks like opportunity," countered their friend Ruan Trevaskis. "Everyone I talked to in Galena said there are rich veins of mineral running through these ridges."

The Pascoes had met Ruan, a Cornish blacksmith, on the ship. The three men had gotten along so well that they all traveled on through North America together. They'd landed in Quebec, then continued down the St. Lawrence River, on through Lakes Ontario and Erie. They'd ridden the cars through Cincinnati to St. Louis, and steamed up the Mississippi River to Galena, Illinois. It was a rugged town with its muddy streets, gambling dens and saloons, and noisy crowds of swaggering river men, fur trappers, miners, and Indian traders.

From there, the Pascoes and Ruan had trudged fifty miles in three days, dragging the cart holding what they'd brought from Cornwall along narrow trails and rutted roads. They'd seen only hardscrabble little mines and a few shabby settlements. They'd passed through ridges dotted with rocky outcrops and valleys running with rivulets and rivers. Some of the land was prairie, undulating oceans of tall grass and flowers she was only learning to identify—purple coneflower, yellow sunflower, red gayfeather. They already knew how to spot the dark purple lead plants said to indicate the mineral they'd traveled so far to find.

It had been a difficult trip. But Ruan laughed often and had lifted the Pascoes' spirits with funny stories. He had an unruly mess of black curls and blue eyes so surprisingly bright that when he looked at Mary, she felt as if he found whatever she was saying incredibly important. His arms and shoulders were massive, and he'd trundled the handcart much of the way. When they camped at night, he often appeared at just the right moment to push the end of a fallen log farther into the fire, or to lift the heavy iron kettle away from the flames.

At first Mary was uncomfortable with Ruan's help, not sure what to make of it. She was used to taking care of herself, swatting away the unwanted attention of some of the men she'd worked with at Wheal Blackstone. But nothing in Ruan's words or manner suggested anything more than kindness.

Now they stood on one side of a barren ravine marked with rumpled hills and limestone cliffs. As far as Mary could see were shallow pits, small piles of tailings, wagons, windlasses, and the scars made by pick and shovel. A few buildings in the distance marked the infant town of Mineral Point, but clearly many people lived out here. Scattered among the diggings were makeshift stone huts, dugouts, tiny cabins, shelters made of sod, holes in the ground covered with brush. Some had barrels as chimneys. Cookfires flickered as the miners settled in for their suppers. The faint chords of an instrument she didn't recognize drifted over the hill.

Mary felt a wave of panic. She'd come from a place of century-old homes and tales of King Arthur on winter nights. Of lichened gravestones in the Methodist churchyard, and Sunday School picnics at the North Cliffs where her parents had, as children, also watched waves crash below. Of Midsummer Eve bonfires on the same tor where her ancestors had danced long ago. This country felt raw.

Andrew rubbed his chin. "Let's make camp."

They settled down in a secluded spot next to a rock wall. Jory and Ruan went in search of fuel. Mary pulled her skillet and an almost-empty sack of barley from the trunk.

"Mary." Andrew's voice was subdued. Melancholy, even. He sat on the ground, knees drawn up, staring down the ravine at the ramshackle community of miners. "Cornwall seems very far away."

So he felt it too. "It does. What I hate the most is—is leaving them all. Mama and Papa, Elizabeth and Loveday..." Her throat grew thick.

He nodded.

A hawk circling overhead cried shrilly, bringing Mary back from the precipice of regret. Cornwall's ancient terrain was steeped in comforting customs and traditions, but those were also the very things that made it almost impossible to rise, to change paths. She blinked hard and lifted her chin. "We made the best decision we could, Andrew."

"I know. This was my idea, and most of the time I don't brood. For some reason it came over me just now."

"We'll do all right here."

He nodded, and she tried to swallow the lump in her throat. Their mother's voice whispered in memory: *Oh, Mary. I do so want a different life for you.* After Loveday died, Mary had agreed to leave only because America offered a chance to become the woman her mother had dreamed she might be. The overtime wages she'd saved had made it possible for her and Jory and Andrew to purchase passage. Hard as all this was, it felt right.

Mary thought of Mrs. Bunney of the Christian Welfare Society, who had ordered Mr. Penhallow around and been so unkind to the mine girls. Mary had learned a great deal from Mrs. Bunney.

She glanced up at the racing clouds. Mama, she promised, I am going to be a new person here. I'm not going to be a bal maiden forever.

When Mary walked down the hill to fetch water, a man with hints of gray in his dark hair walked along the lane beside the creek, leading a small donkey cart loaded with cut wood. He was dressed as roughly as a miner, but wasn't as dirty. "Good day," he greeted her, tipping his hat with a flourish. "Jago Green, wood jowster, at your service. I offer dry wood and fair prices."

Mary introduced herself, eyeing the cordwood in his cart. Wood was scarce here where dug earth and prairies stretched toward the horizon, and timber was needed to shore up mines, but Andrew carried their money. "I may buy, but not today."

Mr. Green briefly looked forlorn, then rallied. "How would you like to have a portrait painted? I'm a good artist." He pulled a large pad from a satchel hanging over one shoulder. "See here. The newspapers back east are using my sketches to make engravings." He flipped through, showing detailed pencil sketches of miners handling a windlass, a lone man swinging a pick, two women washing ore, a smelter. "I can paint too."

"I have no money to spend on fripperies," Mary said firmly.

Undaunted, the man grinned and slipped his pad away. "Perhaps another time." He ambled on.

Mary found her spirits higher as she filled her buckets and trudged back up the hill. Green's cheer was contagious.

Jory and Ruan found only enough fuel for a quick fire. That's fine, Mary decided. Barley half-boiled would make a clacky meal, sticky and chewy, that filled their bellies better than barley mush.

Ruan had made arrangements for a freighter to haul his forge and a supply of iron by oxcart from Galena. "Until my supplies come," he told Andrew and Jory as they ate, "I'll help you look for a good claim."

"No way to know but to dig," Andrew said, "so we appreciate the help. When we hit something promising, I'll find the government office in town." Miners had to lease land from the government agent.

Men they'd met in Galena had explained that lead was to be found in cracks and crevices in the limestone. Some veins dribbled out quickly; others ran a mile or more. The first men to mine lead here had looked for float—lead visible on the ground, which needed only to be collected. "Can you imagine?" Andrew had asked, shaking his head in wonder.

But the easy surface pickings were mostly gone now. Some of the early miners had also come and gone. "These Americans don't dig more than ten feet before giving up," Jory observed, sounding bewildered.

Andrew laughed. "That just means it's time for hard-rock Cornishmen to take over. There's no deep hole in all the world that doesn't have a Cornish miner at the bottom."

———

Andrew, Jory, and Ruan ranged over the hillsides, searching for a promising spot to sink a shaft. They looked for lead gravel, digging so they could study the soil. It took two weeks of prospecting to find a promising show of mineral. They laid claim to the plot by staking its boundaries. Then Andrew went to file the location at the land office in town.

He returned with a new ladder, and told them the rules he'd promised to obey. "Jory and I are only permitted to lease six hundred square feet of land. We are not permitted to farm or cut timber."

"Not much timber to cut," Mary observed dryly. None, to be exact.

Andrew shrugged. "Whatever we mine has to be sold to a licensed smelter, who will hold ten percent of the yield back as rent to the government. Last, we forfeit the claim if eight days pass without any work being done."

They moved into an abandoned badger hole near the claim, the roof made from brush. While the men began sinking their shaft, Mary used a shovel to lift squares of sod from the ground. She laid these over the branches, and by the time she was finished, they could sleep dry in all but heavy rainstorms. It'll do for now, she thought.

They met more Cornish men, some who'd brought their wives, which was a comfort. There were a few slaves at the diggings too, brought here by owners who evidently dreamed of wealth but didn't care to actually work for it. But most of the miners working nearby were Americans from Illinois, or southern states like Tennessee and Kentucky and Missouri. They were hard men, used to living rough. Disputes were settled with fists or Bowie knives. Still, most of the miners were friendly enough to the newcomers, and generous with advice.

Several weeks after they'd come to Mineral Point, the freighter arrived with Ruan's forge and iron. "I'll try my luck right here, for now," he decided. "The miners won't have to go far if they need a new gad. When business is slow I can help dig mineral. Besides, I've been eating a whole lot better than if I had to rely on myself." He glanced at Mary, his eyes crinkling.

Mary's mouth twitched with her own hint of a smile. Their meals had been paltry, for their supplies were dwindling, and their funds too. But she didn't mind having Ruan linger at the Pascoe camp.

ELEVEN

ROELKE SAT ALONE AT the officers' desk, finishing the paperwork triggered by Michelle Zietz's arrest and conversion to confidential informant. With Chloe away, it was a good time to be doing this kind of thing. And taking Libby and the kids to Justin's T-ball game tonight would fill the evening. Funny, he'd lived alone for years and never given it a second thought. Now the farmhouse he and Chloe shared seemed ... hollow, sort of, when she was gone.

She's doing her history thing, he thought. Finding the skeleton in Adam's house was disturbing, but she was working at Pendarvis now. Spending time with a colleague she liked, far away from Ralph Petty. Be glad for her, he scolded himself. She deserved to have some fun.

———

Chloe crouched in one corner of the badger hole as the rain poured down. She wore khaki trousers, which turned clammy, and a thin wool sweater over a cotton blouse. Warmest when wet, she thought, fastening every clasp with trembling fingers, but it was small comfort when she was soaked and shivering.

Sooner or later the rain would pass, but what then? She hadn't been able to climb out of the badger hole when it was dry; she certainly wouldn't be able to climb out now. Chloe hated to think of how worried Tamsin would be. At what point would she call someone? Who would she call? Claudia? The police?

Chloe buried her face in her hands. Of the many stupid things she'd done in her life, this was the stupidest. Who would find her? Gerald, next morning? Oh, he'd love that. Or ... oh God, not Loren, please. Instead of impressing the director, she was going to be humiliated. The story would spread all over Mineral Point. All over the state historical society. All over Old World Wisconsin. It would make the local newspaper: Visiting Curator Falls Into Hole During Monsoon. How would she ever explain it?

Wait. Chloe thought back to that last moment on the edge. *Something* had pressed briefly, lightly, against her back. Had she been too close to the edge when a thrashing branch startled her, throwing her off balance? Or ... had it been a hand? Had someone actually pushed her?

Chloe looked up abruptly, squinting against the streaming rain. No one was there.

Her teeth chattered as she considered. There had been something ... hadn't there? She hadn't just lost her balance. The brush was thick near the badger hole. Someone might have heard her coming and hidden there, or behind the limestone outcrop, and taken advantage of the moment ...

No. She was being ridiculous. She'd been smacked by a branch, or buffeted by the furious wind. After all, who would do such a thing?

Well, Gerald, maybe. He'd certainly been —

Craa-ack!

As wood splintered Chloe instinctively raised her arms over her head. She shrieked as a limb fell, leaves and slender boughs slapping and scratching as it landed beside her.

When the rustling stopped she gingerly raised her arms, her head, and studied the heavy branch. That thing could have killed me, she thought, wiping her face against rivulets of water.

Then she narrowed her eyes. As tools went, the limb wasn't much. But it had more to offer than tissues or hard candy.

She stood, put one foot on the limb, grabbed a secondary branch, and pulled. When it snapped she landed on her butt in the slurry pooled on the bottom of the badger hole. But she had a stout stick about ten inches long clutched in her dripping hands.

Kneeling, she scratched a mark in the slimy wall and jabbed the stick at it, over and over. She didn't stop until she had made a depression a good six inches deep and six inches wide. Then she moved up and over six more inches and started again.

It took a long time. Rain sluiced her face, dripped from her nose and her earlobes and her saturated braid. Drops pittered against the leaves overhead, drummed against the earth. Her teeth clattered uncontrollably. Her clothing clung to her skin. The gloom grew, and she didn't know if twilight was descending or the storm was growing worse or both. Don't think, she told herself. Just keep at it. This has to work. It has to.

Eventually she had half a dozen toeholds carved into the wall. She cast the stick aside, stood, and once again planted her forearms on the surface. The ground was slick now, and she took a moment to find the best spot, to settle her weight. Then she wedged her right foot into the first slippery-slick toehold. When her foot felt truly jammed she held her breath and eased her weight up. The toe-hold held. She found the next gouged hole with her left foot and moved up again.

As her body edged over the badger hole's lip she got excited, moved too fast, and felt the toes supporting her start to slide. *"No,"* she insisted, teeth clenched, muscles tight, toes cramping, refusing to lose ground by sheer will. Finally she got a knee over the edge. For a moment she paused there, catching her breath, terrified that if she put weight on the knee it would slip backwards. She wiggled it for a moment, trying to dig a depression in the mud. Then, with a final heave, she threw herself onto the ground.

She lay there, gasping for breath as rain beat upon her. The air smelled of mud. She tasted mud. She was drenched and freezing and bruised and covered with mud. All she could do was laugh.

Finally she dragged herself up to hands and knees, lurched to her feet, and started back down the trail.

———

Justin was thrilled when Roelke showed up to take him, Deirdre, and Libby to the T-Ball game. "*Really*? My dad came to my last game."

"We're all proud of you, sport."

"Say, Roelke." Justin grabbed his hand. "Next Thursday is Career Day at my school. Will you come talk about being a policeman?"

"If I can," Roelke told him. "I'll have to check with my chief."

"What's it like to be a policeman?" Justin asked, head tipped back, eyes earnest behind his glasses. "Do you like catching criminals?"

"Lots of days I don't actually catch any criminals."

Justin was clearly disappointed. "Oh."

"I do different things on different days. That's one of the best parts. I never get bored."

"But what's it *like*?"

Roelke hesitated. Then he crouched and put his hands on Justin's shoulders. "You know how sometimes your mom tells you to stand up straight? That's what being a cop is like. It's something in your anatomy—something inside—telling you that slouching is no longer an option."

Justin thought that over. Finally he said, "O-oh," again, his tone now suggesting that he and Roelke were in complete accord.

"Time to go," Libby called. "Wear your jacket, Justin." She shepherded the others out the front door. When Roelke passed she leaned against him for a moment, shoulder to shoulder.

Roelke drove to the field. They got good seats on the bleachers, the rain held off, and the kids played their hearts out.

After the last inning Roelke treated his family to frozen custard. Spirits were high by the time they got back to the house. "Thanks," Libby said, as Justin and Deirdre ran ahead. "This was just what we needed."

"It was fun," Roelke said. Justin's team had actually won the game, and Raymo had not presented himself. Maybe that really is the end of the trouble, Roelke thought hopefully.

"Justin's definitely improving, which is *great*," Libby was saying. "Very good for his self-esteem. I think … " She stopped walking.

"What's the matter?"

Libby pointed to the purple tricycle with matching plastic streamers trailing from the handlebars just visible in the yellow glow cast by the light over the front steps. "When we left, that was on the other side of the walk."

"It was?" He couldn't remember.

Libby scanned the shadowed yard. "And my flowerpots have been moved around."

"Are you sure?"

"Of course I'm sure!" Libby hissed. "It was him, Roelke. Dan was here."

"We don't know it was Dan," Roelke said, even though his nerves were prickling. He squinted, trying to see through the gloom as he slowly pivoted. If Raymo was watching, he was well hidden.

Something cold balled in the pit of Roelke's stomach. Was this *his* fault? Had Raymo seen him sitting outside his office this morning? Roelke realized only now that he'd wanted Raymo to see him. Wanted to send a clear message without breaking his promise to not talk to Libby's ex. But he'd screwed up.

"Mom," Justin called impatiently, hand on the doorknob.

"Get the kids inside," Roelke muttered.

In the house, Libby kept the children corralled in Justin's bedroom by reading a story. Roelke crept through the house with his off-duty gun in hand, but he found no sign of Raymo. He stowed the gun back in his ankle holster and returned to the bedroom. "Clear," he murmured to Libby, and saw her shoulders ease with relief. "All doors and windows locked."

She got the kids ready for bed. After good nights were said, cups of water were fetched, and more hugs and kisses delivered, Roelke and Libby retreated to the kitchen. "Take a hard look around the house," Roelke instructed. "Tell me if anything's been tampered with."

Ten minutes later Libby returned. "Nothing's been touched in here. I'd know." She stepped to the back door, flicked a light switch, and stared into the night. "The patio chairs have been moved, though." She turned to face him. "Oh God, Roelke. He was in the back yard too. What if the kids had been out there?"

"I don't think he would have ventured into the yard if you'd been home," Roelke said. Which was disturbing in its own way, suggesting that Raymo was keeping an eye on the house, watching his children and ex-wife.

"Sneaking around, trying to mess with me, is more his style." Libby sounded angry. "I swear, sometimes I just want to shoot him and get him out of our lives once and for all."

The fervor in her voice was as shocking as the sentiment. "Libby, do you own a gun?"

"Of course I don't own a gun," she snapped. "I wouldn't keep a gun in the house with my children."

"We should talk to the local cops."

"They'd think I'm nuts." Libby began to pace. "A tricycle moved three feet? The blue flowerpot where the yellow one should be? Hardly menacing to anyone else. Besides, I can't prove it was Dan."

Roelke knew she was right. He'd been on the receiving end of such calls himself. *Yes ma'am, but if someone was here he's gone now. It was probably just some kids playing pranks… Probably nothing to worry about… Probably it won't happen again, but if it does, call us back.*

"Things will calm down," Libby said. "Adam came over last night."

Roelke did not let on that he knew that.

"I told him it wasn't going to work out between us." She leaned against a counter and massaged her forehead. "He left."

Roelke chewed that over. Had Raymo seen Adam come by Libby's house? Is that what had triggered the little psychotic game of moving things in the yard? If so, Raymo was fast moving from asshole status to official stalker.

Roelke didn't like the way this was going. "Want me to spend the night?"

"No, thank you," Libby said. "The house is secure. The kids and I are fine."

He *wanted* to spend the night, but he couldn't figure out how to push the issue without giving her more to worry about. "I'll talk to you tomorrow," he said instead.

Once back in his truck, he drove to the Palmyra Police Department. It was a small department, much like the EPD. He knew everyone who worked there because officers from neighboring villages called on each other if backup was needed. He was glad to see a light on.

Officer Troy Blakely looked up from his typewriter when Roelke opened the door. Good, Roelke thought. Blakely had been around for a while. He was thoughtful and steady and built like a weightlifter.

"Officer McKenna!" Blakely got up to meet him. "You're obviously not on duty"—he gestured to Roelke's jeans and t-shirt—"so what brings you here?"

"My cousin, Libby Raymo, is having problems with her ex." Roelke explained what Raymo had said, what Libby had found at the house that night.

"I know Raymo." Blakely looked disgusted. "I've pulled him over for speeding in that Firebird more times than I can count. Got him once for a bar fight, and another time on weed possession. Real mouthy."

"That's him."

"Tell your cousin to call if anything else happens. We can at least get a report written, establish some paper trail, in the event such a thing is needed."

"She didn't want to call you, but I'll keep trying. Don't tell her I stopped by, okay? I wanted to ask if you'd keep an eye on the house." He wrote down the address.

"Will do," Blakely promised. "Either Raymo will de-escalate on his own, or he'll screw up and go too far. If he does, we'll nail him."

"Thanks," Roelke said. "Let me know if anything happens."

Blakely promised, and Roelke had to content himself with that. He gave me the same line I gave Libby and Adam, Roelke thought as he went back outside. But nobody wanted to specify what "going too far" might mean.

———

Rain was still falling when Chloe arrived at Tamsin's door looking like she'd just belly-crawled from a hog wallow. Before she had a chance to knock, her hostess opened the door. "When I got back from visiting Lowena and you still weren't home, I got worried!"

Chloe had decided that the best explanation would be short and sweet. "I'm *terribly* sorry. I went for a hike on Dark Hill, got caught in the storm, and slipped and fell in the mud."

"Well. I'll get a plastic garbage bag for your clothes." Tamsin bustled away, fussing under her breath.

After a hot shower, and a supper of homemade vegetable soup and apple bread, Chloe felt better. When dishes were done Tamsin, with the aid of a magnifying glass, worked on a nativity scene done in cross-stitch. Chloe wrapped up in an afghan and settled into Tamsin's antique rocker with her notebook, and pretended to work. The chair was gorgeous, black with ornate red and gold embellishments. She really shouldn't sit in such a fine piece, but the chair felt comforting, somehow. Right now she'd take whatever comfort she could find.

When ten o'clock rolled around, and long distance rates went down, she said good night and retreated to the guest room. She plopped on the bed and called Roelke.

He answered on the first ring. "Hello?"

She sat up straight. "It's me. Is everything okay?"

"I thought it might be Libby. She … she had a bad evening."

Chloe listened with growing dismay as Roelke shared the latest. "Has Libby's ex ever stalked her before?"

"No. He made the divorce as hard as it could be, but nothing like this. Libby thinks things changed when he saw her with Adam. Raymo was content when he thought she was lonely and miserable. Seeing her happy, moving on, made something snap."

"That's sick." Chloe closed her eyes. "And Deirdre and Justin are right in the middle. I don't like this at all."

"Believe me, I don't either," Roelke said grimly. "I'm going to keep an eye on them. I asked the Palmyra cops to do the same."

"Good. Say, have you heard any more about that training thing?"

"My interview with the Police Committee is tomorrow morning."

"You'll do great."

"We'll see," he said. "How are things in Mineral Point? Any more backlash about Old World Wisconsin?"

"Not really. I spent the afternoon helping Claudia with collections stuff, which was good." Compared to what Roelke was worried about, an unpleasant freelance historian, and her own tumble into a soggy badger hole, seemed unworthy of mention. "I miss you, though."

"I miss you too."

After hanging up, Chloe stared at the wall, thinking about Libby and the kids. She hoped that Dan Raymo, having had his fun with flowerpots, would retreat back into his hole. But the whole business of creeping into Libby's yard, just to mess with her, was frightening. If Raymo really wanted to hurt Libby, and went after the children …

Chloe popped to her feet. "Okay, that's enough of that," she muttered. If she didn't distract herself she'd be awake all night imagining things she really didn't want to imagine. She had unread research files from Pendarvis, and decided to get one and retreat under the covers.

When she opened her totebag, however, the first thing she saw was an unfamiliar piece of folded paper. She pulled it out, opened it, and stared at the words printed in ink:

Go back to Old World Wisconsin or you'll be sorry. You are not wanted here, bitch.

Chloe had read the note several times before she realized that her skin was prickling and she felt mildly nauseated. Don't be such a wuss, she told herself. This was the stuff of fourth grade playgrounds. Honestly, she should laugh it off.

But a memory popped unbidden into her mind—the sensation of a hand against her back earlier as she stood braced against the whipping wind on the edge of the badger hole. *Had* someone pushed her? If so, had that person also written this half-stupid, half-chilling note?

She tried to consider who could have left such a thing for her to find. Like an *idiot* she'd left her totebag in the entry room for much of the day, providing easy access to any staff member, volunteer, or visitor. Gerald was the most vocal in blaming Old World Wisconsin, and by extension her, for the threat to close Pendarvis. But others might be harboring just as much resentment, and keeping it to themselves.

TWELVE

"Why are you angry?" Andrew asked.

Mary looked up from the skillet she was scouring with sand. "Angry?"

"You're scrubbing that like the devil." He gave her a crooked smile. "I know you."

She sat back on her heels. Since settling into the diggings something *had* been building inside, but it wasn't anger. Resentment, more like. And it wouldn't do to keep it to herself.

"I apologize," she told him. "And ... you're right. I do have something on my mind."

Andrew scraped the last bit of porridge from his plate. Jory had left for the mine, and Ruan was firing up his forge near the badger hole, but Andrew had lingered. "Best get it out, then."

Mary looked at the ridge Cornish miners called *Mena Dhu*, ugly and scarred. "Mining lead is your dream, Andrew. Yours and Jory's. I have my own." Her dream had been born of her mother's whispered words, shaped in the presence of Mrs. Bunney, nurtured during the long journey from Camborne to the territory.

Andrew frowned. He and Jory had been digging a shaft, pitching out the lead they found, but the deeper they went the harder the work. "We need you to work the surface, Mary. If you cob and clean what we send up, we'll be able to get it to the smelter sooner." Lead didn't require as much surface labor as they'd been accustomed to in Cornwall, but there was still a need to break large rocks down to manageable size, and to remove clay and debris from the mineral.

"I'll gladly help this afternoon," Mary said quietly. "Just not all day."

It was rare for Andrew to express irritation, but he did now. "Winter will be here before we know it. We need a windlass, and they cost forty dollars!" Until they could get a windlass in place, which would let them haul stone from the shaft efficiently, the men had to climb up ladders with an achingly heavy bucket in one hand.

"I said I will help." Mary folded her arms. "But I have another idea. Just give me a chance."

After Andrew stormed off to the mine, she picked her way down the ravine, paying attention to the camps she passed. She saw miners spooning cornmeal mush, or gnawing at blackened bits of skillet-fried cornmeal cakes. She was betting that many of them would be willing to pay her for a taste of real bread.

Sweat trickled down her spine as she walked for the first time into Mineral Point. She passed "The Mansion House"—several crude cabins linked together by walkways—operated by a fat Cornishman. Fiddle music, drunken laughter, and angry voices screeched from the open doors. I'd rather sleep in a badger hole, Mary thought, and kept walking.

A handful of log cabins and stone structures stood, with men putting up more. The place smelled of dust, horse and oxen droppings, and rotting garbage. Mary passed drovers carrying long whips coiled over their shoulders, French trappers in greasy leathers, a few better-dressed men who might have been geologists or Yankee businessmen. Or possibly lawyers, Mary thought. She'd heard that a court had been established here. Lawyers and businessmen hoped that when Wisconsin became its own territory, the settlement would be named the capital. Some passersby spoke dialects she recognized: Cornish, Irish, English. Other snippets of overheard conversations were incomprehensible.

She passed several boarding houses and shops, trying to puzzle from signs which sold boots or mining tools or groceries. She ventured into a log cabin that appeared promising, but inside she found only a man dispensing grog from behind a board propped on two barrels. Several men sat drinking in morose silence. Two more were playing cards on a barrel in one corner, and a fat man lay snoring in another.

Mary approached the bartender and spoke carefully. "Do you sell food?"

"Only the liquid kind." The man looked her up and down with a suggestive leer.

She ignored his lewd look. "Where can I buy food?"

He said something she didn't understand, tugged on his vest, and sent a stream of tobacco juice to the dirt floor.

"Where?" she demanded.

Scowling, the man held up two fingers and jerked his thumb: *Two doors up, that way.*

Mary went back outside. She found the store, such as it was, set up in one corner of another log building. Food for sale sat in kegs, barrels, and sacks. The rest of the room was living space, with a bed built into one corner, a small table, and empty kegs that served as seats. The room smelled kewny—sour and rancid.

"I need wheat flour and salt," Mary told the storekeeper. He had sunken eyes and was cadaverously thin, a combination that did not inspire confidence.

"A bushel of salt is twenty dollars," the man said. "Flour, one hundred fourteen dollars per barrel."

Her jaw dropped. "Aye?"

"It ain't easy or cheap to haul food out here." He shrugged, unmoved by her distress. Then he reached into a barrel of cornmeal and lifted a handful, letting it sift down through his fingers. "Just ten dollars and forty cents a bushel."

Mary turned away. Maybe, she thought, I should just get cornmeal. But her plan didn't involve cornmeal.

Wheat flour it must be. Her stomach twisted nervously as she contemplated Andrew's dismay when he learned how much money she'd spent. I'll make it work, she promised herself, and emptied their cash pouch of the bits of mineral that passed for currency in the diggings. The storekeeper weighed it and fetched as much salt and flour as she could afford.

Back in camp, accompanied by the metallic clang of Ruan's hammer on anvil nearby, she fetched the cup where she'd been nurturing a sourdough starter, made with the last of her barley flour. The wheat flour she'd purchased was of poor quality, full of lumps. She tried sifting it through her finest ore sieve. Finally, flushed and furious, she took her cobbing hammer to the hard bits. Once the flour was of reasonable consistency she mixed up a batch of bread dough and put it in the sun to rise.

When the dough was ready she put it into her spider—an iron pan with three legs—and nestled it over the glowing chirks of her cookfire. She put on the lid, covered the lid with more coals, and left it to bake.

The large loaf that emerged from the makeshift oven was golden brown, crusty, and fragrant. With the bread wrapped in her apron and a knife in hand, Mary set out, meandering through the scattered huts and mines. She offered miners slices of the steaming bread, slipping their coins and lead gravel into her pouch. In ten minutes her apron contained only the three slices she'd saved for her brothers and Ruan.

At their mine site, she found Andrew dumping stone from the bucket. "I brought you a snack," she called.

He was still annoyed with her, but he accepted the bread. "Wheat bread? You spent money on flour?"

"Just tell me if you like it."

He took a bite. "It's very good," he admitted grudgingly.

"The Yankee miners seem to think so too." She held up the plump pouch.

Andrew stared at her, eyes widening. "You've been selling … ?"

"I have. Most of the men on this hill have been cooking for themselves all summer. Flour is dear, but I can make money doing this, Andrew."

"Mary Pascoe, you are clever." He shook his head.

"I'm determined," she said. This was just the beginning. One day she would offer saffron buns and clotted cream, and tea served in pretty china cups.

But she wasn't there yet. "Now I can work," she told Andrew, pulling her cobbing hammer from her basket.

The men dug down thirty feet, cribbing the shaft with timbers to prevent rock falls. They followed horizontal veins east and west as they appeared, looking for a good drift—a horizontal run of lead branching off from the main shaft. They had some success, more disappointments. "I thought this one was promising," Andrew said one evening, clearly tired and discouraged. "But it petered out."

They were sitting around their campfire beside the badger hole, sharing a supper of boiled rice and treacle-smeared bread. A breeze stirred up the rotten egg smell drifting from the smelters. The wood-fired furnaces burned impurities from the ore miners brought by the barrowful. The melted lead was formed into ingots, ready for market. Smelting was necessary, but Mary hated the smeechy yellow smoke and stink.

"We'll find a better drift," Jory said. Mary had to smile. Jory was a miner in his heart, in his bones.

Ruan stood, climbed down into the badger hole, and emerged again with something in his hand. "I made you a sticking tommy," he said, holding out the candleholder. The brothers only had one between them.

"Thank you," Jory said with a delighted grin. "Say, it's a fine one." He passed it to Mary.

Mary hadn't paid much attention to Ruan's smithing, but she saw at once that he did good work. He had taken the time to put a few decorative twists and flourishes in the iron. She'd never seen a sticking tommy that was beautiful as well as functional.

"Do you think it's silly to decorate a tool, Mary?" Ruan asked.

"Not at all." She ran one finger over the twists before passing the candleholder to Andrew.

That night, in the badger hole, Mary lay awake and listened to the boisterous shouts and drunken laughter drifting over the hill, and to the deep breathing of the three men sharing this shelter. Some of her friends from Wheal Blackstone were already married mothers. Mary hadn't given much thought to marriage. She'd been too busy trying to take care of her brothers. Besides, she'd always known that when Mama had spoken of *her* dreams for her eldest daughter, she wasn't talking about marrying a laborer and settling down.

But a blacksmith's skills would always be needed. The work was safer than mining. And, Mary thought, Ruan is a good man.

———

The next morning she followed her new routine: make breakfast for her men, then begin mixing dough. She wished she had butter or jam, but those niceties would come in time.

When the bread was baked she set out in a different direction. She sold bread to a miner manning a windlass, and to another who was shoveling ore into a wheelbarrow. It was a fine day, not as hot as the past few had been. Fluffy white clouds dotted a sky as brilliant a blue as Ruan's eyes.

She passed by the entrance to a small stone shelter built into the hillside, assuming that it was empty at this hour. Then she heard the unexpected sound of a thin and shaky child's voice. "Good morning."

Mary stooped by the entrance, trying to see into the gloom. "Who's there? Will you come out?"

"My papa says I can't."

"Is your papa there?"

"No. That's why I'm not allowed to come out."

"How about if you stay inside, but come closer to the entrance so I can see you? I've got some nice fresh bread with me, and I'd like to give you a piece."

For a moment there was no response. Then Mary heard a little shuffling sound. Finally a girl with enormous brown eyes appeared. She looked to be maybe five or six years old. She wore a faded cotton dress that had probably once been deep green. Her brown hair straggled down her back, in desperate need of a comb. One thumb was in her mouth.

Mary felt as if someone was squeezing her heart in a vise.

Her hand trembled as she sliced off a generous piece of bread and extended it toward the child. The girl hesitated before taking it. She took a tentative nibble, then gobbled the rest. "Thank you," she whispered.

"My name is Mary Pascoe. What's yours?"

"Ida Penberthy."

"Is your father working a mine?"

Ida nodded.

"Where's your mama, Ida?"

"She died last year." Sudden tears glimmered in her eyes, visible even in the shadows.

So, Mary thought, this child is likely left alone in a cave all day, every day, while her father works his mine. And right this minute, there wasn't a thing she could do about it.

"It was that nice to meet you, Ida," she said. "I'll come visit again, all right?"

Ida put her thumb back into her mouth and nodded.

Mary thought about Ida for the rest of the day. After feeding her men at suppertime, Mary walked back to the cave. Ida and a man sat by a small cookfire outside. The aroma of fried salt pork sizzled from a skillet. Ida waggled her fingers in greeting before leaning shyly against her father.

Mary introduced herself. "Are you Mr. Penberthy?"

"I am." Mr. Penberthy got to his feet. He wore buckskin pants, a filthy red flannel shirt, and moccasins. He looked puzzled but pulled his shapeless hat respectfully from his head.

"I was passing your shelter this afternoon and met Ida—who did not step outside, as you'd instructed her. I'd be happy to watch her when you're working."

Mr. Penberthy looked startled. "You would?"

"Our camp's naught but a five-minute walk from here. You could bring her by in the morning and pick her up when you're through with work for the day."

"Now, why would you be making such an offer?"

"Because that's what neighbors do. And because I would enjoy Ida's company."

Mr. Penberthy's fingers were tight on his hat brim. "I'll allow, it's no good for her to be here alone. But I can't take her into the mine with me, now can I."

"Of course not," Mary said gently. "You're obviously doing the best you can in a difficult situation."

Mr. Penberthy looked down at Ida, who was listening with owl eyes. "Would you like to visit with this lady while I'm down in the mine?"

Ida grabbed the leather of her father's trousers. But she nodded.

Mary blew out a breath she hadn't realized she was holding, and smiled.

THIRTEEN

AT THE BREAKFAST TABLE, Tamsin eyed Chloe over her cup of steaming tea. "I do hope you've recovered from your mishap."

The words were solicitous, but Chloe didn't miss the faint hint of once-a-mom, always-a-mom censure. "Again, I'm *so* sorry I worried you," she said earnestly.

"Are you coming down with something? After getting soaked, I wouldn't wonder."

"I'm just tired." Chloe had spent much of the night wondering who had left her the nasty note. Who was that angry, and that cowardly.

"I don't think it was wise to go for a stroll in the woods when the storm was threatening, dear," Tamsin said. "You might have—" Her voice broke when someone knocked on the door.

"I'll get it." Chloe scrambled to her feet, willing to defer learning what additional calamities might have befallen her.

When she opened the door, Investigator Higgins stepped inside. "Good morning, Ms. Ellefson," he said. "Miss Tamsin, I hope it's not too early to come by." He snatched his hat from his head. Chloe wondered if Tamsin had taught him in third grade too.

"Not at all," Tamsin said. "Would you like a saffron bun?"

"Well, I wouldn't say no," Higgins admitted. He took a seat. Chloe got him a plate from the cupboard before taking her own chair again.

He sampled his bun and smiled appreciatively. "Delicious. Now. I wanted to let you know that we have not been able to find any link between the remains and an open criminal investigation."

"Do you know how old the bones are?" Chloe asked.

"I hate to hypothesize before we get the official report. I can say that unembalmed bodies buried without a coffin take about eight to twelve years to decompose to a skeleton. Although I didn't touch the bones, they looked dry. Sort of crumbly. And the smell—"

"I'll get more coffee," Tamsin announced, and marched into the kitchen.

Looking apologetic, Higgins lowered his voice. "There was no smell. All I smelled was earth. It was an old burial."

An old burial, Chloe thought. That narrowed things right down.

"One of the crime scene guys speculated that the victim was an adult male, older than thirty-five." Higgins reached for the butter dish. "We also found some broken china among the bones."

"Right among the bones?" Chloe sipped her orange juice, thinking that through. "What did the china look like?"

"It's just small pieces. White and dark blue."

Chloe sucked in her lower lip. Blue Willow, maybe? "May I see the shards?"

He looked startled. "I'm afraid not. They could become evidentiary, and so will remain in police custody until the case is closed." He drummed his fingertips on the tablecloth much the way Roelke often did. "And you have to understand, this is a *very* cold case. I can request an agent from the crime lab to help with the investigation, but given the age of the remains, it won't be a high priority. Even if the lab could spare someone, it's unlikely that person would be trained to do the kind of research we need."

Tamsin returned with the coffee pot just in time to hear that. "Chloe's already looking into the death. She's trained."

Chloe squirmed. "In history. Not—not forensics or anything."

Higgins gave her a long look. "Well, let me know if you discover anything." He wiped his mouth on a napkin and got to his feet. "Thank you, Miss Tamsin."

Chloe fiddled with a spoon. She was curious about the china shards found with the skeleton, but it seemed unlikely she'd ever get to see them. Had Investigator Higgins taken everything that Adam had found into custody? She understood the need, but still, that was unfortunate.

Suddenly she remembered the sticking tommy she'd borrowed from Adam before the skeleton was found. She wanted to see if there was anything like it in the Pendarvis collection. It was a shame to see that disappear into police custody forever.

Roelke's stern voice was almost audible inside her head: *Turn it over to the investigator.*

Chloe tried to tune him out. It *really* would be nice to identify the blacksmith who'd made the piece. Artifacts mattered, and there was power in matching object with creator. It was respectful—a way of saying *What you did was important* to the long-gone craftsman. Each connection made added another piece to the ongoing research puzzle of mining days in Mineral Point.

I'll turn the sticking tommy in as soon as I check records for evidence of the maker, Chloe decided, and felt only a little guilty.

Roelke waited to call until Marie was on the phone and he knew Libby was home from taking the kids to school. "Hey, it's me," he said when Libby answered. "Everything okay?"

Libby hesitated. "Well…"

Roelke sat up straighter. "What happened?"

"When I opened the front door this morning, there was a yellow rose lying on the welcome mat." Libby's voice was tight.

"Aren't yellow roses—"

"Yes. My favorite flower. Were. I carried them in my wedding."

Roelke cursed under his breath. So much for Dan Raymo de-escalating. "Anything else?"

"No. But it makes me *sick* to know that Dan was here again."

It made Roelke sick too. He drummed the desk with an unhappy thumb. "He's trying to get a rise out of you. Chances are good he'll get tired of playing these games if he doesn't get rewarded with a reaction." He wasn't sure who he was trying to convince. "But Libby—*please* call the Palmyra police and tell them what's been going on. They'll write a report. If Raymo doesn't settle down it might be good to have some documentation."

"I feel like such a girly-girl," Libby muttered. "I'm capable of taking care of myself, Roelke."

He pressed a thumb to his forehead and closed his eyes. "I know you are. But as you said, the kids are involved…"

"Oh, all *right*. I'll call the cops."

After hanging up, Roelke sat brooding. There had to be something he could do. He felt twitchy with the need to confront Raymo. The SOB may not have threatened Libby, but he was harassing her.

Chief Naborski's voice rang in his memory: *You're a good cop, Roelke. But if you want this one you gotta fly straight. Do you understand me?*

It's just my luck, Roelke thought darkly, that Raymo starts acting up again right when I've got this training opportunity on the horizon. When Chief and Dorothy Blevins and the rest of the Village Board's Police Committee were watching him. When Chloe's maniacal boss Ralph Petty was, for all Roelke knew, trying to set him up.

Roelke desperately wanted to be a good cop. He'd been working hard on standing straight, keeping his anger in check in even the worst situations. But this mess with Raymo was personal. That made things a whole lot harder.

———

As she walked to Pendarvis that morning Chloe stewed about the note she'd found in her totebag. The day before, worries had disappeared for a few hours as she and Claudia made plans to improve collections storage and care. Now, trouble loomed large again. Chloe wasn't sure how she'd look anyone in the eye without wondering, Was it you? Was it *you*?

She also wasn't sure what to do about the note. She knew Roelke would tell her to report it to the cops. At the very least, she should show the damn thing to Claudia and Loren.

All I wanted, Chloe reminded the cosmos as she turned onto Shake Rag Street, was a pleasant week. Time away from her micromanaging, ever-critical boss. Time to boost her professional confidence. Seriously, it didn't seem so much to ask.

Investigator Higgins's breakfast visit had made her a little tardy. She hurried into the office at eight fifteen with an explanation for

Claudia at the ready, but Evelyn was alone. "Good morning," Chloe told the receptionist. She tried to picture this patrician, gracious woman slipping a nasty note into her totebag. Ludicrous, Chloe thought, and felt a little better.

"Good morning." The older woman's voice was tight.

"Evelyn? Is everything alright?"

"It's these calls!" She grabbed a fistful of message slips. "I came in early to get organized, and a reporter called at seven forty-five. He wanted to know how it felt to hear that Pendarvis was closing."

"So much for the facts," Chloe said sympathetically.

"I just hung up from a woman who wanted to know if our artifacts would go up for sale if the site closed, and if there was a way she could get a preemptive bid in on the portrait in Pendarvis House."

"No, there isn't," Chloe said—a bit tartly, because she liked that particular painting a lot, and it wasn't going anywhere. She tried to lighten her tone. "Want me to answer the phone for a while? I won't mention my employment status to callers."

"Thanks, but no." Evelyn managed a shaky smile. "I promised Claudia I'd help with all this, and I will."

"Speaking of Claudia, do you know where she is?"

"She was here earlier. Dr. Miller was here too—"

"That woman is a serious pest," Chloe murmured.

"Dr. Miller said Loren had given her permission to go into Polperro House. He and Gerald are over on Dark Hill, so Claudia went with her. I haven't seen her since. Winter was here a few minutes ago, looking for her."

"Winter? Winter the potter?"

"She wanted to show Claudia a prototype for some reproductions they've talked about. She said she'd come back another time."

The phone rang, and Evelyn picked up the receiver. "Good morning. Pendarvis Historic Site."

Chloe glanced at the clock. The day was already skidding off the rails, and the site hadn't even opened yet.

———

Roelke had studied for the Police Committee interview. He had Wisconsin drug law down cold, and he'd thought carefully about responses to expected questions. But the interview felt perfunctory, and the questions were simplistic: *What do you like about serving the Village of Eagle? Why do you want to take the specialized training? How will it help you perform your duties?* He walked out of the town hall, where the meeting had taken place, with no idea if he'd satisfied the committee or not.

Back at the Eagle PD, Chief Naborski beckoned Roelke into his office. "I saw your report. Tell me about Michelle Zietz."

Roelke was glad enough to forget the Police Committee altogether. He summarized his arrest.

Chief Naborski listened without interruption. "Well done. You're confident this young woman will perform as a CI?"

"I believe she will. She lives with her parents, is counting on financial aid to get through college … she's highly motivated."

The older man tipped his chair backward. "What's your plan?"

This was one of the things Roelke appreciated about Chief Naborski—when it was warranted, he let his officers run with things, instead of micromanaging. It occurred to Roelke for the first time that the timing of this investigation couldn't be better—if all went well, this would be a big bust for the EPD. Assuming everything wound through the courts successfully, the department would eventually get half of whatever drug money was siezed. That could only impress the Police Committee.

Roelke tried to sit a little straighter. "I'll have Zietz make three buys. That way we'll establish a pattern, and the dealers can't claim they only sold once to pay grandma's medical bills or something. I'll beg the money from the village board president."

Chief nodded.

"If all goes according to plan, I'll request a search warrant after the second buy in anticipation of the third. Once Zietz confirms that third buy we'll hit the house. We'll need all our guys and then some. I'll request mutual aid from Palmyra and Mukwonago."

"This is all very promising, Officer McKenna," Chief said. "Make it happen."

———

Chloe tried to think where Claudia might be. Maybe she'd gone to greet the interpretive staff.

In the gift shop she found Rita, the recent college grad, talking to Audrey, who sold tickets and souvenirs. Gerald joined them, already muddy and sweat-stained. Was it one of you? Chloe asked silently. Her gaze lingered on Gerald. "How's the badger hole coming?"

Gerald scowled. "Some kids were messing around in there."

"Kids will be kids," Chloe said blithely, hoping no one had happened to notice her emerging from the woods in the downpour yesterday evening. She excavated Adam's sticking tommy from her bag, and unwrapped the towel.

Gerald's scowl deepened. "Is that from our collection?"

"No, Gerald. If it was, I assure you I wouldn't be wandering around with it clutched in my hot little hand. It belongs to a friend and I hope to identify the maker. Does this decorative work look familiar?"

He barely glanced at the artifact. "Nope."

She slipped it away again. "Has anyone seen Claudia?"

No one had. "But we've already got the tour schedule," Rita said. "It's going to be a very busy day."

Well, Chloe thought, maybe I'll find her in Polperro House. Claudia might have been unwilling to leave Dr. Miller alone in the historic home. She was probably standing sentinel, impatiently waiting for Miller to look at whatever she'd come to see. Awk-ward.

Chloe left the front line staff to start their day. When she reached Polperro she found the door to the lower floor unlocked. "Hello?" she called. No answer.

She wanted to compare Adam's sticking tommy with the ones on display while she was here, and so headed for the second room. None of the workmanship suggested the same maker. Oh, well. So far she and Claudia hadn't found any additional candleholders in storage, but Loren might recognize the workmanship in Adam's piece.

Instead of retracing her steps, Chloe decided to go upstairs and get a better look at the kitchen and living quarters she'd only glimpsed earlier. She opened the door to the staircase leading to the second story...

And the body of Dr. Yvonne Miller, Ph.D., tumbled down the last step and landed on Chloe's feet.

FOURTEEN

CHLOE LEAPT BACKWARDS WITH a wordless squawk. Her heart thumped wildly against her ribs. The woman lay in a most unscholarly crumple at the foot of the stairs. Her eyes were open but vacant. One arm was flung high. Her knees were bent. One shoe—a well-polished loafer—lay lonely on a step halfway to the second floor. Her large briefcase had landed on its side.

Something hot and sour rose in Chloe's throat. She pressed one hand against her belly and took several deep breaths. Then she approached the body and went through the motions of looking for a pulse.

But she knew it was too late. Yvonne Miller was dead.

Chloe whirled and raced outside. She spotted a man repairing a plank on the walkway and swerved to meet him. "Call 911," Chloe gasped. "There's been a terrible accident in Polperro House." The maintenance man left his toolbox and took off toward the row house.

When she turned back, Gerald was leading twenty or so school kids toward Polperro. She cut him off. "You can't go in there—someone's hurt—"

Gerald turned to his charges. "How would you like to learn some games kids played a hundred and forty years ago?" The children cheered, and Gerald shepherded them away.

Chloe was pacing in the yard outside Polperro House when she heard sirens. A truck emblazoned with MINERAL POINT RESCUE SQUAD arrived first, followed by a police car. She felt an overwhelming desire to see Roelke McKenna jump out, uniformed and ready to take charge.

Investigator Higgins emerged instead. He trotted toward her with the EMTs on his heels. "Ms. Ellefson? What happened?"

"Dr. Miller—she's in there." Chloe led them into Polperro and pointed. "That door to the stairway was closed when I came into the building. When I opened it, she just … sort of … fell out."

Chloe retreated outside just as Loren Beskeen, once again in period clothes, jogged from the woods on Dark Hill. He must have heard the sirens. When he got within earshot he demanded, "What's happened?"

"There's been an accident. Dr. Miller fell down the stairs in Polperro House."

His jaw went slack. "Is she badly hurt?"

Chloe hesitated, but there was no help for it. "I'm sorry, but I'm pretty sure she's dead. The EMTs are inside with her now, and Investigator Higgins."

Loren looked stunned. "Dear God."

Investigator Higgins emerged from Polperro and joined them. "I'm glad you're here, Mr. Beskeen—"

"She can't really be dead," Loren said. "Not here."

Investigator Higgins put a bracing hand on Loren's shoulder. "Could you wait for me over there? I'd like to speak with Ms. Ellefson for a moment."

"I—it's just that … of course." Loren walked away.

Higgins turned to Chloe. He didn't look like the man who was Adam's friend, and who'd dropped by Tamsin's apartment to eat a saffron bun and share the news. He looked sterner, older.

Abruptly, the refrain of "With A Little Bit Of Luck" from *My Fair Lady* began echoing in Chloe's head. Honestly, the investigator even looked a bit like Rex Harrison playing Henry Higgins in the film version. Why hadn't she seen the likeness before? Same height, same hair swept back from his face. Same—

"Ms. Ellefson?" he said, interrupting her mental foray into something much more pleasant than a dead freelance historian.

"Sorry. I, um … what did you say?"

"I asked if you touched Ms. Miller, or moved anything in the area."

"I tried to find a pulse, but couldn't." Chloe shoved her hands into her pockets. "Otherwise, no, I didn't touch anything."

He scribbled in his notebook. "I know you're a friend of Adam's and Miss Tamsin's, but why are you here at the historic site?"

"I'm a visiting curator. I'm also employed by the State Historical Society of Wisconsin."

"How did you know the deceased?"

"I only met her two days ago. She's writing a book and has been doing research here. That's about all I know. When I got here this morning Evelyn mentioned that—"

"Who is Evelyn?"

"The volunteer receptionist. She said Dr. Miller had already stopped by the office, wanting to get inside Polperro House. Claudia

Doyle, the curator, took her. When I went inside the house I called, but nobody answered."

"Where is Ms. Doyle?"

"I don't know. I haven't seen her today." The admission made her feel a little squirmy, but Claudia had to be around here somewhere.

"Thank you, Ms. Ellefson, you've been very helpful." Investigator Higgins slid the notebook away. "I will want to speak with you again … "

Why? she wanted to ask. What more do you need to hear from me? Dr. Miller suffered a tragic accident and died. But Chloe lived with a cop, and she knew the answer. Any unattended death was considered suspicious until proved otherwise.

" … so please," he was saying, "don't leave the site."

———

Interview over, Chloe retreated to a quiet bench. The shock and adrenaline had faded. Melancholy filled the void. She hadn't liked Yvonne Miller. Now that the woman was dead, she felt guilty for not liking her. Not that Yvonne gave anybody much of a chance. Still, Chloe thought, I could have tried harder. It seemed terribly sad that the woman who'd died so young had been, it seemed, a very unhappy person.

Chloe watched a butterfly dancing through the native plantings nearby for a few minutes. Then she took a deep breath and headed up the hill.

In the row house office, Evelyn turned to greet her. "What's going on?"

Chloe sat at Claudia's desk. "I went into Polperro right after the site opened, and I'm sorry to say I found Dr. Miller at the bottom of the stairs. It looked like she'd fallen. She didn't survive."

"*What?*" Evelyn pressed a hand over her heart.

"Don't be surprised if the police want to talk to you. It's just routine. Has Claudia been here?"

Evelyn shook her head. "I haven't seen her."

Claudia's absence was fast sliding from odd to worrisome. She hadn't shown up to brief her staff before opening, hadn't left a note or message for Chloe. "I'll go look for her," Chloe told Evelyn.

Outside, she headed for the gift shop. Audrey, the cashier, shook her head when asked about her supervisor. "Haven't seen her."

Chloe repeated the "terrible accident" summary. "Unless Loren tells you otherwise, I think we need to tell any general visitors who show up that the site is temporarily closed. Once the coroner has come and gone, and the police have finished studying the accident site, you can welcome visitors again."

On the lower property, Investigator Higgins was still talking with Loren. Chloe skirted Polperro House and checked Pendarvis and Trelawny Houses. Both empty.

There was nowhere else to look. Claudia, Chloe thought, where on earth did you go?

———

Roelke stayed out on patrol until half past noon. Back at the station, he walked straight to the refrigerator. Breakfast had been a long time ago. "Hey, Marie."

The phone rang before the clerk could answer. "Eagle Police Department ... Officer McKenna? He's right here."

Roelke put his sandwich aside and picked up the receiver. "This is Officer McKenna."

"Roelke? He took my baby girl!"

It took him several seconds to realize that the shrill voice belonged to his cousin. Every muscle clenched. "Libby? What happened?"

"Deirdre!" She began to sob. "Dan, took, Deirdre!"

Oh *Jesus*. "You're at your house?"

"Y-yes—"

"I'll be there as soon as I can." He slammed down the receiver. "Family emergency," he told Marie, who was watching with concern. "I'll be back as soon as I can."

His truck was in the garage a block away, so he slid into the squad he'd left parked out front. Mistake, whispered a faint voice in his brain, but it was too late; he was already tearing down Highway 59 toward Palmyra.

When he got to Libby's house, she ran down the front walk to meet him. Her eyes were red-rimmed and puffy. "Come inside," he said. He put an arm around her shoulders and led her toward the house, wondering if Raymo was nearby, watching his ex-wife dissolve.

In the living room he settled her on the couch. He pulled a single chair close and sat down, leaning forward, elbows on knees. "Okay. Tell me what happened."

"I went to pick Deirdre up at preschool, just like always. And when I got there, she was gone! I kind of went a little nuts, and her teacher said that Deirdre's father had just left with her."

"The teacher let Raymo walk out with her?" Roelke demanded. Of all the stupid, irresponsible—

"Well, I'd never told her that Dan *couldn't* pick up Deirdre. Why would I? He's never even been to her preschool before. He's never asked to spend time with her. Half the time he doesn't even show up for his court-appointed visits."

"Where's Justin?"

"I called his school. The principal said he'd ask for a cop to come for the rest of the day, just in case Dan shows up."

"Good." But Roelke didn't believe Raymo would show at Justin's school. Raymo would expect Libby to have warned the principal, and he was way too clever to walk into a trap.

Tears welled in her eyes. "Oh God, Roelke. What if he hurts her?"

"He won't."

"What if he never brings her back?"

"Dan Raymo doesn't want to be a full-time dad. He'll bring her back." Roelke got to his feet and prowled the room. "Do you have a recent picture of Deirdre? We should—" Movement out the window caught his eye. "*Wait*. He just pulled up."

"He's got her?"

Roelke watched Raymo pull Deirdre from the back seat and deposit her on the lawn. "He's got her." He felt almost light-headed with relief.

Libby ran to the door, flung it open, and started down the front walk. "Deirdre? Deirdre, come here!" Deirdre ran to meet her. Libby snatched her up and buried her face in the little girl's hair.

Then she looked over Deirdre's shoulder at Raymo. "Don't you *ever* take one of my children without permission again." Her voice was low and fierce.

Her ex stood by his car with a smug expression on his face. He's pleased with himself, Roelke thought. Libby freaked out: mission accomplished.

Dan Raymo was lean and dark. He'd been in trouble since his teens. Roelke had never liked him, never understood what Libby had seen in him. He must have satisfied some rebellious streak within her, or maybe he was just great in bed. He ran his own business now, and wore suits instead of tight jeans, but he'd never let go of his high school sneer. Or his sense of entitlement.

Roelke locked one hand around Libby's arm in an iron grip. "Take Deirdre inside and shut the door. *Go.*" He physically propelled them back toward the house. He stared at Raymo in hard silence until he heard the door close behind him.

Then he walked down the sidewalk until the two men stood a foot or so apart. He was aware that he shouldn't have this exchange in public, while in uniform. He shouldn't give Raymo opportunity to claim that an on-duty Village of Eagle police officer had accosted him. But what was he supposed to do, go home and change?

The hell with it. "You," Roelke said grimly, "have crossed a line."

Raymo went all innocent. "What line is that, officer? I wanted to see my little girl, so I stopped by her preschool. I was just planning to peek into her classroom, but she spotted me and got *so* excited. She said she wanted me to drive her home. I could hardly disappoint her, could I?"

"You've made a career of disappointing your children," Roelke growled. "Besides, that fairy tale is utter bullshit. No way would Deirdre get all excited just because *you* showed up at preschool. No way."

Raymo's eyes narrowed, but not before revealing a flash of triumph. "Want to take her back to family court and have her questioned by the judge?"

Dammit. Roelke struggled to keep his cop-face in place. Raymo had quickly out-maneuvered him, and they both knew it. Dragging Deirdre into the argument, having strangers question her, was much more likely to harm her than her father. To a stranger, his innocent tale could sound plausible. A judge might deliver a slap on the wrist—*Your motives may have been good, Mr. Raymo, but from here on I expect you to stick to the visitation plan worked out at the time of the divorce*—but that would almost certainly be all.

Raymo sauntered closer, until only inches separated them. "So, Mr. Policeman, whatcha gonna do now?"

Roelke's hands curled into fists. Don't give in, he ordered himself. He leaned closer. "You have been harassing Libby. I expect it to stop. At once."

"Or what?" Raymo leaned in too. The self-satisfied tone flickered and died, replaced with suppressed rage. "It's bad enough that all I ever hear is 'Roelke says this' and 'Roelke does that.' *I* am Justin and Deirdre's father. Not you, not Bolitho, not any other scumbag Libby drags home."

He knows Adam's name, Roelke thought. Not good.

"And there's not a damn thing you can do to change that," Raymo hissed. "I have a right to take part in my children's lives."

They were so close that Roelke could smell the man—aftershave, a faint stink of sweat. Roelke's fists trembled with the desire to punch the bastard in the gut. Don't do it, he willed himself. Don't. *Don't.* You're better than that.

Raymo broke first. "Sucker," he whispered, but he turned away.

Roelke watched as Raymo slid into his Firebird, started the engine, and drove off. He stood still even after the car had disappeared around a corner. All the things that had disappeared during the confrontation eased back: the smell of fresh-cut grass from the lawn next door, the harsh bark of a dog down the way, the everyday sight of a woman pushing a stroller.

Roelke took it in, trying to anchor himself in *normal.* He couldn't calm Libby down until he'd calmed himself down.

FIFTEEN

"Be calm," Mary muttered to herself, using a long-handled spoon to stir up the glowing chirks left from her breakfast cookfire. It was a chilly morning—the sun just a pale blur in a gray sky, the ground still rimed with frost. Andrew and Jory had already left for their own digging, and Ruan was at his forge. But Ida and Mr. Penberthy were inexplicably late.

Ida had become Mary's shadow, helping with baking and other chores, roaming the crumpled hillsides with baskets of bread. Mary loved to hear the girl laugh, loved watching her little fingers struggling to knead a mass of dough, loved the smell of her. Andrew and Jory provoked helpless giggles with jokes and funny stories. Ruan had showed her how to make a game of tossing small iron rings over sticks pounded into the ground.

Now Mary looked over her shoulder again—and felt a spasm of panic. Mr. Penberthy was approaching, without his daughter.

Mary's heart raced like a runaway colt. "Where's Ida?" she cried. Bad things—illness, accident, death—could snatch little girls all too quickly. And the man's eyes were red, as if he'd been crying.

"She's well." Mr. Penberthy fished a red kerchief from a pocket and mopped at his nose. "The thing is, my brother and me, we're done digging."

"Oh," Mary said softly, as her heart crumpled like fisted paper. She hadn't let herself dwell on this possibility. Well, now she must face it.

"We're game for the work but don't seem to have the knack of it. We don't have nearly the earnings most of the boys have. I've heard they might be hiring dockhands down south on the Mississippi."

Mary managed to get words past the lump forming in her throat. "May I come say goodbye to Ida?"

Mr. Penberthy tucked his woolen muffler more snugly beneath his shirt collar. He glanced away, shifting his weight from one foot to the other. Finally he met her gaze. "Ida's taken quite a shine to you. I can see the change in her. Ever since her ma died I've given my girl a rough life, sure enough. And I've no call to think that will change. I'd almost forgotten what her smile looks like, but she smiles when she speaks of you." He shifted his weight again. "It breaks my heart in pieces to ask, but might you see your way clear to taking her in?"

A muffled explosion cut through the morning as some miner nearby fired carefully placed gunpowder down below to blow open the stubborn rock. The sound echoed in Mary's mind as she tried to assure herself of his meaning. "You mean ... to raise her?"

"Everything would be different if her ma hadn't died." His voice was husky. "But she did, and I'm no good for Ida. I know it's a lot to ask. But I'd be that grateful."

Tears of joy and pity welled in Mary's eyes. "I will happily raise your daughter. My brothers will agree, I know."

He nodded.

"I don't have a lot to offer Ida, Mr. Penberthy. But I *will*."

"Well, then." He swiped at his eyes. "I'll go fetch her."

———

Mary's family moved into the stone hut where Mary had met Ida, which opened into a small cave in the hillside. It was fearfully damp but provided protection from snowfall. Ruan decided to stay with them. The miners overwintering would work whenever the weather permitted. They'd need sticking tommies for their tallow candles. They'd need pigtails—iron corkscrews used to hang buckets from windlasses. They'd need powder spoons to deliver gunpowder into a crevice they wanted to blow open.

Sometimes Ida cried for her papa, but that happened less and less as the winter descended. Mary cooked and scoured dishes, baked bread and made the rounds, selling to miners with runny noses and homesick eyes. She took satisfaction from the growing hoard of lead chips and coins. She had a little girl to raise now.

The Cornish Methodists gathered on Sundays for prayers and hymn-singing. Ruan had a surprising tenor voice, and it pleased Mary to discover that he knew all the words to some of her favorites. Sometimes the women sat together in a hovel, sewing and chatting. Sometimes they trundled barrows of ore to the stream and sieved away grit with chapped fingers.

But sometimes Mary and Ida just rumped up together in their blankets, dozing, whispering to each other. On truly bad days, the men huddled inside the dim dugout too. They shared tales of their boyhoods back in Cornwall, and regaled Ida with legends that had been shared around Cornish hearths for generations. Ruan had a surprising dramatic flair, and he delighted in making Ida laugh.

One sleety January morning, after Andrew and Jory had left for the mine, Ruan sat down near the smoky fire as Mary and Ida began mixing bread dough. "Mary?" he asked, strangely hesitant.

She sat back on her heels. "Yes?"

"It's some cold out."

"It is." Mary couldn't imagine what he was getting at.

"With all the sucker diggers gone for the winter my business has slacked off, so I had some time on my hands, and ... " He thrust a metal box into her hands.

"Why, it's a foot warmer!"

"One day maybe you'll use it in a cutter. Now, you can warm your blankets."

"Oh Ruan, what a thoughtful gift. And so beautifully made." He'd constructed the rectangular box of thin sheets of iron, set in a wooden frame with carefully carved corner posts. He'd punched holes in the iron so once the box was filled with coals, heat would escape. And ... Mary held her gift closer to the meager flames for a better look, and felt her cheeks flush with embarrassment or pleasure, or perhaps both. Etched into the iron was a series of interlocking hearts.

"It's beautiful," she said again, not quite able to meet his gaze. "And it will be wonderful to have this winter. Thank you."

"You're welcome," he said, and left her alone with Ida.

Mary traced a finger over the hearts and thought about Ruan. Theirs was a strange courtship. If it even was a courtship. Ruan and Mary never spoke of marriage, of the future. But it seemed that a wordless understanding was growing between them. With every story told they learned more about each other. As they endured howling blizzards or still days of bitter cold, they learned more about each other. They were at ease together in a way that felt ripe with promise.

Most mornings, Ruan fired up his forge while Andrew and Jory trudged from their hut with collars turned up and heads bent low. Some days they struggled through drifted snow. The two of them would descend into their mine, cold and wet but at least sheltered from the shrieking wind. They had a windlass now, and Ruan would leave his forge from time to time and go wind up the heavy ore buckets. With Andrew loading below, Ruan manning the windlass, and Jory emptying the buckets, the work proceeded well. When Ruan was at the site he could also lower her brothers back into the mine. They rode with one foot inside the bucket and the other free to kick away from the shaft walls. Mary liked knowing that instead of creeping down a slippery ladder, her brothers' safety was in Ruan's strong hands.

SIXTEEN

By noon Investigator Higgins had documented the scene and asked to speak with Chloe again. They sat at a picnic table in the sunshine near the row house. "Just a few more questions, Ms. Ellefson. Are you aware of any animosity that might have existed between Ms. Miller and anyone here on staff?"

Chloe tried not to fidget. "Well, Ms. Miller was very critical of the site and the way it's interpreted. She even said so at a town meeting Monday night. So ... I suspect she isn't anyone's favorite person. Wasn't."

"What was the nature of Ms. Miller's criticism?"

"She seemed to believe that her vision of the interpretive approach at Pendarvis was the only correct vision."

"I see."

"But people here are professionals," Chloe assured him. "Claudia Doyle was quite polite in the face of Ms. Miller's negativity."

The investigator looked unconvinced. "And have you seen or spoken with Ms. Doyle since you and I talked earlier?"

"No," Chloe admitted. Claudia's continued absence was making her increasingly anxious.

Once the detective released Chloe, she checked quickly with Evelyn. "Any sign of Claudia? Or did she call?"

Evelyn shook her head. Her face had a pinched look. "I called her house, thinking maybe she got sick and went home. No answer. I'm worried. This isn't like her."

Chloe chewed her lower lip. She didn't know where else to look.

"You had a call," Evelyn reported. "Midge at the Mineral Point archives, wondering if you were planning to stop by today."

"Oh Lordie." Nothing like having a body literally fall at your feet, Chloe thought, to drive all else from your mind.

"You go on, if you want." Evelyn reached for her cane. "The interpreters will spell themselves, but I'll give Audrey a break in the gift shop."

Chloe hesitated. She hated leaving the site when Yvonne was dead, Claudia was missing, and everyone was upset. Still, she couldn't think of anything truly helpful she could do here if she skipped her lunch break and stayed. Besides, she was aware of a clock ticking in her brain. She wanted to bring some morsel of comfort—or at least information—to Tamsin. "Thanks," she told Evelyn. "I guess I will."

Chloe gobbled the cheese sandwich she'd brought with her before dashing back to the public library. Midge greeted Chloe warmly.

"I don't have a lot of time," Chloe said apologetically, "but I'd like to pick up where I left off with the 1930s newspapers."

"No need. I reviewed everything from 1930 to 1936."

Chloe's mouth opened with astonishment. "You *did*? But … "

Midge shrugged. "I'm a professional snoop. I'm also Tamsin's friend, and intrigued by the discovery of human remains in her old house. You obviously didn't have a lot of time for the search, so I thought I'd give you a hand."

"That is incredibly kind," Chloe said. "Any luck?"

"I'm afraid not. There was no reference to a missing person."

"Darn." Chloe perched on the edge of one of the tables. "I need a new strategy. I have to narrow the search parameters somehow."

"There might have been another period when the house was vacant," Midge said.

"Or it's always possible that someone who lived in the house in the early years was responsible for the burial." Chloe rubbed her temples. "I think the next step is to compile property records, and then see what I can discover about each owner. Where would you suggest I start?"

Midge tapped a pencil against her notepad thoughtfully. "Given how old that cottage is, it's a bit complicated."

Of course it is, Chloe thought.

"The government originally leased all mineral land, but that system was pretty corrupt and difficult to monitor. That led to people settling where they shouldn't, so good luck sorting *that* period out. The feds gave up in 1836, and gave people who'd been settled on a plot first right to get a patent certificate, but lots of men got their patents and then turned around and sold them for profit. Historians estimate that three-quarters of the land sales were illegal."

I need a month, Chloe thought.

"Subsequent deeds are filed at the county courthouse in Dodgeville. Mineral Point was incorporated as a village in 1844, four years before statehood, and we have tax records from that point on. Now, if we can come up with names, it would be good to check marriage and birth indices in Madison. Census records are peculiar."

Of course they are, Chloe thought.

"Territorial censuses were taken in the 1830s and '40s, when the bigwigs were keeping close count with an eye toward statehood, but the information they gathered was erratic. It's worth checking, but there were so many people coming and going, so many people living out at their mines or boarding wherever they could find floor space, it's tricky to get a good picture."

Chloe began mentally composing her apology to Tamsin for finding absolutely nothing.

Midge grinned. "Would you like me to look into it for you?"

"I would be eternally grateful," Chloe said humbly.

"I'll get started. The register of deeds is a friend of mine. But there are other people who know a lot about Mineral Point history, and might have heard a story that I have not. You could start with Evelyn Bainbridge."

Chloe remembered Claudia saying that Evelyn had lived her whole life in Mineral Point, but it hadn't occurred to her to consult the volunteer receptionist about the body in *Chy Looan*. "I will, thanks."

Chloe spent the rest of her lunch break flipping through faded photocopies in the *Crime* and *Mineral Point—General* folders in the vertical files, without finding any reference to a missing person or suspected foul play.

"I'll try to get back tomorrow," she told Midge. "Thank you again for your help."

———

Inside the house, Roelke found Deirdre playing with her dollhouse in the living room. Libby was curled on the sofa watching her. He sat down beside her. "He's gone," he murmured. "Is she okay?"

162

"She's fine. A little confused, maybe. I don't think she knew what to do when Dan showed up. But you know how easygoing she is."

"Are you going to be okay?"

"Yeah. I need to be solid when Justin gets home."

"You *will* talk to the Palmyra police about this. They've already had the call from Justin's principal."

Libby swiped her eyes with the back of one hand. "Yes. I will."

"Did Deirdre say anything about what happened?"

"She said they just drove around before he brought her home."

"He only wanted to keep her long enough to panic you."

She looked at him with still-damp eyes. "What am I going to do, Roelke? I can't keep the kids locked in the house all the time."

Roelke scrubbed his face with his palms. He was a cop. He was supposed to have answers to questions like this. And he did not. "The first thing to do is see what the Palmyra cops recommend." It was not much of a response.

He pushed to his feet. "I have to get the squad back to Eagle. Call me if anything else happens, and I'll talk to you later for sure. Lock the door behind me."

"Thank you, Roelke, for always being there for me and the kids." Libby got up, too, and gave him a quick, hard hug. "All I could think to do was call you."

Roelke was glad Libby had called him. He would have been upset if she hadn't. But, he thought as he slid behind the wheel, he hadn't done a damn thing. He hadn't been successful in warning Raymo off. He hadn't been able to put Libby's fears to rest.

"Sometimes," he muttered, "I suck at being a cop."

———

When Chloe got back to Pendarvis she started toward the office, but veered when she spotted Loren sitting alone on a bench, staring across Shake Rag Street toward Dark Hill. He'd yet to change from period garb to director-casual clothes. He looked like a dejected miner.

"Loren?" she asked hesitantly. "Am I disturbing you?"

"What?" He looked up, clearly startled. "Oh. No."

She glanced at the empty curb. "It looks as if everybody's gone."

"Yes. The coroner came and went. The investigator left. The school groups have even come and gone."

"Is the site open?"

"We are, yes." But his voice was flat, as if it didn't matter to him one way or another. Chloe couldn't help wondering if he'd had more of a relationship with Yvonne Miller than anyone knew.

"No one's found Claudia," he said. "It doesn't look good."

"What's that supposed to mean?" Chloe demanded, then swallowed hard. "Sorry, it's just that—you can't believe Claudia had anything to do with Dr. Miller's death."

"No, of course not. But Investigator Higgins knows that Claudia accompanied Dr. Miller into Polperro House this morning. Soon after that, you discover Dr. Miller's body, and Claudia has disappeared."

He's right, Chloe thought reluctantly. It didn't look good. She rubbed her palms on her trousers. "I'm worried about her."

"I am too." Loren shook his head. "And I'm worried about the damage this tragedy will do to Pendarvis. I don't mean to sound crass or unfeeling, but the timing couldn't be worse."

It took a moment for Chloe to catch on. "Because of the budget mess? But this has nothing to do with *that*."

"No, but it's bad publicity."

"This will pass," Chloe tried. "Dr. Miller's death was a horrible tragedy, but it was surely an accident."

"I had high hopes for new programming," Loren said, as if she hadn't spoken. "But nothing is going according to plan. Gerald and I have worked hard to establish the badger hole on Dark Hill, but this morning I found evidence that kids got in there and messed around."

Chloe's cheeks grew hot. Toying with Gerald was one thing. She'd been so relieved to get out of the damn hole that it hadn't occurred to her that the toeholds she'd hacked into the wall would alarm Loren.

" … clearly been down in the hole," he was saying. "And the stakes and safety rope we'd rigged around it were ripped up and tossed into the bushes."

"Wait … what?" Chloe looked up sharply. When she'd left the badger hole the evening before, the safety rope had been in place. "They were?"

"They were." Loren sighed. "Well. I need to get back to my office."

"I know I'm a guest here," Chloe said, "but please let me know how I can be helpful."

"I can't think of anything right now," he said. "But thank you." He trudged away.

Chloe frowned after him. Yes, Loren had a whole lot to worry about. But as site director, he also needed to rally the troops. Sitting on a bench and brooding was perhaps not the best way to bolster staff morale.

And … what was going on at the badger hole? It had stormed off and on for most of the night. Who would have ventured up there in the rainy darkness? Or had someone slogged there at dawn to vandalize the badger hole? It didn't make sense.

She remembered the sensation she'd had the evening before, right before tumbling ass over teakettle into the badger hole, of someone putting a hand against her back. *Had* she been pushed?

This morning, by the lemon light of dawn, the idea had seemed preposterous. But now Dr. Miller had taken a fall too …

"Um, Chloe?"

Chloe looked over her shoulder and saw Rita, carrying something wrapped in a shawl. "Hi, Rita."

"I don't mean to interrupt, but I saw you sitting here, and it must have been just horrible to find Dr. Miller this morning, and … I just thought you might like a cup of tea." She looked over both shoulders before producing a Thermos. "We've got an electric pot."

"How thoughtful!" Chloe accepted the plastic cup carefully, absurdly touched by the kind gesture. Her thoughts had been going in a dark direction, and the distraction was welcome. "Can you sit for a few minutes?"

"Um, sure." Rita seemed surprised by the invitation. "There aren't any visitors on site." She perched on the bench. "What happened to Dr. Miller is just so—so *awful*."

"It is," Chloe agreed. "Did you know her well?"

"No. I'd met her, of course. She's been around a lot. She … she went on one of my tours one time." Rita's mouth twisted. "She didn't say a word on the tour, but she kind of chewed me out afterwards."

Chloe sighed. "Why on earth … ?"

"She said I neglected a lot of important information about Mineral Point's early years." Rita tucked a stray strand of blond hair under her cap. "But all the things I talked about were themes from the interpretive plan."

"I'm sure it was a fine tour," Chloe said firmly. "Claudia was telling me how glad she was you were able to stay through the fall. I know you're looking for a permanent job in the history field. The market's tight, so try not to get discouraged."

"I'm trying." Rita slouched back against the bench, sounding and looking extremely discouraged. "My father didn't want me to go to college at all. He said it was a waste of money. I was determined to prove him wrong, so I went where I most wanted to go, which was Marquette."

Which was much more expensive than a public school. "I can only imagine how scary it is to know the historical society is considering closing Pendarvis," Chloe said.

Rita nodded. "I'm really sorry that Gerald's been rude to you. He's a nice guy, actually. He's just angry about the situation."

"I know." Chloe sipped her tea. "It makes me angry too. But I was really impressed by all the good energy at the meeting Monday evening. I can't believe the society will really close the site, not in the face of so many people determined to save it."

"I hope not."

"Loren and Claudia have lots of good ideas, new initiatives ... " Chloe waved her free hand at Dark Hill. "I love the idea of an interpretive trail and prairie restoration. That hill fascinates me. Maybe it's simply knowing that it was once covered with miners."

"I hope they don't ask me to do any interpreting over there." Rita looked dubious. "I don't think it's safe."

Chloe eyed her over the mug. "Loren feels it is."

"I grew up on a farm near here, and I guess I just heard too many stories about people getting lost in old mines, or hurt or killed in cave-ins. Once my dad was plowing in a field we'd used for years, and his tractor broke through and landed in a mineshaft. Fortunately it was shallow and he was okay." She got to her feet. "Well, I better go. I need to dust in Trelawny House."

"Thanks for the tea, Rita."

She smiled. "You can just take the cup back to the kitchen in the office when you're done."

Sipping her tea, Chloe couldn't help thinking that she'd done a lousy job of lifting Rita's spirits. But truth was, Chloe felt as if she were clogging in quicksand. It was Wednesday already, and other than the work done in the collections storage area the day before, she hadn't really been of much help to Claudia. She hadn't learned anything remotely helpful about the skeleton found in *Chy Looan*, either.

A delivery truck rumbled down Shake Rag Street, startling Chloe from her reverie. Okay, that's enough brooding for you too, she admonished herself. She should be setting a good example as well. Back to work. A quick look-see around Polperro House seemed like a good idea.

The police had searched the historic home, leaving a few items out of place. Chloe refastened the rope intended to keep visitors from the root cellar, inched a large crock back out of the traffic flow, smoothed a wool blanket into place on a bed. It could have been worse.

She later found Rita in Pendarvis House with several senior citizens, and Gerald in the re-created pub with a small homeschool group. The gift shop was empty except for Audrey, who was reading a paperback romance behind the counter. "Everything okay?" Chloe asked.

"It is," Audrey said, "but I appreciate you asking."

In the office, Evelyn was clattering away at the typewriter. "Have a good visit to the archives?"

"Actually, no luck so far. I'm trying to discover if there are any tales about an unsolved murder, or a man disappearing, floating around Mineral Point."

"Is this about the skeleton Adam found in Tamsin's old place?"

I don't know why I even aim to be discreet, Chloe thought. "Yes. Adam and Tamsin are friends of mine. The cottage sat empty in the early thirties, but the newspapers don't mention anyone disappearing during that period. Midge suggested I ask if you remember any old stories about a murder, or a missing person."

Evelyn looked pleased to have her grasp of local history acknowledged. "Actually, I think you're on the right track, regardless of newspaper reports. Consider the times, Chloe. Zinc and lead prices collapsed after World War I, and lots of men lost their jobs. The biggest employer in the area, a smelter, shut down in 1929. The local bank failed three times. Those were bad years for Mineral Point."

"Those stone cottages were already a century old," Chloe mused.

"Here's my theory," Evelyn said. "Most of those crumbling cottages emptied, people moved away, and hoboes and tramps passing though claimed squatters' rights. They were hard men, mostly. Not local. I suspect two men sheltering in the cottage Tamsin and her husband eventually purchased got into a fight. One killed the other, buried him right there, and no doubt left town."

"It certainly could have happened that way," Chloe said slowly. She'd been so focused on identifying a specific and horrific crime that she'd overlooked the context. Some historian *I* am, she thought. Still, she liked Evelyn's theory. It had been rather horrid to think that someone who lived in *Chy Looan* had committed murder.

"I doubt if anyone from Mineral Point was even involved," Evelyn added, as if unsure that Chloe had grasped the moral of the story.

Chloe hid a smile. "I know your Mineral Point roots are deep, Evelyn. Were your people Cornish?"

"Oh, no. The first of my ancestors to arrive in the lead region, my great-great-grandfather, came from Missouri in the 1820s."

"Yikes. That's early." Chloe sat down at Claudia's desk. "He must have been a rugged soul."

"He was. And he became quite the local leader," Evelyn said with quiet pride. "In 1832, when the Black Hawk War broke out, he served as a lieutenant under General Dodge. And later he served as a judge. Dodge gets all the credit—Dodgeville, Governor Dodge State Park—but my great-great-grandfather was his equal. There's an elementary school named for him south of here."

"Pretty cool," Chloe agreed. She was generally most interested in the lives of people who didn't have schools named after them, but she would never say so to Evelyn. "Was his wife with him when he came, or—"

The phone rang. Evelyn picked it up. "This is Pendarvis ... Claudia!"

SEVENTEEN

CHLOE JERKED UPRIGHT.

"Where *are* you? We've been worried sick." Evelyn listened for several moments before nodding. "I'll let Loren know ... Yes, Chloe's right here. I'll transfer your call. Please take care of yourself. And Holly. Talk to you soon." She punched a button, and the phone at Chloe's elbow began to ring.

She snatched it. "Claudia? Are you okay?"

"I am." The other woman sounded weary. "Holly had a crisis this morning. I spotted her on the site when she should have been at school."

"Is she alright?"

"I think so. And I do know what happened at the site after I left."

Chloe was relieved that she didn't have to share that news again.

"Listen, I'm not coming back in today. I left my briefcase by my desk. Would you be willing to bring it by my house this afternoon? It's a five-minute walk."

"Sure."

"Thanks." Claudia's voice trembled as she dictated the address. "Come whenever it's convenient."

After hanging up, Chloe swiveled in her chair to look at Evelyn. "Claudia asked me to bring her briefcase to her house. I'd like to check on her. Do you mind if I leave again?"

"No problem," Evelyn assured her. "I'm worried about Claudia too."

———

Claudia met Chloe at the door of her small brick home on the edge of the historic district. "I really appreciate you coming over. Can you stay a few minutes? Want a glass of iced tea?"

"You're my boss this week," Chloe reminded her. "Tea would be good."

Claudia ushered her into a comfortable living room. Chloe took a chair and—curator's habit—studied the space. A collection of silk fans was displayed in a high shelf. Otherwise the room was furnished with modern pieces, stylish but comfortable. Family photographs were scattered about—old black-and-whites of people probably long gone, a wedding picture of Claudia and her new husband, lots of pictures of Holly.

"Here you go." Claudia returned with two glasses and handed one to Chloe before dropping onto the sofa. "Thanks again for bringing my briefcase."

"I brought your mail too." She handed it over.

Claudia quickly flicked through the mail, and pulled out a manila envelope. "This needs to go to Loren, actually." She gave it back.

"No problem," Chloe assured her. "But enough with the mail. Are you really okay? Is Holly back at school?"

"She is."

"It must have been disconcerting to see her at the site this morning."

"I easily could have missed her too. I'd realized I'd left a file I needed at home, and after leaving Yvonne Miller at Polperro House, I decided to dash home and grab it. That's when I spotted Holly."

"Did she seem okay earlier this morning?"

"When she left for school, everything seemed fine." Claudia kicked off her shoes, brought her feet up, and wrapped her arms around her knees. "Something happened to upset her. Probably another kid made fun of her or something, so she ran away. I think she reached Pendarvis before realizing that I wouldn't be thrilled to see her when she was supposed to be in school. Anyway, when I tried to find out what happened, she got hysterical."

"Poor kid," Chloe said.

"It happens." Claudia made a weary gesture. "I needed to get her away, so I took her for a walk on Dark Hill. It took me an hour or more to get her calmed down. Then I took her to school, where I had to wait a while to meet with the principal. At that point I was still planning to get back to the site once Holly was settled in her classroom."

"And ... what happened to change that?"

"Stopping at home and finding one Investigator Higgins waiting for me."

"Oh." Chloe considered. "Well, he talked to everyone he could find at the site this morning, so I guess that's not surprising."

Claudia gave her a level look. "No. But as bad as it was to hear that Yvonne Miller died in Polperro House, it was much worse to realize that the investigator is obviously wondering if I pushed her down the stairs."

"That's absurd." But Loren's voice echoed in Chloe's memory: *It doesn't look good…*

"I have no way to prove what really happened or where I was. Holly and I didn't pass anyone else on Dark Hill." Claudia pressed the heel of one hand against her forehead. "Yvonne and I weren't exactly friends. Honestly, I can hardly blame him for suspecting me."

"He has to begin by eliminating people from consideration," Chloe said. She'd heard Roelke say that more than once. "Now that he's interviewed you, he'll move on."

"I don't even know if I *want* him to move on." Claudia abruptly rose and began to pace.

A light prickle ghosted most unpleasantly over Chloe's skin. "What are you talking about?"

"If I tell you something, do you swear to keep it a secret?" Claudia sat again and leaned forward, elbows on knees.

Chloe could almost hear Roelke saying *No. Absolutely, positively do not swear to keep* anything *a secret.* And Chloe trusted him on this. Even she knew that, given the circumstances, making that particular promise was a very bad idea.

For a moment the room was silent. A car with a bad muffler drove by. Then Chloe heard herself say, "I swear."

"Chloe, when I took Yvonne into Polperro this morning, we had words. For reasons known only to her, she wanted to measure the root cellar. I *swear* she diddled around, because I could have taken measurements twice in the time she was in there. After measuring I thought she was done, but she just stood there, scribbling in that green journal of hers, totally ignoring me. Finally I said I had to go, and to please not touch any artifacts. I wouldn't normally leave anyone alone in one of our buildings, but Loren has given her a lot of latitude, so—"

"What happened then?"

Claudia took a deep breath. "Yvonne said something along the lines of not needing me to dictate proper behavior, that she knew more about managing historic buildings and collections than I could ever hope to."

What *was* that woman's problem? Chloe wondered for the umpteenth time.

Claudia's gaze was distant. "I said 'Look, I don't know what I did to offend you, but I really need you to stop being so hostile.' She said, 'I am not willing to take orders from an incompetent fraud.' I swear, Chloe, that's what she called me. I sort of... sort of snapped."

Oh *God*. Chloe's gobbled lunch curdled in her stomach. "What did you do?"

"I told her that I would not *tolerate* any more of her verbal abuse. Then I turned my back and left the building."

"Then..." Chloe wasn't following. "What's the secret?"

Tears welled in Claudia's eyes. "It's possible that Holly was already on site by then. It's possible she heard the exchange. But if nobody saw her near Polperro, I don't want anyone to know."

"But... what did you tell Investigator Higgins when he asked why you left the site this morning?"

"I told him the truth about leaving the site to run home and get the file I'd forgotten. But I sort of implied that I found Holly at home, not at Pendarvis."

Chloe sucked in a harsh breath. This wasn't just keeping a secret; Claudia had lied to Higgins. And now I know that, Chloe thought. Lovely.

"I'll admit, I got flustered." Claudia's gaze beseeched Chloe to understand. "But if Higgins knew Holly was on site this morning he'd want to question her, probably alone. I don't know what that would do to her, Chloe, and I am not willing to find out."

"But if someone else saw Holly on site this morning…"

"I know, I know, I could get caught in a lie. I didn't think of that until after he left." Claudia's shoulders hunched, as if she was expecting a blow. "All I could think about was protecting my child."

Chloe looked at a framed photograph of Holly on a nearby end table. The girl was wearing her pretty yellow 1840s dress. She stood in Polperro's side yard, gazing away from the camera. If the picture hadn't been printed in color, it could almost have been mistaken for a period piece.

"Would you keep your ears open? Just let me know if somebody mentions seeing Holly at the site this morning."

Chloe hesitated. She should never have agreed to keep a secret when a death was being investigated.

But the memory of Holly's warm weight at the meeting on Monday night was still vivid. The girl had already managed to wrap her fingers around Chloe's heart.

"Sure, Claudia," she said weakly. "I can do that."

———

Back at the site, Chloe found the director's office door ajar. "Loren?" No answer. She poked her head inside. No Loren. Chloe pulled out the envelope Claudia had given her and slipped into the office to leave it on his desk.

Delivery complete, a framed photograph caught her attention. It showed a younger Loren in nineteenth-century farmers' garb, holding a grub hoe in front of an old house. Two other interpreters flanked him. All three were grinning at the camera. The glimpse of this happy Loren provided sharp contrast to the man she'd seen this week, and it tugged at her heart. Chloe suspected that Loren had become the kind of permanent employee who fantasized about retiring so he could forget administrivia and volunteer at his favorite historic site as a low-level interpreter. *I know the feeling,* Chloe thought.

She was turning to leave when the label of a file on Loren's desk leapt at her: *SITE CLOSURE.*

On a good day Chloe might have taken the high road. But this was not, by any stretch of imagination, a good day. She glanced over her shoulder, then flipped open the file. It contained a stack of stuff: budget summaries, notes from a site directors' meeting, correspondence Loren had exchanged with the Historic Sites Division administrator arguing that it was folly to even *consider* closing Pendarvis. *Way to go Loren,* Chloe thought.

Then, rifling down farther, Chloe found a photocopied letter from one Dr. Yvonne Miller written to the director of the State Historical Society of Wisconsin. Skimming, Chloe found familiar complaints: inadequate interpretation, no discussion of territorial leaders, etc., etc.

Damn. Chloe closed the file again, wishing she'd left well enough alone. It made her angry to imagine Miller voicing her condemnation to the society's director, but she didn't believe that one letter would have influenced the decision to consider closing Pendarvis. Much worse were the other implications.

Loren had obviously seen Miller's letter. Had Claudia? *If I could find it so easily,* Chloe thought, *so could she. If Claudia* had *seen it, she would have had one more reason to be royally pissed at Miller.*

Chloe heard the outer door open, panicked, and leapt away from the desk. She managed to find a modicum of composure before walking into the entry room, where Loren was shrugging out of a jacket.

"Claudia asked me to leave some mail on your desk," she said blithely, and walked on.

In the second office, Evelyn was still faithfully minding the telephone. Chloe settled at Claudia's desk again and began to type up her scribbled notes about artifact storage. Tried to, anyway. Between what Claudia had told her and what she'd seen in Loren's office, it was hard to focus.

She abandoned that task in favor of paging through the binders of collection inventory forms. An hour later, she admitted defeat. There was no record of any cast iron tool made with decorative details.

Someone knocked on the door. "Ms. Ellefson?" Investigator Higgins asked. "May I speak with you?"

Chloe almost yelled, *Claudia Doyle's daughter wasn't anywhere near Pendarvis this morning!* but managed to swallow the disclaimer in time. "Of course," she said instead, in her most pleasant *I am a consummate professional* voice. "Why don't we step outside so we don't bother Evelyn."

She followed Investigator Higgins from the building. They stopped a short distance away where they wouldn't be overheard. "How can I help you?" Chloe asked.

"I understand you had an altercation with Dr. Miller yesterday morning."

Chloe blinked, panicked all over again. "I did?"

"Standing on the sidewalk?" he prompted.

"Oh! Oh, right." That incident seemed like ancient history. Who had observed her discussion with Yvonne? Someone on the staff, or the poodle guy who'd walked by? It could have been anyone. Chloe tried to collect herself. "Except it wasn't an altercation. More like a discussion."

"What were you discussing?"

"Interpretive theory. As I said before, for some reason Dr. Miller thought very poorly of the programming here. I truly do not know why."

"Talk me through the exchange."

The man really did look like Rex Harrison. Chloe looked away, trying to keep another *My Fair Lady* chorus from swelling with orchestral splendor in her brain. "Just You Wait," maybe. She'd always liked that one, and—

"Ms. Ellefson?"

"Sorry. I was heading up to the office yesterday morning, and saw Dr. Miller on the sidewalk, just staring at Polperro House. I stopped to say hello, and asked how her research was going. She got started on how the site should be interpreted differently. I reminded her that at any site, there are many ways to approach interpretation. Our conversation might have become…" She discarded several words before settling on "animated. But I assure you, that's all there was to it." She thought back, trying to remember any pertinent details from the exchange. "Would it be possible for me to see her journal? I might catch something that you missed."

He frowned.

Chloe's cheeks flamed. "That came out wrong. I just meant that you're not a historian."

Her explanation did nothing to ease Higgins's frown. "I haven't seen any journal."

"Really?" Now Chloe's brows drew together. "That's odd. She had it on every occasion I ever saw her, including the town meeting Monday night and our conversation on the sidewalk. It wasn't in her briefcase?"

"It was not. What did this journal look like? Spiral, three-ring binder, one of those black-and-white bound kind?"

"No, it was distinctive. Expensive, bound in a beautiful green leather. Not that I'm a particular fan of leather."

The investigator gave her a quizzical look. Chloe reminded herself that he really didn't care whether she was a fan of leather or not. "And the cover was embossed in gold."

"That's helpful," Higgins said. "Now. How long have you known Claudia Doyle?"

Chloe didn't like the direction this interview was taking. "Almost a year and a half. Until this week, I'd only seen her at Historic Sites Division meetings in Madison."

"And you had no idea where Ms. Doyle was this morning?"

"No, I did not," Chloe said, as calmly as humanly possible. "I didn't know where she was until she called the site from her house early this afternoon."

"Very well, Ms. Ellefson," Investigator Higgins said. "Thank you for your help."

Chloe watched him walk away. She felt more discombobulated than she wanted to admit, and fervently wished that Claudia had never mentioned lying to Higgins about where she'd found Holly that morning.

Had whoever reported seeing the altercation/discussion on the sidewalk that morning made *her* a suspect? Or, if Claudia was prime suspect, had the investigator concluded that she, Chloe, was somehow covering for her friend?

You're being paranoid, Chloe told herself. Unless... She watched a squirrel bound across the lawn. Unless Claudia had lied to *her* too. Maybe the prospect of Holly being questioned was not the real reason Claudia was so frantic. Maybe what really worried her was something more dire. Holly might have overheard her mother arguing with Yvonne. Did that argument get physical?

No. No, freaking, way. Chloe did not believe her friend had anything to do with Yvonne's death.

So … if Claudia hadn't shoved Yvonne down the stairs, was it possible that *Holly* had somehow been involved in Yvonne's death?

A sick feeling pooled in Chloe's gut, and she tried without success to banish the thought from her brain. Holly was very close to her mother. She might have walked the back trail down from the upper property and approached Polperro's second-story entrance. If she'd overheard Yvonne being mean to Claudia … would she have acted? If Yvonne had been standing at the top of the steep staircase, with her back to the door, it wouldn't have been difficult for an angry nine-year-old to send the woman tumbling.

Was *that* what had so troubled Claudia? Why else would she ask Chloe to keep her ears open? Investigator Higgins had already interviewed the staff members. Since he'd asked about Claudia's disappearance, if anyone had seen Holly, they surely had already mentioned it.

Chloe clasped her elbows. Should *she* break her promise and contact the investigator herself? Should she try to convince Claudia to talk to him again? But this theory about Holly is pure speculation, Chloe thought. And she did believe that Claudia had told her all she knew. Claudia might wonder if Holly had been involved, but she didn't know for sure. No way, Chloe thought, am *I* introducing Holly into a police investigation without more to go on.

Besides, what had happened to Yvonne's ever-present green journal? She'd had it in the root cellar. If Yvonne had tripped and fallen down the stairs, her journal would have either fallen down with her or been found in her briefcase.

Was there something in that journal that had worried someone? If so, who? And what on earth had that person been worried about?

Evelyn had left for the day when, at four thirty, the phone rang. Chloe let it ring three times, hoping Loren was still around and would pick up. On ring four she snatched the receiver. "Pendarvis Historic Site. May I help you?"

"I'd like to leave a message for Chloe Ellefson."

Chloe recognized the voice. "Midge? It's me, Chloe."

"I've got a list of property owners for the old Bolitho place."

Chloe's eyebrows shot skyward. "Really? That was fast."

"My friend at the courthouse owed me a favor. It's not a long list, and all I've got are names and dates, but it's a start."

"Names and dates will be great." For now, anyway.

"Switch the machine over to take a fax and I'll send it over."

After hanging up Chloe struggled for several minutes to figure out how to make the switch. She held her breath and punched a button, hoping she hadn't just erased all phone service to the site or something. Almost immediately the printer began to purr, and a curling, shiny piece of paper emerged.

She snatched the page and scanned it quickly. Well, Midge was right. It wasn't a long list. But awesomely, the first date was 1836, when the US government began selling mineral land to the miners and their families.

EIGHTEEN

Since sinking their first shaft, Jory and Andrew had mined enough mineral to pay their expenses and invest in a few tools, but little more. One raw day in February, however, the brothers came home from their digging elated.

"We hit what looks like a good drift this afternoon!" Jory reported. He dropped in front of the small fire and fanned raw fingers toward the flames.

"We have no way of knowing how far it runs," Andrew cautioned, although even he was grinning. "But we'll have a sizeable haul just from the pocket we found."

"I hope it runs a long time!" Mary exclaimed. "I don't want to spend another winter here."

"We won't," Andrew promised.

That night, Mary and Ida shivered as they finished washing dishes. "I'll fill the warming box with hot chirks from the firepit," Mary said. They huddled together beneath their blankets with the warmer Ruan had made wrapped in her shawl and nestled between them, but the temperature was plunging. Still, Mary couldn't help smiling. "Next winter will be better, Ida," she whispered. "We won't have to live in a cave anymore."

"Are we going to get a house?"

"Yes," Mary said firmly. "We are going to get a house."

———

March brought days when water dripped from the stones, and the diggings turned to a sea of mud. A bilious fever swept through the mining camps, hitting those without adequate shelter or food especially hard. Mary helped nurse some of the nearby families through the worst of it, all the while praying she didn't take the illness back to Ida. "You're an angel, Mary," whispered a gaunt mother who had watched one child die, but three more survive.

"No, I'm just a neighbor." Mary pulled a blanket more snugly over the woman's shoulders. She was bone-weary but tried not to show it. "You'd do the same."

As the days lengthened, some of the sucker miners returned from their winter haunts. Mixed among them were inexperienced but eager new diggers, dreaming of quick and easy riches. Mary got back to baking, and business picked up accordingly. The fresh scents of spring mingled with the stink of burning sulphur as smelters increased their firings.

"Can I carry the basket to Jory and Andrew?" Ida asked late one afternoon, when she and Mary were almost finished with their rounds.

"Just be careful in this sucking mud." Mary didn't want her lovely bread and biscuits to land in the muck.

As they made their way, she heard an angry shout. Several new-comers had been digging test pits downslope of her brothers' mine. One of them, a red-haired, barrel-chested man, was advancing on a boy who couldn't have been more than ten. "You're going to have to do better than that!" His speech was harsh American English. "Why should I waste money feeding you?"

The boy was skinny as a gad. He stood with hunched shoulders, arms hugged across his chest, head bent.

"Did you hear me?" The man backhanded the boy across the face so hard he landed on his bottom in the ooze. As the boy staggered to his feet, two miners who'd been digging nearby laughed uproariously.

"Ida, go to Jory and Andrew's mine and wait for me there," Mary whispered. The men were likely underground, but she trusted Ida to follow her instructions. Ida nodded and hurried away.

Then Mary marched toward the group. "Here now! Surely there's no need to beat the boy."

"This ain't your concern," the red-haired man growled. He had a thin scar running from the end of his left eyebrow to his chin.

Mary thought of how Mrs. Bunney had ordered Boss Penhallow about, and tried for the same tone. "I have a baking business." She removed the cloth in her basket to reveal what was left of her offerings.

"Not interested," the man said, although his gaze lingered on her treats.

"Newcomers get a free sample," Mary said. "If you're satisfied, you can buy tomorrow. I make the rounds almost every day." She gave him a biscuit, light and tall and golden brown. Then she grabbed a second and thrust it into the boy's hands. He was barefoot and shivering.

"None for him," the man began, but the boy was already cramming the biscuit into his mouth.

Mary struggled against the urge to snatch the boy's wrist and drag him away. "Has your son misbehaved?"

The man turned his head and spat on the ground. "He's my sister's boy, not mine. She died and I got stuck with him. Will ain't worth nothing, far as I can tell. I got the expense of feeding him with nothing to show for it."

"It doesn't appear that he's been fed well," Mary observed. "And perhaps you should try encouraging Will instead of—"

"Don't meddle!" The man's eyes narrowed.

Another digger tossed down his shovel and joined them. "What's going on?"

Mary struggled to tamp down her anger—at these man for abusing a child, at herself for pushing too hard. Should she retreat now, or stand her ground?

Then footsteps sounded behind her. "Good afternoon!" Ruan stopped so close to Mary that their shoulders touched. "I don't believe we've met. Ruan Trevaskis, skilled blacksmith. I'm well accustomed to making what diggers need." His words were pleasant, but his tone held a note of warning.

The miners eyed him. Anyone digging lead was strong, but they were new to the work, and Ruan—who could shoe the most stubborn ox with ease—was brawnier than any of them. Neither moved.

"Mary, Ida's waiting for you." He took her arm and led her away. He waited until they were out of earshot before muttering, "What was that about?"

"Did you see that boy with them?" Mary said indignantly. "His uncle, the man with a scar, knocked him to the ground. That poor child has no shoes. No warm clothes. Not enough to eat."

Ruan stopped walking. "What do you want to do about it?"

Something inside of Mary squeezed tight with gratitude. There was no one else she'd rather build a future with. "I want to help Will. Take him in, if I can."

"Taking in a boy is no small thing. And the uncle may not be willing to let him go."

"His uncle said Will wasn't worth anything. He begrudged the boy food. Maybe he'd be that happy to give the child away."

"Do you need to think about it?" Ruan's face was serious. "This child is a boy, and American. Do those things matter to you?"

"Not at all."

"Then you best talk to Andrew. And Jory. But I expect they'll agree, at least to the asking."

She looked up at his startling blue eyes, trying to understand beyond the words. "What do you think?" It seemed terribly important.

Ruan smiled. "I think it's a fine idea."

———

Next evening, as twilight smoothed over the hillside's scars, Mary, Ruan, Andrew, and Jory presented themselves at the Americans' worksite. Three men sat hunched by the fire, shoveling cooked beans from tin plates. A raw wind made the campfire flames writhe and whipped smoke this way and that. It took Mary a moment to spot Will, who sat alone in the deeper shadows.

"Good evening!" Andrew said in a friendly voice. He introduced himself and Jory. "We've claimed a mine site just up there." He waved an arm. "I believe you've already met my sister Mary and our friend Ruan. Welcome to the Mineral Point diggings."

The man with the scar got to his feet. "Hiram McCreary," he said in a grudging tone. "Them two are my cousins." The other two men nodded.

"Well, I'll get right to it," Andrew said. "Jory and me, we know how hard it is to get started here. Maybe you'll hit a good vein tomorrow, maybe next week, maybe six months from now. The digging's hard and the money can be scarce."

"What's all that to you?" McCreary asked.

"My sister says you have a boy that you took in to . . ." Andrew searched for the right word. "To honor your sister's memory. That's a good, Christian act. But she also says the boy isn't up to the work. That you have to feed him and tend him, which can't be easy in a place like this."

Mary stood rigid, hands clenched in the folds of her cloak. She and Ruan and her brothers had agreed how to handle this. But it was hard to listen to Andrew sympathize with Hiram McCreary.

"So," Andrew continued, "we're wondering if you'd let us take the boy off your hands."

McCreary widened his stance. "Why would you want to do that?"

Andrew shrugged. "Truth is, my sister took a shine to the boy. We're better settled. One more mouth to feed won't make much of a difference. Don't worry, I'll put him to work."

McCreary snorted. "He's a lazy thing."

Andrew shrugged again. They all waited. A distant shout of "You cheated!" rose from a poker game at a nearby camp.

"I'm Will's only living kin," McCreary added. "He wouldn't want to go off with strangers."

Mary couldn't listen any longer. "Will," she called. "Would you like to come with my brothers and me?"

Will, who'd been listening intently, stood and moved closer. In the flickering firelight his eyes were wary. His cheekbones were sharp angles above hollow cheeks. "Come with you to ... to live?"

"That's right. You'll have plenty to eat and warm clothes. No one will ever hit you—"

"Listen, you can't just take a man's blood nephew away!" Mc-Creary scowled. "Get away from that boy, or I'll call the law."

One of his cousins got to his feet and kicked the other cousin, who reluctantly stood as well. McCreary's hands curled into fists, and he shifted his weight as his kin came to stand with him. Mary's mouth felt dry.

Then Ruan stepped closer to the men. "You're new here, so let me help you understand something," he said softly. "There's not a whole lot of law in the territory. Sure, you steal a man's horse or shoot somebody, you're going to end up in jail. But out here in the diggings, men mostly take care of things themselves. And the men here aren't likely to sympathize with anyone who mistreats a child."

Tension built in the air, as if flames were racing down a fuse toward a pocket of gunpowder. "Come along, Will," Mary said.

Will didn't even look at his uncle, just scurried past and joined Mary. She turned and led him away. After a long moment of silence she heard her men follow.

Back at their stone hut, Mary introduced Will to Ida. The two children stared at each other silently. Jory built up the fire. "I'm going to heat up some supper," Mary told Will. "You'll feel better after you eat. We'll find you some warm clothes too."

Will didn't answer. But he accepted the plate of beans she offered and began to eat.

After the children were settled down for the night, Andrew cocked his head toward the entrance. "We all need to talk."

Mary didn't like his flat tone, but she followed her brothers and Ruan outside. The dark night was raw, and she hugged her wool cloak tightly around her shoulders.

"Mary," Andrew muttered, "I thought you were going to let me do the talking."

"I meant to, but—"

"You've made an enemy," Andrew said unhappily. "I fear you've made an enemy for all of us."

"What would you have had me do?" Mary demanded in a hushed tone. "Simply leave poor Will to a life of misery?"

"No. But I might have been able to get McCreary to give up Will without infuriating the man. It's not good to have enemies out here." He ran a hand through his hair. "I think Jory and I should start sleeping at the mine site. Keep an eye out."

Mary fisted her hands in her skirt. Back at Hiram McCreary's camp, nothing had seemed more important than getting Will away. But Andrew was right. An angry miner could destroy her brothers' windlass, steal equipment, turn the smelter operators against them with a gift of whiskey or a few whispered words. "I'm sorry, Andrew. I should have left it to you."

Andrew blew on his fingers. "It's not just me and Jory I'm concerned about. We were on the edge of a brawl back there when Ruan stepped in. I'm grateful"—he looked at his friend, who nodded—"but unlike Jory and me, Ruan depends on the miners for his business. He can't afford to have anyone speaking against him."

Mary's shoulders sagged. "I didn't mean to … Ruan, I'm sorry if I caused you any harm."

"You didn't," he assured her. "And I've news. I've made arrangements to rent a building in town. It's time I set up a proper smithy, with a proper forge. There's more business than I can handle in town, I wager. I'll sleep there, but … " He looked around the circle, and his gaze lingered on Mary. "I won't be far away."

Some of the tension left Andrew's posture. "Congratulations, Ruan. And I have news too. If Mary keeps insisting on bringing strays home, we're going to get crowded out of our shelter here. I've hired a stonemason to build us a house."

Mary stared at him. "Aye?"

"You've seen those cottages built on the far side of the ravine? They're the work of a Cornish mason. We're next on his list."

"Oh!" Mary's heart overflowed. Ruan had not only saved her brothers from a fight they might not have won, he'd managed to turn this conversation to something cheerful. She had not one but two children to care for and keep safe. And now, a proper Cornish cottage! Besides, moving down to the bottom of the ravine and across the creek would put more distance between her family and Hiram McCreary.

She leaned closer to Jory, who hadn't spoken at all. "Do you mind that we took in Will?" Mary whispered. "What do you think?"

Jory drew deeply on his pipe and exhaled smoke. "I think we all need to be careful, because we made an enemy tonight."

NINETEEN

ALONE IN THE OFFICE, Chloe studied the information Midge had found.

Andrew Pascoe, March 1836–February 1858

That gives us a pretty secure date for when the cottage was built, Chloe thought. Adam would be pleased with that.

Mary Pascoe, February 1858–June 1911

Open-mouthed, Chloe stared at the short line. A woman had owned *Chy Looan*—and for a long time! Had she been Andrew's widow? Had she left the emotions lingering in the cottage?

Whenever Chloe felt discouraged, she thought about the lives of women who'd lived long ago. Most of them faced challenges she couldn't imagine, and their strength and tenacity were inspiring. It had been difficult to do that here in Mineral Point because the records were so scanty. The women who'd arrived during the territorial period had remained blurred, indistinct.

Chloe looked out the window toward Shake Rag Street, trying to imagine it in 1836. This street had been a rutted lane that often flooded, lined with stone cottages and a few log cabins. The woody growth on Dark Hill had not existed. The prairie savannah had been obliterated too, replaced by rubble cast aside by hopeful men with pickaxes and shovels. Men who thought nothing of brutal labor, of living like badgers for months on end, all for the dream of lead.

What had Mary Pascoe thought of this place? Chloe didn't know, but having her name, knowing she'd lived in Adam's cottage, made Mary feel more real. And with a name, she could more easily search for documentation. Claudia would be delighted if Chloe could add information about an early Cornish immigrant woman and her family to the research files.

This was good news for Tamsin and Adam as well. *Chy Looan* had been in the Pascoe family for... Chloe tried and failed to do the math in her head, and so grabbed a pencil and did it on the page. Seventy-six years. She felt inordinately pleased by that. If the property had been owned by a lengthy string of owners, it would be impossible to gain any sense of identity for the cottage and its occupants.

She looked back at the list.

Ann Trezona, June 1911–October 1930

Another woman! Chloe tapped the name with a finger, wondering. Had Ann never married? Was she a widow?

Before Chloe blew off her obligations and settled in for a full day of research, she reminded herself to focus. None of this shed any light on the poor soul who ended up buried in Adam's root cellar with a bashed-in skull.

Although, she thought, it did offer some interesting perspective. Perhaps Evelyn's theory of a fight-gone-bad between hoboes during the Great Depression was spot-on. It seemed likely that the killer had been male. Striking the vicious blow, digging the grave, handling the body...had that been the work of Andrew Pascoe's hands?

Chloe pinched her lips together, stymied. Even if she had a lot of time—which she did not—it was doubtful that they'd ever know what had happened.

Tamsin spoke in her memory. *I shouldn't have asked. I can't bear the idea of being the subject of gossip, so I just hoped... well. I'll think of something.*

"I won't give up, Tamsin," Chloe promised. She wanted something to show her new friend. Besides, now *she* was curious about the cottage's early occupants.

The remaining names scrawled on the page were familiar:

John and Tamsin Bolitho, June 1936–May 1983

Adam Bolitho, from May 1983

Chloe glanced at the wall clock, grabbed the phone, and called the archives.

"You almost missed me," Midge said. "I was heading for the door."

"I won't keep you, then. I just wanted to thank you for the list of property owners. What time do you open in the morning?"

"Officially the archives aren't open at all tomorrow morning. But if you want, I'll meet you there before you need to be at Pendarvis."

"Really? That's very kind of you." As a night owl, Chloe gave extra credit to anyone who showed up bright and early if they didn't have to.

"I'll be there at seven o'clock."

Chloe winced. "Perfect. I'll see you then."

When she got back to Tamsin's place, the older woman was on the phone. "Chloe just walked in," she said, beckoning her guest over. "Hold on." She held out the receiver. "It's Adam."

Chloe slipped her totebag from her shoulder and pulled the old rocking chair close to the phone. "Hey, Adam."

"Hey. How are things going down there? I saw something on the news about that woman falling down the stairs at Pendarvis. I'm so sorry. You're having a terrible week."

"Kind of," Chloe agreed. She'd held everything together at the site, but Adam's sympathy made her feel weepy. "Especially since I'm the one who found Dr. Miller's body."

"Oh my God."

Chloe swiped at her eyes. "On a different note, thanks to Midge at the archives, I now have a list of people who owned *Chy Looan*."

"Really?"

"Only three people owned it before your grandparents purchased it in 1936. Hold on." She put the phone down and fished the list from her bag. "Andrew Pascoe owned it from 1836 to 1858, when it passed to Mary Pascoe. Then a woman named Ann Trezona owned it from 1911 until October 1930. Any of those names mean anything to you?"

"Can't say they do," Adam said.

Chloe stood and began to pace, tethered by the phone cord. "I *could* look in the phone book, and call anyone with the surnames Pascoe or Trezona, but I'm not sure how I'd broach the topic. 'Hi, are you aware of your ancestor killing somebody and burying him in the root cellar?'"

"That does not seem to be the best approach."

"I'll see what I can learn about Andrew and Mary Pascoe, and Ann Trezona. But honestly, I feel like I'm letting your grandma down."

"You're not letting Grandma down," Adam said firmly. "How's she doing?"

Chloe glanced toward the kitchen, where Tamsin was busy with dinner. "Okay, I think."

"Still, I'm glad you're there this week. Thank you."

"My pleasure," Chloe assured him.

Tamsin carried a big bowl of salad from the kitchen just as Chloe hung up the phone. "Did you have a nice chat with Adam, dear?"

"I did." Chloe fetched silverware and began to set the table. "I also told him that I asked Midge at the archives to come up with a list of people who owned *Chy Looan* before you and your husband bought it, and—"

"I think this is a good evening to make pasties," Tamsin declared.

Chloe blinked, bewildered by the abrupt change. "Make pasties?"

"Make pasties."

"But…"

"We both need to take a break. Would you like to help in the kitchen?"

Just the thought lifted Chloe's spirits. The heck with all things gloomy and morbid for a few hours. "I would *love* to help."

As soon as they'd eaten and washed up, Tamsin set Chloe to chopping vegetables while she prepared the pastry. "I like to think I make traditional pasties with traditional ingredients," she said in a conspiratorial tone. "But the truth is, poor women put anything they had into their pasties. Pasties could conceal tough or spoiled meat—whatever scraps of food they had. The old-timers used to say that the devil would never show himself in Cornwall for fear of ending up in a pasty."

Chloe put an arm around the other woman's shoulders. "Thank you, Tamsin. Making pasties was just what I needed this evening."

Being here with Tamsin made her feel as if she was slipping into a continuum. For centuries, women had found solace and strength in their kitchens, among the company of other women. She imagined Mary Pascoe making pasties in the big open fireplace at *Chy Looan*. Cornish women in early Mineral Point may not have left helpful diaries behind, and they may not have had any belongings precious and sturdy enough to be saved through the generations. But their food traditions were passed down, and remained a living link to their time here.

When everything was ready, Tamsin rolled out the pastry and cut out circles. Chloe carefully spooned filling onto each before folding the pastry over in a half-moon shape. "Now, crimping the edges together is the most important part," Tamsin explained. "We're having a pasty supper at church on Saturday, and I guarantee you, if I don't keep a sharp eye on some of these young people in the kitchen, we'll have filling oozing out through the edges." She flapped a hand in disgust.

"Oozing is bad?"

"Men working deep mines couldn't climb out for their dinner break, so they tucked pasties into their pockets. When it was mealtime, they had no way to wash their filthy hands, so they needed a pasty they could handle just by the crust. If their woman hadn't crimped the edges with care, the crust would break off, or the filling would spill all over. Now, watch how I do it ... "

It took some practice, but finally Chloe prepared what Tamsin declared was a proper crimp. "Maybe you have a bit of Cornish blood."

Chloe thought of her mother, all-things-Norwegian Marit Kallerud, and suppressed a smile. "I'm one hundred percent Norwegian-American. But I'm glad to think I know how to make a pasty that would satisfy a Cornish miner. As hard as they worked, they needed every morsel."

"True enough." Tamsin nodded sagely. "But they relied on the pasties to keep them safe too. You know about the knackers, right?"

Chloe slid a pasty onto the baking sheet. "I'm afraid not," she admitted. There clearly was no end to her ignorance.

"Knackers are ugly little creatures that live in mines. Some say they are the spirits of miners who died in underground accidents, lingering to warn others of danger."

Chloe rubbed her arms.

"Knackers could help a miner, or cause all kinds of mischief, so the men were sure to drop their pasty crusts on the ground when they were through eating. If the knackers were satisfied with the offerings, they would protect the miners by making a knocking or tapping sound in warning if a tunnel was about to collapse. But if the knackers felt slighted, they'd hammer away at support beams and *cause* a cave-in."

"Yikes." Chloe was pretty sure that if she was working below ground and relying on the knackers' goodwill, she'd have felt compelled to offer whole pasties. Chocolate cake too.

"They say the timbers in a passage, and the earth itself, creak and groan before collapsing," Tamsin said. "That's probably where the whole notion came from."

"Probably," Chloe agreed. It was folklore, plain and simple. Charming, in its own way. Still, just thinking about mine cave-ins gave her the willies.

———

Roelke and Chloe had worked hard to fix up the old farmhouse, and despite the mismatched furniture, the place had a good feel.

That didn't keep Roelke from feeling lonely when Chloe was out of town, though. He missed her.

"You too?" he asked as Chloe's cat Olympia joined him on the sofa that evening. He was still getting used to living with a cat. Olympia had stopped trying to settle on his lap, but she seemed content to curl up on a plush towel beside him. To his surprise, he liked it when she did.

He grabbed the phone when it rang at ten o'clock, putting his book aside. "Hello?"

"It's me," Chloe said. "Boy, am I glad to hear your voice."

"Bad day?"

"Somebody ... a woman died at the site this morning." The words tumbled out faster and faster. "It was an accident. At least I think it was an accident. She fell down a steep set of stairs. I was the one who found her. She was already dead. I don't know what the cops think. The investigator is asking a lot of questions. But they always do that, right?"

"They do, yeah." Roelke became aware of aching fingers, and deliberately loosened his death grip on the receiver. Olympia abandoned her post, possibly because his knee was bouncing hard enough to vibrate the sofa. "Are you okay?"

"Yeah. I'm okay. It's just sorta unnerving, you know? I wish ... "

"Do you want me to come get you?"

"No," she said, in a stronger voice. "I want to see my week here through."

Roelke tried hard to figure out how to be in two places at once. "I'd come down anyway, if it weren't for Libby—"

"Did something else happen?"

Roelke hesitated. "Well, things with her ex are *not* calming down." He told her about Raymo taking Deirdre from preschool.

"Libby must have been frantic."

"That's one word for it."

"Listen," Chloe said. "What happened at Pendarvis this morning was upsetting, but I can handle it. What's most important right now is that you take care of Libby and the children."

"I love you," he said, because there were no other words for what was brimming in his heart.

After hanging up he sat unmoving for so long that Olympia deigned to return. She bumped her head against his arm, a move he deciphered as *Pet me*. "Your mom had a hard day," he told her, absently stroking the thick fur. "I want to go down and be with her. But I can't."

There was little that would keep him away from Chloe when she was upset, but Raymo stalking Libby made the list. Roelke was worried about his cousin. He'd never seen her frantic like that. During the divorce things had been plenty ugly, but just between Dan and Libby. Dan had fought her in the courts, and hurled verbal abuse at her. Libby had been grim, drained, hollowed out, exhausted by it all. But Roelke had never seen her cry. Never heard her shriek. Never seen the terror he'd seen in her eyes when Deirdre was missing.

But then, Raymo had never done anything like he'd done today.

Part of Roelke still longed to feel his fist meeting Raymo's jaw. No doubt Raymo had been thinking the same thing. He hadn't stood so close just for the fun of taunting Roelke. He'd done it in hopes of goading Roelke into making a final mistake. Thank God I held it together, Roelke thought. Punching Raymo would have been the end of his career.

"Didn't get your wish on that one, you SOB," Roelke muttered. Hard as it was, he was playing this one by the book.

TWENTY

On Thursday morning Chloe dragged herself out of bed at six sharp. Tamsin was already busy in the kitchen, and greeted Chloe with a plate of scrambled eggs and a bowl of grapes. "Sit," Tamsin instructed. "The coffee's almost done."

Two minutes later she set a steaming mug beside Chloe's plate and slid into the opposite chair. "So-o," she said in a tone so casual that if Chloe had been wide awake she would have sensed trouble. "You're off to the archives?"

"I am."

"I want you to stop looking for information about the people who once owned *Chy Looan*."

Chloe sat back in her chair. "You … what?"

"I want you to stop looking for information about the people who once owned *Chy Looan*." The elderly woman rewarded Chloe's scrutiny with a bland smile before digging into her own eggs.

Geez, it was way too early for this. "Why do you want me to stop?" Chloe asked. "I understand if you don't want to dwell on the body, but to not even search for information? You were the one who asked me to look into it."

"I shouldn't have," Tamsin said.

"But … but I don't mind, truly."

"No, thank you," Tamsin said politely.

Chloe was stymied. It was one thing to take a break, as they'd done the evening before; it was quite another to quit altogether. She tried to tell herself that with all the turmoil at Pendarvis, deleting one major item on the week's to-do list was a *good* thing. But here she was, up and at 'em in the dark, bleary-eyed but poised to go do research. She could hardly cancel on Midge now.

Besides … *she* was curious, especially after reading the list of property owners. She wanted to learn whatever she could about the Pascoe family. "Um, okay," Chloe mumbled. "Since I'm up, though, I'll take advantage of Midge's kindness. I'll do some research for Pendarvis."

Tamsin beamed. "More coffee, dear?"

Chloe did her best to make coherent conversation over the remainder of breakfast. Two cups of coffee later, she headed out.

Midge was looking particularly colorful in a flowing purple top, reading glasses with orange rims, and a turquoise headband. "At this point you're searching for information about previous cottage owners, right?"

"Right," Chloe said, ignoring the memory of Tamsin taking her off the chase. "I don't expect to find a confession of murder, but I would like to learn as much as I can. I admit, I'm especially curious about Mary Pascoe. It's intriguing to know the name of a woman who lived in Adam's cottage for so long."

"At one time, she was well-known," Midge said.

"She was?"

"I don't know a lot about her," Midge said apologetically, "but the name is familiar. A pillar-of-the-community type, active in church and civic affairs. I encountered her while doing research about the cholera epidemics in 1849 and 1851. She helped nurse her neighbors, and evidently saved many lives."

Chloe tried to reject the wretched images of cholera epidemics conjured in her imagination. "That must have taken courage." She felt a growing need to go back to *Chy Looan* and think about a strong woman named Mary Pascoe.

Midge perched her reading glasses on her nose. "How about I work on the census records, and you scan early newspapers? We've got some 1837 issues of *The Miners' Free Press*."

"Seriously?" That was only a year after Andrew Pascoe had purchased the lot and had the stone cottage known as *Chy Looan* built. "That's amazing."

"It is, isn't it?" Midge asked happily. "I'll get the reel."

Chloe worked at the microfilm reader as long as she dared, but didn't get far. The print was difficult to read, and she kept getting sidetracked by irrelevant but intriguing tidbits. At eight fifteen she reluctantly rewound the reel and switched off the light. "I haven't found any references to Andrew or Mary Pascoe," she told Midge. "But it's fascinating. Everything from articles about Napoleon Bonaparte to notices for runaway oxen."

"I found Andrew Pascoe in the 1836 territorial census, listed as head of household," Midge said. "But that only confirms what we already knew."

"I'll be back as soon as I can," Chloe said. "Lunchtime today, I hope. Thanks very much for coming in so early."

When she dashed to Pendarvis, Evelyn was alone in the curator's office. "Claudia's not coming in today," she reported. "She has a migraine."

Chloe frowned. "Oh." Was Claudia truly ill, or had yesterday's events left her too upset to come in? Roelke often said that when investigating a crime, cops looked for changes in a suspect's routine. Guilt made people act in ways they normally would not…

Stop that! Chloe ordered herself. This was Claudia she was thinking about. Claudia, who would never harm a soul.

Claudia, who had already lied to the police. Claudia, a mother who would do anything to protect her child—

"Chloe?" Evelyn asked. "Are you alright?"

"Sorry." Chloe was grateful for the interruption. "And I'm sorry to hear about Claudia's migraine. I'd better check in with Loren." She grabbed her totebag before heading to the next office.

Loren was at his desk. "Good morning, Chloe. Come on in." He waved her toward a chair.

She perched on the edge. "I just learned that Claudia called in sick. I've got plenty to keep me busy, but is there anything you'd like me to do?"

"Could you handle the staff briefing?"

"Sure. I'm glad to help."

"Thanks." Loren slumped back in his chair. "But I don't think anyone can truly help."

And how was a lowly visiting curator supposed to respond to *that*? Chloe wondered.

"When I was hired three years ago, I was told that I would be expected to increase attendance by twenty percent." He gave a mirthless smile. "Needless to say, that has not happened."

"Twenty percent?" Chloe echoed. That was a big number.

Loren steepled his hands in front of his chin. "I haven't met expectations. Now Pendarvis is being threatened with closure."

"It's not that simple," Chloe protested. "At any historic site, everything from bad weather to the price of gasoline can affect attendance."

"True," Loren allowed. "But the bean counters look only at the bottom line. I find myself obsessing over everything. Will such-and-such increase attendance?"

Chloe shifted in her chair. She sympathized with Loren, but she wasn't used to such candor from administrators.

"I was thinking about Dr. Miller last night." Loren picked up a small foam ball from his desk and began squeezing it in one hand. "Part of me was relieved that her book will never be published. Isn't that terrible? I was worried about more negative publicity."

"Do you know what the focus of her research was?"

"No, but she was certainly studying Pendarvis with a microscopic and a critical eye. Odd, since she wanted to work here."

"Yvonne Miller wanted to work here?"

Loren nodded. "She applied for Claudia's job."

"I did not know that," Chloe said slowly. It explained some things, though. Such as why Dr. Miller had harbored such resentment toward Claudia.

"She was very knowledgeable about local history," Loren said. "A lot more knowledgeable than Claudia was, actually."

"She seemed more focused on territorial politics and the Black Hawk War than on mining and immigrants," Chloe observed. "There's nothing wrong with discussing the territorial governor and his cronies, of course. And Native American history is critically important. But interpreting the lives of everyday Cornish people is important too, especially since your site is comprised of working-class homes."

"I agree." Loren shrugged. "In any case, academic knowledge is only part of the equation. I needed a curator who could get along with volunteers and interpreters and donors. A curator who could suit up and give tours, and be equally effective with senior citizens and children. Yvonne Miller looked good on paper, but Claudia presented herself much better. I've never regretted my decision."

"Claudia's great," Chloe agreed, and stood because she didn't want to talk about Claudia anymore. "I'll go meet the interpreters. Oh, wait." She pulled the sticking tommy found in *Chy Looan* from her totebag. "This belongs to a friend. I was struck by the decorative work. Nothing I've found in the Pendarvis collection matches it. Have you ever seen ironwork like this before?"

Loren took the candleholder and whistled. "This is a beauty! But no, I've never seen work like this. Have you shown it to Gerald?"

Chloe remembered Gerald accusing her of carrying about one of Pendarvis's artifacts. "Only briefly."

"He knows a lot about mining tools." Loren rotated the sticking tommy with more animation than Chloe had seen since arriving in Mineral Point. "You might also want to show it to someone at the Mining Museum in Platteville, or the Shullsburg Mining Museum. Both are excellent resources, and an easy drive."

Only if you have a car, Chloe thought. Those excursions would have to wait. Maybe she'd see what kind of a mood Gerald was in, and try again. "Thanks for the suggestions," she told Loren, and escaped.

In the gift shop, Gerald stood with arms belligerently crossed over his chest as Chloe thanked the staff for their help in the wake of Miller's death, announced that Claudia was ill, and reviewed the school tour notes with what she hoped was a knowing air. Rita listened politely. Audrey nodded along, probably eager to wrap things up so she could get back to her novel.

Chloe dismissed the staff with a chipper "Have a good day!" Then she added, "Gerald? Do you have a moment?" He turned back, looking unhappy, and she held out the sticking tommy. "I didn't have a good chance to show you this yesterday. Have you ever seen this kind of workmanship on an iron mining tool? I'm hoping to identify the maker."

"This is a fine piece," he said grudgingly. He took it, and while examining it closely, his eyes lost their accusatory glare. "But I've never seen anything like it." He handed it back.

"Thanks anyway." Chloe tucked it away.

Gerald folded his arms again. "Why are you here?"

"Oh, for heaven's sake," Chloe snapped. "As you already know, I'm here to help Claudia."

"No, I mean why are you *really* here? Are you the advance guard, come to assess the site before it goes into mothballs? The society's already made the decision to close us down, right?"

Chloe felt steam rising inside. "Okay, you know what? I've about had it. I am heartsick about the possible closure of Pendarvis. All I know is what I read in the newspaper on Sunday. I will do anything I can to help keep the site open." She pointed a finger toward his chest. "I hope you took that in, because I'm not going to say it again."

For a few seconds she thought she'd gotten through. Then Gerald's eyes narrowed with contempt. He whirled and went to meet the first tour group.

I give up, Chloe thought. There was no getting through to the man. She retreated to Claudia's desk and settled down to type up her notes from surveying the storage area in Trelawny House.

Some time later, as she rolled a new piece of paper into the platen, she became vaguely aware of voices in the entry room. A firm knock on the office door made her swivel in her chair. Loren and a policeman stood in the doorway, and another cop was visible behind them. Chloe and Evelyn exchanged quick, wary glances. Loren looked even more morose than he had earlier.

"Pardon me, ladies," Loren said wearily, "but you must vacate the premises. These officers have a warrant to search Pendarvis staff offices."

———

Evelyn went home. Chloe didn't blame her. Evelyn was a loyal volunteer, but enough was enough. Chloe settled on one of the picnic tables on the grounds to wait out the search. As the officers got to work, she could tell that this search was going to be much more involved than the preliminary one yesterday had been.

Chloe put her elbows on the table and her head in her hands. Fleeing Pendarvis appealed to her too. All I wanted, she thought, was a peaceful and pleasant week away. Had that really been so much to ask?

You are a guest here, she reminded herself. What was it she'd told Roelke when they were driving down on Sunday? *I will not get involved in anything that's faintly problematic or controversial. If something comes up, I will refuse to take delivery.*

Well, things hadn't turned out that way.

Under the circumstances, could anyone blame her if she just went home? Not to Tamsin's apartment, but to the farmhouse she shared with Roelke and her cat. The thought was so appealing that Chloe's throat ached. Surely somebody could come get her. If not Roelke, maybe her friend Dellyn. Claudia was distracted, Loren was melancholy, and the cops had just closed the site. There was nothing left to accomplish here.

Except…that wasn't true.

With a mammoth sigh Chloe sat up straight. She truly cared about Pendarvis, and Pendarvis was under siege. If she stayed, at the very least she could draft a decent plan for collections storage.

And although the investigation into Yvonne Miller's death may not be her problem, it was Claudia's problem. Maybe the most important thing to do was help her friend navigate a crisis. Maybe the timing of this trip was actually fortuitous.

And, Chloe thought, a bunch of unsettling things have happened to me. She hadn't had a chance to tell anyone about the note she'd found in her totebag. Should she pass it on to Investigator Higgins? Compared to finding a skeleton in *Chy Looan*, and Yvonne Miller tumbling to her death in Polperro House, the note seemed silly. But it was creepy, and someone at Pendarvis had left it for her.

I can't go home yet, Chloe thought. There are too many unanswered questions.

So. That being the case, she better get busy.

An officer had poked through her totebag, which she carefully kept with her now, before allowing her to take it from the office. Now she pulled out her notebook—an inexpensive spiral-bound number made with recycled paper instead of animal skin—and turned to a fresh page. If she was going to look for answers, she needed to organize her thoughts.

- *Someone may have pushed me into the badger hole*
- *Someone removed safety rope from around badger hole*
- *Someone left a threatening note in my bag*
- *Yvonne Miller was found dead at bottom of Polperro House stairs*
- *Yvonne's journal is missing*

- *Cops seem suspicious that Yvonne's death not an accident*

Chloe stared at the list, considering. *If* someone had shoved Yvonne down the steps, the deed had been done before the site opened. Who'd had access to Polperro House that morning? Who might have been angry at Yvonne—angry enough to snap?

- *Claudia*

No, Chloe thought again. Claudia would never do such a thing. Besides, Claudia had won the curator job, the job Yvonne Miller had evidently very much wanted. If anything, it was more likely that Yvonne had wanted to push Claudia down the stairs.

- *Holly*

The idea made Chloe sick to her stomach. But … it was possible.

- *Gerald, Rita, Loren, Evelyn, Audrey, et al.*

All of the employees and volunteers Chloe had met were devoted to, and protective of, Pendarvis. Loren knew that Miller had been involved in the effort to shut down the historic site. Even if no one else had seen the stupid letter, Miller had seemed awfully damn pleased about that possibility. Her public comments about the site had surely rankled a lot of people.

- *Everyone in Mineral Point who needs tourism dollars*

Restaurateurs, innkeepers, gallery owners, artists … "Oh!" Chloe suddenly remembered something. Evelyn had said that Adam's friend Winter had stopped by yesterday morning, looking for Claudia. Had Evelyn thought to mention that to Investigator Higgins?

Maybe a visit to Winter was in order. If anyone knew about undercurrents of anger, it would be the woman organizing the effort to keep Pendarvis open.

Since she wasn't permitted in the office and the interpreters clearly didn't need her, Chloe asked Investigator Higgins if she could leave the site. He granted permission, which was reassuring in a selfish kind of way.

But instead of heading straight to High Street's commercial area, she made a quick detour to Adam's cottage. Midge's tidbits about Mary Pascoe's reputation were tantalizing.

Chloe paused in the cottage doorway, then stepped inside. She let herself become receptive. After being so focused on the murdered soul found in the root cellar, it was a relief to once again feel a sense of contentment in the main living space.

It must have looked just like this when Mary moved in, Chloe thought, glad that the house was presently devoid of modern furniture. She squeezed her eyes to slits, imagining a woman crouched by the hearth, baking pasties. Or slipping into bed on a cold night, the room dimly lit by a waning fire. She imagined laughter echoing from the walls. Or excited chatter in Cornish dialect when friends gathered to sit and knit and sew and share news from the old country. There would be no letters for people who couldn't read or write, but stories would be passed from neighbor to neighbor. Newcomers would be welcomed with heartfelt enthusiasm, treated to saffron buns, and begged for news of Cornwall.

It was perhaps a simplistic picture, but until she could find more information about Mary Pascoe's life, it pleased Chloe to imagine it that way. Mary, she thought, you lived here longer than anybody. I hope your time here was happy.

TWENTY-ONE

JULY 1836

Mary Pascoe paused in the cottage doorway, then stepped inside.

Andrew came in behind her, grinning. "What do you think? I want you to be happy here, Mary."

"I will be. We all will be. I think it's almost perfect."

"Almost?" His grin faded. "What would make it perfect?"

"Living here!"

He shook his head. "You do have odd notions sometimes, Mary."

She put a hand on his arm. "Truly, Andrew, it's a fine house. Don't misunderstand. After a full year of living rough on the hill, I'm more than grateful. And to think, you *own* it!" The Pascoes had never owned property before.

"One of the first property owners of Wisconsin Territory," Andrew said with quiet pride. Population had risen in the area so much that politicians had voted to create the new territory. "Wouldn't Papa be proud." Then Andrew's eyes shadowed. He hesitated, shrugged.

Mary felt a familiar twinge of guilt. "You've done well—in spite of me. You had a rough spring after we took in Will."

As they'd feared, Will's uncle had tried to make trouble for the Pascoes. The Cornishmen on the hill rallied around them, and most of the Yankee men had no use for Hiram McCreary and his cousins either. But a few miners were always happy to drink hard and get wild—the kind who jumped into other men's brawls and thought nothing of stealing a man's gad or pick. Jory, Andrew, and sometimes Ruan had spent several cold, often wet months sleeping at the mine site. They were all relieved when the McCrearys packed up and disappeared, evidently discouraged.

"I'm not sorry we took in Will," Andrew assured her. "I'm that pleased with him. Once he got used to eating enough food, and wearing warm clothes and boots, he proved an eager miner."

Mary smiled. Will did love setting out to work with Jory and Andrew. Sometimes he went into the mine and they were glad of his help. Sometimes he did surface work, cobbing and washing the ore, and Mary was grateful. "He's trying to show his gratitude, the only way he knows how."

Andrew put a hand on her arm. "You did right to give him a family, Mary. And Ida too."

"Thank you." Mary squeezed the words past a salty lump in her throat. "It's extra mouths to feed, I know."

"I miss Elizabeth and Loveday too," Andrew said huskily.

I know you do, Mary wanted to say. The girls, though, had been her responsibility. She was the one who'd failed them.

But there were no words for that. She curled her hands into fists, letting the nails dig into her palms.

He cleared his throat. "Well, Will and Jory are no doubt wondering if I've left the day's digging to them." He kissed her cheek. "Think about naming the house."

"I've already chosen a name," Mary told him. "*Chy Looan.*"

That brought a true smile to his face. "*Chy Looan* is a fine name. I'll chisel it into the stone this evening."

Mary watched him cross the creek on the board bridge, and start up the hill with long, confident strides. Jory would be glad enough to have four solid walls and a roof between him and the weather, but it meant more to Andrew. He'd seemed to stand taller as they'd watched the stonemason and his helper raise the walls for their home. Mary hadn't realized how keenly Andrew had felt the burden of being eldest sibling, of needing to provide for his family. She and Jory were his responsibility.

This cottage was proof that he'd done right by them.

Did Andrew feel released now? Lately Mary had seen him talking with the daughter of a London-born smelter. He walked her home after Sunday services, found reasons to stand beside her at informal gatherings.

The girl appeared to be thrifty and modest and pleasant. Mary didn't doubt they'd all get along well enough if Andrew married her. Still, she was glad she had the chance to keep house at *Chy Looan* for at least a while before Andrew's wife moved in and took charge.

And it truly is a fine cottage, she thought, leaning against the doorframe. Mary liked the mason. "You've got to understand the stone," he'd said, caressing a block with a scarred hand. "It's a sacred gift you've got to respect. The stone lives, you see. It breathes, it shrinks and swells with the weather. You have to make mortar that will live in harmony with the particular stone. God help the man who tries to build without knowing that."

Still, what she'd tried to suggest to Andrew was true. She'd grown up in a cottage where the hearthstones were blackened from a century of use, and the sweet earthy scent of burning gorse was imbedded in the rafters, and the thick vines twined on strings around the windows had roots that stretched back generations. *Chy Looan* felt cold, hollow.

Several girls washing ore in the creek started splashing each other, shrieking with laughter—and reminding her that she'd left Ida alone at the camp. Mary took one last look over her shoulder. Just imagining Ida in the cottage made the room feel warmer. We will soon enough be making our own memories here, Mary reminded herself. God willing, they'd be good ones.

———

It took all morning for Mary and Ida to transfer their things to the new cottage—Ida staggering under unwieldy loads of wool blankets, Mary's hands aching from the weight of her iron spider and kettle. By the time they finished, the little girl's face was flushed from heat and exertion.

"Go cool off in the creek," Mary suggested. "Just stay where I can see you."

Ida raced from the cottage. Mary stepped to the open door and watched her wade into the creek, skirt held to her knees.

"Miss Mary!"

Mary turned and waved to the familiar figure leading his mule down the lane.

"Good day!" he greeted her, as he always did. "Jago Green, wood jowster, at your service. Dry wood and fair prices."

"I am in need," Mary told him. "For my first hearth fire."

"This is your home now?" Jago surveyed the cottage appreciatively. "It's fine."

He unloaded and stacked the wood. After paying him, Mary handed him a slice of bread smeared with wild raspberry jam.

"Delicious," he decreed, offering his infectious grin. "How about a portrait today? To celebrate your new home."

Mary shook her head, as she always did when Jago asked. "I've no spare money for such a vanity."

"Perhaps another time." Jago pulled his hat from his head and made a courtly bow before ambling down the lane.

Mary had salvaged several wooden packing crates discarded by a freighter, and they served to hold spare shirts and cooking utensils. Andrew and Jory had made a bench, which she positioned near the hearth. They'd also made a bed in one corner for Mary and Ida, but they still needed to buy the rope required to string the frame, and make a straw-filled tick to sleep on. Will, Jory, and Andrew would sleep on the floor upstairs in the narrow space beneath the eaves.

She was arranging cooking utensils when she heard footsteps outside. "Mary?" Ruan called. He stopped at the open door, blocking the sun. "Anyone home?"

Mary's heart lifted. "Ruan. How nice that you've come." He'd moved to his new smithy in town two months ago. Although he still came out to the diggings every few days to lend a hand or join the Pascoes for supper, she missed him.

"I had to see the new house." He held out a pair of andirons. "And I wanted to give you these."

She accepted the heavy pieces with pleasure, admiring the craftsmanship. The two were identical, and he'd taken the time to add decorative twists and curlicues to the iron. "Thank you! Fires burn so much better if the wood is off the floor." She crouched and settled them in the empty hearth. "Your gift is especially kind because I was just thinking that if I could only have a gorse fire, I would feel at home. Now when I build a fire I'll think about you instead."

He shrugged, looking both embarrassed and pleased, and surveyed the room. "This is nice."

"We need quite a bit, yet. Chairs and a table, to start. A cupboard. But that will all come in time."

He stepped to the mantel, a quizzical look on his face. "A candlestick, and the warmer I made you … and a cobbing hammer?" He touched the tool.

Mary's cheeks grew warm. "It's a reminder."

"Of the mine?"

"Of … of what I want."

"And that is?"

"I want to do better here, Ruan. I want Ida and Will to have more than we had."

Ruan's forehead creased. "You want to be wealthy?"

"I don't want to scrape for every turnip, but it's not that, it's … " She groped for words. "Andrew and Jory and I were destined for the mines from the day we were born. I'm not ashamed of that. But I want Ida and Will to know they have choices."

"That's a fine thing," Ruan agreed. He smiled, and his eyes crinkled, and Mary's insides went all crinkly too. "And what do you want for yourself?"

"Well … " She hesitated. "I want to serve tea."

"Serve tea?"

"Yes," she said stubbornly. "I want to serve a proper tea to Cornish people far from home. I want to bake saffron buns, and have plum preserves and clotted cream, all served on pretty china." She stood straight, holding his gaze, daring him to laugh.

He didn't laugh, but he was silent for a long moment. The sound of children playing floated through the open door. Finally he said, "Well, that's all fine. But I was hoping there might be something else you dream of." He stepped closer.

"Oh?" The word was barely audible.

"Mary Pascoe, you must know I want to marry you."

Now she couldn't manage even a whisper.

Ruan took her hand. His fingers were warm and strong, and made her feel safe in a way she hadn't even known she wanted. "I have dared hope that you might want the same."

She licked lips gone dry. "I do."

He leaned down and kissed her, with one arm behind her back to hold her close. Mary rested against him, smelling the sweat and coal dust of him, putting one hand behind his neck. It was all quite unexpected and delicious.

Finally he released her and stepped back, looking quite pleased. "Good. I'll speak to Andrew."

"When?" Mary asked. "When shall we wed?"

"When I'm better settled."

"But … when will that be?" She would have wed Ruan that day if he'd been willing.

"I can't say. I want to buy my smithy, and that will take some time. And I thought to add a floor above, for living space. I can't expect my wife to sleep in a corner behind the forge, as I've been doing."

Mary shook her head. "We've done all right so far. I'll get back to baking for the miners. I've made arrangements to sew shirts for the new storekeeper, because the bachelors all need ready-made. You could pick up a little extra work with my brothers, and live here with us." Jory had already suggested it.

"No," Ruan said firmly. "I won't take a wife if I don't feel certain I can take care of a family."

"But—"

"*Properly* take care of a family. You'll be bringing two children to our marriage, mind. And with God's blessing we'll have more."

Mary wanted to argue. She wasn't afraid of hard work or lean times, or—hard as it would be to leave this cottage—even of sleeping behind the forge. But she could see how important this was to Ruan, and that deserved her respect. "Very well, Ruan. We'll wait."

His face split in a wide grin. "Thank you, Mary." He started for the door, then paused. "But don't forget, you are promised." Then he was gone. Mary heard him whistling as he walked away.

I am promised, she thought. That notion was even more precious than she had imagined.

TWENTY-TWO

Winter's sales gallery, Winterware, was located in an old building on High Street. When Chloe stepped inside she was immediately distracted from her mission, tugged off-course by the pots, plates, casserole dishes, bowls, mugs, and candlesticks on the shelves. Most of Winter's pieces were glazed in soothing tones of brown, green, and blue. Chloe particularly liked a series decorated with clay maple leaves.

"May I help you?" Winter had emerged from a back room.

Chloe turned. "Oh, hi, Winter. I was just admiring your work."

The potter stood wiping her hands on a cloth. Her usual uniform of denim overalls was streaked with clay. Her hair was piled loosely on top of her head, and enamel dragonflies dangled from her ears. "It's Chloe, right? Adam's friend."

Her demeanor seemed more polite than friendly, but maybe Winter was merely in greet-the-public mode. "That's right. I'm also a guest curator at Pendarvis this week. I know you stopped by to see Claudia yesterday morning, and—"

"It was day before yesterday."

Chloe's eyebrows rose. "Evelyn was very specific."

Winter shrugged. "That's right, it was yesterday. I got confused."

"Anyway, Claudia's home with a migraine today, and I thought I'd come by and see if there's anything I can help you with." That last line was a stretch; she could just have easily called, and it was unlikely that she could help Winter with anything anyway. Still, it gave her a vaguely professional reason to begin a conversation.

"It wasn't anything urgent. We've talked about reproducing some Klais pottery, and I've got a prototype to show her."

"Ooh! May I see it?" Chloe asked, with honest enthusiasm.

Winter hesitated, then made a *Why not?* gesture. She disappeared back into her workroom. A moment later she returned and set a flowerpot on the counter.

"That, is, *gorgeous*." Chloe leaned closer. The pot was glazed in a soft yellow with random decorative brown streaks. "I'd love to see a bunch of these put to use on the Pendarvis grounds."

"Unfortunately," Winter said coolly, "there is no money in Claudia's budget for reproduction pots. And if we aren't able to convince the powers that be to keep Pendarvis open, it will all become a moot point anyway."

"I'm so sorry that Pendarvis is being threatened—"

"*I'm* sorry that developing Old World Wisconsin drained all of the Historic Sites Division's resources."

"I don't think it's fair to blame Old World Wisconsin for the decision."

"The newspaper article made it quite clear!" Winter countered. "Pendarvis, and probably all of the smaller sites, have been ignored lately because of all the time and energy and money that went into *your* site."

Chloe took a deep breath. "Listen. It's true that a great deal of money was spent to move and restore the buildings that are now at Old World Wisconsin, and to operate the site."

"I'd say." Winter sniffed disdainfully.

"But that's *not* the reason Pendarvis is in the crosshairs. Pendarvis is in the crosshairs because the state has not fulfilled its obligation to protect Wisconsin's historic treasures. The stories told here, and the buildings preserved here, are no less and no more important than the stories told and buildings preserved at Old World. Pitting one site against another is counterproductive."

"But—"

"And blaming *me* is counterproductive. All of us need to keep fighting for the resources we need to maintain Wisconsin's historic sites. *All* of them."

Winter opened her mouth, closed it again. Chloe held the other woman's gaze.

At last Winter looked away. "You have to understand," she said stiffly, "that my livelihood is at stake. I own this building. A lot of artists in Mineral Point have invested in their shops because they want to stay here. If Pendarvis closes, it will affect the whole town."

"I know," Chloe said quietly. "And I'm truly sorry. I'll do anything I can to support the cause."

Winter concentrated on scraping a bit of clay from one fingernail, but gave a grudging nod.

The doorbell tinkled, breaking the awkward silence. Three women wandered into the shop and began ooh-ing and ah-ing over Winter's handiwork.

"Well," Winter said, "tell Claudia she can see the flowerpot any time."

"I will. And if you do ever make more, I'd love to buy one. I also want to purchase that bowl with the leaves…"

Chloe left Winterware with the tissue-wrapped bowl tucked into a sturdy shopping bag. She hoped that if nothing else, she'd cleared the air a bit, provided a new perspective to consider. Chloe didn't blame Winter for being angry.

The real question was, just how angry was she? Had Yvonne Miller's comments at the meeting Monday evening pushed the potter over the edge? Had Winter been walking down the upper property path yesterday morning and spotted Claudia and Yvonne entering Polperro House? If so, she could have lingered outside long enough to see her chance for a confrontation when Claudia left Yvonne alone.

Chloe rolled her eyes. It seemed preposterous.

And yet… Winter *had* tried to weasel out of admitting she'd visited Pendarvis yesterday morning. Maybe she'd truly been confused. Maybe she'd lied.

This situation is sucking more and more, Chloe thought, and headed for the library.

"You again!" Midge said in cheerful greeting. "What can I get for you?"

"I thought I'd look for Mary Pascoe's obituary. Do you have newspapers from 1911?"

Midge looked disappointed, in an *Oh come on, give me something challenging* way. "Sure." She fetched the reel of microfilm.

Chloe settled at the reader. The property owners list indicated that *Chy Looan* had passed from Mary Pascoe to Ann Trezona in June 1911. That didn't necessarily mean that Mary had died in June of 1911, but it was a good place to start.

Chloe spent ten minutes scrolling through pages of articles, advertisements, letters, notices. And then—"Found it!" she yelled. She turned to grin triumphantly at Midge, and only then discovered that the archivist was helping an elderly man who'd evidently tip-toed in. "Sorry."

Died—At Mineral Point, on the 17th ult. Miss Mary Pascoe, a respectable spinster and an inhabitant of this village. The deceased was a native of Cornwall, England. In her youth she left Cornwall in company with her brothers, miners Andrew and Jory Pascoe, who, having heard of the lead mines in this part of America, and feeling a strong desire to try their fortune among them, found their way to Mineral Point.

Midge appeared at her shoulder. "You'll want to print that. It's a dime a page."

Chloe looked up. "Mary wasn't Andrew's widow, she was his sister!"

"Does that make a difference?"

"Oh, not in any meaningful way," Chloe admitted. She was impressed by any single woman who managed to make a go of it in the nineteenth century. "Just lining up facts. There was a second brother too."

"Ah," Midge said, in the polite tone archivists used when patrons enthused about genealogical details.

Midge showed her how to send a selection to the printer. Chloe snatched the page as soon as it emerged and read the remainder.

The Pascoes commenced with little save strong hands and industrious habits. Miss Pascoe was well known for the Cornish teas served in her home in the Shake Rag district for many years, attracting her fellow countrymen and women, and others, from as far away as Dodgeville, Platteville, and Madison.

She served tea! Chloe thought happily.

All who knew Miss Pascoe can speak of her gentle manners
and her service to the community and the Methodist Church.
She nursed the sick and is known to have saved many lives.
She was especially fond of children, and many residents can
well recall visits to "Miss Mary's" cottage for play or
refreshments. She also took in a number of orphaned or
destitute children and raised them as her own. Many
Mineral Point residents are mourning the loss of a
remarkable woman.

Chloe leaned back in her chair. Way to go Mary, she thought. Obituaries were intended to emphasize the positive, of course, but it was impossible to not be impressed by a single woman who ran a tea shop and adopted needy children.

This new information also had interpretive potential for Pendarvis. Bob Neal and Edgar Hellum had opened the Pendarvis House Restaurant in the 1930s, serving first traditional Cornish teas and later, full pasty dinners. The unusual ambiance and high-quality food had attracted nationwide attention. Chloe could hardly wait to tell Claudia that a century earlier, a Cornish-born woman had been doing the same thing in a cottage nearby.

———

It was sprinkling as Chloe circled the Pendarvis rowhouse on the upper property and entered the staff-only area. The police cars were gone—always a good sign—and a murmur of voices from the re-created pub let her know that a tour was in progress. Her mind was still full of Cornish tea parties when she opened the door to the entry room … and stopped, open-mouthed. The police hadn't trashed the place, but they'd moved *everything*. Coffee supplies and stray cups had been pulled from the cupboard. Pieces of period clothing once neatly hung on racks were now lying in a heap on the table. The staff reference library had been removed from the shelves, the books now stacked on the floor.

Loren's door was closed and locked, so Chloe moved on to Claudia's office. It was a disaster.

Chloe felt stricken. This little cluttered room had become her home-away-from-home this week. Seeing the aftermath of a professional search was worse than hearing that it was going to take place. She was glad Evelyn had gone home, and glad Claudia wasn't here to see this either.

There was nothing to do but start setting things to rights. The fact that Chloe didn't know exactly where a lot of things belonged made cleanup difficult, but she was determined to at least have things tidy before the other women returned.

Fortunately, the flood of anxious calls about the threat to Pendarvis had slowed to a trickle. As Chloe worked she occasionally heard voices as an interpreter led visitors to the rowhouse, but that normalcy was reassuring, not an interruption. She was trying to remember how Claudia had shelved her books—by topic? alphabetical by author?—when the phone rang.

"Good afternoon, Pendarvis Historic Site. How may I help you?"

"Chloe? Oh, thank God."

Chloe's fingers locked on the phone. "Claudia? What's wrong?"

"This morning cops came with a warrant and searched my house." Claudia began to cry, and her words came out between little shuddering heaves. "Thankfully Holly had already left for school. She would have freaked *out*."

Chloe pressed the heel of her hand to her forehead. This was bad.

"Why?" Claudia demanded. "Why would the cops do that? I have no idea what they were looking for."

Chloe dropped into the desk chair. "I think they're looking for Yvonne's journal. It wasn't found with her briefcase after she died. It seems to me that if there was something damning in there, whoever took it would have destroyed it by now, but I guess they had to try. Did they take anything from your house?"

"No."

"Well, that's good." Chloe hesitated. "They came here too, and searched the offices. I don't know if they found anything."

"They made me sit in a cop car while they searched my house. Neighbors were peeking out their windows. I have never been so humiliated." Claudia's voice was rising. "It took a long time, and all I wanted was for them to leave so I could go inside and lock the door. But then Higgins said he wanted me to come to the police station for questioning. I'm still here."

"Are you under arrest? Did Higgins say you had to go?"

"No. But I don't have anything to hide! All I want is to get through this as quickly as possible so I can go home."

"You should ask for a lawyer."

"I don't need a lawyer! I've told him what happened."

Except for Holly showing up on site, Chloe thought. "What does he want to know?"

"He keeps asking where I was yesterday morning when I left the site. Over and over. Evidently someone heard me arguing with Yvonne when we were in Polperro House."

Shit. "Who?"

"I don't know."

Chloe rubbed her forehead with her free hand. It could have been one of the interpreters. Or the maintenance man. Or a garden club volunteer, for all she knew.

"Chloe, I have a huge favor to ask. I don't know when he's going to release me, and Holly will get home at about two forty-five. Could you please go meet her? Maybe take her for a walk or something? I don't want her to go inside and find a mess. I know it's a lot to ask, but Holly seems to like you. I don't know who else to call."

This is a train wreck, Chloe thought. But ... at the center was a little girl. "Of course I'll go meet Holly."

"*Thank* you." Claudia sniffled. "If you need to get in, there's a spare key beneath the blue flowerpot with the yellow chrysanthemums."

After hanging up, Chloe went to the site director's office. Still no Loren. For God's sake, she thought, did he go home too? What was the matter with him? She wrote *I had to leave for a family emergency* on a slip of paper and taped it to his door. Truthful, in a way.

Then she walked around to the gift shop. It was empty except for Audrey, perched on her stool behind the sales and ticket counter. "Is everything okay?" Chloe asked. The shop looked tidy. "Did the cops search in here?"

"They did." Her face wrinkled with distaste. "That was a first."

"Did they find anything?"

"Not that I saw. But I had to wait outside."

"Did they leave a mess?" Chloe surveyed the tidy room. "If so, you did a masterful job of straightening up."

"Well, we like things clean and orderly," Audrey said pertly. "They flipped through inventory on the shelves, and spent some time going through stock in storage. Looked in all the cupboards, that sort of thing. As soon as they left I straightened up."

"Excellent," Chloe said. "Audrey, there won't be anyone in the offices, at least for a while. Loren appears to be out, and I have to leave unexpectedly."

"No problem. I'll listen for the outside phone line. Our school kids are gone, and with this drizzle, I don't expect many other visitors. If Loren's not back by four thirty I'll close out the cash register and make the deposit. Seasonal workers aren't supposed to, but I've done it before."

"O-kay," Chloe said. Clearly this veteran had things well in hand. "Great. Thanks." She left Audrey to her domain.

Chloe got to Claudia's house early, settled uneasily into a comfy wicker chair on the porch, and watched rain drip from the gutter. She wondered how much trouble Claudia was in. She wondered if the investigator would arrest Claudia, and what would happen to Holly if he did. She wondered if Holly would have a meltdown when she saw Chloe, or run away.

Chloe was well down the road to panic herself when she heard children's voices. Two boys about Holly's age turned onto the street. One was banging the other with a violin case. School was definitely out.

Holly appeared a minute or two behind them. Chloe was so used to seeing her in period attire that it took a moment to recognize her in jeans. She wore a yellow rain jacket, but the hood was down. Her dark braids hung over her shoulders. She stopped when she saw her company. Chloe waved. Looking uncertain, Holly walked slowly to the house.

"Hi, Holly," Chloe said cheerfully. "I'm Chloe, remember? Your mom's friend. She got called away this afternoon, and she asked me to meet you."

Holly's huge eyes glistened. She trembled. She shook her hands with agitation. After an obvious struggle, she choked out a question: "Is—she—coming back?"

"Oh sweetie, yes, of course." The assurance popped out. Chloe hoped like crazy that she hadn't spoken too quickly. "I thought we could take a walk while we wait for her. Maybe to the woods on Dark Hill? I don't mind a little rain, do you? I think it's okay if you leave your schoolbag here on the porch."

Chloe zipped up her own jacket and walked down the porch steps. Please let Holly be okay, she thought fervently. *Please.*

She held her breath until she sensed Holly joining her. Chloe caught the girl's eye and smiled. "This will be an adventure."

Holly didn't answer, but Chloe felt a small hand slide into hers. The gesture—half trusting, half needy—made her feel even worse.

TWENTY-THREE

"Do you want me to go over it again?" Roelke asked.

Michelle Zietz shook her head. "No. I got it."

He gave her a steady look, trying to appear reassuring. "Just go in, make the buy, come back, and meet me here. I'll be listening the whole time."

"I *know*." But the young woman hesitated, gnawing her lower lip.

"You remember your safe word?"

"I'm not an idiot!" she flared. She scowled out the window before muttering, "Thunder."

"You say the word 'thunder' and half a dozen cops will be inside before you can turn around. The only difference between this buy and your previous buys is that you'll be a whole lot safer today."

She got out of his truck and swung into her car. She tossed the purse holding the money he'd given her on the passenger seat, started the engine, and drove away.

Roelke watched until she was out of sight. They'd met three blocks away from the drug house on Hackberry. He was dressed in civvies and he had two other guys out of uniform and three in blues already in place around the house.

This first buy would be the most challenging for Zietz. The desperate eagerness to get out of trouble she'd displayed after her arrest had given way to a *Let's get this over with* edginess.

Roelke felt edgy too. He wanted to make Chief Naborski proud. And he really, *really* wanted to shut the dealers down.

The next five minutes passed very slowly. Roelke sat in his truck listening, both thumbs tapping an impatient beat on the steering wheel. What was Zietz doing? Had she lost her nerve? What the hell was taking so long?

Finally he heard her car door slam, a doorbell ring, a mutter of greeting. Zietz was inside.

The transaction went without a hitch. Fifteen minutes later he saw her Ford Fiesta pull up behind him. She parked, got out, walked to his truck. He tried to read her expression as she opened the passenger door and slid onto the seat. "Are you okay? It sounded like everything went according to plan."

She took a deep breath, staring straight ahead. "Yeah. I bought the crack, I left." She pulled a small plastic bag holding the ivory-colored lumps of crack from her purse and handed it over.

"Well done." Roelke passed her a clipboard holding a blank pad. "Write down everything that happened, starting with meeting me here. Sign it and date it."

She took the pad. The scratchy sound of hasty scribbling filled the cab. A car pulled into a nearby driveway and a boy in a Cub Scout uniform got out and ran toward the front door. Then Zietz handed the clipboard back to Roelke and started to get out of the truck.

"See you tomorrow," he reminded her.

"I *know*." She slammed the door.

Roelke scanned the statement—clear and concise. *Yes*. This thing wasn't done yet, not by a long shot. But they'd gotten off to a promising start.

———

Chloe began having second thoughts about wandering Dark Hill as soon as she and Holly began the climb. A misty gloom cloaked the wooded hillside. The sense of industry she had conjured on her first foray here was gone. Instead, all she could imagine was homesick miners huddled in leaking shelters, lonely and cold and discouraged.

Okay, she thought, this will not do. "I've wanted to explore over here all week, but haven't had the chance," she told Holly. "I'm counting on you to be my guide."

Holly led her up the footpath through trees and brush as raindrops pattered softly down. When they reached the badger hole that Gerald and Loren were digging Chloe saw that, once again, the safety tape staked around the hole had been ripped up and tossed aside.

Who is doing this? she wondered, as a sliver of ice seemed to slide down her spine. The sensation of a hand brushing against her back returned. She cast an uneasy glance over her shoulder. Leaves trembled, as if someone unseen had just disappeared into the undergrowth.

It's just the rain hitting them, she told herself. Still, she wanted to get out of there. "Come on, sweetie." Skirting the hole, they continued on their way.

Holly took her tour guide responsibility to heart. She pointed out an oriole nest hanging from a limb. She knew where to find abandoned mining equipment, rusty and forlorn and almost covered with brambles. But Chloe felt relieved when they'd carefully picked their way back down the ravine and crossed Shake Rag Street.

At Holly and Claudia's house, a lamp was glowing in the front window. Claudia opened the door before Holly and Chloe even reached the porch. Holly's face lit with a joyful smile as Claudia scooped her up. "There's my girl," Claudia said, kissing her. "But you're wet, and heavy too." She let her daughter slide to her feet. "Go inside and change into dry clothes, alright?"

"Bye, Holly," Chloe called. Holly waved before disappearing into the house.

"Thank God I had time to tidy up her room," Claudia muttered. "Both of our bedrooms were taken apart, Chloe. In mine, everything—every book, every memento, every pair of underwear—had been handled and dumped on my bed. I feel violated."

Chloe rubbed her arms. "I don't blame you."

"I got a lot put back together in the kitchen, and I just shut my bedroom door. Was Holly okay?"

"At first she was afraid you weren't coming back. I reassured her, and we went walking on Dark Hill." Chloe put a hand on her friend's arm. "But I've been worried about you."

Claudia's usual Gibson Girl bun was slipping, and she shoved stray pins back into place. "After going over the same ground umpteen times, Investigator Higgins drove me home."

"That will probably be the end of it, then. He found no reason to arrest you."

"I don't think I convinced him of anything." Claudia shook her head, her eyes bleak. "What am I going to do, Chloe? I really think Higgins believes I had something to do with Yvonne's death."

"He can't prove anything, because there's nothing to prove," Chloe said. "You're innocent."

"I am," Claudia said stoutly, as if reminding herself. Then she paused. "But … "

"But what?" Chloe's tone was sharper than she'd intended.

"But if Higgins starts looking at Holly, I'll take the blame."

Chloe was tempted to put her fingers in her ears. "Claudia, don't—"

"I'll say it was an accident. I'll say Yvonne slipped, and I panicked."

"Stop!" Chloe hissed. "Just, stop." She didn't want to hear this. She didn't want to wonder what *she* would do if Claudia confessed to a crime she hadn't committed. Would she tell Investigator Higgins the truth? Or was protecting Holly from the legal system more important than anything else?

Chloe didn't want to confront that moral quandary right now. "Surely Holly had nothing to do with Yvonne Miller's death," she said. Although right that moment, she wasn't sure of anything.

Neither woman spoke for a moment. Then Claudia managed a tiny smile. "Forget it. I was just rambling."

"Have you called your husband?" Chloe asked. "Let him know what's going on? I'm sure his business trip is important, but supporting you in a crisis is important too."

Claudia was already shaking her head. "*No.* Things between us are sticky enough without dumping this on him long-distance. I can handle it."

Since Claudia clearly wasn't going to budge, Chloe reluctantly said goodbye. There was a lot yet to do at the site.

At the office she called Tamsin, explaining that she'd be late. That meant missing, once again, the chance to visit Lowena, but it couldn't be helped. It took another hour to make the place look somewhat presentable.

After locking up the building, and the main gate too, Chloe walked down to Shake Rag Street. The sun had set, and Dark Hill loomed black against the charcoal sky. Just as she was about to turn toward Tamsin's place, a light blinked on the hill.

Chloe froze, rain dripping from the hood of her jacket. After a moment she saw the light again. It flickered, as if someone with a flashlight was walking behind trees. Then it abruptly disappeared.

What the hell? Chloe thought as she turned to walk to Tamsin's place. Why would anyone be up there after dark on a rainy night?

———

Well after midnight, Roelke stood across the street from Libby's house. A waning moon cast long shadows, and he kept to the darkness beside a tall lilac bush. He'd been there for two hours, and seen only a few passing cars. Shortly after he'd begun his vigil, a Palmyra cop car had slowed in front of Libby's house, the driver taking a good look around before moving on. Roelke was grateful.

He had no reason to believe that Libby's ex was planning to move flowerpots, or to leave another menacing "gift" on Libby's front step. There'd been no sign of Dan Raymo's Firebird. The only thing Roelke knew for certain was that he wanted to catch the SOB in stalker mode. He'd gone too far, and the Palmyra police couldn't intervene unless Roelke could prove that Raymo was acting in a threatening manner.

Libby's tired ranch house was dark, quiet. Dawn was still hours away. Roelke's eyes felt gritty. His knees ached. He needed to move.

He hurried silently across the street to Libby's place and slipped into the deeper shadows beside the side fence. He crept to the back yard and took a hard look around, alert for any slight movement, a whisper of footfall on grass. Nothing.

Roelke wasn't afraid of the dark. But Libby's back yard was a place for barbecues, and croquet with the kids, and relaxing with friends. The silence, the deep shadows, the reason he was here … his nerves were ratcheted tight.

He stood by the fence for some time, listening, watching. A fretful breeze rustled through the maple trees nearby. Somewhere in the distance a cat yowled, then went quiet. The night smelled damp, as if rain were coming. A cloud cloaked the moon, blurring the shadows.

Then he heard a distinct *crack*, as if someone farther back in the yard had stepped on a stick. He tensed, straining to see, to hear.

Then, a louder rustling. Every fine hair on his body rose. Someone was creeping along the back fence through Libby's flower garden.

Roelke launched toward the sound, feet pounding the grass. Then he sensed movement behind him. As he turned his head, something flashed on the patio. A gunshot cracked the stillness.

The ground slammed into him before he realized he was falling. He twisted to his knees and snatched his handgun from its holster. Where was Raymo? *Where*? Ahead? Behind? Roelke couldn't find a target.

Roelke's heart thudded. His mouth tasted metallic. He was pretty sure he'd been shot, but the pumping adrenaline blocked the pain and he didn't know where. He patted himself down with his free hand. It came away sticky-hot when he tested the left side of his belly.

Someone approached from the house, footsteps soft in the grass. Roelke pointed his gun at the shadow, but the adrenaline was subsiding and a firecracker of pain exploded in his side. He wavered, managed to stay up on his knees.

The figure stopped a few feet away, arms stretched forward, pistol pointed at Roelke. Words came in a low, furious hiss. "You son of a bitch!"

An inarticulate groan escaped Roelke's clenched teeth. Jesus Holy *Christ*.

Dan Raymo was not the shooter.

Chloe tiptoed from the guest room without turning on a light and settled into the antique rocker. She felt uneasy and hadn't been able to sleep. She was worried about the threat to close Pendarvis. She was worried about Claudia, and the whole mess surrounding Yvonne Miller's unexplained death.

And she was worried about Roelke. When they'd talked that evening he'd sounded tense, distracted. Things were still bad, he'd said, with Libby and her ex.

He'd also told her that the raid of the drug house was scheduled for Saturday, and that Adam had offered to bring Chloe back from Mineral Point when he returned from his weekend visit on Sunday. "You okay with that?"

"Sure," Chloe had said. "Maybe I'll help with the pasty dinner at Tamsin's church Saturday night." Honestly, though, she was disappointed that Roelke couldn't pick her up on Friday evening.

Now her thoughts pinged from Claudia to Libby, from the un-identified skeleton to Yvonne Miller, from Holly to Mary Pascoe. And to Roelke, always back to Roelke. She wished they weren't apart right now. He was struggling, and she was struggling, and the bed in Tamsin's guest room felt empty.

———

"For God's sake, Libby," Roelke gasped. "It's me!"

" … What?" Libby slowly dropped to her knees. "*Roelke*? Oh God. Did I hit you? Oh my God!"

A second-story light appeared in the house next door. "Be quiet," Roelke whispered harshly. "Don't move."

"But—"

"Shut up!"

Libby's breath came in tiny pants but she swallowed whatever she'd been about to say. The night ticked by. When the neighbor's bedroom went dark again Roelke forced himself to count to one hundred before moving. "Okay," he grunted. "We need to get inside. Fast."

"Oh Roelke," Libby quavered. "I'm so sorry! I thought it was—"

"There's no time for that." Roelke winced as he lurched to his feet. "Come on. Stay low. Do *not* turn on any lights."

Stumbling, hunched over, he managed to make it to the house. Libby opened the back door and they slipped into the kitchen.

"Bathroom." The word squeezed out between clenched teeth. "Don't wake the kids. Get a flashlight." He heard a drawer slide open, slide closed again.

In the bathroom he made sure the blinds were closed, the curtains drawn, and the toilet seat lid down before dropping. Thanks to a nightlight's soft glow the flashlight wasn't needed. He was clutching the wound with his right hand. Blood seeped between his fingers, stained his shirt. He forced himself to loosen his grip. A burning sensation throbbed in his side, but it looked like a flesh wound. The bullet had grazed him just below his rib cage. An inch higher would have splintered bone. Two inches to the right would have torn through organs.

"Oh my God," Libby moaned. "I'm so sorry. I'm *so* sorry. We've got to get you to the hospital—"

"No hospital."

"You're going to the ER!"

"No hospital," he insisted. "I'd have to explain where I got a gunshot wound. You want me to do that?"

Libby began to cry. "I want to make sure you're alright!"

"I'm alright." He grabbed a towel hanging by the sink and pressed it hard against his side. With his left index finger he eased the blind away from the window, just a bit. The street was dark and still.

Libby collapsed onto the rim of the bathtub, leaning over with her face in her hands, weeping uncontrollably.

Roelke wanted to reassure her but every ounce of energy he had left was focused on the street. A minute passed, maybe two. He was just beginning to hope that they'd get away with this debacle when he saw headlights. A sedan crept slowly down the road, parked in front of Libby's house. The Palmyra PD, responding to the neighbor's call.

Libby sobbed.

"Shut *up!*" Roelke breathed. "There's a cop outside."

The cop switched on his bright searchlight and scanned the front yard. After a moment the beam flicked off, and the squad car door opened. Roelke didn't dare touch the blinds again and so tried to mark time in his head as if he were outside, gun in one hand and flashlight in the other. He'd clear the front yard first, checking behind the bushes, before creeping down one side and to the back yard. Then he'd take another good look.

Roelke closed his eyes. How much of a mess had he and Libby left in the back yard? There was surely blood, and the spent bullet. But with any luck this inspection would be cursory. If it were *him*, he'd want to assure himself that there was no dead body among the tulips, no pet injured by a stray shot. Then he'd come back at first light and take a much harder look around.

Time crawled. Libby wept. Blood soaked into the towel as Roelke sat rigid, terrified that the cop would bang on the door. Thanks to his own informal request to keep an eye on Libby's place, the guy was likely to be more suspicious than usual. But after a painful eternity, Roelke heard a car door close, the engine rumble to life. He dared one more peek out the window and saw the street brighten as headlights came on. The cop drove away.

Roelke counted to a hundred again. "Okay. I think we're clear. Get some first-aid supplies.... Libby? Libby!" He snapped his fingers in her direction. "First-aid supplies!"

She blinked, stood, fumbled in the medicine cabinet. "We *have* to go to the ER. You need stitches. I don't care if I get in trouble—"

"Then you're not thinking straight. There are two children asleep just down the hall, and you're all they have."

"But..."

"I'm all right, Libby." Roelke leaned sideways against the sink. "Turn on the light and patch me up. Then you're going to get some sleep. You have to pull yourself together, do you hear me? In just a few hours the kids will be up. Do you understand?"

Libby nodded and flicked the switch. Roelke winced at the harsh flood of light. Through squinting eyes he saw tears rolling down her cheeks.

She cleaned the wound as best she could, dabbing at the welling blood before applying several butterfly bandages. Then she pressed a thick pad of gauze against the hole, fastening it in place with medical tape. "We'll have to keep an eye on it." Her voice was all shuddery. "We'll probably need to change the dressing."

Roelke nodded. All he wanted to do was lie down and pretend the last hour had never happened. But the question had to be asked. "Libby, where the hell did you get the gun? You told me you'd never have a gun in the house."

"He—he was here again," she quavered. "Dan. I sat up last night, trying to watch out the window, but I fell asleep. This morning I found...I found a dead yellow rose." A new wave of tears began. "And two dead rosebuds."

Roelke's marrow turned to slush. Raymo had just threatened to kill Libby and the kids. "And you didn't call me?"

"I was afraid you'd go after him and do something that would wreck your career." She swiped at her eyes. "This isn't your problem, Roelke."

"The hell it isn't!" He took care of the people he loved.

"So after I took the kids to school I drove to Waukesha, and I ... I went to a gun store."

"Were you planning to kill him, Libby?" Roelke demanded in a harsh whisper. "What would happen to Justin and Deirdre then, hunh? What were you thinking?"

"This has to stop." Libby lifted her palms in a helpless gesture, let them drop. "That's what I was thinking. This has to stop."

Roelke had nothing left. "I gotta lie down," he muttered. "You do too. Set your alarm, because everything needs to be tidy before the kids wake up." His bloody shirt and two soaked towels were in the corner, and he'd no doubt dripped blood on the kitchen floor.

He wound a beach towel around his midsection in hopes it would catch any seeping blood. In the living room he gingerly lowered himself to the sofa and curled on his right side. His wound still pulsed painfully. There were things to do, but first, he had to get some rest.

But sleep eluded him. The night's events played through his brain like a movie. Libby had shot him. Libby had actually *shot* him. His cousin, the person he knew better than anyone else, had become an armed stranger, wild-eyed and sobbing.

Roelke felt a hollowness in his chest like he'd never known. It came partly from anger, but partly from fear too.

TWENTY-FOUR

ROELKE FELT GROGGY WHEN he staggered from the sofa on Friday morning. Had he slept at all? It didn't feel like it. Maybe he could call in sick. No, that wouldn't work. He needed to oversee Michelle Zietz's second set-up buy today. It was his case. It wouldn't be fair to ask Skeet to handle it, even if he wanted to. Which he didn't.

He gingerly unwrapped the towel. The bandage was stained, but dry. The wound didn't seem to be bleeding anymore. Good.

The house was quiet, which meant the kids were still asleep. He found Libby in the kitchen. Her face was haggard, and when she looked at him, her eyes filled with tears.

"Knock that off." Roelke put his arm around her.

"I could have killed you!"

"But you didn't." He stepped back so he could look her in the eye. "Listen, you *have* to pull it together. I'm going to leave before the kids get up. I don't want them to know that anything's wrong. And there's a good chance that a Palmyra cop will show up—"

Panic flared in her eyes. "Why?"

"It's what I'd do if I got a 'shot fired' call in the wee hours. I'd knock on the door and ask if everything was okay. If that happens, you have to convince him that you did not hear *anything*." Roelke struggled to appear calm. He was urging his cousin to lie to a police officer.

Libby studied her fingers. "I don't know if I can convince anyone of anything."

He let his voice get sharp. "Do you know what will happen if the fact that you shot me last night becomes public knowledge? Your ex will suddenly have some interesting new information to take to a judge about your fitness as a parent."

She took that in, stood straighter, squared her shoulders.

"You can handle this." He kissed her cheek. "I'm going home to clean up before work. Where's the pistol?"

Libby pushed a step-stool in front of one of the cabinets and retrieved the gun from the top shelf.

Roelke slipped it into a pocket and then zipped his dark jacket all the way up to cover his bare chest. "We'll talk later." He let himself out the kitchen door and quickly surveyed the back yard. No evidence of the wild shot.

As he circled to the front yard, a Palmyra cop car pulled up and parked. Officer Troy Blakely stepped out. Here we go, Roelke thought, and went to meet his colleague.

"Hey, McKenna," Blakely said. "What're you doing here?"

"I spent the night. Just keeping an eye on my cousin's place until this foolishness with her ex settles down."

"Any sign of him last night?"

"Nope."

"When I got in this morning, I found a note from the third shift guy. The neighbor"—Blakely cocked his head toward the next house—"called at two a.m. and reported hearing a gunshot. You hear anything?"

"A gunshot?" Roelke held Blakely's gaze, trying to look surprised and perplexed. Libby's pistol was a hot weight in his pocket. "No, I didn't hear a thing. And if Libby heard a gunshot, I'm sure she would have mentioned it to me this morning."

Blakely exhaled slowly. Finally he nodded. "Well, I wanted to check it out. Especially since Raymo's been harassing your cousin."

"I appreciate it."

"Don't worry. In the end, justice will be done."

"Sure," Roelke said, but only because he wanted the conversation to end. When it came to Raymo, justice was proving elusive.

"Raymo's so-called hunting club is meeting at Mickey's Tavern on Sunday afternoon," Blakely said. "I arrested him there once after a brawl. I've also nailed him for drunk driving a couple of times after one of these gatherings, and once for possession of marijuana. I'm sure he does harder stuff too. He thinks it's all a game. The asshole actually taunts me."

The thought of Raymo maybe messing around with drugs around the kids made Roelke feel sick. "Sounds like him."

"I'll look for him on Sunday. If he's inebriated, I can search the car." Blakely fiddled with the baton on his duty belt. "Say, how's your drug case going? You still looking for backup tomorrow?"

"I am. Everything's going according to plan."

"See you tomorrow, then."

"Great." Roelke turned away.

"Hey, McKenna," Blakely called. "Where's your truck?"

Roelke turned back. "Down the street. I didn't want the kids to know I spent the night. Libby and I are trying to keep them out of this mess with their father."

Blakely nodded and walked back to his squad. Roelke felt a flood of relief when his friend, the man he'd asked to keep an extra eye on his family, drove away.

He walked to his truck and climbed stiffly into the cab. Then he sat. Now *he'd* lied to a cop. He'd betrayed his training, his oath, everything he believed.

And it hadn't solved the larger problem. He had no reason to hope that Raymo was finished stalking Libby and the kids. Did I hear a squirrel along the back fence last night, Roelke thought, or had it been Libby's ex? Had her shot scared him off—or made him even angrier?

———

Chloe plodded from the guest room that morning feeling bleary-eyed and dull. She gratefully accepted a cup of coffee from Tamsin and snuggled into the antique rocking chair.

"Breakfast is almost ready," Tamsin said cheerfully.

Chloe tried to put bad thoughts aside and face the day with at least a dollop of good cheer. She tucked the cheerful blue and yellow crocheted afghan over her lap and gently rocked. "I love this chair," she told Tamsin. "It's comfortable, and beautiful, and it just makes me want to curl up with a good book." Today would be great for that. A soft rain was pattering against the windowpanes. The room smelled of the saffron buns Tamsin already had in the oven. It was all much more appealing than the threat of closure, and the troubling aftermath of a suspicious death, that were waiting for her at Pendarvis.

"I've spent many an hour in that chair," Tamsin told her. "Rocking my children, knitting, thinking. It's seen me through some hard times."

Chloe tucked her toes under the afghan. "Is it a family heirloom?"

"Not really." Tamsin put a pitcher of orange juice on the table. "We found it in *Chy Looan* when we moved in. Someone had left it in the crawl space above the second floor."

"Seriously?" Chloe stopped rocking. "Why didn't you tell me that before?"

Tamsin looked startled. "Well, I don't think about it. I've had that chair for ... almost fifty years."

Chloe stood and stared at the rocker. Had Mary Pascoe owned this chair?

Probably not, Chloe cautioned herself, before she could get too carried away. This style of rocker dated back to the 1820s, but it seemed unlikely that Cornish immigrants would be able to afford such a piece very soon after their arrival.

"Knowing where the chair came from wouldn't have helped your research," Tamsin added.

"No. Still, I'd like to figure out who made it, or sold it," Chloe mused. "Claudia is looking for furniture documented to Mineral Point. Perhaps there are business records in the archives. It's a long shot, but maybe I can even confirm that *Chy Looan*'s original occupants owned this chair."

"I told you yesterday that I didn't want to learn any more about the people who lived in that cottage." Tamsin filled one glass and moved on to the second.

Chloe hesitated. "I remember, but ... I don't understand why."

Tamsin wiped some nonexistent crumbs from the tablecloth. After a long moment she said, "You left the list of property owners sitting by the phone after talking to Adam the other evening. I took a look, and ... " Her voice trailed away.

"And what?"

"Andrew Pascoe is actually an ancestor of mine. On my mother's side."

"Really?" Chloe absorbed that news. "And when you bought *Chy Looan*, you didn't know he was the original owner?"

"I had no idea."

That was an amazing coincidence, but it didn't explain anything. "And?" Chloe prompted. Tamsin's anxiety suggested knowledge of something ghastly.

Tamsin pleated her apron with her fingers. "We don't know when that man was buried in the cottage. I don't want you to find anything that might tarnish the record of someone on my family tree. Please, Chloe. I want to forget the whole sordid incident."

Chloe wanted to point out that no one could blame Tamsin if some dark story actually came to light. Everyone had unpleasant stories on their family tree. If Andrew *had* killed a man and buried the body in his root cellar, the crime dated back one hundred and fifty years.

But one glance at the older woman's troubled face made Chloe swallow her protest. This wasn't about *her* family. What mattered were Tamsin's feelings.

"I understand," she lied. "But your Boston rocker is still an amazing piece. And very valuable."

"Is it, dear?"

"The elaborate decorations have held up remarkably well." Chloe leaned closer to the chair. "Whoever painted this piece did some graining on the surface, using a comb to put red over the base black to make it resemble expensive rosewood."

"I always thought it was pretty."

"My best guess is that some of the embellishment was stenciled and some painted freehand, but it's all done by an experienced artist. The metallic gold detailing is spectacular. Would it be okay if I look at the bottom?"

"Certainly." Tamsin waved a permissive hand.

Chloe put her coffee down and gently eased the rocking chair onto its side. Her mouth dropped open. "There's a signature penciled on the bottom."

"Gracious!" Tamsin sounded duly impressed.

"It looks like…" Chloe squinted. "'T. George/Min. Point.'" She looked up. "Do you know that name?"

"Can't say I've ever heard it."

"I would have guessed that anything of this caliber would have been shipped in from Madison or someplace," Chloe mused. "If a 'T. George' is known to have been making furniture in town, it would be *huge*."

A timer dinged in the kitchen, and Tamsin hurried away. "Breakfast is ready."

Chloe returned the chair to its rockers and gently draped the afghan over the back. She couldn't wait to get back to the archives.

And if being there gave her the opportunity to learn more about Mary Pascoe, so much the better. Chloe was willing to give up on the skeleton found in the root cellar. But now she was on the hunt for an immigrant woman's life, and it would take more than Tamsin's reticence to make her stop.

————

When Chloe reached the Pendarvis rowhouse that morning, she was almost bowled over as Holly plunged out the door. "Good morning, Holly!" she said, stepping backwards. Holly, looking adorable in a period dress made of pinstriped blue cotton, flashed her a smile but kept running.

If that child pushed Yvonne Miller down the stairs, Chloe thought bleakly, I don't want to know.

Claudia stood in the door, watching her daughter race away. "Sorry 'bout that."

"She's not in school today?"

"No school due to teacher in-service. Holly's happy roaming the site. Thank God Loren doesn't mind." Claudia straightened her shoulders. "Let's go make some more progress on the collections storage inventory."

Chloe could feel the strain that morning as she and Claudia worked on the second floor of Trelawny House, identifying items that most desperately needed better storage conditions. Claudia went through the motions but seemed so preoccupied that Chloe finally put a hand on her friend's arm to catch her attention. "Are you okay?"

Claudia stared at the shawl she'd been examining. "Not really. I feel a bit ... besieged."

"I suspect the investigation would have been closed if Yvonne's damn journal hadn't disappeared." Chloe pounded one fist against her knee. "It's probably long gone, but I sure wish it would turn up." Preferably in the hands of the person who had, the police seemed to believe, given Yvonne Miller a fatal shove at the top of the Polperro House staircase.

"I'm sorry your visit has gone so badly." Claudia's eyes brimmed with unshed tears. "But speaking selfishly, I don't know how I would have gotten through the last few days without you."

"Don't worry about it. That's what friends are for." Chloe didn't point out the obvious: this was the last day of her residency at Pendarvis, and they'd accomplished far less than hoped.

That could bite me in the butt, Chloe thought. She didn't think Loren would make a bad report, but with everything going on he wasn't likely to make a good report, either. He didn't appear to be particularly interested in her contributions one way or the other.

But that seemed inconsequential in the face of Claudia's problems. When I'm gone she won't have a friend, Chloe thought. She hated the idea of leaving Mineral Point with Claudia still under suspicion.

At noon Claudia left to run some errands and Chloe made haste to the library. She was selfishly pleased to see that no other patrons were in the archives. "I've got something for you, Midge," Chloe said without preamble. She described what she'd found on the bottom of Tamsin's chair. "Does 'T. George/Min. Point' mean anything to you?"

Midge checked the card catalog. "Nothing."

So much for finding business records.

But Midge's eyes—behind fuchsia readers today—narrowed thoughtfully. "Give me two minutes. If I'm not mistaken…" She disappeared into the storage room and returned with a roll of microfilm. Once seated at the reader, she found what she was looking for in about thirty seconds. "Ha!" She got up and let Chloe take a look.

The reader was focused on an advertisement for a furniture store owned by one Theophilus George, cabinetmaker. "Oh my."

"That's 1866," Midge said. "It will take some time to determine the exact period he was in business."

"I suspect that Claudia will be thrilled to do the digging." Chloe glanced at the clock. "With the time I have left, I'd like to go back to the early newspapers. I'm still hoping I'll find a reference to one of the Pascoes."

A couple of high school students wandered in, looking for help with a school project. Chloe went back to skimming the *Miners' Free Press*. She tried not to get sidetracked today, focusing instead on finding "Pascoe" or "Cornish" within the columns of blurry type. She was so focused, in fact, that she passed over something intriguing, and had to scroll back.

Information Wanted—A man by the name of Parnell Peavey left his home in Columbia, Missouri, in April, 1838, with the intention to return to the vicinity of Mineral Point, where he had successfully exploited a mine claim the summer before. He was seen at his customary boardinghouse in Mineral Point on April 19th. From that time to this his friends have not been able to discover any trace whereby they could form any conjecture to what end he has made. He was light in complexion, quick spoken, of steady habits, active and industrious. Any intelligence of his fate communicated by letter, directed to the address below, will be immediately handed to his disconsolate wife.

Chloe leaned back in the chair. This was exactly the kind of notice she had naively hoped to find when she started this quest. Honestly, though, miners must have disappeared with some frequency—perhaps due to accident while traveling, perhaps due to foul play, perhaps due to abruptly setting out for some distant diggings in order to escape a debt.

Chloe had only tried to solve the mystery in the first place because of Tamsin's distressed pleas. Trying to connect poor Mr. Peavey's unknown fate to the skeleton found in *Chy Looan* was a fool's mission. Trying to find evidence that Andrew Pascoe had killed someone and buried the body in his root cellar was equally so. Evelyn's theory about vagrants during the Great Depression, when the cottage was empty, was the most likely explanation.

Chloe printed the Peavey notice anyway. But she'd trade a dozen notices of missing persons for one honest insight into Mary Pascoe's life.

TWENTY-FIVE

"How can I help you, Miss Pascoe?" the storekeeper asked. "You need more flour?"

Mary pushed her shoulders back. "Not today. I've come to buy your teapot there on the shelf. And the serving platter, and two cups and saucers." She pointed. The man had a full set of white ironstone china available, but she wanted pieces from a more expensive set with blue decorations.

"I see!" His eyebrows went up. "Well, you've made a fine choice. Fine indeed."

"I thank you for hiring me to sew for you." That had made the difference. The money Mary made with her baking business went into regular household expenses. She'd paid a carpenter to build a corner hutch for *Chy Looan*. She'd purchased shoes for the children, and picked out cotton cloth to make them new clothes. Last Christmas she'd spent an exorbitant amount to buy Ruan a pocket watch.

Now it was time to buy herself the gift she'd wanted since the day Mrs. Bunney came to Wheal Blackstone so many years ago. Mary watched with pleasure as the storekeeper packed the china into her market basket, nestled in straw. Once outside, she resisted the impulse to swing the basket like a happy child.

In the two years since the Pascoes arrived, the village had grown tremendously. There were general stores and dry goods stores and grocery stores. There were three public houses, a brewery, a courthouse and jail, and a bank. A Temperance Society had formed, and an Odd Fellows lodge. On Independence Day everyone had turned out for speeches, foot races and horse races, and a picnic.

Now, instead of going straight home, she walked farther up the main business street. The morning smelled of woodsmoke and ox dung and the sulphur ghosting from the smelters. Carpenters banged mallets at building sites. Drovers shouted at their animals. Boisterous laughter came from a tavern. A wagon creaked by, jouncing among the ruts.

Ringing faintly among the noise was the metallic clang of hammer on anvil. Mary found Ruan making a gad at his forge. She stood in the shadows, watching as he shaped the iron, studied it, pounded it again. Evidently satisfied, he plunged it with a fierce hiss into a tub of water to cool. Then he reached for the bellows handle and fanned the flames.

"Good morning," Mary greeted him, stepping closer.

"Mary!" He grinned at the surprise. Sweat glowed on his face and stained his limp cotton shirt. Mary leaned in for a quick kiss. She breathed in the irony forge smell imbedded in his clothes, saw the black rings around his fingernails, and knew without doubt that this was the man she wanted to marry.

Her brothers already treated him like kin, but on Sunday afternoons Ruan and Mary usually walked out together, slowly getting to know each other's dreams and fears; discovering the disappointments and opportunities that had shaped them. Mary had found the words on one windy day to tell Ruan about her two dead sisters, and the guilt she carried for her poor choices. "I hope one day you put that burden down," he'd said, but that was all.

Now she said, "I came to invite you to tea."

His eyebrows rose. "When?"

"When can you get away?"

"I don't know." He ran one hand over his face, leaving a black smear on one cheek. "Orders are backed up."

Mary felt a twinge of disappointment but reminded herself that this was all good news. "The sooner we can marry," she said lightly.

"Yes indeed." Ruan's eyes glowed with pleasure. "I've made the arrangements with the stonemason. He's got three houses to build ahead of ours, but he believes he can do it before the snow flies." Ruan had decided that lodging even above the shop wasn't suitable.

"You don't have to build a house for me," Mary said gently. "With Andrew gone, we've plenty of room at *Chy Looan*. Jory thinks it would be fine if you moved in."

Ruan stared down at the anvil, but Mary suspected he was not considering the offer so much as finding the words to disagree. They'd had the conversation before. When Andrew had wed his sweetheart the past spring, her father surprised the couple with the wedding gift of a small home of their own. Instead of the new bride moving into *Chy Looan*, as they'd all expected, Andrew had moved out.

"I was content enough to throw my lot in with your family's when we were new-come to Wisconsin," Ruan said finally. "But this is different, Mary. When we wed, I will become a husband and father. I want to provide for my own."

"I understand." And loved him for it.

He nodded toward her basket. "You've been shopping?"

She brushed aside some of the straw and displayed her purchases.

"Fancy," he observed.

"I want to serve tea to guests. And to the children. I want..." She tried to find the words. She wanted Ida and Will to know they had worth.

"I know." Ruan stole another kiss, grinned, and reached for the bellows handle again.

"Come when you can," she told him. "Ida and Will have been asking for you."

She walked back to *Chy Looan*. Ida was at school and Will working with Jory at the mine, so the cottage was quiet. Mary gingerly unwrapped her new china pieces and put them in the center of the mantel. A candle, and the foot warmer Ruan had made, were on the left. She reached for her old cobbing hammer, thinking it no longer had a place on display, then hesitated. In the end she let it be.

Then she stepped back and proudly surveyed the room. The cottage was becoming what it had not been when they moved in a year earlier—a home. Her brothers' laughter had echoed from the stone walls. Ruan's boots had dried by the fire. Black smoke stains smudged the hearth. The room smelled of wool and baking bread. And now, her china gleamed blue and white on the mantel.

Mary built a fire and hung a kettle of water over the flames. When Ida came home from school, they had tea.

———

Mary got a late start with the day's baking, and twilight was falling gray over the hills before she was ready to pack baskets and head out on her rounds.

"I can help," Ida said. She said that every day.

"Of course you can." Mary handed her a basket filled with slices of still-warm wheat bread. She looped another basket over her arm and picked up a tin lantern.

The two crossed the creek and began climbing the hill, zigzagging from camps to mine sites, stopping wherever there were men about. Soon the baskets were almost empty.

"Let's take this last bit to our mine," Mary told Ida. "Jory and Andrew will likely work longer." Daylight didn't matter to men working underground.

After digging all the lead from their first mine, Mary's brothers had recently sunk a shaft on a new site a bit farther away. In June they'd hit a promising drift and were now digging horizontally into the hill. Andrew wanted to do well for his new wife. As for Jory, well, as long as he had a roof overhead and food on the table, tobacco for his pipe and money for a mug of beer on Saturday afternoons, he was content.

Mary and Ida turned toward the new mine. Campfires flickered on the hill. The smell of frying potatoes popped from iron skillets. A few newcomer Cornish were singing "Camborne Hill."

"My father used to sing that song," Mary said—then paused, tipping her head. "Did you hear that?"

"What?" Ida tipped her head too.

"I thought I heard … it sounded like someone crying."

A hot wind gusted over the hill. For a long moment Mary didn't hear the sound. Then it came again. It sounded very much like a sobbing child.

Mary felt a tightness beneath her ribs. She took Ida's hand. "Come along."

They walked briskly toward the sound. It came and faded, but gradually grew louder. Mary finally stopped at a mine site that had been abandoned for the day. Piles of rubble surrounded the shaft, which had been dug just downhill of a limestone wall. An ore bucket dangled from a windlass over the hole. There was no ladder in the shaft and no one in sight, but a shuddering wail rose from the depths.

Mary leaned over the hole but saw nothing in the inky blackness. "Hello?" she called. "Are you down the shaft?"

The wail broke off sharply. Then, "I'm sorry! I'll do better!" It sounded like a boy's voice, shuddery with tears.

Mary pressed a hand over her mouth. Dear God. Someone had left a child at the bottom of the mine.

"I'll do better!"

She glanced at Ida, who was watching with worried eyes. "Ida, do you know how to find our mine from here? It's just over that rise." She pointed.

Ida nodded solemnly. "I know."

"Take the lantern and go fetch Andrew and Jory and Will. If no one is on the surface, try hollering down the shaft. Bring them back here."

Ida hurried away.

"Help is coming," Mary called down the shaft. No answer.

She was pacing with agitation by the time Ida returned with her brothers and Will. Mary ran to meet them. "There's a child left in the mine. I don't know if he's hurt, but he's certainly frightened."

Andrew and Jory exchanged a hard glance. "Peavey," Jory muttered.

"Who's Peavey?"

"Parnell Peavey owns this plot," Andrew said. "Just got started a week or so ago. We stopped by to say hello." He hesitated.

"And?" Mary demanded. She had no patience for this.

"Peavey's a sucker, originally from Missouri." Andrew looked around, as if expecting the man to materialize from the shadows. "He's well-known among the old-timers. He first came to the lead region years ago, and fought in the Indian wars. Did some mining near Dodgeville."

"He *calls* himself a miner," Jory said derisively, "but he's never hefted a shovel or pick. He's got slaves to do it for him."

"Slaves?" Mary echoed, although she understood. Slavery was officially prohibited in the territory, but no one seemed to care when slave owners brought their black men to labor in the diggings.

"He treats them rough," Andrew said grimly. "Jory and I stay clear of this place."

"Their camp can't be too far away," Jory said. "Although Peavey likely leaves a boss in charge, and boards in town."

"We need to get that child out of the mine," Mary said. "He hasn't made a sound for a while, and that frightens me. After that, we'll decide what to do."

Andrew studied the windlass. "That's a heavy ore bucket. Will, I think it best if we send you down. Are you willing?"

Will nodded and patted his shirt pocket, lumpy with candles. He was a sturdy boy now. Mary had made him attend the winter term of school, but all he really wanted to do was help Andrew and Jory. He was still quiet, but steady and capable.

Mary's brothers gripped the heavy windlass handle and braced their feet. At Andrew's nod, Will climbed into the bucket. He left one leg free to keep the bucket from banging mercilessly against the walls. Andrew and Jory turned the crank, and the bucket slowly disappeared from sight.

It seemed to take an eternity before Will yelled, "I'm down!"

"Did you find anyone?" Mary called. What if the terrified child had fled deeper into the mine? She hugged her arms across her chest, tense with anxiety.

"There's a boy down here. He's hurt."

Mary closed her eyes.

"Can you get him in the bucket?" Andrew hollered.

Will's voice floated from below. "I think so." Another long pause. "Ready!"

Andrew and Jory resumed their stance and wound the crank on the creaking windlass. Finally Will's head and shoulders appeared, then the whole bucket. Jory spread his feet and leaned back. "I got it."

Will leapt from the bucket, leaving a brown-skinned boy— maybe eight or nine years old—huddled alone. Mary lifted the lantern and stifled a horrified cry. The back of the boy's shirt had been sliced to ribbons. The tatters were crusted dark with blood.

Andrew reached for the boy. "Let me help you."

The boy cringed. "I'll do better tomorrow! Please tell Massa Peavey I won't be so lazy no more!"

"Oh, child," Mary whispered. Her heart felt heavy as a lead ingot. "We just want to help you. What's your name?"

"Ezekiel." It came out a whisper. Tears tracked through the dust on his cheeks. His hair was clipped close to his head. His feet were bare, and his patched trousers were tied around his skinny waist with cord.

"There, now," Andrew said softly, as if gentling a nervous horse. He reached into the bucket and eased the trembling boy into his arms. Ezekiel cried in pain. Andrew settled the child on his hip, avoiding pressure against his back.

Jory locked the windlass in place, then stepped away. "A pox on the man who'd flog a poor lad so," he muttered. "Did Peavey do that to you?"

"I'm sorry!" Ezekiel whimpered.

"Let's sort that out later," Mary said urgently. "We need to tend to him."

"I'll take him to my house," Andrew decided. "The rest of you, scatter. We shouldn't all be seen." He turned away.

"Andrew," Mary began.

He looked back impatiently. *"What?"*

"*Chy Looan* is closer," she said. "Take him there."

TWENTY-SIX

CHLOE GOT BACK TO the Pendarvis office at quarter after one. "So sorry I'm late," she began, pulling off her rain jacket.

Evelyn nodded hello from the typewriter. Claudia swiveled in her chair. "No problem."

"I have a gift for you." Chloe scootched the spare chair close to Claudia's desk. "Tamsin has this gorgeous old Boston rocker, and this morning I found a maker's signature penciled on the bottom, and guess what?" She held out the photocopy she'd made of the ad. "Midge found him! He was a cabinetmaker, and owned a furniture store in Mineral Point in the 1860s and 1870s."

"Really?" Claudia snatched the copy. "This is *exactly* the kind of thing I've been searching for! Do you think Tamsin will let me see the chair? Document it?"

"I'm certain she won't mind," Chloe assured her. It was wonderful to see Claudia excited. I've done at least one good thing here, she thought.

"I've been so distracted by crises I haven't even asked how your *Chy Looan* research is going." Claudia looked remorseful. "Any luck identifying the victim who ended up in the root cellar?"

"No," Chloe admitted. "It was an unrealistic goal, I think." She brightened. "But I did learn something interesting along the way. The first owners of the cottage were named Pascoe. Mary Pascoe owned it for over fifty years. Isn't that cool?"

"Mary Pascoe?" Claudia mused. "I've heard that name. Oral tradition suggests she was a real trailblazer. The local Cornish Club members all speak her name with pride."

"I found her obit, and it's glowing."

"A grad student looking at the economic impact of the 1839 financial crash found a story about Mary Pascoe baking bread and giving it to hungry families."

Awesome, Chloe thought.

"She didn't leave any written records behind, of course, but—" Claudia's phone shrilled, and she reached for it. "Hello? ... How many? Where's Gerald? ... Oh. Has Rita gone home? ... Oh. Okay, I'll take it." She hung up and looked at Chloe. "A surprise group of homeschoolers just arrived. Rita was scheduled to leave early this afternoon, and her ride is on the way. No one knows where Gerald is. He took a late lunch, but he should be back by now. I need him to be available for general visitors."

"You deal with the homeschoolers," Chloe said. "I'll go find Gerald." She grabbed her jacket and totebag and headed out.

The rain had tapered off, but more dark clouds were building overhead as Chloe quickly searched the site. Gerald wasn't anywhere in the rowhouse. He wasn't in Polperro House, or Pendarvis House, or Trelawny House.

She glanced toward Dark Hill. Had Gerald spent his lunch break working on the badger hole? Might as well check, she thought, and hurried across the street.

Wind whipped tree branches as she started up the path. The brittle brown fists of dead Queen Anne's lace flowers bobbed angrily. A squirrel stopped in the trail as if shocked to see a human before scurrying back into the undergrowth. The air smelled dank.

Chloe was nearing Gerald and Loren's badger hole when she heard the snuffling sobs of a crying child.

She froze, pulse racing. *You've tapped into a local legend,* Claudia had said. *Every once in a while someone comes down from the hill saying they've heard a child crying.*

No way was that a bird, or a rabbit, or anything else that lived in the forest. *But,* Chloe told herself, that did not mean she was hearing some ghost child echoing through time. School was not in session today. What if a couple of bored kids had gotten into some kind of trouble?

Chloe nibbled her lip, then took a cautious step forward. Two more steps and something unexpectedly bright, blue and white, blinked from the muted forest floor. A lonely domino peeked from beneath a fallen leaf.

Her mouth went dry. Dear God, when she'd searched for Gerald, she hadn't seen Holly on the site proper. "Holly?" Chloe shouted, looking wildly about.

No answer.

"Is someone hurt?"

More weeping.

Chloe followed the sound to a mounded shrub growing against a limestone upthrust. Echoing off the rock, the whimpering cries sounded odd. Hollow, sort of. Chloe's nerves tingled. "*Holly!*" she yelled. She felt gooseflesh rise on her skin and rubbed her arms. The woods were dim. The air felt oppressive. But nobody was here.

Then she spotted a broken branch dangling from the right side of the shrub. *Somebody* had recently forced their way past. Chloe did the same, squeezing between the shrub and the rock face. Branches raked her jacket. She sheltered her face with one bent arm.

She was so focused on minimizing blood loss that she didn't think about her footing … until solid ground became open air. Caught off-balance, she stumbled backwards with an inelegant screech.

A black hole, almost hidden beneath the shrub, had opened at her feet. Chloe took a deep breath to steady herself. *Geez.* She'd come very close to falling into a freaking mineshaft.

How far back did it date? Her head filled with visions of sweating Cornish miners, digging deep where the Americans had contented themselves with easy pickings.

But that was irrelevant now. She knelt and peered into the hole. Propped against one edge of the very old shaft was a very modern aluminum ladder.

Who had found this shaft, brought the ladder, and gone exploring? Whoever it was hadn't mentioned the discovery to Loren. Unless maybe … maybe Loren *was* the explorer. And/or Gerald.

A whimper rose from the shaft.

"Holly?"

More whimpers.

Chloe silently cursed whomever had left the ladder to beckon Holly or whatever curious child had found it. The sound was fading again. Was the child seriously hurt? Or moving deeper into the mine?

Chloe hesitated, torn between investigating herself and going for professional help. She was definitely not eager to venture down that ladder into the dark unknown. But how long would it take for her to get back to Pendarvis and make the call? To wait for help, and then guide the responders here? What tragedy might conclude in those extra moments?

"Dammit!" Chloe muttered. She twisted to her knees and began the awkward maneuver of getting situated on the ladder. "Hang on," she called to the depths. "I'm coming!"

———

"Chief's waiting for you," Marie told Roelke as he came through the door. He nodded, grabbed a folder he'd left on the officers' desk, and went into the chief's private sanctum. Officer Skeet Deardorff was already there. Roelke took the empty seat, gritting his teeth to keep from wincing. At least sitting straight down wasn't as painful as climbing into his truck had been.

"Did Zietz complete the second buy?" Chief Naborski asked.

"She did."

Skeet thumped one fist against his palm. "Excellent."

Chief Naborski tipped his chair back with a small, satisfied smile. "Alright. Talk us through what happens tomorrow."

"Tomorrow is the final buy. Assuming all goes as planned, we hit the house right away. I've already requested the warrant."

"Backup?" Skeet asked.

"In addition to the three of us plus Conroy"—one of the EPD part-timers—"Troy Blakely from Palmyra is going to assist, and one officer from North Prairie. We should be good." Roelke opened the file, produced the map he'd drawn of the property on Hackberry Lane, and outlined his plan for hitting the house.

When the talk-through was complete Chief Naborski banged his chair back down on four legs. "Well done, Officer McKenna. It's your show tomorrow." He paused. "Officer Deardorff, will you give us a minute?"

Once the door had closed behind Skeet, the chief gave Roelke a level gaze. "Roelke. Are you alright?"

Dammit. "Yessir."

"You don't look good."

Roelke fought the urge to look for a spreading bloodstain. "I'm just a little tired."

"This is way too important to screw around with. Will you be good to go?"

"Yessir. I will be good to go."

"Very well."

Roelke knew a dismissal when he heard one. He rose with as much ease as possible and made his escape.

In the main room, Skeet was busy at his locker. "Say, Roelke," he said over his shoulder. "You had your interview with the Police Committee about the advanced training gig, right?"

"Yep."

"Have you heard anything?"

"Nope."

"I suppose we'll know soon enough."

"I suppose so." Roelke pulled out the desk chair and went through the sitting-down-without-groaning routine again.

But once settled, the question nagged. Well, hunh, he thought wearily. On Monday, winning the opportunity had seemed incredibly important. But honestly, since his interview on Wednesday, he'd forgotten all about it.

———

Chloe hadn't climbed down very far before the meager light from above vanished. It was disorienting to descend into darkness. A bit spooky too. She'd considered turning on her penlight, but she needed both hands for the ladder. So down and down she went, moving one hand or foot at a time. Her fingers began to ache, and she realized she was clutching the metal convulsively, but couldn't seem to stop.

After ten minutes or an hour, she wasn't sure, one foot hit solid earth. Chloe pulled her totebag from her shoulder and scrabbled inside. Her fingers first found the iron sticking tommy she'd been carrying around, and she almost laughed. "My kingdom for a candle or ten," she muttered. She also found the foil-wrapped herby pasty Tamsin had given her for lunch, and her notebook, and several pens. Finally she found the slim flashlight and gratefully flicked it on. The tiny beam wasn't nearly as bright as she wanted, but it was better than nothing.

She stood beside the ladder—the only space where she *could* stand. A passage led off to the left, but it was no more than four feet high. It was colder down here, and damper. Moisture gleamed among the gravel beneath her shoes. She could hear water dripping on stone.

What she didn't hear was the childish weeping that had brought her down here in the first place.

"Hello?" she called, her voice echoing strangely against the stone. "Holly? Is anyone there?"

No answer. Chloe rubbed her chin. Was the child hiding? Should she climb back out? But what if the child was unconscious, or bleeding to death? I've come this far, Chloe thought. She couldn't weenie out now.

For fortification, she did delay long enough to gobble part of the pasty. She threw the crust off to one side. If some of the knackers Tamsin had told her about lived in this mine, she might as well stay on their good side.

Then she bent over and got moving.

Chloe quickly realized that every mining scene she'd ever imagined was a fantasy. She hadn't expected Mammoth Cave, but she had imagined easy-to-navigate passages. Now she remembered the short shovel she'd seen on display in Polperro House, and Claudia's comment about the men digging on their knees. The men who'd worked this mine had surely spent a lot of time on their knees, because there wasn't room to stand erect. Chloe crept along with knees bent and back hunched, occasionally banging her head against rock anyway. She wished whomever had left the ladder had left a helmet behind too.

The passage was narrow and twisty. At times she splashed through shallow streams because there was nowhere else to put her feet. Water dripped from the ceiling and trickled down the irregular walls. Chloe also had to inch past—and, once, over—piles of rock debris. But that made sense too—why would miners waste energy and time hauling every bit of rubble to the surface? If what they hacked from the earth didn't contain lead, they simply shoved it aside, or behind them, and kept going.

Every few steps she paused. "Hello? Holly? Anybody?" Her calls bounced from wall to wall, and were never returned.

Progress was slow, so Chloe knew she hadn't gone far when a voice in her head said *enough*. She didn't want to give up, but it would be foolish to keep going. The silence was ominous. No one knew where she was. She had to go back and get help. She knew what she'd heard, and she wouldn't back down until someone believed her.

Frustrated, she studied her surroundings. Had she been so focused on forward motion that she'd missed some side passage branching off? A frightened child might have found a hidey-hole among the rock that she hadn't seen. As she began retracing her steps, Chloe paused every few feet and let the narrow beam of light play over the rough rock.

Suddenly the light flashed on something pale and shiny—just a glimpse between two jags of stone. Stepping closer, Chloe discovered a cleft in the rock maybe eight inches wide, about as long as her forearm. Something was wedged into the crevice. A bunch of somethings. The shininess was a row of plastic storage bags.

"What on earth?" She drew one out—the type of gallon-sized reclosable bag she used to freeze leftovers. This one was packed with smaller plastic bags. She removed one of those. Her penlight revealed the contents: some sort of small white lumps.

Oh, God. She was holding a bag of crack cocaine.

She'd never actually seen crack cocaine, but she lived with a cop and had heard his descriptions. She'd also heard him talk about the need to educate those who believed that small towns like Eagle—and Mineral Point—were immune to the danger. Now she remembered the light she'd seen, and then not seen, on Dark Hill the night before. She remembered the safety rope repeatedly removed from around the badger hole, as if someone was discouraging Loren and Gerald from returning.

She also flashed on something Investigator Higgins had said the day they'd met: *We've got our share of domestic abuse calls, speeders, kids on drugs…* Evidently some of those kids kept their drugs right here.

Except there was way more here than some teen user would need to stash. Chloe stared unhappily at the crack. This was more likely to belong to a dealer.

A gnawing fear replaced her apprehension. She didn't want to think about why she'd heard a child crying in a mine frequented by a drug dealer. All she wanted to do was get out of there and call the cops before said dealer showed up.

Her hand trembled as she re-zipped the bag and stuffed it back into the crevice. There were bags of pot stashed in there as well. Then the flashlight beam touched on something else. A cheap spiral notebook was stashed here too, also enclosed in plastic to protect it from moisture and mud.

Chloe looked over her shoulders and listened. Nothing suggested that she was not still alone. She extracted the notebook.

Only a few pages had been used. Scrawled in columns were dates, names, and figures—probably quantities purchased and money paid. She hastily skimmed the list of names. Near the end, one line jumped from the page as if highlighted in neon marker: *Yvonne Miller.*

Chloe's jaw dropped. Dr. Yvonne Miller, Ph.D., had used pot or crack cocaine? That was almost unbelievable. But Miller had been an unhappy person. Maybe she'd been looking for something, anything, to ease whatever caused her unhappiness.

Chloe jammed the notebook into her totebag. Cops could come down here and fetch the goods, and the notebook would prove her story. Quivering with the need to get the hell out of there, she scurried as fast as she could back in the direction she'd come.

"Hey!" a man bellowed up ahead.

Chloe went still. Had help arrived? Or a drug dealer?

"I'm talking to you, bitch!"

Ice formed in her veins. Questions answered.

She tried frantically to think through her options. Problem was, she didn't have options. The man was between her and the mine entrance. As desperately as she wanted to reach the ladder, she wanted even more to avoid the man.

"I know you're down here!"

Chloe turned again and scrambled deeper into the winding passage. Maybe there was another exit up ahead.

She tripped and fell more than once. She banged her elbows and konked her head. Her feet were soaked from splashing through wet patches and her chinos clung clammily to her ankles. She shivered uncontrollably.

Just keeping going, she ordered herself. She crawled over a rubble heap. The passage opened up a bit, and she rounded a corner ... and hit a dead end.

"No, no, no," she whispered, madly shining her measly light over the jagged rock walls. Up, down, left, right. There was nowhere to go, and the man hunting her was closing in.

TWENTY-SEVEN

CHLOE'S FLASHLIGHT FLICKERED. SHE convulsively punched the *Off* button, plunging herself into depthless blackness.

"That's not gonna help," the man scoffed. "I don't like snoops. And nobody in this town is gonna miss you."

He wants to kill me, Chloe thought. She realized she was panting, and forced herself to slow her breathing and *think*. She'd reached a dead end. Her only chance to escape whoever this was, and whatever he had planned for her, was to somehow get past him and beat him back to the ladder.

She was in a space not much larger than a phone booth. She pressed herself against the rough rock just beyond the final turn, to the right of the straightaway. Then she slipped her hand into her totebag and drew out the only remotely weapon-like item she carried. Don't think about it, she ordered herself. Just be ready to *do* it.

The light from the man's flashlight was growing brighter. She saw the beam's lead edge. "There's nowhere to go," he sneered. "You're at the end of the line, lady." His voice was close.

Chloe clenched her teeth and forced herself to stay silent as the arc of light got bigger. She held her breath, feeling every thudding beat of her heart, and slowly raised her arm.

The first thing she saw was the man's hand gripping the flashlight, held in front of his body. As he stepped into view Chloe tightened her hold on the sticking tommy and swung her arm with all the force she could muster.

When the cast iron point struck flesh he screamed and dropped his flashlight. In the crazy swing of light she glimpsed a young man's contorted face. One hand was pressed against his left shoulder. A bandana was tied pirate-style over his head.

"Bitch!" Rita's boyfriend gasped, sounding as incredulous as he did angry.

Chloe struck again. Bandana Man stumbled backwards. His head struck stone. He grunted and slumped to the ground.

She leapt over his legs and started back through the passage. She punched on the penlight but was rewarded with only a feeble yellow thread. I should have snatched his light, she realized, but no way was she turning around. Cell-deep instinct urged her forward: *Go, go, go.* Scrabble through this tunnel. Squeeze through this narrow bit. Scramble over this pile of rocks.

Her light flickered again.

She had no idea how close she was to the ladder. Maybe I can pull it up after me, she thought. She'd race back to Pendarvis, call 911, show the rescue squad and the cops the way to the hidden mine. Maybe Bandana Man wasn't badly hurt, just unconscious.

Her foot caught on a rock and she landed hard on one knee. The penlight slipped from her grasp. It blinked and went out. The blackness was overwhelming, without depth or shadow.

An inarticulate bellow came from behind her. *Shit.* Bandana Man was after her again.

Frenzied, Chloe pawed the gravel and mud around her. When she finally found the light she pushed the button. She punched it over and over, as if urgent need might override the physics of dead batteries. Nothing.

She tried to rise, banged her head, fell back down. Glancing over her shoulder she saw the edge of her pursuer's powerful light. He could see where he was going; she could not. No way could she outrun him. He'd be on her in moments, a whole lot angrier than he'd been before.

———

"It's good to be here," Libby said. "The farm feels like a safe place."

"It is a safe place," Roelke said. He and his cousin were sitting in lawn chairs behind his farmhouse, watching the kids play. Libby held a Leinies in one hand. Roelke was drinking iced tea, poured from a large jar in the fridge. Before going to Mineral Point, Chloe had made sun tea with mint sprigs for him. It was the kind of thing she did. Having even this ephemeral connection with her right now was good.

Libby swirled her bottle, watching the lime wedge she'd pushed into the beer. "You're sure you're healing okay?"

"Yes."

"No sign of infection? Or bleeding?"

"No."

"We could still go—"

"It's okay, Libby. I'm being careful."

Justin ran over to join them. "Is dinner almost ready?"

"Nope." Libby ruffled his hair. "I haven't even started the grill yet."

"Oh." He looked disappointed, but turned and ran back to his sister. Justin chased Deirdre toward the garden, but before he could tag her she whirled and began chasing him. Justin paced his steps, running slowly so the little girl didn't get discouraged.

"Say, I promised to do a Scout thing with Justin on Sunday afternoon," Libby said. "If you're free, would you mind watching Deirdre for a few hours? I could leave her with a neighbor, but I'd rather leave her here."

"Sure," Roelke said. "Chloe expects to be home by noon. She made Deirdre some kind of ballerina skirt, and has been waiting to give it to her. I know she'd be happy to babysit if I get called in to work or something."

"Everything go okay with that drug thing you're working on?" Libby asked.

"Yeah. The young woman made another buy today, no problem. Assuming the same thing happens tomorrow, we'll hit the house. It could be big." He was eager to stop this particular flow of drugs into Eagle. And if they found a big stash of cash, so much the better. A portion of whatever he found would eventually come back to the Eagle Police Department. Maybe next time the PD could afford to send two officers to special training programs, without having to beg the Police Committee for funds.

"Just be careful, okay?" Libby asked quietly.

"I'm always careful." He saw the fear in her eyes and amended, "But I'll be extra-careful tomorrow."

"Sorry." She stared at the trees in the distance. "I'm just feeling ... " She lifted her free hand and let it drop.

"Vulnerable?" This was the new Libby. Roelke wanted the old Libby back.

The kids' laughter floated over the lawn. It was a gray afternoon, clouds dulling the first bursts of gold and crimson in the forest beyond the fields. Something about it made Roelke's heart ache.

"Actually," Libby said finally, "I feel helpless."

Roelke looked away. He felt defeated. All he'd ever aspired to do was be a good cop and take care of his family. It had never before occurred to him that he couldn't manage both.

And he'd been so damn cocksure. What had he told Adam? *We have to trust the Palmyra cops to deal with Raymo if he goes too far. The fact that Libby is family doesn't change that.*

But the Palmyra cops couldn't touch Raymo. Worse, Raymo had bested *him*.

Justin was chasing Deirdre, making roaring noises, hands raised like predatory claws. Deirdre laughed so hard she could hardly run.

As Roelke watched the two children he loved, his bleak melancholy sparked to a hot flash of anger. He didn't have the luxury of defeat, or fear.

Something inside him shifted. He felt it so clearly that he was surprised that Libby hadn't heard the *click* as everything he held sacrosanct, inviolable, hitched into a new alignment.

"It'll be okay," he told her. "I really think it will."

———

I, Chloe thought, am screwed. She sank onto her butt, hearing her ragged breath in the stillness, sucking in stale air. She still clenched the sticking tommy, but he knew she had it now. It would be a lot tougher to land another blow.

Suddenly she heard a primal groaning that emanated from the earth itself. Old support timbers shrieked as if in pain. A knocking sound pounded in her ears. She threw herself forward, half crawling, half scuttling, her free hand feeling the way in front of her. Something like hail pelted her. Dust swirled in the air, thick and gritty.

Then a deafening roar filled the mine. Larger stones bounced against her. She curled into a fetal ball, arms tucked over her head, as the roof caved in.

Chloe heard fearful little cries and realized they came from her. She expected a crushing blow any second. There was nothing to do but wait.

After an eternity the noise faded as quickly as it had come. Dazed, Chloe lifted her head. She tasted grit and was wracked with a coughing spasm. Evidently she was still alive.

She tried moving her arms, her legs. She felt battered and sore, but everything seemed to work.

"Hey!" she yelled.

No answer.

Chloe crawled backwards and quickly hit rubble that had not been there before. She patted the huge stones, trying to get a sense of this new reality. She couldn't find an opening. The collapse had plugged the passageway. "You okay back there?"

Still no answer. Was Bandana Man trapped on the other side of the cave-in? Had he been buried? She had no idea, and there was nothing she could do for him.

"Okay," she said aloud. "Get moving." It would not be easy to reach the ladder in sooty blackness, but she had no other choice. With one hand tracing the rock wall beside her, and the other extended high in front in hopes of preventing a fatal cranial blow, she inched toward the entrance.

She'd been closer than she'd dared hope. Almost imperceptibly, the darkness eased. One foot hit the ladder. She grabbed it with both hands. For a moment she leaned against the cool metal, half laughing and half crying. But she couldn't linger.

Climbing was a struggle. Chloe was scraped and banged and, frankly, trying not to freak out. "You can do this," she muttered. Grab, step. Grab, step. She kept her head tipped back, gulping lung-fuls of fresh air, heartened to leave the inky darkness behind and below. When she reached the surface she felt as triumphant as Syl-vester Stallone climbing the museum steps in *Rocky*.

Miraculously, the day looked much as it had when she'd left it. She stumbled down the hill, and jogged across the street and up to the row-house. The entry room was deserted. When she lurched into the sec-ond office, Evelyn and Claudia turned shocked faces her way.

"Call 911," Chloe gasped. "Tell them an old mineshaft on Dark Hill collapsed, and somebody's either trapped inside or ... " She took a deep breath. "Or dead."

TWENTY-EIGHT

EVELYN REACHED FOR THE phone.

"Dear God, Chloe, what *happened*?" Claudia looked aghast. She still wore an 1840s dress and tidy white cap. "Who got trapped?"

"Where's Holly?" Chloe demanded. "Have you seen her lately?"

"Why, I saw her not twenty minutes ago," Claudia assured her. "Holly's fine."

Thank God, Chloe thought. Limp with relief, she dropped into a chair. She held a palm up, waiting until she knew help was on the way. Then she explained how her search for Gerald had led her up Dark Hill, and how the sound of a child crying led her down the ladder.

"An open mineshaft?" Claudia's eyes were round. "On Pendarvis land?"

"It's very well hidden. And I swear, the sound of weeping was coming from it. I was afraid it was Holly. I found one of her dominoes near the entrance. But ... there was no child down there." Chloe hadn't figured that part out yet. Her brain felt foggy. "I think I need to talk to the police before I say anything more."

"But . . . a cave-in?" Evelyn sounded horrified. "Dear heavens."

Claudia closed her eyes for a moment. "We've had so much rain this fall . . . "

"I've got to meet the first responders so I can show them where to find the shaft," Chloe said. "Where's Loren?"

"I don't know," Evelyn said helplessly. "He's been out all afternoon."

"He'll show up sooner or later," Claudia said. "Come on, Chloe. I'll come with you."

They walked down to Shake Rag Street to wait for the responders—Investigator Higgins and a cop Chloe hadn't met, rescue squad, firefighters. After giving a condensed version of her underground escapade, she led half a dozen people to the mineshaft.

Claudia shook her head when Chloe held back branches and pointed to the hole. "Unbelievable."

"Holly and I walked by yesterday without noticing anything," Chloe mused. "She must have dropped the domino then."

"Ms. Ellefson." Higgins beckoned her aside. "Let's let the experts take it from here. I'd like to go back down the hill and get your statement."

Once back on Shake Rag Street Chloe told him in more detail what had happened. "I didn't get a good look at the guy chasing me. He wore a red bandana tied over his head, just like Rita's boyfriend."

"Rita, the interpreter here?"

Chloe nodded. Rita's possible role in this mess was a sickening disappointment. She brought me tea! Chloe thought. She wanted to believe that the young interpreter was innocent, kept in the dark by her bad-boy boyfriend. But Rita was deep in debt, and earning minimum wage at a historic site that would soon close for the season—or altogether. She'd told Chloe she didn't think it was safe to work on Dark Hill, which might have been part of the campaign to discourage visitors. Had Rita left the nasty note? Had she or her boyfriend been on the hill when Chloe ended up stuck in the badger hole, or the evening she'd seen the flickering light up there?

Well, Chloe thought, all I can do is provide facts. She'd assumed the man in the mine was Rita's boyfriend, but maybe not. Maybe lots of men in Mineral Point wore bandanas. The cops would sort it out.

"Rita left early this afternoon," Chloe told the investigator.

"We'll track her down."

Chloe was happy to let the cops pick the sordid tangles apart. "Anyway," she concluded, "here's the notebook I found hidden with the drugs." She handed it over. Higgins had already confiscated the sticking tommy.

"Well done," he said quietly. "You can provide a written statement later. Right now, I want the EMTs to check you out."

Chloe felt battered, and knew she probably looked worse. "Okay."

After cleaning Chloe's abrasions and bandaging the worst of them, one of the EMTs gave her a thumbs-up. "It's all superficial," he assured her. "You'll ache for a while, but you're fine."

Chloe was sitting on the back ledge of the rescue squad truck. "Thanks," she said. "I appreciate it." She stood, trying not to wince, and looked at Dark Hill. "Any word from the mine?"

The man shook his head. "Nothing yet."

Chloe nodded. She felt strange. A little lightheaded. Things had been moving fast, but now she didn't know what to do. Claudia remained with the responders as site representative, but Chloe felt no desire to go back herself. She needed time to sort out what had happened up there.

The cave-in had come exactly when and where she needed it. If it hadn't happened, she'd likely be dead by now. Chilling thought.

Maybe the recent incessant rains had, as Claudia suggested, caused part of the ceiling to collapse, and the timing was pure coincidence. Maybe an old miner had been looking out for her. Heck, maybe she'd been protected because she'd tossed her pasty crust aside for a starving knacker.

She would never know. But she did understand that the Cornish miners had named the hill well. *Mena Dhu*, she thought, staring across the street. Dark Hill.

She glanced at her watch. The site was due to close soon. I better check in with Evelyn, Chloe thought. Then she could go to Tamsin's place, take a bath, call Roelke, and go to bed. That notion was so appealing that tears brimmed in her eyes. She swiped them away and plodded up to the rowhouse.

"Still no sign of Loren," Evelyn reported, glancing toward the director's silent office with a hint of reproach.

That was odd. "Did Gerald show up?"

"Haven't seen him."

Chloe had no idea what to make of that, either. But she was too tired to worry about it. "Okay. Claudia's still on the hill. I'm going home."

"Um ... " Evelyn looked apologetic. "The woman in the gift shop called right before you got back. She wanted to know who's taking responsibility for the cash."

"Audrey told me she's handled it before."

"Audrey isn't on today. It's someone new."

There's no one else, Chloe thought wearily. Claudia was on the hill. Loren and Gerald had disappeared. Rita was, for all Chloe knew, in police custody. Lovely. "I'll take care of it."

"Thank you." Evelyn nodded.

Chloe walked around to the gift shop entrance and found a plump woman with longish brown hair and an impatient expression waiting expectantly behind the counter.

"You can go," Chloe said without preamble. She didn't have the energy for chitchat.

"Oh!" The other woman clearly hadn't expected that. "Thanks."

Chloe had no idea what the procedure was for checking for errors and depositing the money. She also didn't know how to use the cash register, which was old enough to be accessioned. She walked around the counter, settled on the stool, and tried to open the register. No cheerful ding, no cash drawer sliding from the inner regions. Shit. Well, the cash would just have to stay where it was.

Although the shop was officially open for another half hour, no one else was there. Chloe closed her eyes, trying to center herself in the blessedly peaceful stillness. But her thoughts whirled like a cyclone. What was happening on the hill? Was Bandana Man dead or alive? How much damage had she done with the miners' candlestick? The feel of iron spike meeting flesh and bone had become a visceral memory, the moment replaying in not just her mind but her hand and arm, her muscles and bone. He threatened to kill me, she reminded herself, but that didn't make her feel better.

She hoped the cave-in hadn't buried the drug cache. At least she'd saved the notebook that seemed to label Dr. Yvonne Miller as a buyer. Her bizarre druggie status presented a new angle for Higgins to investigate. Had Miller not paid Bandana Man what she owed? Had she threatened to expose him? Had he slipped onto the site Wednesday morning, caught her alone, and pushed her to her death? It was possible.

"But it's not that simple," Chloe muttered. If Yvonne Miller's death was related to some deal-gone-bad with a crack seller, there was no good reason why her green journal had disappeared. Surely Miller wouldn't have documented drug use in a journal she'd used for academic notes.

Claudia had seen Yvonne with her journal the morning she died. By the time the cops arrived, the notebook had disappeared. Cops had searched the site without finding it.

Chloe thought about that for a while, unmoving. Finally she straightened, pulled her own notebook out, and opened to the page where she'd made notes about Miller's death. Yvonne Miller had been using the green journal to compile research notes for her book. Her research must have uncovered something so disturbing that someone was willing to steal, and perhaps even to kill, to get it.

Chloe chewed on the end of the pen.

- *Book might tarnish Pendarvis's reputation, providing fuel to those who want to close the site*

Most people in town didn't want Pendarvis to be closed. If it was possible for someone to slip onto the site unseen that morning to accost Yvonne, that theory pointed suspicious fingers at Winter, Pendarvis staff, and a whole lot of local residents.

Chloe chewed her pen for another few minutes.

- *Book might cast aspersions on Cornish community*

Chloe remembered Miller's sarcastic *It's all Cornification* comment. The woman seemed to resent stories told about the early Cornish immigrants, and there were still plenty of descendants in

Mineral Point who wouldn't appreciate their ancestors being portrayed poorly.

- *Book criticizes some local hero*

Perhaps Miller had fixed her academic sights on some particular revered figure. It was safe to assume that some of the local leaders in the territorial days, even educated professionals, were hard, rough men. A mining frontier was filled with restless souls who relieved their lonely labor by boozing, gambling, and brawling. Slavery was accepted. Settlers fought with brutal zeal to drive Native Americans from the area. Those things, heinous as they were by modern standards, were widely accepted at the time. So … had Miller discovered something else?

Chloe slapped her notebook closed, slipped it away, and came around the counter to pace. The gift shop was, as Audrey had said, tidy. Immaculate, actually, with merchandise aligned on shelves and tourist brochures stacked neatly. How had Audrey managed to straighten the shop so quickly after the official search? It had taken Chloe ages to make some semblance of order from the chaos left in the cops' wake.

Perhaps the cops hadn't been quite as thorough in here.

Folding her arms, Chloe considered. Claudia had said that this space had once been used as a workshop and reception area for Bob and Edgar, the two creative men who had managed to save the Pendarvis buildings from destruction. What else had Claudia said? *A natural spring runs under the building, and they created a little fish pond right in the floor. We have it covered now…*

The fish pond entrance was probably covered by a bookshelf or something, completely inaccessible. Still, there was no harm in looking.

Chloe walked down the shop's first aisle, keeping her gaze down, studying the floorboards. No sign of a hidden fish pond. But in the central aisle, a woven rag rug covered much of the floor. It was an odd choice for a gift shop, where visitors were likely to rumple, if not trip over, the rug. Chloe kicked it aside—and saw a trap door in the floor.

She crouched and raised an iron ring that sat flush in a well in the wooden hatch. She got a good grip on the ring and pulled. The door was more awkward than heavy, and she raised it with only a brief struggle.

Water still flowed beneath the building. Bob and Edgar's little pond no longer held fish, but it still existed. The space was rectangular, about two feet deep. Several iron bars helped support the trap door. The men had added a cement liner. Gravel lined the bottom. Larger stones were piled on one side, out of the water. Perhaps they had once supported potted plants.

Today, they supported a journal bound in green leather.

TWENTY-NINE

CHLOE REACHED THROUGH THE iron bars and grabbed Dr. Yvonne Miller's journal. Someone *may* have pushed the scholar to her death, but someone had *definitely* stolen her journal and hidden it away.

Chloe shoved the trap door back in place and smoothed the rag rug over it. Back at the counter, she flipped through the journal. Miller's handwriting was tight and dense. It would take hours to read everything, but on one page, several words and phrases were underlined: *slavery*…*child abuse*…*Parnell Peavey*…

Parnell Peavey? Chloe closed her eyes, trying to remember where she'd seen that name before. It came back in a flash—he was the subject of the Missing Persons notice she'd found in the *Miners' Free Press*. But she'd been studying the newspapers in hopes of learning something about the body found in Adam's cottage. It seemed extraordinary to find his name in Dr. Miller's notes.

Then snippets of remembered conversation exploded in her brain like popcorn. Her gut knotted. "No," she whispered. It couldn't be.

Could it?

There was one fact she could check. Chloe grabbed the phone book and flipped through until she found the section she wanted. She ran a finger down the page. *There.* There it was.

This isn't proof, she reminded herself. And whatever the answer, it was not her place to investigate.

She slipped the journal into her totebag. Then she grabbed the phone and dialed 911. "I need to get a message to the Mineral Point police," she told the clerk who answered.

"Is this an emergency?"

"Yes! I'm at Pendarvis Historic Site, but not up with the rescue team at the mine. I really need to talk with Investigator Higgins. If he can't come right away, please send another officer. I'll wait at … um … Trelawny House." She didn't want to wait here, where she'd found the journal. If anyone saw her disappear inside Trelawny, they'd just think she was working on the collections storage project.

"Can you spell—"

The shop door opened. Chloe hung up the phone and tried to compose herself before turning to greet whomever.

"Chloe?" Evelyn called. "I'm heading home. Shall I lock up the office?"

"Sure," Chloe said. She was so conscious of the notebook that she half expected her totebag to spontaneously combust.

"Are you all right?" Evelyn tipped her head. "You've had a wretched day. Maybe you should just lock up the shop and go home too."

"I think I will. I don't expect we'll get any last-minute shoppers." Chloe mustered a faint smile. "Have a good evening."

After Evelyn left, Chloe locked up and hurried down the path toward the lower property. The clouds were low and dark. Thunder cracked the sky. More rain was on the way. Just what the team on Dark Hill needed.

But what was happening on the hill, and what had happened to *her* on the hill, were receding. She imagined Miller's green journal pulsing in her totebag like Edgar Allan Poe's telltale heart. Had she screwed up? Her overpowering instinct had been to simply keep the damn thing safe until the cops arrived, but she probably shouldn't have taken the journal. Shouldn't have even touched it.

The trail came out behind Pendarvis House, middle of the three homes on Shake Rag Street. She started to walk past, then stopped. Had anyone thought to lock up the house? Probably not, she thought with an inner sigh. Nobody on staff was even around.

Her hand was on the doorknob when a roll of thunder shuddered through the afternoon. It almost, but not quite, hid the *crack* of a gunshot. Splinters of stone flew from the wall.

Chloe threw the door open, leapt into the small kitchen, slammed the door behind her, and turned the bolt. Her pulse raced. Who the hell was *shooting* at her?

She dug the site master key from her pocket with shaking fingers. A discreet modern lock had been installed beneath the doorknob left from Bob and Edgar's day. She fumbled the key into the lock and managed to turn it.

But any sense of security was illusory. The shot had come from the site's upper property behind her. If the shooter had a key, she'd just trapped herself in Pendarvis House. Claudia had said the front door was sealed. There was no other way out.

Chloe's mouth felt dry as cotton. She had to find a weapon or a hiding place. Preferably both.

The kitchen had nothing to offer. She plunged into the parlor—and stopped short. "*No,*" she moaned.

Holly sat on the floor in the middle of the room with her dominoes, staring at Chloe with obvious concern.

Chloe had known fear in the mine, when Bandana Man threatened to kill her. She'd known it moments before, when someone fired a shot at her. That fear paled compared to the cold, soul-crushing terror that came as she realized she'd trapped herself in Pendarvis House with this little girl.

She scanned the room frantically, then snatched an iron poker from a set of fireplace tools on the hearth. As she turned her gaze landed on the portrait above the mantel. The woman seemed to stare across the room with special intensity. *Protect the child.*

Chloe looked toward the far wall. The room's only bed sat in one corner. Above the bed was the small ceiling hatch she'd noticed before.

She darted across the room. "I'm sorry," she muttered as she leapt onto the gorgeous white-with-red quilt covering the bed. She dropped the poker.

Holly pointed in horror at the bed: *You're not supposed to touch!*

"Come here, Holly. It's an emergency. Leave your dominoes for now. Just for now. *Hurry.*"

Holly must have understood the urgency, because she jumped up and climbed onto the bed. Her eyes were wide, the pupils dark as midnight.

"There's a bad person outside." Chloe reached above her head and shoved on the hatch cover. It moved easily. "I'm going to boost you up there to hide, okay?" She laced her fingers together and held her hands out for Holly's foot.

Chloe wouldn't be able to eel through the hatch to the crawl space without a ladder, but it wasn't difficult to get Holly up. The little girl's head and shoulders disappeared. She managed to get one knee over the edge, and she scrambled from sight.

"Put the cover back in place," Chloe hissed, but Holly was already sliding the door back where it belonged.

Someone rattled the doorknob.

Please don't let them have a key, Chloe begged the universe. She jumped down and slapped at the quilt to hide any sign of recent activity. She shoved her totebag holding Yvonne Miller's journal between the bed and the wall.

Then she grabbed the poker again, dropped to the floor, and squirmed beneath the bed. Floor or trundle? Trundle, she decided, and wriggled onto the small bed. She was too tall for it, and so lay on her back with knees bent and legs pressed sideways against the quilt covering a lumpy straw-filled mattress.

Then came a few moments of silence. Was her pursuer leaving? Chloe scrunched her eyes closed, every muscle rigid, hoping against hope. Maybe a patrol car had pulled up in front of the house, scaring the shooter away. Please, please, *please*...

In the stillness, the metallic rattle of a key turning the deadbolt sounded shrill. Then came a faint squeak as the kitchen door swung open, and the emphatic thump of it being closed again.

A slow footstep creaked on a kitchen floorboard. Chloe was scarcely breathing. Thunder rumbled a warning overhead.

The next deliberate footstep moved toward the parlor door. Chloe opened her eyes. Who *was* it? Was the shooter a friend of Bandana Man's, who somehow knew that Chloe had found the cache of drugs? Was it Rita?

Chloe gritted her teeth so hard her jaw ached. The fireplace poker was clenched in both hands, resting on top of her belly. What would happen to Holly if she, Chloe, were killed? And shouldn't a cop be here by now?

The shooter's first step into the parlor was tentative, probably entering with caution to be sure that Chloe wasn't waiting just inside the room. A small bureau beside the doorway hid the person from view.

With one more step her pursuer cleared the bureau. Chloe stared with disbelief at feminine pumps and shins enclosed in nylons. Even knowing what she knew, she had not expected *this*.

The woman stopped, perhaps considering the room. There was only one place to hide in the parlor itself—under the bed—and she figured that out fast. "Chloe, come out. I know you're there."

Chloe's fingers throbbed against the poker. Come closer, she willed. If the woman crouched and fired from the center of the room, there was no help for it.

One step. Two. Three. Chloe heard a faint rustle of fabric, as if her pursuer was leaning over to peek under the bed.

Now. She thrust the poker sideways. For the second time that afternoon she felt a cast iron point meet flesh and bone.

The poker caught Evelyn in the side of her left knee. She screamed a horrible scream and crumpled to the floor. Her cane fell with a clatter. A small pistol hit the floor too, and slid a few inches away.

Chloe thumped from the trundle and rolled from her hiding place, slamming into Evelyn. The older woman was already reaching for the pistol. Chloe shoved with her toes, stretching for the gun. Evelyn got it first but Chloe grabbed her wrist and squeezed with all her strength. Whimpering, Evelyn hung on to the gun. Chloe slammed Evelyn's hand against the floor. The pistol spun away and this time, Chloe grabbed it first. She leapt to her feet, pistol held in both shaking hands and pointed at Evelyn.

The volunteer receptionist was almost unrecognizable. The shellacked hairdo was in disarray. Her pink suit was smudged with dirt. Her nylons were ripped and blood spilled from one knee. Evelyn's normally placid face was twisted with pain and, maybe, despair. An inarticulate keening filled the room. She stayed on the floor, clutching her knee.

The kitchen door banged open, and heavy steps hit the floor. *Please* be a cop, Chloe thought.

It was not. From the doorway, Gerald gaped at the tableau in the parlor.

"Where have you *been*?" Chloe demanded, which was not what she'd meant to say.

"Taking the maintenance man to the hospital after he had an accident in the shop," Gerald said. "Do I need to go back? What the hell is going on?"

Chloe licked her lips. "Evelyn shot at me."

"What?"

"I think Evelyn pushed Dr. Miller down the stairs in Polperro House. I found Miller's journal hidden in the gift shop. I think Evelyn figured out that I'd found it, and came after me."

"*What?*" Unmoving, Gerald gazed from Chloe to Evelyn and back again. He looked stupefied. And unconvinced.

"I didn't push her," Evelyn quavered. "We had an argument, that's all. I'd only brought the gun to scare her. I had to make her listen to me! But she stepped back, and she … she fell."

"You were trying to do more than scare me just now," Chloe snapped. Her hands were shaking more than ever. "Who was it about, Evelyn? Parnell Peavey? I just saw the listing for Parnell Peavey Elementary School in the phone book."

"Who's Parnell Peavey?" Gerald demanded.

"He was one of your ancestors, right, Evelyn? What was Dr. Miller going to write about him? What did he do?"

"It wasn't true," Evelyn wept.

"Evelyn told me that her earliest ancestor here was prominent enough to have a school named in his honor," Chloe told Gerald. "Now I'm trying to figure out what she's so ashamed of. Some of the early leaders massacred Indian people. A few of them owned slaves. But those things were generally accepted in territorial days. So, what could be even worse? Murder, I suppose. Or pedophilia, or other types of child abuse—"

"That story isn't true!" Evelyn insisted. "Parnell Peavey was a great man. You sound just like Yvonne. When I loaned her some of my family records, all she wanted to do was twist the facts and make it something ugly."

"Jesus." Gerald looked stunned.

Evelyn put one palm against the floorboards, as if intending to rise. "Do, not, move," Chloe warned, but her knees were starting to wobble. This afternoon had just been too damn much. "I could use a little help here, Gerald!"

Gerald crossed the room and crouched by Evelyn. "Sit up. You can lean against the bed." He helped the elderly woman reach a sitting position. He sat beside her and gripped her arm. Then he looked up at Chloe. "Go call the police. I'll stay with her."

Chloe chewed her lower lip. Could she trust Gerald? She decided she would, but she was hanging onto the gun. She also fetched her totebag from its hiding place. No way was she leaving that behind.

Then she backed from the room, through the kitchen, out the door. At that instant the heavens, once again, let loose. Rain drummed the cottage, the flagstone walkway, and her. And Chloe did not care, because a police car pulled up to the curb.

She waved down the officer. "In here." Back inside, she pointed at Evelyn. "She shot at me, and came after me to shoot again. She's admitted to threatening Dr. Yvonne Miller just before she fell down the stairs on Wednesday too."

The cop's eyebrows rose as he considered the elderly woman sitting on the floor and weeping piteously.

Chloe didn't waste time with more details. Instead she threw the bed quilt back and jumped onto the mattress.

"*Chloe!*" Gerald cried.

She pushed on the wooden hatch. This time she felt resistance.

"Holly, it's all right," she called. "A police officer is here. It's safe to come out now."

The hatch moved. A moment later Holly's frightened face appeared above her.

Chloe looked over her shoulder. "Gerald, help me."

He climbed up on the mattress. Together they caught Holly as she slithered through the hatch.

Somehow the girl ended up in Chloe's arms. She sat on the bed hugging Holly close, rocking back and forth. Holly patted her knee. Chloe began to cry, shock and anger and relief and gratitude all mixing together. There was a lot of malice to sort out, but at least the child was safe.

THIRTY

At least the child is safe, Mary thought, but the severity of the whipping he'd received worried her.

By candlelight Mary had eased the shreds of cloth from his back and gently dabbed away the blood with a damp cloth. Ezekiel had finally fallen into an exhausted sleep, belly-down on the bed.

"Should we fetch a doctor?" Jory asked uncertainly.

"I think not," Mary said. "For the boy's safety. A doctor might go straight to Peavey."

Andrew paced the small room. "By law, we need to tell Peavey that we're tending the child."

"You'd pass Ezekiel back to the hands of the man who beat him half to death and left him down a mineshaft?" Mary hissed.

"Not willingly." Andrew's face was set in hard lines. "But if Peavey learns that Ezekiel is here, he'll send the sheriff. We could be arrested for stealing his property."

Mary felt sick. And enraged. "I'll take that chance."

"Me too." Jory spoke from the shadows.

Andrew crouched in front of Ida, who stood near the bed. With a stricken expression she'd watched Mary clean Ezekiel's wounds, once softly patting his hand when he whimpered in pain. "Ida," Andrew said quietly, "a very mean man hurt Ezekiel. We want to keep him safe and let him heal. That means you can't tell *anyone* that Ezekiel is here. Can you keep it a secret?"

Ida nodded. She looked frightened, but resolute.

"Will?" Andrew asked.

"I won't tell." His voice was low but firm.

Andrew straightened. "Maybe we can keep this a secret while Ezekiel heals. But what then?"

"We give him a home." Mary didn't see any other choice.

Jory folded his arms. "Maybe we can do that. Maybe we can find a safer place for him, somewhere else. But we can't let him go back to Peavey."

Mary opened her mouth but swallowed her words. For now, they were agreed. But she didn't want Ezekiel to go anywhere else.

She looked at the boy. She had never been so close to a Negro before, never touched black skin. But what did it matter, when a child needed comfort? How could anyone do anything but wipe away tears and blood? Keeping him safe was all that mattered.

"We're agreed, then." Andrew nodded. "I do think we better take him upstairs."

Mary grimaced. "I hate to move him."

"For his own safety," Andrew said, "he needs to be out of sight."

———

Mary was washing dishes the next afternoon when Jory walked into *Chy Looan* and closed the door behind him. Her heart tightened with dread. "What's wrong?" He should have been at the mine.

"You need to know what's happening."

She dried her hands on her apron. "Tell me."

Jory reported that when Peavey arrived at his mine that morning, he'd been enraged to find no sign of Ezekiel. "He stormed all through the diggings, looking for the boy."

Mary smiled a small, mean smile. "Well, he didn't find him."

"No," Jory said grimly, "but even in the dark, somebody evidently saw Andrew carrying him down the hill. Peavey's already been to Andrew's house. Frightened his wife half to death. She let him search the place, which was probably for the best, and then came to find us. But I doubt this is over."

Mary sat down heavily. She'd been so focused on Ezekiel's care that she'd let herself believe that there wouldn't be trouble.

"I'm going to stay home with you this afternoon," Jory said.

"You can't do that! The mine ... "

"The mine can wait. Andrew and Will are working." He sat down at the table. "How's Ezekiel?"

"I think he's dazed by his turn of fortune." She blew out a long breath. "But he's clearly still frightened. I've tried to reassure him, but I don't know how much he really understands. Most of the time he sleeps."

Jory reached for the latest copy of the *Miners' Free Press*. Mary finished washing up. Although bread was baking in the spider, she decided she wouldn't make her rounds. It was best she stay clear of the diggings today.

She was chopping potatoes and swede for pasties when a fist pounded on the door.

Jory jumped to his feet. "Go upstairs."

Mary didn't want to go upstairs. She stood still.

Her brother opened the door, but only as wide as needed. "Yes, Mr. Peavey?"

"Do you have that boy in there?" The furious voice was high, nasal, inflected with the drawl Mary had heard from other Southern men. She took a step closer.

"Our boy Will is at our mine—"

"*My* boy!" Peavey screeched. "That boy is my property."

"I have no idea where he is."

That was the first lie Mary had ever heard Jory tell. She couldn't have been prouder.

"Then you won't mind if I take a look around." Peavey edged closer, stepping into Mary's view. He was a slight man with an aggrieved, pinched face. Dark hair shot with gray hung in strings to his shoulder. He didn't look like a miner. His clothes—a dark suit and red vest—were not crusted with dirt. His hands were clean, uncalloused.

"I do mind." Jory blocked Peavey's way. "Go. Now."

"I have a right!" Peavey shoved against Jory, clearly planning to force his way into the cottage. Jory was shorter, but he was a miner—powerful and strong. He moved so fast that Mary scarcely saw the blow. One moment Peavey was trying to muscle his way inside; the next, he was falling backwards down the front step.

He leapt immediately to his feet, slapping dust from his trousers. He pulled a kerchief from his vest pocket and dabbed gingerly at his nose, which was bleeding. His eyes narrowed as he stared at the blood staining his kerchief. Slowly he looked up at Jory, who'd stepped outside, and Mary, who stood in the doorway.

"I'll find that boy," Peavey spat. "I'll make him sorry he didn't stay where I left him. And I'll be sure that whoever helped him lives to regret it too."

———

When someone else knocked on the door a short while later, Mary pressed her lips into a tight line to keep from crying out. Jory lifted a hand in her direction: *Wait. I'll get it.* He walked to the door and cracked it open—then swung it wide.

Ruan stepped inside. "What's this? Why the closed door on such a fine afternoon?"

"Oh, Ruan." Mary went to him and let her cheek rest against his shoulder. *Safe.*

His voice softened. "Here, now. What's happened?"

She drew back and, with occasional commentary from Jory, told her fiancé about hearing a child crying on *Mena Dhu*, and what had happened since.

"That's a cruel trick, leaving him in the mine." Ruan looked disgusted. "But—what are you going to do with him?"

"Keep him, I hope," Mary said. "Raise him in a kind home."

Ruan was silent. Mary watched him glance at the ceiling, as if imagining the child sleeping fretfully in the loft. Then he spoke to Jory: "You'll stay while I take Mary for a walk?"

"Of course."

Mary grabbed her shawl from its peg and they left the cottage. For a long time neither spoke. They walked up Shake Rag, lifting hands in greeting to women hanging laundry in their tiny yards, children racing about, a miner who'd suffered a broken leg and now spent most daylight hours on his front step where he could see the diggings.

Ruan's silence made Mary uneasy. She was bone-weary after watching over Ezekiel all night, running up and down the steep stairs over and over. Parnell Peavey had frightened her, and she was even more frightened of what he might do next.

Finally Ruan felt moved to speak. "Mary. You know you can't keep that boy."

She frowned. "The first thing is to help him heal."

"But … where Peavey comes from, he's entitled to own human property. You're breaking the law."

"It's a law worth breaking!"

"Keep your voice down," Ruan muttered. He nodded pleasantly at a woman walking down the lane with a market basket. "Mary, you have a charitable heart. It's one of the things I loved about you, right from the beginning. You are kind and good. But surely you can see that this is a bad idea."

"No, I don't see." She pulled her hand from the crook of his elbow and walked on with arms crossed over her chest. "I'll never give Ezekiel back to the man who abused him so. Slavery is an evil that should be abolished—"

"Yes, it should. But like it or not, slavery is generally tolerated in the Wisconsin Territory."

She walked faster.

"Mary!" Ruan's low voice held a note of something hard. "How can you speak of raising this boy? Is that a decision for you to make alone?"

"Well, I—"

"I was happy when you took Ida. When you took Will from his uncle, I helped you. But this? No. You may *not* take this boy in."

"I already have."

"What will people think?"

Mary stopped and whirled to face him. "I don't know how it's all going to work out. But I do know I will never return that child to slavery."

"You won't have to. The sheriff will find out and seize the boy."

"I'll hide him." Tears stung her eyes. Ruan wasn't being fair. She hadn't had time to figure everything out. "My brothers will protect him."

Ruan's mouth tightened. "Be sensible! You came here with a dream of doing well. To rise. And you're doing so! *We* are doing so. Do you want to undo all of your hard work?"

"I don't care."

"Every friend you've made will shun you."

"I don't care!"

Ruan walked away, turned again and came back. "Mary, think about what you are saying. You are my intended. I will happily welcome Ida and Will into our home. But that is all."

"If you would come meet Ezekiel, see how badly—"

"No."

Mary stared at the man she loved. She'd thought, after two years, that she'd *known* him. And that he'd known her. It was hard to breathe. She pressed one hand against her chest. Her heart had broken when she'd first seen how badly Ezekiel had been hurt. Now the broken pieces were shattering to bits, as if struck by a hammer. "I thought..."

Ruan tried one more time. "Mary. He's naught but a slave boy."

His words came as another blow, filling her with more sharp edges. "No, Ruan. Ezekiel's naught but a *child*."

A muscle in Ruan's jaw twitched. The eyes that so often crinkled with laughter seemed hooded.

He turned and walked away. This time he didn't come back.

THIRTY-ONE

"I STILL CAN'T BELIEVE everything that's happened." Adam rubbed a hand over his face. "In fact, I still don't even understand it."

Adam had arrived in Mineral Point the day before and found Shake Rag Street crowded with police cars and other rescue vehicles. By the time the police were finished with Chloe, and she finally got back to Tamsin's apartment, she'd been too exhausted to do more than provide Adam and Tamsin a quick summary of her day, call Roelke, and go to bed.

The three of them were now ensconced in a booth at the Red Rooster Café, ready for breakfast. The Saturday newspaper was on the table. Much of the front page was devoted to Pendarvis. Chloe picked it up and frowned at the headline: *Drugs Found In Abandoned Mine On Dark Hill; Shot Fired In Historic Pendarvis House.*

"The shot was fired *at* Pendarvis House, not in it," she observed, and put the paper down.

Adam eyed her. "Roelke must be apoplectic."

"Actually, that's a bit of an understatement," Chloe admitted.

A young waitress appeared at Chloe's shoulder with insulated pot in hand. "Coffee?"

Adam and Tamsin nodded. "Definitely," Chloe said, and turned her white mug over to receive the aromatic offering. She'd been too shaken up to eat much the evening before. She was still shaken, actually, but she was also hungry. She ordered scrambled eggs with hash browns, toast, and a tall OJ.

When the waitress had departed Adam said, "Let me make sure I've got this straight. What happened in the abandoned mine yesterday was not related to what happened in Pendarvis House yesterday?"

"I don't *think* so." Chloe reached for the pitcher of cream. "Here's what I know. Rita, a young interpreter at Pendarvis, has been dating a guy who is evidently a drug dealer. Somehow he or Rita discovered the hidden entrance to a mineshaft on Dark Hill that hadn't been sealed, and he decided it would be the perfect warehouse for his stash. *I* went in because I thought a child, maybe Holly, might have gotten into trouble down there."

"But there was no child?"

"Nope." Chloe concentrated on stirring cream into her coffee. She still didn't know what to make of the cries that had lured her into the mine, but she didn't want to talk about it. "I did find a stash of what I think is cocaine, and some pot, and a notebook where the dealer kept track of customers."

"And then the dealer found you." Adam's frown was accusatory.

"I didn't know there were drugs in the mine!" Chloe protested. "And I didn't know he'd seen me go into the mine." Although the crowded café hummed with conversation, she lowered her voice. "Actually, I wonder if Rita saw me start up Dark Hill from Pendarvis, and called him. When the dealer showed up I managed to get past him, and was heading for the ladder, when the mine caved in. He got trapped on the other side."

"Too bad he didn't get trapped underneath," Tamsin muttered.

"Grandma!" Adam looked shocked. Tamsin looked unrepentant.

Chloe began creasing her napkin. "It took the responders a while to get him out. They'd heard my story by then, of course, and took him into custody."

"What about Rita?" Adam asked.

"I don't actually know if Rita was involved." Chloe still hoped that the young woman was guilty of nothing worse than falling for a jerk. "It seems hard to believe. And yet … " She sighed. "No harder to believe than Evelyn Bainbridge shooting at me."

Tamsin leaned back against the red upholstery. "Evelyn is on the board of the Mineral Point Historical Society. She's active in the church. She's got deep roots in this town."

"I think that's the point," Chloe said gently. "You helped me understand that, Tamsin. When you saw Andrew Pascoe's name on the property owners list, you decided it would be better to stop searching than to discover something disturbing about your ancestor."

"Well, it's just that … I thought … " Tamsin picked up a spoon and began rubbing at an invisible spot of tarnish with a napkin.

"When I talked to Evelyn about the skeleton," Chloe added, "the only possibility she would entertain is that two hoboes passing through in the early 1930s, when *Chy Looan* was empty, had brawled."

Tamsin looked up from the spoon. "It could have happened that way."

"Yes," Chloe conceded. "But Evelyn's extremely proud of her ancestors, especially one Parnell Peavey, who was a contemporary of territorial governor Henry Dodge. Those early white leaders are still revered as heroic pioneers, but many were hard, sometimes brutal men. Peavey and Dodge both owned slaves. Both fought to drive Native Americans from the area. Evelyn had shared some of her family records, and also filed the Pendarvis research material Dr. Miller used. Evelyn figured out that Dr. Miller was writing a book that did not depict these white men as heroes."

They were brooding over that when the waitress appeared with their food. Chloe started with her hash browns. Comfort food.

After a moment Tamsin said, "Well, maybe I didn't want to hear that Andrew Pascoe was suspected of killing someone. But even if it was true, I *never* would have done anything to stop someone from publishing that information."

"I suspect Evelyn got concerned when she realized that she might have inadvertently provided family material for what was going to be a hatchet job on the Lead Region's early white leaders," Chloe said.

"But to *kill* the poor girl!" Tamsin moaned.

"Evelyn probably entered the house on the upper level and caught Miller at the head of the stairs." Chloe had spent a lot of time imagining the possibilities. "Evelyn admitted that they argued, and that she'd pulled a gun to scare Dr. Miller, so perhaps she fell. Or perhaps they got into a tussle over the journal or the file about Evelyn's family. Maybe Evelyn tried to talk Miller out of writing her book."

Tamsin shuddered. "I can't bear to think about it."

Adam gestured with a piece of bacon. "Either way, Evelyn made a horrible decision when she left Polperro House and pretended nothing had happened, instead of calling for help. She must have been guilty of something if she just left Miller lying at the bottom of the stairs."

"Evelyn's window for confronting Miller was short," Chloe said. "If only someone had walked into the house in time to calm things down . . . " She'd been thinking about that a lot.

"Where was Loren?" Adam asked.

"Loren and Gerald were on Dark Hill, digging a badger hole." Chloe dabbed butter on her toast. "And Evelyn might have seen Claudia taking off. However Miller ended up falling, Evelyn was quick-witted enough to grab the green journal before leaving Polperro House. I'm guessing she panicked, and felt compelled to hide the journal fast. She used to volunteer in the gift shop, and so knew about the boarded-over fish pond."

"It's astonishing that no one saw her," Adam observed.

"At that hour, the shop is generally deserted," Chloe told him. "When I arrived, Evelyn was alone in the office. She was agitated, but when I asked if she was okay, she said she was frustrated because of people calling about the threat to close Pendarvis. The day before we had just as many calls, and Evelyn was calm and cool." She twisted her mouth with regret, wishing she'd paid more attention.

Adam leaned forward, elbows on the table. "But why did Evelyn come after you?"

"Evelyn came into the gift shop right after I found the journal. Maybe she glanced in the window and actually saw me find it." Chloe tucked one leg up on the bench. "At that point she might have figured she was in too deep, and she couldn't let me pass the journal on to—"

"Why—hello!" Claudia stopped beside the booth. "I see we all needed sustenance this morning." Holly waved energetically at Chloe from her mother's side. Claudia was in jeans. Holly wore period clothes.

"Want to join us?" Adam asked.

Chloe, sitting across from Adam and Tamsin, scooted all the way to the wall. "Slide in." Holly wriggled onto the bench beside her and carefully smoothed her skirt. "You look extra beautiful this morning," Chloe added, thinking, Holly is okay. She really is okay.

Then she looked at Claudia. "Have you heard anything about Rita? Was she involved?"

"I haven't heard," Claudia said. "But I do have news. Loren's resigning as site director."

"Resigning?" Chloe echoed. "Because of the closure threat? What happened yesterday wasn't his fault."

"He disappeared yesterday afternoon because, in his words, he'd 'reached the end of his rope,'" Claudia told them. "He's realized he doesn't want to be an administrator. He hopes to find a site that's open year-round and pays a living wage to interpreters."

"Yikes." Chloe took that in. Not everyone would be willing to step down the ladder a rung or three. "But what does that mean for you?"

"I suppose I'll be acting director for a while."

"I'm so sorry," Chloe told her. Claudia had enough problems without assuming huge new responsibilities.

"It'll be all right," Claudia said. "I love the site. I know the site better than anyone. The community support has been amazing. I'm optimistic."

"Good for you," Tamsin said.

"After what could have happened yesterday"—Claudia leaned over and kissed the top of Holly's head—"all the other problems suddenly seem more manageable. I can face anything as long as Holly's safe."

The waitress returned. Claudia ordered an omelet for herself and pancakes for Holly.

"I'd like to order something else," Adam announced. "Figgy hobbin for everyone."

Tamsin looked askance. "Figgy hobbin for breakfast?"

"Oh, yeah," Chloe said. "Absolutely." Poor people in Cornwall centuries earlier might not have thought much of their figgy hobbin, but she'd been wanting to try what Tamsin had called "a sweet version made with raisins and caramel sauce" all week.

———

When they slid from the booth some time later, Claudia leaned close. "Gerald was looking for you after all the commotion yesterday. Did he find you?"

"He did." After seeking Chloe out, the interpreter had scuffed his feet, stared at his hands, and mumbled, "I'm sorry."

Chloe hadn't been sure if he was apologizing for leaving the nasty note, for being rude, or on general principles. "For what?"

Evidently incapable of articulating the deed, Gerald pointed at her totebag.

"*You* wrote that nasty note."

He nodded.

"It was unkind," Chloe had said, "but we're good now." After everything else, the childish note seemed immaterial.

Now Claudia gave Chloe a hug. "*Thank you* for protecting Holly yesterday."

"I'm just grateful that everyone's alright," Chloe said fervently. "And listen, if you start feeling overwhelmed at the site, call me and I'll come down again."

"That would be great."

Chloe dared give Holly a quick hug. "It was wonderful to meet you." Holly smiled.

"Chloe," Tamsin said, as Adam helped her into her jacket, "Midge called from the archives yesterday afternoon. It flew right out of my head last night. She has something for you to see, and said she'd leave it at the library for you."

"I'll stop by," Chloe said. "See you later."

Once alone on the sidewalk, however, she turned in the opposite direction of the library. This was her last day in Mineral Point. There was something she wanted to do.

Ten minutes later Chloe reached the old cemetery. She started walking the grounds, trying to read the cracked and faded headstones. Maybe half an hour later she spotted a familiar name.

Andrew Pascoe had died in 1900 and been buried beside his wife. Just to the right was a leaning stone with a sculpted finger pointed to heaven above a chiseled inscription:

Mary Pascoe

b. 1816, Camborne Parish, Cornwall

d. August 24, 1911

Perhaps this is the moment for which you have been created.

Esther 4:14

Interesting choice of verse, Chloe thought. Had Mary Pascoe met the moment for which she had been created?

Chloe pressed one palm on the cold stone. "I'm sorry I wasn't able to learn more about you," she told Mary softly. "I think you're awesome to have immigrated so early and survived for so long. And done so much good along the way. It can't have been easy."

The stone to the right of Mary's appeared to be much older. Chloe knelt, squinting at the weathered inscription. Finally she tore a piece of paper from the notebook in her totebag and gently held it over what she thought was the name on the stone. She went back and forth lightly with a dull pencil also found in her bag, then considered what emerged. *J, o* … and was that a *v*, or an *r*?

" … Oh, *no*." Chloe realized the obvious with dismay.

With a little more work she decoded the rest.

Jory Pascoe

Born 1817, Camborne Parish, Cornwall

Died March 11, 1838

Chloe sat back on her heels. Jory Pascoe had only been twenty-one when he died. Had his death been the result of an epidemic? A mining accident?

Or—or had Jory Pascoe been injured in a fight? The fight that had led to a man being buried in the *Chy Looan* root cellar?

Chloe thrummed with excitement. With Jory's death date in hand, maybe—just maybe—she could find a newspaper article that would suggest an identity for the skeleton in *Chy Looan* after all.

———

"Any questions?" Roelke looked around the circle of cops crowded into the Eagle station. He didn't expect to find more than two people inside the house on Hackberry Lane, but no way was he screwing this up by not having enough manpower.

Zietz had made her final buy around lunchtime, and all had gone according to plan. He'd made a map of the yard and, with details she'd provided, produced a basic sketch of the interior. He'd assigned his colleagues to locations around the perimeter. He'd talked through who'd do what once inside, and how he hoped it would all go down.

Since no one had any questions, he glanced at Chief. The older man gave him a tiny nod: *You got this. It's all yours.*

Roelke was ready. "All right. Let's go." He led the way out the back door. No point in telegraphing the fact that something potentially big was about to go down in Eagle.

Outside, Blakely caught up with him. "Things still tense between your cousin and her ex?"

Roelke could hear someone chopping up fallen leaves with a lawnmower. "Yes. They are."

The other man muttered something beneath his breath. "All the Palmyra guys are keeping an eye on her place," he assured Roelke. "Sooner or later Raymo will screw up bad enough for us to arrest him. You can bet I'll be waiting for him to leave his hunting club meeting at Mickey's tomorrow. Chances are very good he'll be drunk enough I can at least nail him for DUI."

"That would be good," Roelke said. But nailing Raymo for driving under the influence would be little more than a petty annoyance, one that would do nothing to keep him away from Libby's house. It wasn't enough. Libby deserved to feel safe.

THIRTY-TWO

I just want to feel safe, Mary thought. She eased the front curtain over a smidge and peeked outside. Parnell Peavey stood in the street, arms folded, feet planted wide, scowling at *Chy Looan*.

Mary turned away. The door was barred. There was nothing the man could do. If he was still there when Andrew and Jory came down the hill with Will, they'd run him off. It wouldn't be the first time.

She crouched and added fuel to the fire. It was extravagance, but she needed to drive the chill from her bones. The autumn afternoon was cold, the sun already sinking in the western sky, and Parnell Peavey was waiting to get what—who—he was after.

Then Mary tiptoed up the steps to check on the children. A candle burned in the sticking tommy Jory had stabbed into a beam. In the wavering shadows Ida, who'd been keeping Ezekiel company, was recounting a tale Ruan had once told her about piskies.

Mary paused, feeling the familiar ache flame inside. She hadn't seen Ruan since they'd argued about Ezekiel a month earlier. Part of

315

her longed to run to his smithy and somehow make things right. The other part of her was still hurt, and horrified, that Ruan had made her choose between helping Ezekiel and marrying him. Every time she looked at the boy, she knew she couldn't possibly have made any other choice.

"Are piskies like knackers?" Ezekiel asked.

"Knackers live in the mines," Ida reminded him. "Piskies live on the moors. They lead travelers in circles until they get lost."

"That's mean!"

"They only do that if the travelers are not good people," Ida assured him earnestly. "Piskies are kind to people who are old or crippled. Or hurt like you."

Mary swiped at her eyes and went on up the stairs. The children were both sitting on the mattress. The sight of them together eased her heartache.

Ida had initially been shy about spending time with Ezekiel, but over the weeks she'd crept closer. She volunteered to take him food or water. Then she began lingering, singing him to sleep, telling stories, teaching him a game of her own devising played with colored pebbles. Mary had struggled to understand his dialect, which was melodious but thick and soft, but Ida was already chattering easily with him.

"Neither one of you has to worry about piskies," Mary told them now. "Ida, it's time to start supper. Please go downstairs and begin peeling the potatoes I left on the table."

Once the girl was gone, Mary crouched beside the makeshift bed. "It's good to see you sitting up, Ezekiel. May I see your back?"

He swiveled obligingly, and she lifted his shirt. Although the welts made her sick with fury, the wounds were closed now. "You've mended well."

"Yes, Miss Mary."

"Ezekiel … " She hesitated, but the question had tormented her. "Are there other children working Mr. Peavey's mine?"

He shook his head. "I think he just brought me because my mama died."

"What about your father?"

"Don't know."

Don't know, Mary thought. At least she knew what had happened to the people she grieved. "Tomorrow, I think you can come downstairs for a while. Would you like that?"

"What about Massa Peavey?"

That is the question, Mary thought. "You don't want to go back to him, do you?"

Ezekiel shook his head vigorously.

"We have to keep you hidden, then. I'll keep the curtains closed."

In the shadows, Ezekiel's expression was old beyond his years. "If Massa Peavey finds me now, he's like to beat the life out of me."

"Why did he beat you?"

"He done said I didn't dig fast enough."

"And … why did Mr. Peavey leave you down the mineshaft that night?"

"After being whipped my back be hurtin' so bad I could hardly dig at all. That's why. Said I could think about digging, all night."

There should be laws to protect children, Mary thought. But she knew of no such laws, even for white children. For Ezekiel, Peavey *was* the law.

She put a hand on his head, feeling the texture of his hair. "We'll keep you safe," she promised. She prayed every day for God's help in protecting this boy. "Now, I must go help Ida. I'll bring your supper up later." She stood, hating how the wind whistled around the eaves, and how the stone walls held the chill.

"Thank you, Miss Mary." Ezekiel curled up on his side and pulled the blanket up to his chin.

It was chilly downstairs too. Jory and Will had opened the back wall and were, as time permitted, digging a root cellar into the hill behind the house. But they hadn't hung a door yet, and drafts crept from the cellar.

She crouched by the bed she shared with Ida and groped underneath until her hand hit metal. She drew out the foot warmer Ruan had made for her, inscribed with hearts.

Mary traced them with one finger. She missed Ruan.

Well. A life with Ruan was not to be. She briskly carried the warmer to the hearth, filled it with hot chirks, wrapped it in her old shawl, and carried it upstairs for Ezekiel.

———

Peavey had disappeared by the time Mary's brothers and Will came down the hill that evening, but Andrew stopped inside anyway. "Do you want supper?" Mary asked. "I made potato cakes."

"No, I've got supper waiting at home, but ... " He cocked his head toward the table. "I'll sit with you. We need to talk."

Ida had already set the table with tin plates and cups. "What's wrong?" Mary asked, as she passed a plate heaped with the potato cakes.

"The sheriff sought me out today," Andrew began. "Peavey asked him to search *Chy Looan* for the boy."

Fear, hot and sour, crawled up Mary's throat. "He's coming?"

"No. He told Peavey he had no call to search a home without evidence of some crime. I was seen with Ezekiel, and my home was searched. That's all he'll do without cause."

Jory helped himself to several potato cakes. "Then we mustn't give him cause."

"I agree, but … " Andrew ran a hand over his head. "How long can you hide a child?"

"As long as it takes," Mary said sharply. "Peavey's a sucker, right? He'll go back to Missouri before the snows come."

"Men say he didn't fare well this season," Will put in. He drained his mug and wiped his mouth with the back of his hand.

"I doubt he did," Andrew agreed. "But I don't think he'll give up, Mary. Slavery is legal where he comes from. Ezekiel was his possession. Property worth money. If he can prove the boy is here—"

"We won't let him find proof." Mary pushed her plate away, no longer hungry.

A log in the fire popped. Ida looked around the table with sad eyes. Mary wished she could shield the girl from this horrid situation. But Ida needed to understand it, because Ezekiel's safety depended in part on her.

Finally Andrew said, "I hold God's law above all, and I don't think it Christian to own slaves. But at the same time … you can't keep Ezekiel hidden forever, Mary. That's no life for him either."

Mary inhaled a slow breath, let it out again. Andrew's observation was fair. But she simply couldn't bear to give up on Ezekiel. "It's just for a while. We have nowhere else to send him. Let's wait and see if Peavey leaves."

THIRTY-THREE

ROELKE TRIED NOT TO let his nervous excitement show as they approached the house on Hackberry Lane. He was prepared ... but had no way of knowing for sure what they'd find inside, or how the homeowners might react.

He gestured at the officers designated to stay outside, and they silently fanned out. Roelke trotted up the front steps with Skeet and Chief Naborski behind him. He hadn't been able to get a no-knock warrant because the suspects had no known history of violence. But that was good, right?

He hammered the door three times and bellowed, "Police!" The door opened almost instantly. A man stared at them, slack-jawed with astonishment. Before the man could react, Roelke shoved inside.

The action was over fast. Greg Trieloff made a mad dash toward the back door, and was tackled and cuffed by Roelke for his trouble. Marjorie Trieloff screamed like a banshee, and was cuffed by Skeet for *her* trouble. Once the pair was in custody two of the other cops escorted them to separate squad cars, and stayed to babysit them during the search.

Roelke took the bedroom. He ripped the bed apart first, as he always did; once that was clear everything else in the room could be piled on the mattress. Next, the dresser and—*jackpot*. The idiots weren't even creative, Roelke thought, with a twinge of mild disappointment. The top drawer held a large hoard of marijuana packaged in separate baggies, and a scale, which meant he could make a good case that the weed was intended for resale. In the next drawer he found five, maybe six pounds of crack, also divvied into small plastic bags. And in the bottom drawer he discovered money, rubber banded in stacks. A quick count showed over thirty thousand dollars.

Holy toboggans.

"Chief?" he called. When his boss came into the bedroom, Roelke showed him both drugs and cash.

The older man's craggy face relaxed into a rare, satisfied smile. "Well done, Officer McKenna. Well done."

————

At the Mineral Point archives Chloe found an elderly man on duty. "Oh, yes," he said when Chloe introduced herself. "Midge left this for you." He picked up a small carton on the desk and handed it over.

"Thanks," Chloe said. "Before I dig into this, though, I'd like to see microfilm from the 1838 *Miners' Free Press*."

"We don't have any newspapers from that year."

"You don't?" Chloe felt crushed. "I've looked at 1837."

He nodded. "Yes, we do have those. Then we jump to the *Mineral Point Free Press* for 1843, and then the *Mineral Point Democrat* for 1845, and then—"

"I see." Jory had died in 1838. Evidently any relevant reports regarding his death had died with him.

"It's not like somebody was systematically saving newspapers for posterity back then." The man sounded a tad defensive. "We're lucky to have *anything* from the territorial period."

"Yes, I do understand that," Chloe assured him. "Thank you."

She settled at one of the worktables with the box Midge had left. A scribbled note was taped to the top:

Chloe,

Something nagged at me about Theophilus George.
Bob Neal saved everything he could get his hands on,
bless his heart, and gave us such a large collection of stuff
that we don't have everything cataloged yet. I had this
feeling that something useful might still be hidden
away. I went on the hunt, and voila!

Midge

Chloe removed the lid. The box contained a collection of thin leather ledgers, faded and worn. She opened the one on top and peered at lines of faded, crabbed script. She caught her breath. "Oh my," she whispered.

———

"Yes!" Officer Skeet Deardorff was practically bouncing off the Eagle Police Station walls. He was jazzed.

Roelke had been jazzed too, for the raid on Hackberry had been a thing of beauty. Now, his buzz was fading. He was staring at a mountain of work yet. And something else.

But Roelke didn't want to think about that. "Thanks, Skeet. I really appreciate your work at the house this afternoon."

"Want me to stay and help wrap everything up?" The other officers and the chief had all gone home.

Part of Roelke did want that, wanted Skeet's company every minute until he locked the door behind him.

But he shook his head. "Naw. I got it."

"I'll do the inventory while you do the other paperwork," Skeet suggested. "Otherwise you'll be here for hours."

Skeet was right. Roelke had to write a detailed report that started with the original complaint and went through the raid itself. He needed to inventory the drugs. He needed to record the cash seized, noting every bill's serial number, cross-referencing the numbers on the cash he'd given Michelle Zietz to make her buys.

But he waved a hand. "You've got a wife and kids waiting at home. All I've got waiting is a cat who's aggrieved because Chloe's away."

"Okay." Skeet shrugged and opened his locker door. "It's your funeral."

Probably, Roelke thought, and got to work.

————

When Chloe got back to Tamsin's apartment, Adam answered her knock. She inhaled the heady sugar-cinnamon scent of baking cookies. "Smells good in here."

"Yes, but I advise you to stand clear. Grandma's moving at extremely high speed."

"I heard that, Adam," Tamsin called from the kitchen. "I told the ladies I'd be at church by four thirty with cookies in hand, and I will *not* be late. We've got hundreds of pasties to make for the supper."

"I'll drive you, Grandma." Adam snitched a snickerdoodle from one of the tins on the table and winked at Chloe. "And you can even put me to work in the kitchen."

Tamsin emerged, wiping her hands on a rickrack-trimmed apron. "We'll have to stop at the old people's home to deliver supper for Lowena. There's been so much going on this week I've slighted her, I'm afraid."

"How about if I visit Lowena?" Chloe asked. "I'd be glad to take her supper."

Tamsin's face brightened. "Well, that would solve a problem, if you're sure you don't mind. Her food's all packaged up."

"I don't mind at all," Chloe assured her truthfully. The idea of a quiet hour with Tamsin's half-sister was more appealing than working with a dozen supervisors in a chaotic church kitchen. Besides, she'd wanted to ask Lowena about her memories of childhood in Mineral Point.

"We can drop you off," Adam offered.

"That's okay." Chloe tucked the plastic food containers into her totebag. "I'll walk."

Her route led through the historic district, and she tried not to get too distracted by the stone, Victorian, Federal, and Italianate buildings. I love this town, she thought. Yes, some truly horrid things had happened here this week. But Mineral Point had a fascinating past, and residents clearly cherished their historical and cultural heritage. This evening she felt optimistic that common sense would prevail, and that Pendarvis would remain open to help tell the stories of early Cornish mining families, and the two men who'd saved old buildings and launched the local preservation ethic.

When Chloe arrived at the nursing home she found Lowena's room and knocked on the open door. "Hello?"

Lowena was sitting by the window, knitting a cheerful red shawl. For someone a hundred and one years old, she looked surprisingly vivacious in a teal sweatsuit, with a flowered headband tied over thin white hair. She lifted one hand.

Chloe interpreted the gesture as *Come in.* "Do you remember me? I'm Chloe, Tamsin and Adam's friend."

That *I'm still here spark* was back in Lowena's eyes, and the portrait of her first husband was back on the nightstand. "I've been waiting for you," she said—just as she had when they'd met.

A tingle buzzed down Chloe's spine. She had no idea how to respond. "Um…Tamsin's busy with a church function tonight, so I brought you supper. A pasty and saffron bun and cookies."

"I'll have it later. I'd rather have your company."

Chloe pulled a vacant chair close to the elderly woman. "I was hoping we'd have a chance to talk. I love history, you see."

"Well, child, I've lived it."

"Do you have any favorite memories from your childhood?"

"My early years were not filled with 'favorites,'" Lowena said. "My father abandoned my mother and me when I was eight years old."

"Oh." Chloe sucked in her lower lip. With her first question she'd inadvertently evoked something painful. Lovely. "I'm sorry. Perhaps we should talk of other things."

"It was all a long time ago." Lowena met Chloe's gaze. Behind her glasses, the old woman's blue eyes were still bright. "I don't think I need to keep secrets from you."

Chloe felt the undercurrent in the conversation, but couldn't define it. "Um…no, there's no need to keep secrets."

"I'm tired of the secrets." Lowena flicked a hand as if sweeping them away. "My mother kept my father's behavior a secret. It was a scandal, you see."

Almost a century ago, Chloe thought, I imagine it was. "She must have been terribly hurt."

"And ashamed. To get by she took in laundry, mostly from bachelor miners." Lowena stared out the window. "That's how I remember my mother—bending over a copper wash boiler, perspiration running down her face, with a huge pile of filthy work clothes waiting on the floor."

"That's a hard way to make ends meet," Chloe agreed.

"She couldn't manage. After less than a year she gave me away."

"Oh, Lowena. I'm sorry. Your mother must have been at wits' end."

"I've always wondered if she truly believed I'd be better off, or if I had become a painful reminder of my father," Lowena mused. "She even made me change my name. My father named me Ann, you see. Lowena is my middle name."

"Lowena is a beautiful name," Chloe said honestly. "Did you keep in touch with your mother?"

"Not really. And when she remarried a few years later, she didn't take me back." Her fingers plucked absently at the red yarn. "I don't know if her second husband, Tamsin's father, even knew she had an older child."

Something came clear in Chloe's brain. "Tamsin told me that she never knew *your* first husband. Is that why?"

"Tamsin didn't know I existed until a cousin told her. The Depression had started, so Tamsin was … thirty-six? Thirty-seven?" Her voice was thin and she spoke slowly, as if needing extra time to dig memories from the past. "Somewhere in there. I was almost fifty."

"I'm sorry you two lost so much time together." Chloe tried to imagine what it would feel like to walk the planet for so many years and *then* discover she had an unknown sister. Lowena must possess an indomitable inner strength. Abandoned by her father *and* her mother, widowed twice … and here she was, over a century old and still knitting shawls and eating pasties.

Chloe leaned forward and put a gentle hand on Lowena's arm. "You've had a hard path through life."

"No more so than many." Lowena shifted in the chair, as if trying to sit straighter. "I was fortunate. A very kind woman took me in as a child and raised me like I was her own granddaughter. Mary Pascoe."

Chloe went very still. "Mary Pascoe? You were raised by Mary Pascoe?" She tried to assimilate that factoid into what she knew of the Pascoe and Bolitho families. "Were you … did you grow up at *Chy Looan*?"

"I lived there from the time I was eight until I was fourteen, when I became a nanny. I was the last child Miss Mary took in, and I visited her often after I left. Shortly before she died, she told me she was leaving me the cottage. And that there was something I needed to know."

Chloe leaned back in her chair, totally flummoxed. "But Adam didn't … Tamsin never said … "

"Tamsin and Adam don't know." Lowena's voice was thin as paper; it also held a note of iron. "I didn't move back, you see. I rented it out. Eventually I had a lawyer sell the cottage. That was before Tamsin and I even met."

"You sold … " Chloe pressed fingertips to her temples. This made no sense.

Then—*Ann*. The name rang in her memory like a church bell. She'd been so focused on the Pascoe family that she'd barely considered the other name on the list of *Chy Looan* property owners. "Lowena, before you got married, what was your last name?"

"Trezona. I was christened Ann Lowena Trezona."

Chloe stared helplessly at the old woman.

Lowena smiled. "Mary Pascoe was the kindest, most generous person I ever met. She was involved in many projects, but most of all she helped many children over the years. It was because of her sisters, you see."

"Her sisters?" Chloe asked weakly. "I didn't know she had sisters."

"She had two, both younger. They died before she left Cornwall, and she blamed herself. One died when she got too close to the hearth and her dress caught fire. The other died in a mining accident. A boiler exploded."

Dear God, Chloe thought. It was unbearable to imagine.

Then she noticed that Lowena's eyes had closed. "Would you like a glass of water? Or … should I go?"

Lowena opened her eyes. "I'm growing tired. But I don't have much time left, and I want someone to know."

Know *what*? Chloe wanted to shriek, but forced herself to be patient.

"Before Adam found that skeleton in *Chy Looan*," Lowena said, "I was the only person left who knew there was a body buried in the root cellar."

This time Chloe couldn't help herself. "You *knew*? Who was it?"

"An evil man." Lowena paused again, as if gathering her strength. "Perhaps I will nibble that saffron bun, and catch my breath. Then I'll tell you the story."

THIRTY-FOUR

MAY 1838

A hot ache bloomed in Mary's chest as she arranged saffron buns for her visitor on a china plate. Oh, Jory, she thought. It happened this way often—some stray memory or scent caused grief to strike like a miner's pick. Jory had loved saffron buns.

She was managing. Will was at the mine, trying to fill Jory's boots. "I'll take care of you now, Miss Mary," he'd promised hoarsely the day Jory had died, as tears tracked down his dirty cheeks. Still, Mary expected Jory to walk grubby and tired through the door any moment.

But he will not, Mary reminded herself. Ever again. All they had left of Jory were memories and his shovel, leaning in one corner. His other tools had gone to Will and Ezekiel, but no one could bear to touch his shovel.

Jory had died on a bitter March day when several inches of ice-crusted snow still coated the landscape. The sky was the color of lead, and a bitter wind shrieked around the cottage. Mary had just set some dough to rise near the hearth, and was savoring the yeasty smell mingling with the smoke, when a fist hammered the door.

Mary had felt a sudden, bone-deep chill. Ida shot her a frightened glance: *Is it Mr. Peavey?*

It hadn't been Peavey. The man pounding at the door was a friend of her brothers. "What is it?" Mary had cried, because she couldn't bear to voice the real question: *Who is it?*

"Cave-in," he'd gasped. "It's Jory."

The memory was harsh, and she was glad when a much calmer voice behind her interrupted it. "You have a snug home, Mary."

Mary tried to swallow the lump in her throat, turned, and set the platter on the table in front of her guest.

"Saffron buns?" Kerenza Benallack's eyes went wide. "I didn't expect to taste saffron buns ever again."

Mary found a smile. "I wanted to give you a proper welcome to Mineral Point. Living among so many different kinds of people, Cornish food helps *us* remember where we came from." She reached for her precious china teapot. "May I pour?"

Mary and Ida had met the young woman while making their rounds on *Mena Dhu* with loaded bread baskets. Kerenza and her husband were newly-arrived and camping in a badger hole. Mary had given her some bread, shared tips about outdoor cooking, and invited her to come for tea the next day.

Now Ida emerged from the root cellar, carrying a china bowl of plum preserves with clotted cream. She approached the table slowly, anxious not to spill. When the bowl was safely deposited, she beamed.

"Would you like to join us for tea, Ida?" Mary asked. She glanced toward the stairs, but caught herself. Ezekiel was upstairs, but it wouldn't be wise to call him down.

Ida, however, was happy to be included. As Mary poured tea she thought, as she often did, of Mrs. Bunney's decree: *You have no hope of becoming a decent woman unless you give up mining.* She thought of her mother, who had wanted more for her daughters than *she'd* had.

Kerenza's eyes glistened. "And clotted cream! Just as my mother used to serve."

"One day I hope to have a proper tea shop," Mary confided. She couldn't expect Andrew to support her forever, and despite Will's promise, she didn't want him to shoulder such responsibility so young.

"I thought we were moving to a wilderness," Kerenza admitted. "I underestimated the lead region."

The Pascoes did their part, Mary thought. They and their Cornish neighbors had replaced surface diggings and badger holes with stone cottages and deep mines and, most of all, a sense of community.

Kerenza ate the last morsel of her bun, dabbed her mouth with a napkin, and smiled. "You have lifted my spirits, Mary. Thank you. I must get back up the hill, but I hope I might visit again."

After Kerenza left, Chloe called Ezekiel down. "Have some tea," she told him.

"Yes, Miss Mary." Ezekiel sat down and accepted a steaming china cup. He'd filled out some over the winter. There were no longer hollows in his cheeks, or between his wrist bones. But the ... Mary searched for the right word ... the haunted look in his eyes had not faded. He was jumpy as a rabbit, even in the evening with the door barred and curtains closed and only family at home. He never mentioned Peavey, but twitched and whimpered in his sleep.

When the dishes were washed, Mary met Ida's gaze. "Now the sewing." Ida, generally a willing worker, had resisted Mary's efforts to teach her proper stitching. "See if you can finish hemming your new apron today before it's time to go next door." A family with three daughters lived in the next cottage, and they'd invited Ida for supper and evening games in honor of the youngest girl's birthday.

"I'll try," Ida said with a heavy sigh.

Once Ida was settled, Mary stepped to the window. Most of the suckers had already appeared, trudging north on slushy trails to spend another season digging. So far, there'd been no sign of Parnell Peavey.

If Ezekiel resented his confinement, he never said so. He helped Mary, played with Ida, and sometimes simply sat like a tired old man. Mary suspected that her neighbors here in the Shake Rag district knew everything. But they were friends, and mostly Cornish. The kind of people who helped tend each others' sick children, and chopped firewood for the elderly. After Jory's death they had come with baskets of pasties, crocks of potato soup, even a starry-gazy pie with bass peeking from the crust instead of pilchards. She trusted them to hold their tongues.

Still, worry hung over her like a thundercloud. Every time she passed the log jail in town, or saw a man resembling Peavey, a sliver of ice ran down her backbone. She felt as if they were all holding their breaths, waiting for something to happen.

She turned away from the window. Life kept digging the hole of grief inside Mary deeper and deeper: her parents, Elizabeth and Loveday, and now Jory. And, she thought, Ruan too.

He'd stayed away until the night Jory died. As friends crowded into *Chy Looan* Mary had searched his face, still so familiar to her that even in the gloom she could have traced each tiny line with her finger.

"I'm sorry about Jory," Ruan had said hoarsely. That was all.

Ida spoke, breaking her melancholy reverie. "Miss Mary? I'm finished."

Mary started. Enough mourning, for now. She had three children to tend, and Andrew's family nearby, and good friends. It would be enough.

She sat down to check Ida's sewing. "The stitches are still a little too big, but they are quite even. Well done, Ida."

"May I go next door now?" she pleaded.

"Of course." Mary kissed her forehead.

After Ida left, Mary added a log to the fire. Ezekiel padded over and slipped into one chair by the hearth, stretching his toes toward the flames. Mary picked up her wool and needles, knitted a few rows, and felt herself drowsing. It's been a good day, she thought.

Someone banged on the front door.

Ezekiel was on his feet and gone, up the stairs, even as Mary jumped to hers. She started forward, but it opened before she could grab the wooden bar. With a stab of horror she realized she'd forgotten to bolt the door after Ida left.

Parnell Peavey stepped inside and closed it behind him. He'd cropped his long hair, and traded his suit and red vest for rougher traveling clothes. But his eyes were the same. They bore into Mary like augers.

Mary's pulse raced. "Get out of here."

"I've come for my boy." He scanned the cottage. "I know he's here, woman."

"Get out!" Panic was rising inside. Oh, Ezekiel, Mary moaned silently. He had nowhere to hide.

Peavey shoved past her and looked quickly under the bed. Then he grabbed her wrist in a manacle grip and dragged her, stumbling, to the root cellar. He smelled of stale sweat and cheap tobacco. After a hard look he jerked Mary toward the narrow set of steps leading to the second story.

Mary fought like a wildcat to break his grip. "Get *out*! You have no right—"

He backhanded her across the face. Her head jerked with an explosion of shock and pain, and she stumbled against the wall. Before she could recover she heard feet pounding down the stairs. "*No,*" she begged.

Ezekiel shot from the staircase with a sticking tommy clenched in one hand. "Leave Miss Mary be!" Arm raised, he charged at the man who, by Southern law, owned him.

Surprised, Peavey lost his footing and fell to the floor. Ezekiel stabbed at him viciously. The sharp iron tore through the shoulder of Peavey's coat, drawing blood. Peavey grunted a blasphemous oath and kicked the boy aside. The candleholder slid across the floor, out of reach.

Mary stumbled forward, shielding Ezekiel as Peavey staggered to his feet and whipped a knife from a sheath on his belt. He explored the shoulder wound with his free hand, and glared when his fingers came away covered with blood. His eyes narrowed. "Boy, you just made your last mistake."

Mary heard Ezekiel's rapid breaths behind her and tried frantically to think. What could she do to distract Peavey? To give Ezekiel one last slim chance at escape?

The slaver stood between them and the door, knees slightly bent in anticipation. With no great haste he turned the knife this way and that, admiring its blade in the firelight. "You all think you're so-o clever," he drawled, pointing toward Mary and Ezekiel. "Once I have my boy back, woman, I'm setting the sheriff on you."

I can't go to jail, Mary thought numbly. What would Ida and Will do?

"And hoo-ee, have I got plans for *you*, boy." Peavey flexed his fingers on the knife's bone handle, as if searching for the best possible grip. "You know what happens to slaves who run away? And assault their master? You're going to die, boy, but it's not going to happen quick. First I'm going to..."

Mary stopped listening. Her brain cleared. Her loneliness for Ruan, her grief for Jory, even her fear of this vile man—all disappeared as terror gave way to rage and purpose. Jory wasn't coming home to fight Peavey off. Ruan wasn't stepping in. When the workday ended Andrew would hurry straight home to his wife and infant son. It's up to you, Mary told herself.

But how? Her own sharp meat knife was tucked away in the corner cupboard. The sticking tommy was out of reach. Peavey would be on her in a second if she lunged for either. She didn't have a weapon.

... No, *wait*. She did.

A shudder of revulsion rippled over her skin, but she clenched her teeth against it. She had to try. One of her favorite Bible verses, from the fourth chapter of Esther, came to mind.

The rattle of a handcart with a squealing wheel sounded from the street, and with it Jago Green's shout: "Wood for sale! Wood for sale!"

Peavey glanced toward the door.

Perhaps this is the moment for which you have been created.

Mary snatched her old cobbing hammer from the mantel and was swinging even as the slaver turned back. She landed her blow on the side of Peavey's head. His skull was much easier to crush than stone. The bone made a different sound too—brittle.

Peavey gave one surprised croak before dropping the knife and crumpling to the floor. He twitched. His last breath rattled hoarsely in the room. Then he was still and quiet, his eyes staring vacantly.

Blood thrummed in Mary's veins. The hammer clanged to the floor. She had just killed a man. She looked at the hand that had held the hammer, and hardly recognized it.

Her stomach roiled, and she fought the urge to be sick. She stumbled back to her chair and closed her eyes.

"You all right, Miss Mary?"

Her eyes snapped open. This child needed her. She got to her feet with an effort. "Ezekiel. Go upstairs."

He stood staring at the body. "Peavey come for me."

She crossed the floor and wrapped him into a tight hug. "He—he did. And you were very brave, Ezekiel." Instead of cowering, Ezekiel had run to protect *her*.

For a moment he clung to her. Then he pulled away and crouched by the body. Mary reached for him, but realized that he needed to see this. Needed to know to his marrow that Peavey was dead. "You don't have to worry about Peavey anymore, Ezekiel."

Finally Ezekiel nodded and looked back at her. "What you goin' to do with him?"

"I—I don't know. I'll fetch Andrew—"

"*No.*" Ezekiel spoke in a tone she'd never heard before. It was a man's tone, coming from a child who'd never had a childhood. "Nobody but you and me, Miss Mary. The more people know, the harder a secret is to keep."

Mary understood that she was learning more about Ezekiel, about what he and his kin had endured at the hands of men like Parnell Peavey, than he'd ever choose to tell. She also realized the truth in his words.

"Can't leave him where somebody might find him," Ezekiel mused.

Mary licked her lips. "Maybe...maybe the root cellar?"

"It's the only place," the boy agreed. "I best start digging a hole." He glanced over his shoulder. "It be all right with you if I use Mr. Jory's shovel?"

She felt hysteria rising inside, and fought it down. "Of course. I—I'll help you."

"There's no need, Miss Mary. When I want to, I can dig real good."

That brought hot tears to her eyes. But Mary couldn't leave this to him. Together they dragged Peavey's body into the root cellar. Ezekiel began digging the grave, and Mary scrubbed the floor and hearthstones.

By candlelight, Mary and Ezekiel finished the grave. She scratched the earth with the sticking tommy, and Ezekiel shoveled. Finally Mary straightened. "I think that's deep enough." She tossed the sticking tommy into the grave. She was ready to throw the cobbing hammer after it when Ezekiel shook his head. "Best put it back on the mantel, Miss Mary. Otherwise folks'll ask why it's gone."

Mary scrubbed the hammer and returned it to its place. She and Ezekiel rolled Peavey's body into the grave. Then Ezekiel began to shovel back the dirt.

Mary started shoving soil into the grave with her hands, but stopped as a wave of horrified despair crashed over her. I'll never be able to erase this night, she thought. I'm a different person than I was this morning.

She pitched to her feet, went to the main room, and plucked a china cup from the mantel. Back in the cellar, she hurled it into the grave. When it broke, she started to cry.

She was not, and would never be, a decent woman. Mrs. Bunney had been right all along.

THIRTY-FIVE

When Lowena had finished her tale, Chloe leaned back in her chair in shocked silence. An *elementary* school had been named after Parnell Peavey. How much had Evelyn known?

As for Mary Pascoe, *wow*. She was a much more complex woman than the one celebrated in her obituary. Given the skeleton's crushed skull, everyone had been inclined to believe the killer was male. Shame on me for underestimating a capable woman, she thought. She didn't know if she'd have found the strength and courage to do what Mary had done.

She didn't even know if Mary had done the right thing.

Somewhere down the hall a visiting child squealed, "Hi, Grand-dad!" Lowena wearily leaned her head against the chair.

Chloe stirred. "I'll let you rest, Lowena."

"Thank you, child." The old woman reached out and clasped Chloe's hand in hers. "I've carried that story for over seventy years. You can do with it what you wish."

Lovely, Chloe thought weakly. Just lovely.

After leaving the nursing home, Chloe walked darkened streets to *Chy Looan* and sat on the front step. She understood why Lowena had kept the story secret. Mary Pascoe had given her a home when she had nowhere else to go. Mary Pascoe had also been revered for her good works—especially her care of needy children.

Chloe rested her elbows on her knees, and her chin in her hands. What was *she* supposed to do with this information?

She could let the whole thing go. The skeleton could remain unidentified. Mary Pascoe's legacy could remain untarnished.

Or, Chloe thought, I can tell the Bolithos and the police what I've learned. What Evelyn's ancestor Parnell Peavey had done; what Mary Pascoe had done.

Indecision pushed her to her feet. She stepped inside the empty cottage, lit only by the faint glow from a nearby streetlamp. "Mary," she whispered, "I don't know what to do." She tried to be receptive.

And—there it was, the same sense of contentment that she'd felt before.

Chloe walked to the root cellar door. The air felt damper and cooler against her face. The windowless room was black as a lead mine. She retrieved her little penlight, glad she'd already installed new batteries, and scanned the room. Adam had smoothed loose earth back into the empty grave.

Chloe took a deep breath and stepped inside the cellar. Ugliness hit her again like a physical blow. She heard the faint scrape of young Ezekiel's shovel. She sensed Mary's horror as she dragged Parnell Peavey's body across the floor to his grave.

But Chloe clenched her fists and held her ground. There was something *beneath* the bad stuff too. She felt a sense of…of strength in the dank room.

Mary never moved away from *Chy Looan*, Chloe thought. She raised children here. Coming to fetch potatoes or cabbage, she walked over Peavey's grave a thousand times. She must have found some kind of peace about what happened.

Chloe had her answer.

———

After another restless night, Chloe slipped from Tamsin's apartment before dawn and walked back to the old city cemetery. Something still bothered her about Yvonne Miller's death. Miller's journal might hold answers, but it was in police custody. Chloe only had two possible unexplored clues. Miller had been studying the root cellar at Polperro House, and she'd made a rubbing of an old tombstone.

In the cool pale light spreading softly over the hill, Chloe made her way to that grave. It was weathered and blotched with lichen, impossible to decipher. She'd borrowed a small bag of flour and a pastry brush from Tamsin's kitchen. Now she knelt and lightly tossed flour at the rough stone. Then, ever so gently, she brushed it from the surface. Traces of flour remained in the chiseled inscription. She deciphered the name: Ezekiel Miller.

"Oh my God," Chloe whispered. Ezekiel *Miller*. Yvonne *Miller*.

She sat back on her heels. She'd never know for certain, but she suspected that Dr. Yvonne Miller was a descendant of a man who had been enslaved. Sure, Miller was an extremely common name … but *something* had compelled Yvonne to study that gravestone with such intense interest. Something had fueled bitter resentment toward the prominent white men who were still so often simply hailed as heroes—Parnell Peavey in particular. Something had driven her to the root cellar at Pendarvis, even though she'd expressed no interest in analyzing domestic history or territorial food storage. Maybe she'd wanted to spend time there simply to help her imagine one of her ancestor's most desperate moments.

Chloe remembered feeling lofty because *she* was after the stories of people like Mary Pascoe—illiterate working-class people historians often overlooked. But Miller had evidently been after the stories of the most vulnerable, the least likely to leave records behind.

Maybe, like the woman who'd killed her, Yvonne Miller had only wanted to protect her ancestor's legacy.

———

Later that morning, after breakfast, Tamsin hugged Chloe goodbye. "I'm grateful for all you did for us, Chloe."

Chloe had told Tamsin, Adam, and Investigator Higgins everything she'd learned. "Lowena had promised Mary never to share the secret," Chloe stressed, in the face of Tamsin's shock and hurt feelings. "But she didn't want to die with the story untold. I'm a historian, and a friend of yours . . . sort of a neutral party."

Now Tamsin added, "I've been thinking about what you learned about my rocking chair."

"God bless tenacious archivists," Chloe said. The records showing that Theophilus George did indeed sell a Boston rocker to Mary Pascoe hadn't even been cataloged yet, but Midge had ferreted them out.

"I can picture Mary rocking small children, just as I did so many times." Tamsin studied her chair. "I've decided to donate it to Pendarvis."

"Claudia will be delighted." Chloe beamed, and gently sat in the rocker one more time. I'm sitting where Mary did, she thought. So often a search for the people who made or owned an artifact reached a dead-end, which was extremely frustrating. It was a joy to know that something of Mary's had survived, and could be used to tell a broader story about Mineral Point.

"Maybe it will help visitors understand that Mineral Point was not a frontier town for long." Tamsin lifted her chin with pride. "My Cornish ancestors saw to that."

Chloe and Adam left with a Tupperware container filled with currant-studded saffron buns. As Adam drove up Shake Rag Street Chloe felt compelled to help herself, strictly in homage to the Cornish immigrants who'd once labored along this ravine. "Ooh, yummy."

Adam threw her a rueful glance. "Are you sorry you came?"

Chloe considered. "Well, it certainly wasn't the week I'd expected. But Pendarvis is a treasure, and Mineral Point has fascinating stories to tell. I'm glad I had a chance to learn about a few of them."

"Good." Adam flicked on his turn signal. "I hope you'll come back and see the cottage as the restoration progresses. Oh, by the way—I finally remembered to ask Grandma for the translation of *Chy Looan*."

Chloe licked a crumb from one finger. "What does it mean?"

Adam smiled. "It means 'Happy House.'"

———

That afternoon Roelke parked several blocks away from Mickey's Tavern, on the outskirts of Palmyra, and strolled toward the bar. He was off-duty, wearing a jacket over a pullover and jeans.

Raymo's so-called hunting club is meeting at Mickey's Tavern on Sunday afternoon, Roelke's friend Blakely had said. *I've nailed Raymo for drunk driving a couple of times after one of these gatherings … If he's inebriated, I can search the car.*

The parking lot was full, mostly with old beaters and pickups. Dan Raymo had parked his black Firebird near the Dumpster behind the squat brick building. No windows overlooked this alley.

Roelke walked between vehicles to the Pontiac, squatted beside the driver's side, and tried the door. It opened. Raymo hadn't even locked the car. Idiot.

After a quick glance over his shoulder, Roelke reached into one jacket pocket. He withdrew a plastic bag holding a dozen smaller bags of crack cocaine. He had stolen them before inventorying the official haul from his big drug bust, which was now in the evidence locker at the Eagle PD. He'd packaged the crack in a different brand of bags, taking care to leave no fingerprints.

Now he quickly tucked that bag under the driver's seat, with just a corner peeking out the back. He shut the car door, rose, and walked away.

No one yelled after him. No one had seen a thing. He'd anticipated trembling, or nausea, or a dozen other physical manifestations, but he felt steady. Calm, even. What should have been the hardest thing he'd ever done had been ridiculously easy.

He remembered again how glib he'd been that day with Adam: *We have to trust the Palmyra cops to deal with Raymo if he goes too far. The fact that Libby is family doesn't change that.* But when children were involved, that belief was nothing but—Roelke barked a bitter laugh—a cop-out.

Still, once back in his truck, he decided not to go home—where Chloe was babysitting Deirdre—right away. He and Chloe had once promised to never keep secrets from the other. He'd meant it at the time. Believed it was possible. But he was about to break that promise. He couldn't hide his gunshot wound, but what he'd just done would die with him.

He had a little paperwork to finish at the PD. I'll take care of that before going home, Roelke thought. He wanted to see how this new *him* would feel walking back into the police station.

When Roelke arrived, his key still turned in the front door lock. It felt no different to walk into the crowded main room. The only surprise was seeing Chief Naborski's door open. Chief rarely came in on Sundays.

Roelke paused in the doorway. "Afternoon, Chief."

"Ah, Officer McKenna." The older man looked up from his desk. "I wasn't expecting you, but I'm glad you're here. Come in." He gestured toward a chair.

Roelke felt a tightening in his gut as he sat. "Yessir?"

"I got a call last night," Naborski said. "The police committee has made their decision."

"Oh?"

"They decided that Officer Deardorff is the best candidate for advanced training."

"I see." Roelke could think of nothing else to say.

"That's all."

"Yessir." He stood and left the office.

In the outer room he settled at the officers' desk, opened the necessary file, and stared blindly at the contents. Why had the committee chosen Skeet? They *know*, he thought. Which was of course ridiculous, since the decision was made yesterday. So … what had happened? Had they decided that after successfully orchestrating the huge drug bust, Roelke was less in need of specialized training than Skeet? Had Ralph Petty, Chloe's deranged boss, influenced the decision? Had Chief Naborski read Roelke's intent regarding Dan Raymo in his eyes?

No way to know.

Roelke forced himself to concentrate and do what he'd come to do. Then he left the station and drove home.

The sight of his farmhouse relaxed the tightness a little. He needed to put away the garden hose and clean the gutters and insulate the windows before winter settled in, but none of that mattered right now. Generations of Roelkes had called that farm *home*. In a remarkably short time it had become an oasis for him, and for the people he loved.

Including the two children he would do anything to protect. Laws and police officers were supposed to shield children from harm, but when they didn't and couldn't... well, he'd taken justice into his own hands, and done what he had to do.

Roelke parked in the driveway and cut across the front lawn. As he approached the house he heard music. Chloe had put some classical record on the stereo.

On the front porch step he stopped, looking in the living room window. Chloe was dancing around the room, a pretend ballerina in jeans and wool socks, her long blond hair swaying as she dipped and turned. Tied over Deirdre's jeans was the skirt Chloe had made from gauzy layers of turquoise and purple. The little girl copied Chloe's every move. When the piece ended, and Chloe curtsied, Deirdre wobbled too low and landed on the floor. Chloe fell beside her. Carefree laughter drifted from the room.

Roelke's inner calm shattered into a thousand pieces, sharp and small. He sat down on the step, put his elbows on his knees and his face in his hands, and cried.

THIRTY-SIX

JANUARY 1866

"Goodbye, my dear." Mary kissed Ida's cheek. "I always love seeing you and the children, and I love my new lace collar too."

"Happy fiftieth birthday. And Miss Mary..." Ida hesitated.

Mary tipped her head, considering the woman who had once—decades ago—been her ward. Ida was thirty-six now. "Is something troubling you?"

"You're as kind to my children as you've always been to me." Ida twined her fingers together. "I was thinking about my childhood this morning and suddenly wondered if I ever thanked you. I fear I did not."

"There's no need, child," Mary said softly. "You have repaid me tenfold. I'm proud of you."

Ida visited *Chy Looan* often. She'd married a man who worked at the brewery, and now had five children of her own and a small house to keep just a few blocks away. She was a good mother. She taught Sunday School and sang in the choir. When her husband had joined the Union Army, she'd kept her family going by taking in sewing. Today she wore a stylish gown she'd made herself of mauve cotton, draped over a fashionable hooped petticoat—a walking advertisement for her skill. Quite impractical, Mary thought. Still, she was pleased that Ida had become so skilled with her needle. Glad too that Ida didn't have to hem her skirt up because she did heavy labor.

Ida took one of Mary's hands in her own. "Thank you for raising me. And all the others."

"You have been my greatest source of joy," Mary told her. "You … and all the others."

After Ida had left with her three daughters and two sons, Mary checked the baby she was fostering for a young woman with pleurisy. The baby's father had gone west, looking for better prospects, and the mother didn't have the strength to care for the child alone. The baby was sleeping in the cradle near the hearth, one thumb in her mouth.

Then Mary made another cup of tea and settled by the fire, remembering Ida as a frightened child. *And all the others.* There had been many others over the decades, staying for weeks or years, and she loved them all. But Ida had been the first. Then Will. Then Ezekiel … Mary hitched her paisley shawl snuggly around her shoulders. Ezekiel would always have a special place in her heart.

Not that those first weeks and months after she'd killed Parnell Peavey had been easy. She'd moved through each day in a daze, certain that Andrew and her friends and her minister would know with one glance what she had done. The visceral memory of her cobbing hammer hitting Peavey's skull—the feel and the sound and the look and the smell of it—was a constant companion. When something was needed from the root cellar, she sent Will. She was too ashamed to pray. Too ashamed to think of her sweet mother. She'd failed everything and everyone she'd held dear.

And she'd worried incessantly about Ezekiel. The boy had watched her kill a man, and helped bury him. What would that do to him? Would fear hound him through life?

But one autumn morning, months later, something unexpected had happened. She'd sent the children outside to bring cabbages from the garden before heading to the mine or to school. She was sweeping when she heard Ida's happy squeal, and Will's teasing shout. Mary smiled because Will tried hard to be the man of the house, and she loved it when he forgot to be a man and played with Ida.

Then she heard a sound she'd never heard before. She stepped outside to see who had joined her children. But what she'd heard was Ezekiel's laughter. He had joined Will in chasing Ida around the garden. For the first time, he didn't look like an old man trapped in a boy's body. For the first time, he had—however briefly—forgotten his nightmares.

That morning, Mary's horror began to ease too.

Now she sat by her fire, rocking gently in the beautiful chair she'd recently purchased from Theophilus George, a fine craftsman who owned one of the furniture stores in town. No one arriving in Mineral Point today could imagine how rough the diggings were in 1835, Mary thought. But time went by, and things changed. Ruan had left Mineral Point for good when gold was discovered in California, and not having to worry about seeing him had helped ease the lonely ache left from the broken engagement. Andrew had taken a job at his father-in-law's smelting operation, and was raising four sons. Will still mined, and had recently married a shy young widow.

Slavery, long tolerated in the territory, had been abolished when Wisconsin became a state in 1848; runaways had still been at risk, but the Civil War had rendered slavery illegal everywhere. Ezekiel worked at a lumber mill and stopped by *Chy Looan* at least once a week. He'd married a Negro woman with shadows in her eyes, a big heart, and a talent for baking pies. They had a son and daughter Ezekiel adored, and lived in a cottage of their own. He liked to sit out front in the evenings, whittling toys for the children who stopped by to visit. He was a free man. A good man.

And I am a decent woman, Mary thought, not with grandiose pride, but with conviction. She had two tables in the front of the room, and every Friday and Saturday served a proper Cornish meal with pasties, saffron buns, figgy hobbin, plum preserves and clotted cream, and tea. She had opened *Chy Looan* to children in need. She had saved Ezekiel.

She remembered marveling at Mrs. Bunney. She had recognized even then, as a girl, that Mrs. Bunney's air of authority had come from someplace inside. A sense of knowing who she was, and of understanding that she was not beholden to a greasy dobeck like surface mine boss Jake Penhallow.

As I was not beholden to an evil creature like Parnell Peavey, Mary thought. Yes, she had done a *horrible* thing. But when there were no laws to protect children ... well, she'd taken justice into her own hands, and done what she had to do.

"Mistress Mary!" someone called, interrupting her reverie. Jago Green presented himself in her open door. He removed his cap with a flourish and bowed low. His face was lined as a shriveled potato now, and his hair was gray, but he'd lost none of his flair. "Are you in need of fuel today?"

"I'll take a cord of wood, if you have it," Mary said. She usually bought coal these days, but it was dirtier and smellier than wood, and sometimes she indulged herself.

In short order Jago had the wood pitched from his wagon. Mary stood outside while he stacked it in her small side yard. The warm May day was scented with lilacs and mud. "Have you time for a cup of tea?"

Jago beamed. "I do indeed. Say you have a saffron bun too, and my heart will absolutely melt."

Mary led him inside. When he finished the last morsel, Jago sighed happily. "There is no finer baker on my route, Miss Mary, although I'll ask you not to repeat that." He got to his feet. "And might you be interested in a portrait? My talents in the artistic arena are undiminished."

Mary opened her mouth to utter the usual refusal. Then she paused. She'd just turned fifty years old. She had faced much and accomplished even more. Why not?

"I believe I am interested, Mr. Green," she said, and laughed at his look of astonishment.

"Wonderful! That's wonderful! I can't finish a piece in one afternoon, of course, but we shall commence at once. Let me just fetch my satchel from the wagon..."

Mary went upstairs and changed into her best dress. She combed her hair again before pinning it up and covering it with her cap. And she added her new lace collar.

Back downstairs, Jago settled Mary in a chair by the window, where the light was good. Then he stepped back and considered her. "Ah. You are a handsome woman, Miss Mary. But to meet current fashion, I suggest you turn your head to the side. Look down instead of at me." He moved closer and gently guided her chin. "Like so. Yes. Very demure."

Mary smiled, lifted her chin, and met his gaze. "I appreciate your thoughtfulness, Mr. Green. But I want you to paint me just as I am."

THIRTY-SEVEN

"This is nice." Chloe leaned her head against Roelke's shoulder, wishing she could stay there forever. "I'm glad to be home."

"I'm glad about that too."

The two of them were finally enjoying some peaceful solitude on the porch swing. Libby had taken Deirdre home. Shadows slanted across the lawn. Chloe had pulled on a Norwegian sweater against the chill. But the true warmth came from the weight of Roelke's arm around her. If everyone had what we have, she thought, the world would be a much happier place.

Which reminded her of what Roelke had been dealing with all week. "How are things with Libby?"

Roelke took a long moment to respond. "I'm hoping that the situation between her and Adam improves. He'd be good for her. Good for the kids."

Chloe used her toes to gently rock the swing. "What about Libby's ex?"

This time he was silent for even longer. Something's up, Chloe thought.

Finally Roelke said, "You know, it's a beautiful evening and I just got you back home. I'd really rather not talk about Raymo."

Chloe decided not to push. "Sure." She watched a ragged V of quacking ducks flying overhead, aiming for nearby marshland. "Settling in for the night. Just like me."

"You had quite the time of it in Mineral Point," Roelke observed. His voice tightened, and his hand on her shoulder did too. "I remain in awe of the amount of trouble you managed to find in one short week."

"You were the one who discovered the skeleton in *Chy Looan*," she protested.

"True. But I'm talking about what came later. You took foolish chances—"

She straightened to face him. "I did not!"

"You should *never* have gone down in that mine." He frowned at her. "What on earth were you thinking?"

"I was thinking that a child needed help," Chloe flared. "I'm sorry if you have a problem with that."

Roelke jerked as if he'd been struck. "No. I don't have a problem with that." He lurched to his feet and strode across the porch. He stopped at the far side, hands thrust in pockets, looking across the yard to the forest beyond.

Chloe sighed. This was not the homecoming she wanted. When she got tired of waiting she joined him at the porch rail and put one tentative hand on his back. His muscles were corded with tension. "Hey. What are you thinking?"

"I'm thinking how precious you are to me," he said. "And ... about children. Children are precious too."

Chloe let her hand drop.

"Do you ever think about it?" Roelke asked. "Having kids?"

"I'd want to be married first," she said, and immediately felt her cheeks flame. It was true, but she wasn't angling for a proposal.

"Do you want—" Roelke began.

"I didn't mean—" Chloe said at the same time. They both stopped.

A painful silence stretched between them. Finally Roelke said, "The thing is … if you have kids, they have to come first."

"Of course." She watched a squirrel bound up a tree in the side yard, feeling at a loss.

"I'm sorry," Roelke muttered. "It's just that … " He turned to her, eyes glassy with tears.

Chloe didn't know what was burdening him. What she did know was that he didn't need to talk about marriage and kids right now. For whatever reason, Roelke—the strongest person she knew—needed comfort.

She put one palm against his cheek. "Whatever it is," she said gently, "it'll be all right. We'll work it out together."

He wrapped his arms around her. They stood like that for a long time, leaning into each other, and she felt some of the tension leave him. Then Roelke kissed her.

For the first time in a week, everything was right in Chloe's world. "Let's go inside," she suggested. "I'll make a pot of tea."

GLOSSARY

Aye?—What's that you say? I beg your pardon?

Bal maiden—a female mine worker, young or unmarried. ("Bal" means "Mine" in Cornish.)

Chirks—embers

Dish o tay—cup of tea

Dobeck—a stupid person

Dummity—cloudy, overcast, dim

Figgy hobbin—a dessert which includes pastry, raisins ("figgy" refers to raisins or currants, not figs), and caramel sauce

Fitty—proper, properly

Giss on—Don't speak such garbage!

Gook—a large, protective bonnet worn by bal maidens

Gorse—a yellow-flowered shrub

Hoggan—a type of flatbread, sometimes containing bits of meat or potato

Jowster—traveling salesman

Kewney—rancid

Knackers—mythical creatures that live in mines; also knockers or tommyknockers

Pasty—a pie, usually filled with meat and vegetables, often carried by miners

Peat—an accumulation of partially rotted plant material; often dried and used for fuel

Pilchard—small, oily fish once a mainstay of the Cornish diet; also known as Cornish sardines

Pisky—pixie

Mena Dhu—dark hill

Rumped up—huddled for warmth

Smeech—acrid smoke

Starry-gazy pie—a pilchard pie with the fish heads sticking through the crust

Swede—turnip or rutabaga

That—very, as in "I am that sorry."

Wheal—place of work; commonly used to identify a mine, such as Wheal Blackstone

Wisht—tired, weak, faint

1. Polperro House, Pendarvis Historic Site.

2. Pendarvis House (left) and Trelawny House, Pendarvis Historic Site.

*3. Artifacts found in the basement of a home
on Shake Rag Street, Mineral Point, Wisconsin.*

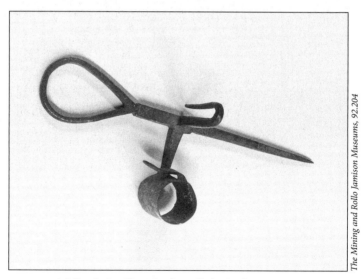

4. Miner's Candlestick, also called a Sticking Tommy.

5. This portrait of an unidentified woman hangs in Pendarvis House.

Pendarvis Historic Site, PD1981.402.342

6. *This type of early teapot would have been a prized possesion for a Cornish immigrant.*

Pendarvis Historic Site, PD1981.401.353

7. *Whoever made this foot warmer took the time to add decorative hearts.*

8. Earthenware flowerpot attributed to Bernard Klais, Mineral Point, 1858–1883.

9. Boston rocker signed by Theophilus George, Mineral Point, 1866–1880.

ACKNOWLEDGMENTS

In 2011 and 2012, I had the great good fortune to be awarded residencies in Mineral Point. I'm grateful to the Council for Wisconsin Writers, the Shake Rag Center for the Arts, and Don and Lisa Hay for making those experiences possible. Although Pendarvis had already been on my list of potential settings for a Chloe mystery, these visits were tantalizing reminders of how much the Lead Region had to offer.

I am indebted to Robert Neal and Edgar Hellum, whose decision to rescue a crumbling old home on Shake Rag Street launched a preservation movement. Thanks to State Historical Society of Wisconsin employees past and present for preserving and interpreting the historic buildings. Special thanks to curator Tamara Funk for her partnership in this endeavor, and to former director Allen Schroeder and former curator Kori Oberle for their help.

Thanks to Nancy Pfotenhauer and Mary Alice Moore for helping me explore the Mineral Point Library Archives, and to Dr. Benjamin Bruch for his insight about Cornish language and dialect. I'm also grateful to Kathy and Dan Vaillancourt and their wonderful team at the Walker House for their hospitality.

I'm grateful for the help provided by education coordinator Mary Huck and curator Stephanie A. Saager-Bourret of the Mining Museum & Rollo Jamison Museum, and to the interpreters at the Badger Mine and Museum, for sharing their knowledge.

Warm thanks to Chief Robert P. Weier of the Mineral Point Police Department and to Sergeant Gwen Bruckner of the Eagle Police Department, for patiently answering questions.

I'm extremely fortunate to have Fiona Kenshole and Sarah Binns of Transatlantic Literary on my team. Thanks to Terri Bischoff, Amy Glaser, Nicole Nugent, and the Midnight Ink crew. I remain grateful to

Laurie Rosengren, Katie Mead and Robert Alexander, and Maddy Hunter for their assistance.

The support and encouragement I receive from my husband and partner Scott Meeker makes everything possible. And finally, heartfelt thanks go to my enthusiastic readers.

Geri Gerold © Kathleen Ernst

ABOUT THE AUTHOR

Kathleen Ernst is an award-winning author, educator, and social historian. She has published thirty-four novels and two nonfiction books. Her books for young readers include the Caroline Abbott series and *Gunpowder and Teacakes: My Journey with Felicity* for American Girl. Honors for her children's mysteries include Edgar and Agatha Award nominations. Kathleen worked as an interpreter and as curator of interpretation and collections at Old World Wisconsin, and her time at the historic site served as inspiration for the Chloe Ellefson mysteries. *The Heirloom Murders* won the Anne Powers Fiction Book Award from the Council for Wisconsin Writers, and *The Light Keeper's Legacy* won the Lovey Award for Best Traditional Mystery from Love Is Murder. Ernst served as project director/scriptwriter for several instructional television series, one of which earned her an Emmy Award. She lives in Middleton, Wisconsin. For more information, visit her online at http://www.kathleenernst.com.